SUNSTRUCK

SUNSTRUCK

WILLIAM RAYFET HUNTER

1 3 5 7 9 10 8 6 4 2

#Merky Books
20 Vauxhall Bridge Road
London SW1V 2SA

#Merky Books is part of the Penguin Random House group of companies
whose addresses can be found at global.penguinrandomhouse.com.

Copyright © William Rayfet Hunter, 2025

First published in the UK by #Merky Books in 2025

www.penguin.co.uk

A CIP catalogue record for this book is available from the British Library.

ISBN: 9781529919790

Typeset in 13.5/16pt Garamond MT by Falcon Oast Graphic Art Ltd

Printed and bound by Clays Ltd, Elcograf S.p.A.

The authorised representative in the EEA is Penguin Random House Ireland,
Morrison Chambers, 32 Nassau Street, Dublin D02 YH68.

Penguin Random House is committed to a sustainable future for our business, our readers
and our planet. This book is made from Forest Stewardship Council® certified paper.

www.greenpenguin.co.uk

Penguin Random House is committed to a
sustainable future for our business, our readers
and our planet. This book is made from Forest
Stewardship Council® certified paper.

Make yourself all honey and the flies will devour you.

PART ONE
Honey

Prologue

The body in the swimming pool doesn't move. Dark hair and white silk fan out around it, arms and legs hanging down like a marionette. I stare down into the inky water for a moment longer. The night around me is muted. The noise of crickets and the music and the laughter from inside are muffled, as if I too am submerged.

And then the world snaps back into focus. Rough grooves of stone scrape my feet. Crickets, water, music, laughter. Every sound swells to a crescendo. There is hot blood in my ears. I look around, hoping someone will rescue us. But no one is coming. It's just the body and me, suspended together.

My clothes are like a second skin around me. I kick off my shoes and strike out towards it. Fists of water clutch at my shirt, pulling me down. I panic as my legs thrash against the drenched linen. I reach the body and try to flip it onto its back like they taught us in swimming lessons. Diving for blocks and waterlogged pyjamas and swimming badges sewn onto bright red towels flash through my mind. The body jerks away from my grasp and turns to face me, taking in hungry gulps of air.

'I knew you'd save me,' she says. Then she winks, pitches forwards, and dives into the blackness.

Tuesday

I wake to a sound I know well. Grandma singing tune-lessly and the clang of pots and pans. It is the sound of an island I have never visited. My phone tells me it's 3.36 in the morning. Still over an hour until the first of the five alarms I have set will go off. Part of me wants to go back to sleep but I am too restless, so I wrap a towel around my waist and pad down the narrow corridor to the bathroom. The boiler groans in protest at the early start as I step into the jet of hot water, bowing my head to fit in the cramped shower. Grandma says I'm too big for this house.

My collar is damp and water drips from my hair as I lean against the doorjamb and ask her what she's doing up. She wants me to eat. She has cooked a huge pot of spiced porridge, the nutmeg and vanilla and cinnamon curling through the house. She places a steaming bowl on the counter, so thick the spoon stands upright. I am too nervous to eat so I push the oats around the bowl.

'Sweetness,' she purrs, 'you haffi eat someting before you go jet-set off. No grandson of mine a guh France pan a hempty stomach. Me nah haf them rich folk think I cyan feed my own grandson.'

Grandma's accent has always been a defiance. A strong

4

Jamaican lilt with creeping Manchester vowels. She lost a job because of that accent once. When she arrived in England, she says, the country didn't seem real. Flying over tiny toy houses, crammed impossibly close, spewing grey columns of smoke into the frigid air. A place further from the lush sprawling hills of St James was difficult to imagine. She tried everything she could to blend in. She hot-combed her thick, kinky hair, and her nursing uniform was always immaculately pressed and starched. But she couldn't keep the waves out of her voice. One morning, she answered back to a white doctor who pretended he couldn't understand her accent. She told him that she spoke better English than him and he'd better open up his ears. She was fired before midday. She confided in a friend, who had made the crossing a few years earlier, who told her that maybe it would be best if she just kept her head down, tried a bit harder to fit in. She refused. I am proud of her for this, but I have never told her.

I push away the bowl and see the disappointment skim across the clear skies of her face. She fumbles in her purse for a ten-pound note.

'Grandma, it's fine. I'm fine. I have to go. I'll see you soon.' And then, after a pang of guilt, 'I love you.'

It's too early for the train. I drag Grandma's battered floral suitcase in the opposite direction. The cold of the plastic bench soaks through my jeans. I take out my passport, running my finger along the embossed gold lettering before flicking to the photo page. A slightly younger version of me stares back. There is a question in his eyes, a hopefulness. I want to reach out and touch his face. The photograph was taken about three years ago when I last left England for the freedom and mayhem of the Magaluf strip with sixteen other boys from school. The trip was a total disaster. Drunken arguments, a broken nose. I started university friendless and bruised.

'*Please*. Please, please, please, please, please, please, please. Wait! Hold your head right there, you look wonderful,' Lily Blake said, poking her head around the large canvas between us, her tongue jutting out of the side of her mouth, mirroring the movement. 'You'll love it, everybody loves it. And besides,' she said cautiously, retreating back behind the canvas, 'I may have already told Mummy you were coming.'

We were in my room at university, three months earlier. We would often find ourselves here, ensconced within the peeling paint and grubby corkboard. Lily had her paints spread out across the desk and on the floor, tiny pots of blue and violet and yellow carefully placed among my discarded socks and the detritus of a bedsit half packed for the summer holidays.

'Oh Lil, you didn't,' I protested. 'Now I'm going to look so rude if I turn you down, but I can't cancel on Jazz. I'm meant to be staying with her family in London in August and looking for flats togeth—'

'Stay still, you're the worst subject ever, you know. Come on, you know you deserve the holiday. London and Jasmine and flats will still be there when you get back.'

6

I could feel the animosity dripping from the name. Jazz, who proudly called herself my 'only Black friend', had an instinctive mistrust of Lily and her boarding-school clique. This was met with haughty disdain from Lily, although I privately suspected this was more likely hurt than malice. Sometimes it felt like my two closest friends were pulling me in opposite directions. I let the silence linger.

'And after you've paid for flights it's basically free because everything is already paid for.' She spoke so quickly that the words smeared into one another.

I tried to claim it wasn't about money, but even as I said it, the heat of shame burned the tips of my ears. I still felt a small sting every time she wordlessly paid for our drinks or a meal, when she would slip off to use the toilet and take care of the bill on her way. For Lily, money, like laughter, was something that flowed as freely as water. Her wealth had never taught her to be embarrassed about money, just to never talk about it. Throughout university, people who didn't think twice about spending money made me uneasy: girls shielding their hair from the rain with expensive laptops, private-school boys with cars and credit cards and cocaine habits. I never really got used to their carelessness.

I shifted uncomfortably on the bed. 'I can't come, I've got a family thing.'

'All summer?' Lily said, raising an eyebrow. 'Look, you'll have the best time ever, I promise. And once you get there, I swear you'll never want to leave! I have so much to show you and everyone is really looking forward to meeting you. Dot and Felix will be there, and it's my birthday. I won't take no for an answer.'

'I'll think about it,' I said, and booked the flights as soon as Lily left my room.

I am jerked awake for the second time today by a sad-looking flight attendant wearing an orange-and-white uniform and bright coral lipstick. The lurch of a mid-morning hangover hits me as the plane tilts and curves around to land.

She's telling me to put on my seatbelt, flashing her white teeth in a humourless smile. I click the belt into place and sit back, wishing I had ordered water. At the time, two pints of lager at six in the morning had seemed like a clever idea. But the nervous knot in my chest, which had loosened slightly with the drinks, is now tight again, mingled with nausea and a headache. I close my eyes against the rumble and lurch of the landing, gripping the armrests tightly. Eventually we emerge into a fierce heat that blazes up from the smooth, hot tarmac.

The airport is small, a single corrugated iron-and-glass building. I lean against a pillar, embracing its coolness against my damp T-shirt. A small boy runs a toy car along the dirty tiles, the soles of his bare feet traced in pale dust. After a few quiet minutes, the battered carousel creaks into life and starts spitting luggage onto the rubber slats. I watch as the rest of the passengers collect their things. Grandma's old suitcase, which she lugged all the way from Kingston, is usually unmissable with its garish pink and yellow flowers and purple plastic piping, but it fails to appear. I look around for assistance and, finding none, head over to the kiosk.

'*Excusez-moi, je ne trouve pas ma valise.*' I slaughter the words on their way out, my mouth cutting them down into rough, unusable parts. The woman behind the counter looks up from her magazine with a sigh.

'Try over there,' she says in English. I follow the lazy point of her finger and see a small desk I hadn't noticed before. I try to explain myself in broken French. The man takes down my name, a description of the bag, and the address and phone number of the Chateau – at which he raises his eyebrows, looking me up and down. I make my way to the exit and into the car park, where Lily has told me the 'handyman' would be waiting for me.

He's short and fat and has a round, red nose that looks like it might burst open if it is blown too hard. He's leaning against the bonnet of a rusted yellow car, smoking a cigarette and holding a sign with my name on it. He fixes me with an odd look before breaking into an insincere smile.

'*Bienvenue,*' he growls. 'No baggage?'

'I . . . It got lost. This is all I've got.'

The man gives a noncommittal shrug, as if this must be another inexplicable quirk of one of the strange guests of the Blake family. I squeeze into the remaining space in the back of the car, because the front seat, most of the back seats and presumably the whole boot are taken up by neatly stacked, unmarked white boxes.

9

'*Du vin*,' says the man. He raises a nicotine-stained finger
to tap his nose and gives me a conspiratorial wink. He
climbs into the front of the car, lights another cigarette,
and pulls out of the car park. As we speed through the
countryside, I watch field after field of lavender bushes
flicker past and imagine fat bumblebees lazily chugging
between them in the thick wash of sunshine.

I am about to fall asleep again when the pattern of the
window vibrating against my forehead changes and I realise we are slowing down. I blink, readjusting to the light, as
the car turns into a long, sweeping drive, flanked on both
sides by rows of thin trees. We snake up a small incline
to a rusted green double gate in the middle of a high wall
that stretches out in both directions. Half of the gate is
open and the driver deftly directs the car through the
small gap without changing speed. The smooth rumble
of tarmac changes into a shifting crackle as we pull on
to a courtyard. The house is made of pale yellow stone
with dark green shutters that peer inquisitively down at
me. Where the garden wall and gate had seemed old and
faded, the house itself looks freshly painted. The shutters gleam in the sunlight as if they are wet. There isn't
much to distinguish the Chateau from a very big house.
No crenelations, no moat, no tiny windows for archers
to shoot from. I'm slightly disappointed and smile to
myself at the thought of Lily's face when I ask where the
turrets have gone.

I climb out of the car and into the heat and instantly

regret my decision to wear jeans. I look towards the house and Lily is walking across the gravel in a flowing sundress. She leaps towards me, linking her slim arms around my neck and wrapping her legs around my waist. The nervous knot in my stomach loosens a little.

'Oh, darling! It's so wonderful that you're here! You're just in time for lunch and everyone is so excited to meet you. We thought you'd somehow got lost – Mummy almost sent out a search party and Felix wanted to start eating, but here you are!' She pauses and looks around the courtyard then down at my small backpack. 'Is that all you've brought with you?' I explain about the airport and the carousel and the man behind the counter.

'Oh, how irritating. Don't worry, I'm sure Felix has something that will fit you. Luc,' she says, her tone shifting as she addresses the driver and takes my backpack from my hand, 'would you be a darling and make sure this makes it into the house? Gosh, I'm starving.'

I try to protest but she takes my hand and pulls me across the courtyard, eagerly dragging me like a child wanting to show a parent some discovered treasure at the beach. She leads me down the side of the house. Vines stretch gnarled fingers up the wall and pink flowers pick up shafts of sunlight, marking the way. There is a terrace at the back, where large tables are laid out underneath a wooden arch. There's a chorus of welcomes and the sound of metal chairs scraping back as the Blake family rise to their feet to greet me. A tall boy in dark sunglasses sits at the far end of the table and does not stand with the others.

There are introductions to be made before we eat. A tall, slender woman of about fifty spreads her brown arms wide in welcome. She has thick hair, dark as oiled mahogany, in a loose plait over one shoulder, and strong features that would have looked stern if she weren't beaming at me with warm, walnut eyes. This is Mrs Blake – Annie, she insists: Mrs Blake makes her feel old. She pulls me to her chest; she smells of oranges and sun-cream. Mrs Blake – Annie – releases me from the embrace but keeps hold of my shoulders, leaning back to study me. She tells me I am more handsome than her daughter has let on. I smile awkwardly, the tips of my ears hot. A girl with dark features rolls her eyes and tells her mother not to be so embarrassing. She must be Dot, Lily's younger sister. Dot's face is a quiet echo of her mother's. Where Mrs Blake's features are long and sharp, Dot's are somewhat softened. Instead of Annie's straight Roman nose, Dot's is small and round and slightly sunburnt, her cheeks flushed and full. She surveys me from under her fringe.

'Lily says you're a musician too? Are you going to play something?'

I've heard a lot about Dot from Lily. A musical child prodigy, Dot mastered pretty much every instrument the Blakes could think of by the time she was eleven, and scared off countless music tutors in the process. Dot is what Lily referred to once as 'difficult', having been expelled from two schools before sitting her GCSEs. She's seventeen but the roundness of her face and the sparkle in her eyes make her look much younger.

Lily must see the fluster in my eyes because she cuts in. 'Of course he's going to play something. Everybody has to, it's tradition.'

'Oh, come on, Lil,' the boy in the sunglasses says from the other end of the table, 'you're twenty-one years old. Surely you're not going to make us do La Fête this year.'

'Don't be such a spoilsport, of course we're doing it, and I know you've already been practising because I heard you in your room.' She sticks her tongue out at the boy, who pulls a face back at her, then flicks up his middle finger and smiles.

'Every summer we have a talent show on Magpie's birthday,' explains Dot.

'It's not just for my birthday,' counters Lily. I smile at the nickname, feeling like I've unlocked a new secret about her.

'Yes, but if it wasn't your birthday, it wouldn't be so militantly enforced,' says the boy.

'Anyway,' Dot continues, 'we have a talent show every year and everyone has to perform something. A song, or a poem, or whatever. One year, one of Daddy's friends had a full clown costume and tried to make balloon animals.'

'The less said about that the better,' says Annie with a smile. 'Now, you look like you could do with a large glass of wine, darling. Felix, would you do the honours?'

The boy takes off his sunglasses and stands up. He reaches into the centre of the table and plucks a slender bottle from a bucket of ice, pouring a generous glass of pale pink wine. He walks over to me with his empty hand outstretched. I go to take the wine from him and realise too late that the outstretched hand is meant to be shaken. Clumsily, I cross my arms and take hold of the wine and his hand at the same time. Felix raises an eyebrow and a smirk spreads across his face, pressing a dimple into the corner of his sun-kissed cheek. His face is clear and boyish, handsome in a way that draws a smile from some unsuspecting part of me. His eyes hold no trace of the disdain I sensed from the end of the table. They are bright, inquisitive, the colour of a jar of honey gazed into from above. I feel a little shift inside me, like something important has been discovered.

'Felix Blake,' he says. 'Welcome to the madhouse.'

We sit and start passing around bright bowls of food. As we eat, the family talks about the party that is being thrown at the weekend, who is arriving when, and how much wine is being brought down from the vineyard. I try to smile and laugh along but the combination of the drinks and the heat and the flood of new names and cryptic inside jokes makes it hard to keep up. Instead, I take in the scene around me. A low wall of lemon-coloured stone runs along the edge of the terrace, with a gap in the middle where a few rough stone steps lead down to a sloped lawn and a deep green swimming pool. The surface is as still and smooth as glass. To one side of the stairs, on a small stone plinth, stands a statue of a headless woman. She is draped in a robe, the stone nearly translucent, one of her white breasts exposed. Her hands are by her sides, palms frozen upwards in supplication. I did not know stone could look so soft in person. Mrs Blake must have followed my gaze as her voice drags me back into the moment.

'Oh, you've seen my Venus.'

'I've never seen a marble statue before,' I say and immediately regret it.

'Alabaster,' Mrs Blake replies. 'You can tell by the way the light comes through.'

'Well, it's beautiful,' I say.

'She was, before Felix dashed her head to pieces on the flagstones in a rage.' She looks at me from under thick eyebrows. 'A warning not to get in my son's way.' She says this with a smile, but it barely hides the threat. Her voice is low and warm, like a summer storm, with an almost imperceptible hint of a well-disguised accent.

'It took some serious force to do it as well,' says Felix. He is staring directly at me and I feel a blast of heat wash over my limbs, one that has nothing to do with the summer air. 'The goddess of love is stronger than she looks.'

'That's everyone's mistake, you see. They think love is about softness and beauty, but really love is about power. The most powerful person in *Macbeth* isn't the man himself but—'

'But his "bloody-handed wife". Yes, Annie, I know, I know.'

'I always thought it was the witches,' says Dot.

'Well, you would, wouldn't you, Dorothea?' replies her

mother. 'And you really were very good in that performance, Felix, my dear.'

'Thanks, Annie. I really was,' says Felix.

When we finish eating, I stand to help clear away the plates. Mrs Blake places a hand gently but firmly on my arm and pulls me back into my seat. She reminds me warmly that I am a guest, but asks if I will please pass the wine. I fill both of our glasses, feeling awkward as Luc clears away the mess from around us. A tiny speckled bird with brown feathers and a sharp black beak pecks at the crumbs in the breadbasket.

'Aren't you horribly hot?' Lily is lying by the pool, lazily stroking her hand across the surface. I'm sitting on the edge of a sun lounger, sweat running down my forehead. Lily breaks the calm of the moment, shouting her brother's name three times with increasing intensity.

'I'm fine, honestly,' I tell her.

'Don't be so ridiculous, you must be baking. Felix, darling, would you please lend our guest some swimmers before he collapses from sunstroke?'

'Sure,' says her brother, striding down the lawn. He reaches out a hand to help me up. 'Have you got anything in your pockets?'

'No,' I say, confused. I'm about to ask why when Felix swings his weight around, so that we swap places, and launches himself towards me, pushing me hard in the centre of my chest. I stumble backwards and feel a lurch in my stomach as my foot finds air before I crash into the cold water. Everything is green and black and silver. The water roars around my ears for a moment and then is still. I kick my way to the surface and see Felix bent over with laughter. Lily is laughing too, half of her jet-black hair dripping from the splash.

'No! Did you get him? That's so unfair! It was supposed to be my turn!' says Dot, running down the lawn.

'Sorry, mate, family tradition,' Felix says through a grin, out of breath from laughing. 'But at least now you're fully initiated.'

He reaches out a hand to help me out of the pool, which I gratefully take hold of and then pull, hard. Felix loses his balance and there is a moment of surprise on his face as he splashes down next to me. He comes up gasping for air, the water collecting on his heavy eyelashes and his dark hair stuck to his neck and face.

'Well played.'

We climb out of the swimming pool together and lie panting on its edge. Felix strips down to his underwear and flings his clothes off to one side. He has a golden tan and the hairs on his forearms have been bleached white by the sun. I watch the rapid rise and fall of his stomach. There is a shadow of a tattoo, a sun cut in half by the waistband of his boxers.

'I really wasn't expecting that,' he tells me.

After a while, my black jeans begin to steam. Felix notices and says we should go into the house to change, flicking the water from his hair over Lily's dress as he passes her.

'Ugh, you utter twat! Would you please bring me a beer? From the fridge, not the cooler, they're always too warm.'

We make our way up the lawn, Felix leading me to a side door. I'm about to follow him inside, but he turns and stops me, his palm planted firmly in the middle of my chest.

'You can't come into the house like that. You'll drip all over the floor and Annie will be furious. You have to strip.' I look at him for a moment, waiting to see if he is joking, but he seems completely serious. I start to clumsily peel off my jeans and T-shirt. I am down to my boxers, which have become almost transparent.

'Everything,' says Felix, his face expressionless, hidden again behind his sunglasses.

I'm panicking, my heart pounding, and I reluctantly slip my thumbs into my waistband and start to tug it down.

'Oh God, stop! I was joking! Sorry!' Felix says with a smile. He whirls into the house, staggering a few steps, turning his face away in mock horror. 'Christ! Lily said you were odd, but I didn't realise you were actually mad.' He bursts out laughing and sets off up the corridor. 'Just leave your clothes on the bench! And please, please keep your pants on.'

Blood is thundering in my ears and I think I might pass out. I throw my wet clothes onto a scuffed wooden bench. The corridor is narrow and lined with various coats, hats and life jackets hanging from pegs. I head through the door and into a huge square kitchen with a marble island in the middle. At the far end, above the stone sink, there is a tall stained-glass window. I cross the kitchen and almost trip over Felix. He is crouching down, reaching into a small fridge full of wine bottles, cans of beer and soda water. He hands me two red cans and pops the tab on a third, taking noisy gulps and letting out a long, artificial sigh.

'Help yourself to anything from the kitchen, by the way,' he tells me. 'Just don't open any bottles of wine with dust on them.'

I laugh but he isn't joking. He leads the way out into the hall and up the curve of a wide staircase. The walls are made of the same pale yellow stone as outside and the grey slate floor feels cool against the soles of my feet. I follow Felix up the stairs and down a long corridor with doors coming off both sides. He waves at one with thick black studs in the wood.

'This is you. Don't lock the door, the key is, like, a million years old.' I follow him down a long corridor where an arched window watches over us; fields of vines languish in the distance behind the glass. It feels much more like a castle from inside.

Felix leans his weight against one of the many doors. It creaks open a few inches, then, with a sigh, swings wide and he almost stumbles down a short flight of steps. The room is huge, and mostly bare except for the large unmade bed and a gilt-framed mirror leaning against the far wall. The space is nearly the size of Grandma's house.

Felix gestures towards a battered chest of drawers in the corner and tells me I can help myself to whatever I want. He pulls down his boxers and reaches for a towel on the bed. I try to pretend I'm not looking at the curve of his spine and the line where his golden tan pales and the soft fuzz on his back becomes darker. I think I see him pause for a moment before stepping through into the bathroom. I hear water splash and it is clear he is done with me. I grab a pair of red swimming shorts and head back to the pool with Lily's drink.

When I was fourteen years old, my dad appeared in my life as if from thin air. I didn't even know his name. No one ever mentioned him at home. It had been so long since I'd even thought about him, about having a father, that he didn't look real, standing on the doorstep of Grandma's home. My home. I remember looking at the tall, balding white man smiling sheepishly down at me. He opened his mouth to speak and suddenly I was pulled backwards into the house. I remember the ensuing argument between them which felt like it lasted for hours. Grandma's voice got angrier and louder and her accent thicker until I could barely understand her. I could hear the man I understood to be my dad mumble *But he's my son* over and over. After he left, the door slamming behind him, the house was so quiet that I thought for a while that Grandma must have gone too. I remember walking into the little lounge and seeing her sitting there, her face like a mask. She was silent for a very long time before she said, 'Your father wan fi take you to France.'

It was his first and only attempt to try and have a relationship with me. I remember seeing how much it took for Grandma not to show how much she was hurting. The strain of it was almost physical. But she thought she was doing the right thing. I was never asked what I wanted. So, a few weeks after he'd turned up out of the blue, this strange man arrived to take me out of England for the first time, driving the same battered blue Renault Clio he's leaning against in the only picture I have of us together. In the photograph, he is smiling, holding me, tiny and swaddled, my little brown face peeping out from a bundle of sky-blue cotton.

The small car was loaded with suitcases and beach towels and I was slotted in among the various detritus on the back seat, leaving the passenger seat conspicuously empty.

'How are you, son?' he asked, as if we were chatting at the end of a school day rather than after a lifetime of absence. A wave of shame washed over me every time he called me 'son'. I had never needed a dad before. I had a grandmother and, for a while at least, had had a mother. I had never before considered myself to have an absent father. I hadn't considered my father at all. I was fatherless. But now there he was, eyeing me cautiously in the rear-view mirror and attempting to gloss over the last thirteen years. We slowly pulled out of the drive and I saw that Grandma had already gone inside and closed the door.

'Now, son' – that word again sent a shockwave through

me – 'there's someone I'd like you to meet.' We pulled round the corner – purposefully out of sight of the house, I realised – and my dad slowed the car. 'This is Julie.'

Julie was a towering contradiction of pale white flesh and tight denim. She had chemically curled yellow hair, shiny fingernails, and was beaming down at me with crooked teeth. Where my dad's smile had been timid, Julie's sharp teeth glinted in the sunlight. I immediately hated Julie. I hated her simpering over me and her fawning over my dad. I hated her silly laugh and her glossy magazines. I hated that she dared to refer to me as her stepson to the people we met. And I hated that she was white.

I sat in silence for most of the journey. A long, slow drive, painstakingly counting the streetlights all the way to Dover. The nauseating ferry crossing. When we arrived in Calais, I didn't even feel like we'd left England, except that the signs were in a different language and my dad kept swearing when we approached a roundabout. In the late afternoon, we settled in a campsite outside Boulogne-sur-Mer. I had never put up a tent before, and apparently neither had my dad. Julie sat in a blue-and-white deckchair smoking a cigarette and drinking white wine out of a plastic tumbler. By the time the tents were up it was almost dark, cold air blowing in from the sea. I had packed for a summer trip and didn't have a coat, so I shivered in my jumper. My dad clapped me on the shoulder with a skinny hand and said, 'Isn't this nice?'

The next morning, I woke up and felt like I was drowning. The morning sun had turned the cold tent into a hot, sticky cocoon. I scrambled to unzip the door and let the fresh air in but was greeted by a lungful of plasticky smoke from a disposable barbecue on which my dad was burning some bacon.

'Morning, son,' he said. I had a sudden thought that maybe he was calling me 'son' because he'd forgotten my actual name. Maybe I was just one of his many forgotten children, scattered and nameless. But the look on his face, both cautious and expectant, dissolved this fantasy.

'Good morning,' I replied.

Julie locked both tents with tiny padlocks, as if there were anything inside them worth stealing. We drove down the winding roads into a large town, then out the other side, and eventually arrived at a large and crowded beach. We set off, carrying windbreakers and deckchairs, blown and buffeted by the wind. We eventually came to rest on a small patch of sand between a group of middle-aged topless sunbathers and a sprawling family who seemed to know every person on the beach. I sat in a deckchair and put my earphones in, twisting the white cable around my finger and turning the wheel on my iPod Nano to avoid hearing Julie's machine-gun laugh.

I remember looking down towards the sea and seeing two swimmers emerge from the waves. The men were tall and golden brown, laughing at some joke I wished I could hear. I paused a song to try and catch what they were saying but their words were swallowed by the crashing of the waves. The taller of the two men tripped slightly and fell to his knees. The other man held out a hand to help him up and the taller man stood back up, laughing, the sand carving out the definition of his muscular legs. I couldn't stop watching them as they sauntered down the beach in their briefs-like swimming trunks, laughing and pushing each other. I felt like I was crossing some sort of line, sitting here so close to my dad, enjoying the sight of these two men. His loud voice in my ear made me jump and my heart skipped a beat.

'Just like your old man, eh?' he was saying. I panicked, confused, then realised that the path the men had taken had drawn my gaze directly above the topless sunbathing women. I cast around for an excuse but couldn't think of anything to say. I felt a flush of shame rise up from the depths of my throat.

'How about a cold beer? A boy's first beer should always be with his father.' I was once again struck by his attempts to plaster over his total truancy from fatherhood. I also fought the urge to tell him that I had spent most weekends of the last year drunk in various parks around Manchester with the older goth kids who had taken me under their wing. I just said yes and took the beer from his outstretched hand. It was lukewarm. I sipped it and winced. 'Ah, you'll get used to it,' said this stranger who called himself my dad.

He returned me to Grandma two days later. She never asked me how the trip was, and I didn't offer up any information. The man who called me his son didn't show up again.

*

I pick my way down the stone path and find Lily floating on a lilo in the middle of the pool. I slip into the cool water and wade towards her, offering her the beer. She reaches out for it and looks me up and down.

'I knew Felix would have something for you,' she says after a moment. I look away and wonder if the sudden, inexplicable embarrassment I feel is showing.

'Oh, yeah,' I offer back weakly, and then, 'They don't really fit me, I had to double-knot the string thingy.' Lily relaxes back onto the lilo.

We spend most of the afternoon in and around the pool, laughing and getting slowly but steadily drunk. I fill Lily in on the end-of-year parties at uni, which she missed to fly out here early. I tell her about how Jenny Carmichael passed out on a table at the Psych Soc ball, and how Tim Hollins hit his head so hard in Flares that he had to go to A&E. I don't tell her about kissing Sarah Lacey again on the street outside McDonald's and how I hated myself afterwards. I don't tell her how much I wished she'd been there so I could have cried to her rather than into my pillow. In turn, Lily fills me in on who's who and gives me a rundown of the people arriving for the party at the end of the week. An extensive list which includes Blake family friends, boarding-school roommates, politicians and minor celebrities. I try to keep track of it all but everything she tells me seems to melt into the water and drift off into the shimmering air. My head swims with a whirl of new names and information and my headache from earlier starts to return. I dunk my head into the pool.

'That's so cool,' says Lily. 'The water just rolls right off. Like a duck's back.' She glides her hand through my tight curls and I flinch backwards. She withdraws it, the smile fading from her face.

'Sorry,' I say, 'I just . . .' The thought trails off as I see Felix striding towards us across the grass in white shorts and a navy linen shirt.

'Annie says you two need to get ready for supper.' He casts the words out to us as he walks up to a little outhouse and disappears inside. Lily follows my gaze and takes my lingering look as one of curiosity.

'Ice shed,' she says nonchalantly and rolls off the lilo with a little splash.

When I get to my room, I find it smaller than Felix's but still big enough that my damp footsteps on the floor echo around me. Someone has brought my bag up and placed it neatly by the dresser. My wet clothes and trainers are nowhere to be seen and I realise I must have left them downstairs. There is a tidy pile of dry clothes I don't recognise at the end of the bed. I unfold the crisp white shirt and blue trousers and a folded piece of paper falls to the floor. I pick it up. The note is handwritten in pristine script.

Those shorts looked awful on you.
If you're going to wear my clothes, at least do it well.

I look around for underwear but find none. I'm worried that I'm already late, so I quickly pull on the clothes Felix has picked for me along with a belt and a pair of loafers I find by the door, which fit perfectly.

The house is cool and quiet. And while the thick walls and tiny windows block out most of the sun, the corridors are imbued with golden light. The whole building hums with quiet grandeur. It's as intimidating as it is intoxicating. I want to look behind every door but remind myself that I am already late for tea. I descend the staircase, following the sound of voices through various rooms until I emerge onto the terrace.

The Blakes seem involved in a heated discussion, but as I appear the conversation suddenly trails off.

'And here's the man of the hour!' Felix says wryly and I feel my face colour.

'Stop, Fe, you're making him blush,' says Lily, giving me a warm smile.

'I didn't know you could blush, darling,' says Mrs Blake, tossing her dark hair, which has been loosed from its plait to spill casually over her shoulders. I don't know what to say to this and feel my cheeks flush even more.

'God, Annie, you can't say that!' says Dot, outraged on my behalf. 'It's *such* a microaggression.'

'Don't be so silly, Dorothea, I was just making an observation.' Mrs Blake smiles at me but there is something like a challenge in her eyes. 'You don't mind, do you, darling?'

'Oh,' I say, caught off-guard. 'I mean, no, Mrs Blake.'

*

27

'A microaggression. Come on, seriously? Have you ever read a book? Or, like, been on the internet in the last ten years?' Jasmine shook her head in mock disbelief, her loose curls bobbing around her face. 'It's, like, that subtle racism. That little inkling-sprinkling of racism. The one they think they can get away with and then get all upset when you call them out for.' She gestured towards me with a brown hand, adorned in silver rings and gold bangles. 'It's like when they ask you where you're from and you say, like, Manchester or whatever—'

'Bury.'

'What?'

'I'm from Bury,' I corrected her.

'Whatever. It's like when they ask you where you're from and you say Bury, and they're, like, "No, no, but where are you *from*?" Like they don't care where you were born or what part of England you grew up in. That's not what they're asking with all that emphasis on the second "from". They're asking why you look like you do. They're asking why you're not white.'

'I think that's a bit unfair, Jazz.'

'What's "unfair", babe, is that you're too brainwashed to see it. Like, once you notice it, it's just constant. And the hair thing is just another side of the same politely racist coin.'

We were sitting in the cafe at the students' union. Jasmine was waiting for a disciplinary meeting after telling one of her lecturers to fuck off during a seminar. I'd met her for a coffee before to offer moral support, but

28

it seemed she wanted me there to fire her up. Not that Jasmine ever needed firing up. Born in London to Nigerian parents, Jasmine seemed cool and at ease in every way that I did not. Her Blackness was a source of pride and joy and righteous fury. She wore her hair natural and T-shirts that said stuff like does my sassiness offend you? She (affectionately, I think) called me WhiteBoy whenever I didn't understand yet another Black cultural reference.

'I'm not backing down this time, it's fucking ridiculous.' The incident in question had occurred a few days earlier. They had been discussing African protective hairstyles as an offshoot from a discussion on depictions of 'non-European' features in one of her History of Art seminars, when the seminar leader, allegedly trying to make a point about the 'beauty' of Black hair, had reached forward to touch Jasmine's afro. In response to which, according to Lily, who had witnessed the whole thing, Jasmine had gone 'full Beyoncé'. Jasmine maintained that she'd flinched away, had politely explained why the lecturer absolutely could not touch her hair, and when the tutor had tried to protest, had just as politely told her to fuck off.

'I refuse to compromise my bodily autonomy just because some kaftan-wearing Becky feels like she has a right to run her dutty nasty fingers through my hair.'

'I thought her name was Sarah?'

'No, like, a Becky. Like "Becky with the good hair"? No? Jesus Christ, WhiteBoy, you're a nightmare.'

*

29

'Let's retire to the drawing room.'

'Oh, come on, Mum, people don't actually talk like that anymore, don't be ridiculous,' says Lily from the other end of the table. 'Anyway, it's far too nice to sit inside. And I want to smoke.'

'Those things will make you look old, darling,' counters Mrs Blake.

'Oh, do fuck off,' Felix interjects from the seat next to me, laughing. 'Darling, would you like one?' Mrs Blake laughs too and reaches a ring-encrusted hand across the table to accept the cigarette. Even through the pleasant haze of red wine, I am shocked that anyone could speak like this to their parents. If I told Grandma to fuck off, she'd get the slipper out. Felix holds out the packet of cigarettes to me, but I decline. He passes around a box of matches as Mrs Blake launches into a treatise on the joy of a single cigarette after a meal.

'Looking chic, by the way,' Felix says quietly, nodding towards my borrowed clothes.

'I . . . uh . . . Thanks,' I say.

'Managed to keep your boxers on this time?'

I choke on a sip of wine and Felix laughs. At the same moment we hear the crackle of tires on gravel and Dot jumps up excitedly.

'Daddy's here!' she almost shrieks.

'Great.' Felix's jaw tightens and he pours himself another glass of wine. There is something in this sudden shift in demeanour that makes me want to reach out and take his hand. I hear an approaching mix of voices, a loud laugh, then three figures appear around the side of the house.

David Blake is tall and broad with the same dark golden curls as his son, though where Felix's are loose and carefree, David's are cropped sensibly short and shot through with silver. He is smiling, showing off a set of pristinely white teeth, a soft-looking leather suit-carrier slung casually over one shoulder. His navy tie is loose, and the top button of his white shirt is undone, a practised picture of casual sophistication. He is flanked by a short, ugly man and a tall, beautiful woman.

The ugly man takes my hand in his, which is soft and hot. He tells me his name is Simon Chance, David's business partner, and my skin tingles. There is something about the way he looks at me, like I am a fish he has caught and can't decide whether to kill or throw back. Simon slides a hairy arm around the waist of the tall, beautiful woman, whom he introduces as Celeste.

'I am Simon's . . . good friend,' she tells me. Her eyes are lined with emerald kajal. There are flecks of gold in her brown gaze, which glitters as she speaks. Celeste slinks past me to plant two kisses on each member of the Blake family's cheeks. 'Ah, Fifi!' She gasps and wraps her pale arms around Felix's throat from behind. She plants an exaggerated kiss on his cheek, which he swivels to return. He does not stand to greet his father.

'Annie, you gorgeous creature, how are you? Lily, how's university? Felix, how's whatever it is you pretend to do with your time? Dot, my darling, aren't you blossoming into quite the young woman?'

The Blakes murmur their answers as Simon drops into the chair I was sitting in. Dot says nothing. Her expression is black as thunderclouds, thick brows knitted together.

'Let's have a bloody drink!' Simon shouts. 'Polka Dot, would you do the honours?'

Dot scowls and stays seated, folding her arms across her chest.

'Dotty, don't be so rude,' says Annie. 'Get Uncle Simon a drink.' Dot scrapes her metal chair across the flagstones.

'Let me guess . . . Whiskey. Rocks.' Simon nods.

'Chic, as always.' Felix winks at Dot, who seems to relax a little then trudges off to get the drink. 'And a French 75 for our French 75!' he calls after her.

'Oh Fifi, you are too kind,' Celeste purrs. Dot mumbles something about not using the good champagne and slams the door behind her. A tiny crack appears in the bottom left pane, but nobody seems to notice.

Wednesday

I don't remember going to bed but I must have at some point because that is where I wake up. The curtains are open and a slice of light cuts across my face. My head is hot and my mouth tastes like alcohol. I roll over and wait for my vision to catch up. A full glass of water sits on the small table next to my bed, a naive attempt to stave off the grim reality of the morning. I must have smoked last night because splinters pierce my throat with every breath.

I have never liked cigarettes. I remember Lily once telling me you can become addicted to anything if you try hard enough, which I found incredibly sad. Mum used to smoke. I remember delicate wisps of silver rising up from her brown fingers. When I was little, I used to sneak into her room and sit on the pink satin stool in front of her vanity. I'd slip the top drawer open and slide a cigarette from the blue packet. I'd practise holding it as precisely as her, trying to emulate the graceful arc of her slender wrist with my pudgy one. I would put it to my mouth and suck in my cheeks then slowly let the air escape through lightly pursed lips like she would do when she knew a man was watching her but was pretending not to notice. Once, when I was maybe five or six, I found a silver lighter next to the blue box. As I sucked in, the tip flaring orange against the flame, the glamour of the moment surged up from my stomach and I vomited all over the vanity. For three days afterwards, every time Mum looked at me, she burst out laughing. Cigarette smoke on clothes always makes me think of her, but the evocation is hollow. The base notes of cinnamon and cocoa butter are missing.

'Please tell me you haven't locked this door, darling,' says Lily from behind the thick wood. 'The key is from the thirteenth century and it's really actually just for show.' I have absolutely no idea whether I've locked the door and as I scramble to pull on Felix's borrowed trousers, the catch clicks and Lily tumbles into the room. 'Oh, don't look so stricken, I've seen it all before. Now splash some water on your face and get dressed. We've both missed breakfast, so Felix is going to drive us into town. I'd murder a man for a pain aux raisins.'

'You'd murder a man for much less, Lil,' I reply.

Felix is waiting in a bright yellow Jeep Wrangler. He's wearing electric-blue cat-eye sunglasses and his hair is pushed back from his face. It's careful, considered and looks so casual that I almost fall for it.

'Get in, losers, we're going *le shopping*.'

Lily gracefully slips into the passenger seat and I clamber over into the back. I've barely made contact with the hot black leather before Felix slams his foot down, spraying gravel towards the house. He swings out of the long drive and we speed past fields and small stone buildings. 'Call Me' by Blondie crackles through the stereo.

The winding country lanes eventually give way to proper roads with markings and speed limits.

'I can never remember which fucking side to drive on,' Felix shouts back to me, swerving lazily across both lanes. I muster a laugh but tighten my grip on the door, wishing he'd look at the road. His gaze lingers on mine for a second, then he smiles and there is a light in his eyes that connects to something in my chest. Lily is shrieking with laughter but pulls him back round to face forwards.

'Watch. The. Road,' she says, punctuating each word with a slap to Felix's bare thigh. Mercifully, we slow down as we approach a small town and Felix looks for a place to park. He settles for a tiny piece of pavement between two big blue vans. After two attempts at parallel parking, he yanks out the keys with the back end of the Jeep jutting out at an angle.

'I am good at many things,' he says. 'But parking is not one of them.'

'Or driving,' says Lily, plucking the thought from my head.

I trail a few steps behind to watch the siblings lazily wander down cobbled streets they seem to know so well. They let themselves float down side-streets and alleys, confident they will end up where they need to be. Lily flits between stalls and shopfronts, picking up trinkets. She stuffs a floppy white sun hat over Felix's head and snaps a photograph of him with the film camera she wears around her neck. Felix winks at the old lady sitting by the stall as he hands the hat back to her. She returns his smile. I get the feeling that these two could take anything they wanted and no one would complain. Felix is striding ahead, his curls dancing between brown and gold as shafts of sunlight escape from adjacent streets, eager to greet him. The shutter clicks on Lily's camera and I can see each moment as it will appear on film: Felix between steps, the sun lighting up the hairs on his muscular leg, the rest of his body in shadow. I can't stop watching him, recording every fluid motion of his body. Will photographs ever do it justice?

'Come on, Magpie. I'm going to starve to death,' Felix calls back to Lily, who has stopped at a small stand selling silver and gold jewellery. She is bent forwards, hands clasped behind her back, face screwed up in concentration. She straightens up and picks something off the table.

'Try this on,' she says, reaching for my hand. She loosens her fist and a thin gold chain pours into my outstretched palm like sand through an hourglass. The chain is thin and delicate, its weight barely perceptible in my hand. I slip it around my neck and fumble with the clasp.

'Here, let me.' Felix's hands take over; my stomach tightens at the touch. *Click, click, click.* Lily fixes yet another moment in time, but it stretches out beyond the snapshot. I can feel my heart pounding and imagine that Felix must be able to feel it too, pulsing down the chain to his fingertips. He finishes with the clasp and smooths his hands across my shoulders before giving them a light but deliberate squeeze.

'Oh, it looks so beautiful,' whispers Lily. 'Gold really works with your skin tone. One sec.' She takes my shoulders and repositions me so I'm facing toward the light. 'Perfection.' *Click.*

'Right, you two: food,' says Felix, dragging his sister away from the stall.

'But the necklace—' I say.

'It's already yours, my dear,' Felix cuts me off. The owner of the stall is smiling and pushing some notes into the tin box on the table.

In the main square, the market is starting to wind down. The Blake siblings slide through the dwindling crowd, waving at people like they've known them for years. Maybe they have. I feel very much like an afterthought here. A stranger they are treating kindly for a while. They seem so relaxed while I feel so displaced. Maybe it's my hangover, which curdles in the August heat. I wish I'd brushed my teeth before we left the Chateau. As if he's read my mind, Felix hands me an apple, a bite of which takes away the cottony feeling in my mouth. He chatters away in rapid French to the owner of the stall. Lily drifts down the makeshift corridor, camera clicking as she goes.

We find a cafe on the corner of the square and cluster around a small green table. Felix carefully piles paper bags full of cherries and peaches and green beans between the chairs while Lily orders coffees and pastries, I fiddle with my new necklace.

A stall towards the edge of the market catches my attention. While the others are varying shades of grubby tarpaulin with open fronts showing off beeswax candles and fresh fruit, this one seems closed. A handwritten sign saying bienvenue is the only indication that it is actually in use. I excuse myself from the table and walk towards it. Beneath the neat welcome there is a scribble, barely visible under the glaring sun.

MME DE BENET
TAROT, VOYANCE ET CHIROMANCIE

'Feeling lucky?' says a voice and I jump. A tall woman, presumably Madame de Benet, appears through the curtain. 'You would like to know what your future holds.' Her voice is deep and authoritative. This isn't a question.

I'm not really sure I believe in any of this. Grandma would call it witchcraft and nonsense. Jasmine would say that the occult provides the self-reflection that our faithless society is lacking now. I decide it can't hurt.

I'm not sure what I was expecting to see behind the curtain. Maybe lots of soft cushions and tapestries, the smell of incense. But the inside of the tent is bare apart from a small table and two chairs. Madame de Benet leads me across the concrete floor. She has pale yellow hair with dark roots showing through, a strong, aquiline nose and high, angular cheekbones. She gestures to the empty chair. I sit.

'My French isn't very good,' I start to apologise.

'*Oui, je sais, mon cher.*' She places both of her hands face-up on the wooden table. I do the same. She takes mine, turning them over to study my knuckles, running her thumbs down my fingers. Her hands are warm and rough and dry. She takes a deep breath. My palms are facing upwards now, and Madame de Benet gently traces them. First the deep coarse lines, then the finer ones. Once, twice, three times. Another breath. I realise I am holding mine.

'Such sadness, little boy,' she says. 'And grief. To lose a mother in that way.' I am startled and pull my hands away. She shushes me and takes hold of my hands again, tighter this time. 'Such sadness, so young.' She clucks softly, shaking her head. 'So much love here too, little boy. Not all of it is wise to give, but you give it anyway. And why would cruel Luck deny you? There is power in beauty, and beauty in power. But a mother's hands can cut as well as cradle – she will be the ruin of it all. In or out. The clock ticks on. A house built on shifting sands falls into the sea, *mon cher*. Little birds always fly back to their nests.'

None of this makes any sense at all. I feel too hot in this tent. I stand up and hide my hands in my pockets. I pull out a crumpled ten-euro note and try to throw it onto the table. It falls short and as I bend to pick it up I catch my forehead on the edge of the table. I swear and give the woman the note. I walk back to the cafe where Felix and Lily are waiting with curiosity oozing from their faces. My forehead is pulsating where I hit the table and I think I can hear a faint rumble of laughter linger from the tent. I sit and drink my coffee in silence; I'm no longer hungry.

'You look like you've seen a ghost,' says Lily.

'Maybe he has.'

When we pull in to the driveway, Dot is sitting on the stone wall near the road. Excited, she hops off and races us up towards the house. Her bare feet deftly pick out the mossy rocks as she runs. Felix slows down, his lips curving into a smile. They have played this game before. We obviously have the advantage on speed, but the drive sweeps up to the gates in a long arc while Dot makes a beeline through the trees. The roar of the engine in low gear drowns out the music coming from the stereo. It's too close to call and I think for a moment that one of them will pull out: the narrow opening of the gate is far too small for both Dot and the car to fit through. I involuntarily clamp shut my eyes. The engine roar gives way to Lily's high, terrified scream and the firecracker sound of gravel on metal.

'You stupid, fat oaf!' squeaks Dot, now standing by the car and breathing heavily. 'You could have killed me!' She brings down a flat palm onto the bonnet of the Jeep, slamming it hard.

'You should stay off the fags, Dorothea, they're making you slow,' Felix says to Dot, who scowls.

'Don't. Call. Me. Dorothea,' she says darkly, then spits onto the windscreen. There is a pause before the three of them start chuckling. There is a wild note to Dot's laughter, which reflects in her eyes as she looks at me through the rolled-down window and says, 'I've got a surprise for you.'

She turns and skips towards the house. Her bare feet on the gravel make me wince. The rest of us climb out of the car. Lily and I start unpacking the groceries from the small boot while Felix wipes away Dot's gift and checks the bonnet for dents.

'What in the name of all that is sacred is that?' Felix says, horrified. I follow his gaze to where Dot is picking her way towards us, pulling a battered suitcase behind her. The slightly-faded-but-still-too-bright-to-be-stylish pink and yellow flowers give the game away.

'Oh my God, you found it!' I say, reaching over to take it from her.

'Well, technically EasyJet found it and then they called Mummy who sent Luc to get it,' replies Dot. 'I volunteered to go with him, trying to stay out of the way of the grown-ups. Who you lot left me all alone with, by the way.' Her brother and sister exchange guilty looks as she continues. 'Luckily Simon was busy drooling over his new "friend", and Mummy and Daddy were fighting. But anyway, I haven't let it out of my sight all morning. Except for a brief two minutes when I had to go to the toilet. And I guess maybe another five minutes when I heard you coming and then waited on the wall for the race – which I would have won easily if you hadn't been driving like a total idiot.' She scowls at Felix. 'But anyway, yeah, you're welcome.'

I take the suitcase and Felix sidles up next to me.

'Darling,' he says, 'haven't you heard of Mulberry?'
Then he walks inside, leaving the Jeep blocking the gate.

The air is completely still and the chirp of crickets crackles through the hot air like static. I am sinking into a sun lounger, rereading the same page of my book, fighting sleep and the heat. Somewhere a guitar is being tuned, strummed, paused, retuned. The sun beats down from a cloudless sky and the yellow flagstones kick up lazy ripples of heat. My book slips from my grasp and I do not try to stop it. I let it and myself fall further into the afternoon.

'*Malheur!*'

The sudden shout makes me jump. Celeste triumphantly plants seven tiles onto the green board. They are sitting at a wrought-iron table next to the swimming pool. An invisible insect skates across the water's surface.

'*Ça me fait trente-cinq points,*' she says, regaining her languid composure. '*Et tu as vingt-trois.*'

'*Bien joué,*' growls Mrs Blake, studying the board, sunglasses carefully placed on the tip of her nose. There is a gentle push and pull between the two women. They have been playing this game for hours. Slowly and quietly battling with words, in both English and French, effortlessly switching between the two languages as they chat and gossip and size each other up. My French is GCSE at best, so I struggle to follow, letting the words wash over me until something piques my interest.

'Conniving,' says Mrs Blake after a while.

'What is "conniving",' asks Celeste, the delicate wrinkle of a frown appearing in the space between her perfectly shaped eyebrows.

'I'm sure you know,' says Annie. 'Someone who'll go to great lengths to get what they want.'

'Ah, conniving! Like you?' asks Celeste with a trace of smirk.

'I already have everything I want,' Annie replies. 'And I'm very protective of it. My children most of all. Especially dear Felix.' I feel the flash of her eyes through the lenses. 'You have to be careful around men like Felix.' Her gaze turns to me and I feel heat prickle my face until suddenly her eyes flick towards something over my shoulder. '*Ah! Quand on parle du loup, on en voit la queue!*'

'Never mind my tail, Mother, this wolf's ears are burning,' says Felix, striding down towards the pool. 'Gossiping about me again are we, ladies? What's for lunch?'

Without waiting for either answer, he peels off his T-shirt and dives gracefully into the water, glides the length of the pool, then comes up for air, shaking his head and sending out a spiral of crystal droplets.

'Fifi!' cries Celeste as the water knocks the board to the floor and scatters the letter tiles into the dry grass. She gathers them, turning to look at Felix and rolling her eyes from behind the sweep of straight black hair that has cascaded over her forehead. Felix splashes her with water. A smile tugs at the edges of her mouth. 'Felix, don't.'

He returns her look for a second, the tension between them pulsing through the warm air. Then Felix brings both hands arcing upwards, sending a sheet of water directly into Celeste's face. Dripping wet and suddenly furious, she draws herself up, breathes a long, slow breath, turns on her heel, and marches into the house. Felix whistles, feigning amazement. He winks at me, drawing me into complicity.

'The French can't take a joke.' Felix dips his face half into the water and takes in a mouthful, then spits it towards Mrs Blake.

'Oh, Felix, darling, don't be vulgar.' She picks up her gin-and-tonic, draws herself up to her full height so she looms over her son and pours the remaining two-thirds of the drink onto his head. Felix shrieks at the cold. The slice of lime bobs in the water beside Felix, mocking him. Satisfied, she saunters up the lawn towards the house and disappears.

'It appears', Felix smirks, 'that the Greeks can't take a joke either.'

'Is your family from Greece?' I ask him, suddenly realising that I've always just assumed Lily was straight up Anglo-Saxon.

'Technically Cypriot. Or Greek Cypriot, it depends which uncle you talk to. Just never Turkish, unless you want to end up with a black eye. Although most conversations with Mum's family end up with someone getting a black eye.' I laugh but again it appears he isn't joking. Or maybe he is and I just haven't yet learned how to tell. I

44

think maybe there's a playful light in his golden eyes that is starting to feel familiar.

'Not that Mum talks to anyone from that side anymore anyway. They pretty much disowned her when she swapped Constantinou for Carpenter and ran away to London to reinvent herself. But I suppose I wouldn't be here if she hadn't.'

Something about the name tugs at part of my mind.

'And I guess I wouldn't be here if Dad hadn't walked into that specific jazz club on that specific night and seen her sing. He says he fell madly in love with her within two bars. But so did everybody else at the time.'

'Wait, is your mum Annie Carpenter? Like, *the* Annie Carpenter?'

'Uh, yeah,' says Felix, looking confused. 'Did Lily not say? God, Annie's gonna be furious.' He drags out the last word, savouring the fun he'll have when he tells her.

Growing up with Mum, Annie Carpenter's voice was the soundtrack to our life. I can still hear the satisfying chunky click of the cassette in the deck of Mum's old purple Nissan Micra, the pause before the music started. The swishing hi-hat, the thick thrum of the double bass, the gentle rolling piano, the light urgency of the alto sax. Then that voice. Like a rumble of distant thunder. It slipped so well into the music that sometimes you could barely tell that a woman was singing, the voice just another perfectly tuned instrument. Mum would sit, eyes closed, engine idle, listening to the first track of that album and just breathe. I would try to do the same but would always sneak a peek at her, tall and still and beautiful beside me. At her favourite part of the song – a soaring unaccompanied note rising as if from the depths of the sea – a tiny smile would play at the corners of her mouth. I like to remember Mum like this – peaceful, happy, undisturbed. We would listen to that album all the way through, track by track, on every car journey. And if we reached the end, on longer journeys to rain-soaked seasides, she'd turn the tape over and we'd start again. Hi-hat, bass, piano, sax, thunder, bliss.

'Oh God, you're not a *fan*, are you?' The word drips with disdain.

'Well, no. I mean, yeah. I mean, I like her music. But, like, everyone does, right? I wouldn't say I'm a super-fan or whatever. I just . . . My mum used to listen to her in the car, I guess.' I'm babbling.

'Used to?'

'Uh, yeah, she's . . . not around anymore.' I try to catch the words but they have already escaped. I watch Felix's face change with his perception of me.

'Oh. Man, I'm sorry. That sucks,' he says. He looks at me in a new way. Felix's formality, which I hadn't realised had coloured our interactions until now, seems to have faded away a bit.

'Yeah. It does suck.' I feel a sting of tears and a sharp tug scraping at my chest. I blink and push it down, wiping my face of emotion.

'Let's get another beer and find Lil,' Felix says, lifting himself out of the pool, pausing at the top to allow the water to cascade down around him, framing his body in silver shards of light.

'Yeah, sure, give me one sec.'

As he drips up towards the house, I allow myself a moment of indulgence. I close my eyes and picture my mother next to me: serene, mellow, the sour smoke of the joint between her purple-painted fingers curling up around her, gold eyeshadow and puffball afro, lost in the music. Hi-hat, bass, piano, sax, thunder, smile. Bliss.

When I track down Felix and Lily, they have snapped into host mode. Felix is speaking into his phone in rapid French and Lily hands me a pile of fluffy towels.

'Family emergency,' she says. 'Would you be an absolute knight in shining armour and pop these up to Fizz and Bill's room, please? Apparently, they'll be here in twenty minutes and Luc's in town doing something for Daddy. Mummy's going absolutely spare – I don't think she's made a bed in thirty years.' She disappears off into the house before I can ask who Fizz and Bill are or where their room is meant to be. I follow the sound of absent-minded humming and find Mrs Blake surprisingly making a bed in a room down the corridor from Felix's.

'Oh, you absolute darling, thank you,' she says, taking the stack of towels from me and placing it on a side-table. 'Has Lily put you to work already? Good man. Would you grab the other edge of that sheet? I fear it may be too small for the bed. That's it, now pull.'

The sheet tears as I pull it towards me, causing both me and Mrs Blake to stagger backwards.

'Oh God, I'm so sorry, Mrs Blake, I didn't mean—'

'Egyptian Cotton, my arse! And please, for the love of God, call me Annie. I will not tell you again, my sweet.'

Mrs Blake twists the torn strips of linen into a ball and throws it behind her. She takes a second sheet and unfurls it over the bed. This time we tuck it neatly around the mattress.

'Good God, what else do people need? Pillows!' she barks at me and throws them in my direction with a couple of mismatched cases. 'It really is so lovely to meet one of Lily's university friends. My daughter can be so secretive sometimes, it's like I barely know her. But meeting you has reassured me she's in with a good crowd. Christ, some of the friends Felix brought back from Edinburgh really were dreadful. Now what was her name? Ariadne? Arabella! That's it. Awful girl, so impossibly dull. Being pretty is useless when you have absolutely nothing to say.

'She talks about you an awful lot, you know. Lily, I mean, not Arabella. I think she's very, very fond of you. I can see why, I suppose. You're very beautiful. And there's a gentleness about you that I think she craves. She very much values your friendship, I think. And it's been good to have an outsider here – keeps the lid on family tensions. Felix and David have been out for one another's blood since . . .' She trails off then seems to remember I'm standing there. 'Well, it's lovely to have you.'

I don't really know how to respond to any of this. No

one, except maybe Mum and Grandma, has ever called me beautiful before. I have a thousand questions; about Arabella, about Felix and Mr Blake, but I get the feeling she has already said more than she'd prefer. I feel too shy to meet her gaze but sense that it is fixed on me. 'Thank you, it's so nice to be here. The house is so nice.'

'It is, isn't it?' she says, clearly relieved to be back on even ground. 'Though I do wish people wouldn't turn up to it two damn days early. I'm throwing a garden party, not running a bloody bed-and-breakfast. And where the devil is Luc? I pay him to run the household, not sit around smoking and drinking cognac with my husband.'

She finishes straightening the sheets then surprises me by pulling me into a gentle hug. Oranges again. 'Welcome. It's so good to have you here,' she says for the third time.

I am saved from the need to respond by the sound of tyres on gravel and a commotion downstairs.

Fizz and Bill, it turns out, are the in-joke nicknames of Lily's ersatz godparents (her real ones having fallen out with David Blake over some business deal gone wrong back in the late nineties). Fizz – actually Fiona – a bottle-blonde sixty-something with a smudge of coral lipstick on her front tooth, tells me she got her nickname from her penchant for seeking out the most expensive bottle of champagne in any given location. Bill – actually Frederick – a rumpled former dot-com business mogul with a nest of grey-brown hair, seems to have been given his name because of his habit of funding Fizz's. Fizz

49

grips both my shoulders and surveys me at arm's length like I'm a butterfly under glass.

'Fascinating,' she purrs. 'And how was the flight from Manchester?' She pronounces the name like it's some jungle-wrapped city in a far-flung colony. 'Our daughter read Economics at Manchester. Years ago. Hated the place. Do you have the accent?'

'Can I get you a glass of something cold?' Felix sweeps in to rescue me, knocking me gently to the side with his hips and arching an eyebrow. 'Prosecco maybe?'

'Felix, my dear, you know I'll accept nothing less than champagne!' she replies.

We move out onto the terrace, Fizz leading the way with her glass shimmering in the afternoon sun. Everyone arranges themselves around the table, flopping back into domestic torpor now that their duties are done and the guests' glasses are filled. Bill complains about every step of their journey from Hampstead in excruciating detail. Felix listens but maintains eye contact with me over the rim of his glass, a flicker of laughter dancing across his eyes without quite spilling over onto the rest of his face. The sudden appearance of Dot by my side sends a jolt of unease through me. Felix's gaze casually slips back to Bill.

'Mummy told me to ask you if you'd do me the honour of accompanying me on the piano for La Fête. You can't say no because Lily already told me how good you are, and I told Mummy I'd already asked you and you said you'd be delighted. There's sheet music by the piano, not that anyone really uses it in this house anyway,' she says feverishly. 'Do you know Porter? Of course you do. Everybody knows Porter. Shall I show you?'

She doesn't wait for a reply but instead takes my hand in hers, soft and moist from the afternoon heat, and leads me back up to the house and in through the French windows. The drawing room is cool and shaded. Faded striped pillows are scattered across white settees and in the ornate fireplace a neat pile of pale wood waits patiently for the first drift of cold air. Dot drags me to a gleaming black baby grand piano. A stack of sheet music, warped, ringed and gummed together from years of neglect and countless spilled drinks, splays its notes across the piano's surface.

'Let's see what you've got,' says Dot, flicking through *The Cole Porter Song Book* until she finds what she's looking for. She guides me down onto the stool with excited trepidation.

I stretch out my fingers. Having been home at Grandma's for most of the summer, I haven't sat behind a piano in months. The first few bars of the song Dot has chosen are slow and complicated. Two false starts. She is forced to drag out the first line and a bum note from me pulls her voice unnaturally low. She catches my eye and we both burst out laughing. I slide a frustrated, discordant glissando across the keys.

'Let's go again. Just relax. It is jazz, after all.'

I start again, this time making it through the introduction and opening verse. When we reach the chorus, Dot springs into action and I feel the music open up for us. There is a familiar shift of gear and I stop reading the music, I stop thinking, my fingers glitter across the ivory. I like to imagine this is what it feels like to fly. As we speed towards the end of the song, the excitement carries us both away and Dot starts to spin, black hair whirling around her. Finally, she collapses, panting, holding the edge of the piano. We both laugh for a long time.

'You sound a lot like your mum,' I manage to say between breaths.

Dot slows her breathing and stares at me mischievously. 'It's de-lovely to have you here.'

Thursday

I wander down through stone corridors to the terrace.
It is still early. The sun is over the horizon but only just.
I must have narrowly missed it creep up past the distant
mountains that separate us from the sea. The pale disc,
wrapped in the thin gauze of morning air, gently kisses
the blue hilltops. The crickets hail the new day in hushed
reverence, daring me to break the silence, but I do not.
The golden tickle of light on my face promises another
day thick with heat.

A movement in a field just beyond the boundaries of
the Chateau's far wall catches my attention. The field is a
craggy sun-browned cheek with huge round bales of hay,
or straw maybe, dotted around it. It moves again and my
eyes catch it and follow. The hare is long and sleek and
fast. It pauses as if it heard my sharp intake of breath.
It sits tall, checking for danger. Finding none, it bows its
smooth brown head and nibbles at something I cannot
see. Suddenly, its long ears prick up and its body flattens
against the dry earth, then it darts away across the field,
making a zigzag pattern between the bales before my
view is obscured by the tall trees at the far corner of the
garden. A noise behind me makes me jump.

'Beautiful in the morning, isn't it?' Felix is standing

close behind me. His breath is warm on my neck. I feel a sudden urge to turn and fold into him, but I do not.

'There was a hare.'

'Ah yes, he comes up into the garden sometimes. I leave vegetable scraps out for him if we have any left over. Coffee?'

He holds his mug out to me with his large hand. I take it and sip from the edge of the cup that is already wet with coffee and the memory of his lips.

'I can never go back to sleep once I've woken up,' he says, taking the coffee back and taking another sip from where my mouth had been, his eyes not leaving mine. 'I like to come out here in the morning, where no one can distract me. It's almost as peaceful as still being asleep.'

I start to apologise for encroaching, but he waves my sorry away.

'No, no, I like your company. Come. Sit.'

He climbs onto the low wall surrounding the terrace and sits with his legs dangling above yellowed bushes. He pats a patch of smooth stone next to him. We sit side by side, so close that our arms brush as we pass the mug back and forth. We watch as the sun paints the fields beyond the wall with blond light. A bird with a forked tail swoops and dips to drink from the stillness of the swimming pool.

I help Felix make breakfast. Or, more accurately, I follow his commands, fetching him ingredients and utensils and taking things out to the table when they are ready. There are little wire domes embroidered with flowers to keep the flies away from the food. People come down in dribs and drabs until we are all seated, munching toast and sipping tea and discussing the plan for the day. Mr Blake wants to show Bill and Simon the new fermenter down at the vineyard. Mrs Blake says that she cannot think of a single thing that would bore her more.

'I am entirely uninterested in any step of the wine-making process before it is poured into a glass. Fizzy, let's go into town – there's a gorgeous little place off the square that's just opened up. Oh, and you can have your cards read while we're there.'

'Going to get your hair braided by that gypsy man in the dress, are you?' Simon chimes in from behind the *Telegraph*.

'Actually, Si, she is Romani,' Lily says. 'And I don't think you should talk about people like that.'

'Oh, what's he going to do? Put a curse on me?'

'By the looks of that hairline, Uncle Si, I think she already has.' Felix's joke doesn't do much to ease the tension. There is a moment of silence before Lily breaks it.

'Well, I'm going to show our guest the bathing pool. Any adventurers who think they're up to the journey should report to the kitchen in . . .' She checks her watch. '. . . fifteen minutes, with their togs, some sensible foot-wear, and a can-do attitude.'

'Aye-aye, Captain!' booms Felix, saluting. He gathers up some plates and marches in through the French windows.

*

The three siblings and I gather in the kitchen to divide the chores for our excursion. Felix is wrapping fresh bread, ripe peaches and blue cheese in tea towels, placing them carefully into his rucksack. I am on swimsuit duty, but Lily needs a hand with drinks, so I help her arrange a ridiculous amount of cans and bottles into a cooler. When the essentials are packed, Felix leads us down the garden, past the swimming pool, towards a strip of dry grass. He stops by a huge rusted metal wheel that leans against the wall, the bottom edge of it buried a few inches into the hard ground. A secret escape, he tells me, for a bored prince or a wayward servant. Or both. He climbs the spokes of the wheel then reaches up and pulls himself onto the high wall. He swings his legs over, pauses for a second, then drops out of sight. Lily goes next, looking down at us while we pass her the bags and the cooler, which she drops down to her brother. Then she too disappears. Dot gestures for me to go next. When I get to the top I am looking out on a quiet country lane. There is a ditch on the far side overflowing with green and yellow and orange life. At my feet, there is an unassuming stack of plastic crates, snaked through with flowers. They make an almost perfect staircase down from the wall. A secret escape route.

Felix is already walking down the lane. Though it was Lily who floated the idea, it's clear he is in charge. He leads us through the village, past faded blue and white signs, rust dripping down from the bolts that hold them on to walls the same shade as the Chateau's. Past little houses with unruly gardens, the green shutters flung wide. It is still early, not even midday, but the air buzzes with heat. We walk until we reach the edge of a village. We haven't passed anyone on our way there – there seems to be no one around at all. I point this out to the others.

'This place always feels deserted,' says Felix. 'Even when the locals are here.'

The road ends and we hop over a stile. We walk through a cluster of trees in between large, rolling fields of hay. I notice that the route we are taking is marked by yellow lines, hand-painted on some of the trees and fenceposts. Felix uses a switch of long grass to swat away flies. He tells stories of his childhood, spent running around these fields. Lily and Dot laugh, remember and correct him while I listen. Abruptly, Felix stops and hops over a section of fence onto a disused railway track. I am sweating now. Little beads collect on the curls at the nape of my neck and run down my back. Lily has piled her hair on top of her head to try and stay cooler and Felix has peeled off his T-shirt and tucked it into the waistband of his shorts. The straps of his rucksack leave an impression on his skin when he readjusts it. He catches me looking at him. He asks me if I want to hear a ghost story. Lily complains that she's heard it a hundred times, but Dot insists on hearing it again.

'In the century before this one,' Felix begins, 'before war came to Europe again, and before a tunnel was blasted through the mountainside between this village and the next, the only way to travel between them was

along this track. The train was privately run and trav-
elled only on market days. The villagers had no need to
travel more than this, satisfied with their little lives and
the little places in which they lived. And if they ever did
need to get to the next village over, they could follow the
tracks to exactly where they needed to be. One summer,
the trees on this side of the valley hung heavy with fruit.
Excited, the villagers plucked, preserved and sold what
they could and still had plenty left over. A young woman
came to know of a blight on the other side of the mountain, which had ruined crops and left an entire village sick
and hungry. She was fraught because her lover, a beautiful boy from that village, had not responded to her last
letter. She feared the worst. The family who owned the
railway – who had built it with the same money that built
the house we now call our own – had forbidden anyone
to use the tracks to reach the village, fearful they would
bring the blight back with them. But the young woman
decided she would make the journey across the valley to
see her lover and bring him some fruit, for they still had
plenty spare.

'She did not tell her father where she was going, knowing he would only worry and forbid her from making the
journey. In the night, she packed up a sack of fruit, bread
and wine, hurled it over her shoulder, tied her best purple
spotted scarf around her hair, and set out for the valley.
She knew the way, even in the early morning light when
the village was quiet and the bats and owls were her only
company. But she wasn't alone. The baker's boy saw her

sneaking out and raised the alarm. Soon, half of the village was following her, urging her to stay, warning she would bring the blight back with her. Someone sent for her father. The young woman had some resolve but knew she would buckle at the sound of her father's pleading voice, so she took some wax from around the stopper of the wine bottle and used it to plug her ears. She eventually found the tracks we stand on now and followed them out onto the plain without looking back. The villagers dared not venture onto the tracks and disobey the family's orders. What the young woman did not know was that they had finally taken pity on the neighbouring village. In their generosity, they had decided to send a wagon of fruit and bread and other necessities to help their neighbours. As she disappeared around a bend in the tracks, oblivious to the shouts of her friends and neighbours, the steam engine drawing the wagon was fired up.

'The journey by foot was long, but the steam train sped along towards its destination. Unknowing, the young woman hurried along as the dawn broke across the valley. She thought she felt a rumble, a vibration in the ground, but never having felt this before she paid it no mind. They say her death was quick. But people say all sorts of things. They say the driver did not even see her, slight as she was. It was only when the train pulled into the next village that someone noticed the purple spotted scarf that had become tangled in the front wheels of the train. A crowd had formed when they heard it coming and the woman's lover was among them. The young man saw the scarf and knew what had happened. They say he let out a pained, animal howl. They say he ran up the tracks in search of his love.'

Felix crouches and lies down on the hot ground. He motions to me to do the same. I oblige. His voice hums in my ear.

'Legend says she was lying in this exact spot. And when her lover found her body, lifeless but strangely unmarked, he began to cry, and his tears soaked into the wooden sleepers. People say he began to sing and the song soaked into the tracks. They say that if you listen closely, the rails still sing his lament.'

I try to slow down my breathing, straining to listen despite my scepticism. All I hear is the buzzing of the insects and my pounding heart and Felix's soft exhales. Until a blinding, clanging sound fills my head. I jump up, clamping my hands over my ears. Lily and Dot are both holding big sticks, each of them having struck one of the rails. The siblings collapse in a heap. I cannot bear their laughter and keep my hands over my ears, face down in the dirt. When the ringing finally stops, I pick myself up and brush the dust off my T-shirt. The Blakes look at each other, worried they might have taken it too far. I force a laugh, try to ease the tension, and ask in the most jovial voice I can muster where we are heading next. We walk in uneasy silence until we reach a break in the landscape where the railway bridges a deep ravine. We slip through the fence and start down the steep hillside. The Blakes skip lightly, seeming to know exactly where to place their feet. My Nikes slip and stumble after them. A twisted root almost sends me headfirst into Lily.

'You've got to keep your centre of gravity low,' Lily tells me. 'And take your time – trust me, it's worth it.'

The siblings disappear into the trees and I follow the sound of laughter and snapping twigs. Then there is something else, soft at first, a gentle murmur. It gets louder the further I go until I am suddenly in a clearing and the sound of falling water crashes through the air. The Blake children kick off their trainers and socks and head towards the water.

The pool is round and wide and perfect. Carved deep into the rock by the tumbling waterfall, it's deeper than I expected, the bottom invisible to the eye. The water is a chocolatey black at its centre, fading to gold where it laps gently at the riverbank. There is a barricade of big black stones downstream, where the pool swirls then spills over the rocky lips of the valley and into the river beyond. I reach the edge and offload my rucksack, glad to be rid of its rough, sticky embrace. I open it and search around, then start to panic as I cannot find what I am looking for. Lily, standing at the edge of the pool, notices the puzzled look on my face.

'What's happened?'

'Who had the swimming stuff?' I say, even though I know it was supposed to be me. My mind races back towards the Chateau and I see the costumes languishing on the marble countertop. I bite the inside of my cheek and look down at my feet.

'You're kidding,' says Lily. Her tone is deadpan but there is a smile in her eyes.

'I'm not going in naked!' shrieks Dot.

'Oh, come on, Dorothea! We were there when you were born,' says Felix. 'It wasn't that long ago that you were parading up and down the Chateau, naked, claiming to be the Frog Princess. I think you'll be fine.'

Dot goes beet red. 'That was years ago, and I'll have you know I was the Toad Queen, *actually*. And besides, it's . . . different now.' She blushes even deeper, avoiding my gaze as if it might turn her to stone.

'Dotty. They're just tits. And yours are lovely. You've got Mummy's. I'm stuck with the world's flattest chest and I—'

'Don't talk about my body like that. Just shut up, will you? I'm not going in. I'll watch the bags.' She stalks off up the bank and sits on a patch of dry earth under a big oak tree, facing away from the pool and our rucksacks.

'Suit yourself,' says Lily, rolling her eyes. She peels off her T-shirt, unhooks her bra and shimmies off her underwear. There are pink lines around her back and hips. She hops gracefully onto a large rock that leans out over the pool. Her skin, pale and perfect, glows in the light. She dives forward into the water, coming up for a gasp of air then swimming towards the foot of the waterfall.

'If I didn't know better, I might think you were some sort of pervert.' Felix looks up at me as he bends over to pull down his shorts. 'You know, if you wanted to see me naked so badly, you just had to ask.'

He stands up and I cannot stop my eyes from flicking down to his cock, nestled in a fuzz of curly brown hair. His eyes meet mine on their way back up and he takes a small step towards me. I feel my breath catch. He looks me up and down and it's like I'm already naked. He leans in even closer, so I feel his words on my cheek.

'Are you going to join us or are you going to miss out on all the fun?'

He winks then sprints to the point where Lily dived from, leaping into the air. He pulls his knees up to his chest, his broad back flexing as he wraps his arms around himself. The splash paints the rocks slick and black and causes Dot to turn from her sulk and smile at her siblings. She looks around, peeling off her T-shirt and shorts but keeping her underwear on and her arms folded tightly across her chest. She runs on tiptoes to the water's edge and wades in to join Lily and Felix, who have ducked under the waterfall and are now chatting and laughing. Their voices disappear into the raging water as I step out of my shorts and move towards the pool.

We eat the cheese and bread and peaches, the skin of our hands wrinkly from hours spent in the water. Juice drips from our chins and the sun beats down on the four of us. Felix's and Dot's skin shines deep and golden while Lily's turns into a warmer shade of pink. Dot's knees are pulled up to her chest. Felix tears open a can of Coke, the fizzy foam spilling out over his fingers and down his arms. He laughs, easy and free, throwing back his head and flicking the cold syrupy liquid at me. A precious drop lands on my lips and my tongue darts out to catch it. We are hungry from the walking, the swimming and the heat and we devour our picnic without a word escaping our mouths. In what seems like an instant, the sun shifts from our clearing and a cool breeze tickles the hairs on my body. Felix slaps his bare thighs and says we should head back and we wade across the shallow edge of the pool to where our clothes lie discarded, shadows of our urgency to dive in.

The walk back feels much quicker. The light in the forest is scattered and warm and we follow the river along its course until a steep path leads us up to a different path than the one we walked this morning. The ground rises to meet my feet as we scramble up the bank. I feel a calmness settle in my body, a sense of belonging that takes me by surprise. Lily loops an arm around my neck and kisses me on the cheek. She tells me she loves me, and I say it back, meaning it more than I ever have before. I store this memory away. A sliver of another life, one that I never dreamed could be mine. A bright, urgent feeling surges in my chest and I feel like I might cry. I don't know how much more happiness my body can bear. It is not used to feeling like this; it is almost painful. I grit my teeth and hope the feeling passes, though I know that when it goes, I will hunger for more. The feeling intensifies as we step into the burnished light of the setting sun.

We smell it before we see it. The fetid reek sends my head spinning. Dot coughs then retches. Lily scrunches up her face and asks no one in particular what the hell that smell is. The deer lies in the middle of the dusty road. Its ribcage is torn open and the dark blood in the sandy gravel is barely dry. The vehicle that did this – for only something made by men could wreak such wild and casual destruction – cannot be more than a mile away, kicking up dust clouds, skin and guts and death clinging to its bumper. Felix goes to drag the lifeless, beautiful beast to the side of the road, but its brown fur is slippery. A cloud of flies spirals out of the gaping blackness where its chest should be. Lily shrieks and vomits. Felix stoops to try again, embracing the deer around its sleek middle and heaving its weight out of the way of further harm. When he straightens up, his chest, face and arms are streaked with red. Dot wordlessly gathers flowers from the roadside and places them by the creature's head. She kneels and closes the deer's glassy eyes with her stubby fingers. There is nothing to say so we walk the rest of the way in silence. I try to wash the animal off my mind, but I can feel its unseeing eyes tracking our journey home. Through the languid evening that follows, the scent lingers in my nose and spoils the food in front of me. Whenever I look at Felix, I can still see his hands covered in blood.

I excuse myself after pushing food around my plate for an hour, leaving the Blakes and their guests to play yet another parlour game. They all know its obscure rules and I don't want to hold back their fun by asking them to explain it for a third time. I walk towards the pool and slip my phone out of my pocket. I dial Jazz's number. She picks up on the second ring.

'WhiteBoy, thank God! I was beginning to think they'd mounted your head on a wall or something.'

'It's so good to hear your voice. How've you been?'

'Oh, you know, kissing cuties and getting myself into trouble . . . the usual. But how are you, though? I wanna know everything.'

'I'm good, I'm good. It's kind of mad here. I knew they were posh and stuff but this is next level.'

'You're at a castle in France with a girl whose dad owns half of Kensington. Babe, what did you think it was gonna be like?'

'Yeah, obviously, but, like, at uni Lily's relatively normal—'

'Be fucking for real, WhiteBoy. She once looked me directly in the eye and asked me if I could ski.'

'True. But everything is different here. The wealth feels more real. You can see it everywhere and nobody but me seems to notice. Like it's normal to have servants and marble statues and own a fucking vineyard.'

'That's their normal, innit, the nought-point-nought-nought-one per cent. It's all castles and moats and nose jobs to hide the inbreeding.'

I snort with laughter then feel bad. 'They're really nice though, they've been so welcoming. Everything feels so easy here. I don't have to think about anything.'

'But what are they *like*? You must have some goss. I bet they've got some weird rituals or something.'

'I mean, they did push me in the pool as an initiation—'

'Oh, they didn't! You poor thing! Can you even swim? I can see the headlines now: "black kid drowns at mysterious french castle".' She pauses, letting out a raspy laugh. 'Who am I kidding? They'd bury that story quicker than your lifeless body.'

'Woah, that's a bit dark, Jazz. They're actually nice people.'

'I'm messing, man. Didn't realise you had to hand over your sense of humour when you got there.'

I laugh. 'Fuck off. No, they're cool, really. Lily's mum is so nice. Kind of terrifying, and I wouldn't want to get on her wrong side, but she's been lovely to me so far. There's this creepy-ass guy though, one of their dad's friends? He's proper slimy and has this model girl hanging off his arm but she clearly hates him.'

'What about the older brother? Is he as much of a wasteman as he sounds?' There's a rising sensation in my chest at the mention of Felix. I hesitate over the question. 'What?' says Jazz.

'Nothing. He's . . . he's . . . I don't know. He's Lily's brother.'

'Uh . . . yeah. Oh shit, babe, don't go getting a crush on a Blake.'

'I don't have a crush! I just . . . He's fit. That's it.'

Jazz yawns. It's late, and she has work in the morning. 'Well, just don't fall in love with him, alright?'

'I won't,' I say, but it feels like a lie.

'It's nice to hear your voice, dude. I miss you. Wish you

were here.' I let the implication dissolve in the silence. 'I might have found us a flat, you know? It's cute, cosy . . . Like, fucking tiny, but we'd make it ours. In Tooting, as well, near the station, so I wouldn't be too far from Mum and Dad.' She dives into talk about the flat and the horrible ones she's already queued hours to view. I lie back and listen to her talk. After a while Jazz says she should get ready for bed but asks me to stay on the line. I listen as she brushes her teeth, shouts at her little sister for using her face cream. I listen to the rustles and clinks of her night-time routine. The sounds make me feel closer to her. Closer to home.

Friday

Something about birthdays always makes me sad. There's an unspoken disappointment woven into the fabric of the day itself. The natural downside of the outsized importance and excitement placed on it in the run-up. Mine is invariably wet, grey and lonely. I once wished on my candles to never have another birthday again. Which, on reflection, is pretty dark. The deepest sadness, I think, comes from the feigning of surprise and gratitude at a disappointing gift. The grief of choosing silence when you haven't got what you wanted. Lily, it seems, does not share my disdain.

Last night, after Jazz's breathing slowed to a soft purr, I snuck through the corridors to find Lily. We tiptoed downstairs for a bottle of champagne then sat up for hours, tipsy and giggling, cross-legged on her bed. I gave her my gift at midnight, a little gingham cotton pouch for storing rolling tobacco with a pocket to keep papers and filters on the front. We'd seen it in a craft shop near campus earlier in the year and had laughed at how silly yet practical it was. I could tell she wanted one but didn't want to admit it. When the wrapping revealed it, she hugged me really tight then filled up our glasses and we toasted to being silly. She talked me through the traditions and rituals of Blake birthdays in microscopic detail. At uni, when I previously heard about her family, they seemed distant and inscrutable. Now I feel like I've been given a cipher. I'm beginning to understand the magic.

All families have their rites and customs, the domestic idiosyncrasies that demarcate their little unit from others. The Blakes apparently have hundreds for birthdays alone. I try to keep up, warmed by the dancing glow of their familial love. Lily, a silver plastic tiara perched on her head, shrieks with laughter as she is thrown into the air and caught on her bedsheet twenty-one times. A boarding-school tradition, I am told. Felix, David, Bill and I each hold a corner while Annie, Dot and Fizz cling to the edges of the sheet. Simon and Celeste are notable by their absence. I wonder if they think they are above this or if I've been specially chosen to be included. As we hurl Lily into the air a final time, her dark plaits floating ethereally above her, she catches my eye and for a moment I am distracted. The corner I'm holding slips from my fingers and Lily tumbles towards me, taking me out as she goes. Bill helps me to my feet.

'Got to keep your eye on the ball, my man!'

Downstairs in the kitchen, Felix boils scores of eggs while Dot marches from the oven to the marble island, chopping mountains of toast into a battalion of soldiers. Lily has sent me through from the drawing room – which is what they call the one with the settees and piano in it – to find more celery salt because the drinks trolley has run out. For a moment I'm not sure if I'm being sent on some fool's errand. When I was sixteen, grandma made me work with my Uncle Henry – not a real uncle but one of the many Jamaicans who made the crossing at a similar time to Grandma and was therefore considered family. I turned up to the building site with my packed lunch – cold rice and peas and a Mini Babybel – and borrowed steel-toe boots, terrified and out of place. Kitted out in a hi-vis tabard two sizes too big, I was sent off first thing to the suppliers to pick up some tools: a masonry drill bit, a 17mm combination wrench, some 4mm screws and a glass hammer. The first three were easy enough but then after maybe half an hour of traipsing awkwardly round the shop, I asked the red-faced bald man behind the counter to help me with the hammer. Immediately his eyes lit up.

'Yeah, mate,' he said, 'we keep 'em just next to the chocolate teapots!'

With his laughter ringing in my ears and embarrassment propelling me forwards, I walked out of the shop and straight home. I never went back to the building site and Uncle Henry never mentioned it again.

'Celery salt?' I say cautiously, stepping into the busy kitchen.

'What?' shouts Felix, straining to hear over the music blaring from the radio on the windowsill.

'I've been sent for celery salt . . . CELERY SALT!' I shout back just as Dot turns down the volume.

'Wow, chill out, mate!' says Felix with a backwards nod. 'Over there, cupboard below the spice rack.'

I root around the tins and boxes, pallid vegetables in jars and pomegranate molasses and ras-el-hanout and unlabelled things I can't even begin to identify. Near the back is a dusty silver biscuit tin with the words I'm looking for embossed on a homemade label. I grab the tin and turn to stand up but find myself facing the waistband of Felix's shorts. He jerks his hips back to avoid a collision and drops the carton he's holding. Yolks and shells splatter across the stone floor.

'Careful! You almost smashed *my* eggs too, mate.'

'I'm so, so sorry,' I say, scrambling to stop the eggs seeping into the grooves between the flagstones, catching the thick, slippery liquid with my hands. Felix grabs a tea towel from an upper shelf, picks up the half-empty carton, and wipes the excess egg from the floor. Once damage control is done, he takes a fresh cloth and runs it under the tap. He takes a step closer to me. I can smell his aftershave: cedar and pepper and earth. Felix takes my hands in his, the cloth is rough but his touch is gentle.

'I'm going to have to watch my step around you, aren't I?' he flirts. I tilt my head upwards slightly to meet his eye. A reply starts to form in my mind but is cut short.

'Felix! Fire!' shrieks Dot. Felix spins around in alarm. A thin wisp of grey smoke is rising from a blackened piece of bread between Dot's oven-gloved hands. Felix laughs, takes the toast in the wet tea towel and drops it into the bin.

'Dorothea, you little drama queen.' He smirks at her.

In the drawing room, Fizz has grown bored of waiting for a Bloody Mary and has poured herself a large glass of champagne. She makes a dramatic show of squeezing in a tiny drop of orange juice. The glass is already so full that a trickle slides down onto her hand. She holds the drink triumphantly aloft with one hand, licking the spillage off the other. She reminds me of a beetle. Big unfocussed eyes and thick rings that click against each other. Last night she smudged my cheek with a wet lipstick kiss then licked her thumb to rub it off.

Lily gratefully takes the biscuit tin from me and busies herself making drinks. I take a seat on the piano stool, far enough from the others that I don't have to join their conversation but close enough to Lily that I can see her roll her eyes at them. David is complaining about European export laws while Simon nods like a zealot.

Fizz tries to raise a counterpoint, but Bill places a quieting hand on her leg. *Leave it*, says his gentle squeeze of her knee.

'Oh, it isn't worth it!' says Annie to no one in particular, leaning her head back and shaking out her dark hair in a casual gesture I will come to learn is her way of ending a conversation. It's not clear what exactly she thinks isn't worth it.

'Yes, can we please talk about something less fucking mind-numbing on my birthday?' Lily passes the Bloody Marys around the room then takes a large gulp of her own. 'Ugh, the first sip is always so disgusting. Why does breakfast drinking have to be such a punishment?'

Lily seems much younger here, almost childlike. I suppose that is what happens when we go home. We stop being the person we are trying to become and step back into the role we played before. Homes are always haunted by past versions of ourselves we tried to leave behind. Old photographs, forgotten diaries, heights marked in pencil on the kitchen door frame. At university, Lily is capable and opinionated, people like her and are impressed by her. At the Chateau, she seems petulant and erratic.

She must have noticed my staring. She links her arm through mine and leads us out onto the terrace. The sun hangs low in the late-morning sky but heat is already kicking up from the yellow stone.

'Are you having the best time?' She doesn't leave me any time to respond. 'Everyone adores you and you've just fit right in. You even managed to raise a smile from Felix, who's been a total bore all summer, by the way, ever since he broke up with his girlfriend.'

The revelation knocks me slightly off balance but I keep my face still. The fact that Felix has, or had, a girlfriend fetters a fledgling feeling in my core that hasn't yet fully formed but has been gathering momentum somewhere.

'It had been like three years, on and off. More off than on by the end, but he's done this time. She said some rather awful things to him when he ended it, I think. It sent him into a bit of a spiral. David even threatened the Priory, which is totally outrageous because he was never even that bad. He was just sad, I think. But he's been alright, in a bit of a funk maybe. He seems to have perked up, though, since you arrived.'

Sometimes Lily has a way of saying things that dare

you to press on, to ask the myriad questions she invites. I've already learned that this is usually a trap but this time I feel like taking the bait.

'What do you mean?'

'I don't know,' she says. 'I think he quite likes you. He's opened up again. He's laughing more. Maybe he just needed some male company that wasn't Dad or Simon.' She almost shudders at the name. The Blake children, I have noticed, do nothing to hide their disdain for their father's business partner.

'I don't think that's anything to do with me. He's probably just being friendly.'

Lily laughs. 'You clearly don't know my brother.'

'Well, no,' I say, 'but that's kind of my point.'

'We'll see.' says Lily, squeezing a blueberry from the elaborate fruit platter that sits at the centre of the table, the juice bursting out and staining the immaculate linen that covers it. 'Would you help Dot with that plate before she ruins my birthday breakfast?'

I turn around and find Dot carrying a plate of buttered toast.

'I can do it just fine thank you,' she says, staring her sister down. 'I don't know why everyone still treats me like a baby.' Dot's foot catches the uneven edge of a flagstone and she almost trips.

'Yes, it is a wonder,' says Lily.

Breakfast is a raucous affair. The Bloody Marys were just the start. I am served soft-boiled eggs and soldiers, bowls of berries with honey and icing sugar, and a heaping mound of pancakes covered in thick cream. We drink champagne and wine and Magpies, a syrupy fruit-filled cocktail that Lily invented. Her presents are brought down. Two of them are wrapped in black-and-white paper. Felix and Dot make a show of squawking and flapping their arms and chanting, 'Magpie! Magpie! Magpie!' Lily rolls her eyes at me as if this a completely normal part of a birthday celebration, then tosses the black-and-white packages to her siblings. The chanting dies out. Lily turns to the rest of her presents. She opens them, graciously thanking each person around the table and keeping a note in the back of her diary of which absent friend or relative has sent what. There are so many that, by the time she finishes opening them, we have eaten every scrap of breakfast and almost drunk the two wine coolers dry. As she's noting down the last gift – an engraved silver fountain pen from her aunt – Bill interrupts with a squawk.

'It's not over until the Magpie prizes have been opened!'

The chanting and squawking begins again and Felix and Dot tear open the presents. Dot's contains a glittering crystal flower, which she holds up to the light.

'It's for your hair, darling,' says Fizz. 'I'll show you how to put it in later. You can wear it tomorrow – you'll look so pretty!'

Dot looks absolutely horrified but manages to summon a thin smile. 'Can't wait.'

Felix is pulling a stream of fabric from a box. It is a fierce orange colour that burns in the sunlight. He places the silk scarf around his neck and flips one end over his shoulder, showing the intricate pattern traced in deep ochre thread on the underside.

'It's perfect,' he says, smiling warmly at Lily's god-parents, who both beam back at him.

At some point, Mr Blake and Simon excuse themselves and slink off to discuss work. Celeste says Simon should try to remember that they actually are on holiday. Annie rolls her eyes. I am drunk and it's barely past midday. A question that's been sloshing around in my mind all morning rolls past my lips.

'Why do they call you Magpie?'

'Because she squawks,' says Dot, spilling some of her drink onto the white tablecloth.

'Because I'm bad luck,' says Lily, smirking at me from behind the rim of her coupe glass.

'Because she collects beautiful things.' says Felix.

The summer before I went to university, in a bid to escape the crushing intensity of the lads' holiday I had found myself on, I opened an app, looking for sex with a stranger. A German man in his forties was the fifth person I messaged but the first one who responded to my blank profile. We swapped a few messages back and forth. He seemed handsome enough from his photos, although I suspected they were more than a few years old. A watermark from a defunct version of the app suggested these photos had been screen shotted and re-uploaded more than once. I had a choice, I suppose, but at the time it didn't feel like one. The prospect of another day drinking warm beer on the beach with sixteen boys who hated me didn't seem appealing. So I made up a girl from the night before who had given me her number and wanted to hang out. The boys hollered and made crass jokes. They asked to see pictures of her, but I denied them, saying I wasn't that type of boy. I'm pretty sure they knew what type of boy I was by that point anyway. But I still made up a girl.

I got the German to park a ten-minute walk from my hotel and took a carefully mapped route to get there, making sure none of the boys were following me. At a glance, the German was obviously older than his photos, but somehow more handsome. I think it's true of most people that they look better when they are living and breathing and smiling in front of you. He told me his name and I instantly forgot it. I don't remember if I told him mine. His voice was deep and relaxed and I felt something rise in my chest and a tightening in my shorts. I climbed into the stranger's car and drove away from the boys and the bars. I'd thought we were going to the villa he was staying in, which he'd hinted was somewhere in the hills overlooking the strip, but we turned onto a slip road leading to the motorway along the coast.

'I hope you don't mind going to the beach,' he said. And then, clearly sensing my nervousness, 'Don't worry, it's far away from your friends.'

It was far. We sped along the motorway for maybe half an hour in complete silence. I felt waves of doubt roll up and down my chest. I'd almost cancelled three times on my way to meet him, but now I was here, in this moving vehicle, and was too late to back out. Apprehension swelled into anticipation, underscored by the sense of something done that could not be undone. Something that I couldn't stop even if I wanted to. I watched the sea roll past through the window. The German saw me looking and put down the window so I could feel the breeze on my face. The air from outside was much warmer than the frigid air-con of the rental car. At some point we pulled onto a winding mountain road that took us up and up and up until we crested the peak and the full width of the ocean opened up below us. I think I let out a gasp at the view. The stranger told me he liked the noise I made and squeezed my knee, which made me hard. We descended into a secluded bay, cut off from the rest of the coastline by rocky outcrops, which stood sentinel either side of the vast beach. The German parked up in a makeshift car park and handed me a pair of faded blue speedos. He told me to put them on, though I wouldn't be wearing them for long. He watched me shimmy my shorts down, awkwardly leaving my T-shirt on and feeling suddenly ridiculous. Out of nowhere he took my dick in his hand. I must have jumped because he asked me if everything was okay. I said that it was and tried to relax into it. I reached over into his lap where I could see him getting hard and started to undo his belt.

'Let's save something for the dunes,' he said, and hopped out of the car.

I pulled the blue trunks up and tried to arrange everything so he couldn't tell how excited I was. The German stripped down to another pair of sun-bleached briefs, then pulled out a cooler and a beach bag and headed off into the white dunes. I followed him, awkwardly holding my clothes in my hands.

The beach was a narrow strip of sand, hidden from the road and the mountains above it by rolling dunes. All I could see was blue sky, bluer sea and bronze figures moving slowly across the sand. The German laid out two huge towels and handed me a cold beer. He lay down and motioned for me to do the same and we lay there, propped up on our elbows, sipping our beers and listening to the waves. Eventually, wordlessly, he got up and headed into the dunes. I understood that I was supposed to follow. When he reached some predetermined spot, he turned and kissed me. His lips were soft but the stubble on his chin was rough against mine. I bit his lip, and he bit mine back harder. He pushed me down onto my knees in the sand and drew me into the crease of his thigh. I breathed deep and kissed him there and felt his body stiffen. He guided my face to where he wanted it to be and pushed himself into my mouth. I could hear the waves breaking and falling back into themselves. And then I was on my front, the warm sand sticking to his spit on my cheek. He spat on his hand and then on me. One finger, two and then he was fucking me. The crash and swell of my breath and his and waves of pain but pleasure too and I could feel the surge of the sea in my chest threatening to drag me under. He broke over me and it was done. The warmth of the dune beneath me and his body on mine and the fragmented rhythm of his breath and my breath and the breath of the ocean. The two of us calmed but the waves kept their gasping rhythm.

We walked back towards the shore and his hand bumped gently against mine until I let him hold it. We walked and kept walking until we were swimming and then we swam until the water got deep. I let the air escape my lungs and sank a little beneath the surface. I let the sea swell around me. I let the German hold me in the waves. I let him kiss salt into the mouth of a boy he'd just met. I let him bite the neck of a boy he'd just fucked. I did not let him know that it was my first time.

The walls of the house seem to sweat, heat emanating from them. Breakfast has been cleared away and everyone has been set to work. Except for Lily, of course, who oversees everything from behind Felix's bright blue sunglasses, plastic crown still perched on her head. There is a steady stream of deliveries, and locals laden with boxes of wine and crates of fruit criss-cross through the house while Luc grunts directions at them. Dot is dangling white bunting out of a window and Bill is trying to catch the other end, perching atop a battered wooden ladder. He's leaning too far out and looks like he might fall. Fizz and Annie are supposed to be writing place cards for dinner but instead they are gossiping about each guest on the list, sipping wine, heads pressed together.

Fizz whispers something and Annie leans into her, laughter tumbling out. They both almost fall backwards onto the paving stones. Felix is leaning against the wall of the house, shaded by vines, the beer keg he was carrying lying forgotten on the gravel. He's talking to an olive-skinned delivery boy in a powder-blue polo shirt who is holding a matching package emblazoned with gold lettering. The boy laughs at something and puts down the box, pulling out a pack of cigarettes and offering one to Felix, who takes two and places one between the boy's pink lips. He takes a silver lighter from the pocket of his shorts and leans in close to light the boy's cigarette. The boy looks up and I am caught. Felix tracks his eyes and catches mine. We all look at each other for a moment, trying to decide who, if anyone, has crossed a line. Felix breaks first and beckons me over.

'This is Etienne,' he says. 'We practically grew up together. His mother owns the bakery in the village – they're catering for the party. Etienne, this is a friend of Lily's.'

The truth of the statement, that I am Lily's friend, not his, is hot as a whip. It is soothed, though, by the arm Felix casually slings across my shoulders, my skin tingling where his fingers now sit. Etienne smiles but tilts his head, slightly narrowing his bright green eyes.

'Lily always has such beautiful friends.' His accent is rich and open; he luxuriates over every letter. 'You are coming to the party tomorrow, yes?'

I open my mouth to reply but Felix speaks for me.

'Of course he is. I have a feeling it's going to be a lot of fun.'

Luc shouts something in French and Etienne snaps to attention. He picks up the blue box and strides towards the kitchen door. Before he rounds the corner, he pauses, turns over his shoulder, and looks back at us.

'It was nice to meet you, and thanks for the light, Felix. See you both at the party.'

Then he flicks the butt into the gravel and disappears. Felix pauses, picks up the keg under one arm, and strolls down the lawn to the ice shed, which is being converted into a bar for the night. He doesn't look back but I can feel that he knows I am watching him, his movements slow and calculated. I take out my phone and open an app. At the top of the grid, a few feet away, Etienne stares up at me, green eyes defiant, one brow arched. He has sent me a message, but I don't read it.

I have become the de facto piano accompanist for the Blake family's annual Fête. Earlier, Annie heard me and Dot practising and stormed into the room to say she refused to play her own piano this year and insisted that I take charge. At this, Dot stormed out and Annie told me not to worry. She ambushed me, declaring at lunch today that I'd be playing with her, so I couldn't refuse. It would have been impolite. Which is how I find myself in the drawing room, surrounded by sheet music I've never read, staving off another afternoon hangover with a glass of five o'clock rosé. The condensation from the chilled bottle pools on the marble floor next to the piano stool as I pick my way through unfamiliar notes. I enjoy this stage of reading music. It feels like a first date. We feel each other out, testing the waters, sensing what works and what doesn't. Sometimes it doesn't work out, the piece or I or both decide the other isn't worth the time. But sometimes it clicks, a rush of excitement as we fall into place. This is how it feels today.

'You play wonderfully. Where did you train?'

Annie is leaning against the doorframe, draped in orange silk. I didn't hear her come into the room and have no idea how long she's been there.

'In the music building at school, mostly,' I say. 'We didn't have space for a piano at home. Although my Uncle Henry had one and he used to let me play it sometimes.'

'I see,' Annie purrs, but something in her voice makes me feel as if I've said the wrong thing. 'You're a natural, darling. From the top, if you will.'

I begin to play and, after a time, she begins to sing. *I'm wild again, beguiled again, a simpering, whimpering child again.* The ivory softens in agreement under my fingers. *Bewitched, bothered, and bewildered am I.* The storm in her voice clears into an expansive autumn sky. *Couldn't sleep and wouldn't sleep.* She leans against the open piano. *When love came and told me I shouldn't sleep. Bewitched.* She lifts her chin to appraise me. *Bothered.* I meet her eyes. *And bewildered.* She smiles. *Am I.* The song rolls on and we dance each other through it. During the final refrain she moves to softly put a hand on my shoulder.

'You're something of a marvel. And completely self-taught?'

I nod, struck by how surreal this is. I used to search for a vacant piano at lunchtime and put Annie Carpenter CDs in the Walkman Grandma gave me for my eleventh birthday and listen and listen until I was able to play along. Mrs Blake doesn't know it is her who taught me to play piano. But I can't tell her that, so I tell her how much of an honour it is to play for her instead. She waves this aside with a casual flick of the wrist, then picks up the bottle of wine and pours herself a glass. She fills up mine too, propping it on the lid.

'It really is a shame to let a natural talent like that go to waste. Have you ever thought of applying to the Royal Academy?'

I tell her I haven't. This isn't entirely true. When I was fourteen, I asked my music teacher if you could do a degree in piano. He laughed in my face.

'Well, you should. Luckily for you, Cassandra Quant, who runs the admissions board there, is a very dear friend, and her husband owes David a favour. If you call a rather large and unrepaid loan a "favour",' she says smiling down at me. 'They're coming tomorrow. Remind me to introduce you. We'll have you playing the Royal Albert Hall in no time. It's amazing how quickly you can get business done at a party. Now, you were pretty much perfect, but let's take it from the top one more time to iron out my bum notes. We've got this in the bag though. I think we're going to win, don't you?'

'I didn't realise it was a competition,' I say.

'Oh, it isn't. But there's always a winner.'

This evening's meal is hurried and frantic. Felix is topless, with slicked back hair and kohl around his eyes. I watch him dance around the kitchen stirring a hasty risotto and singing under his breath. We eat standing up and sipping wine. The evening has the topsy-turvy buzz of the opening night of a school play. Fizz is bigging up her upcoming performance to anyone who will listen. We are not going to know what's hit us, apparently. I feel nervous and then feel ridiculous for feeling that way. Dot has been sulking and only appears when dinner is finished. Celeste sneaks off after a single spoonful of rice to change into her costume. Felix, who has procured a red velvet top hat and a gold-topped wooden cane from somewhere, bursts back into the kitchen.

'Ladies and gentlemen, boys, girls and anybody who might be both but is probably neither,' he tips his hat towards Dot, who curtsies back. 'Please, recharge your glasses and make your way into the drawing room, where tonight's festivities are about to begin! And maybe squeeze out a piss on your way because there won't be an interval.'

The room has been rearranged, with the settees and chairs turned to face the French windows, across which heavy velvet curtains have been hastily hung. The piano has been rolled closer to the wall and the room is lit by lamps and candles scattered between chairs and cushions on the floor. When we are all settled, drinks in hand, an old speaker crackles into a drumroll. A cymbal crashes and Felix leaps between the curtains, does a forward roll, lands on his knees, and starts to sing. My lips stretch into a smile.

Willkommen, bienvenue, welcome! Fremder, étranger, stranger. He leaps up and marches around the room. *Glücklich zu sehen, je suis enchanté, happy to see you. Bleibe, reste, stay.* He adopts a hammy German accent. *Meine Damen und Herren.* He bows towards Fizz. *Mesdames et messieurs.* He curtsies to Simon. *Ladies and gentlemen!* He reaches me, turns and bends over, speaking at me from between his legs. *Guten Abend! Bonsoir! Good evening!* He rights himself and turns on a heel into a low crouch. *Wie geht's? Comment ça va? Do you feel good?* He winks at me. *I bet you do!* He taps Bill in the centre of his chest with his cane. *Ich bin euer Conferencier, je suis votre compère. I am your host!* He strides from one side of the makeshift stage to the other. *Und sagen: Willkommen, bienvenue, welcome. Im Cabaret, au Cabaret, to Cabaret!* He spreads his arms wide and bows, the top hat tipping off his head and rolling under Mr Blake's chair. Felix smiles breathlessly at his father who looks back, his face inscrutable. There is an instant, a flash of something like fury in Felix's eyes. But it flares and bursts like the filament in a camera bulb.

'Welcome to the annual Blake Family Fête. Are you sitting comfortably? Good. Then let's begin. First things first! It would be remiss of me not to mention our wonderful and generous patron, the person who makes all this possible, without whom we'd all just be having a delicious dinner and wonderful wine . . . Lady Lily Blake, the Magpie of Marylebone!'

There is a raucous round of applause, cheering and foot-stamping, which Lily graciously accepts. She is wrapped in a fur coat with streaks of golden glitter around her eyes. Her hair, now out of its plaits, is back-combed into a savage black nest, the plastic tiara balanced carefully off to one side. She looks like a nymph or a wood sprite, a wildness threaded through her cool smile. This is the girl I know.

'Alright, alright, settle down. Without further ado, it is my pleasure to introduce our first act of the evening. Please welcome to the stage the magician, the conjurer, the illusionist, the man doing the same three magic tricks he does every year! Put your hands together for . . . Bill!'

There is much whooping and applause. Bill pulls a coin from behind Lily's ear, a string of handkerchiefs from his sleeve and an umbrella from a bag which it couldn't possibly have fit inside. Dot faithfully provides an approximation of a drum roll and cymbal clash for each trick using a tambourine. Finally, Bill reaches into his trousers and pulls out a bunch of fresh roses, which he presents to Celeste, kissing her hand. The room erupts. Apparently, this is a new trick and the crowd goes accordingly wild. Celeste gasps and puts her delicate thumb to her mouth, pricked by a thorn. When he takes his seat, I watch a small trickle of blood run down into Bill's sock. Felix takes the stage again.

'Well, that certainly was a surprise! Apparently, you

can teach an old rogue new tricks,' he says, twiddling his fingers at the room.

'They just need the right muse,' murmurs Annie from her armchair.

'Indeed,' continues Felix. 'Well, anyway, I think it's time for our next act, don't you? Now this performer was due to be accompanied by our dashing young guest, but it seems they have changed their mind. Performing an experimental piece entitled' – he pretends to check a non-existent notecard in his hands – '"Don't Call Me Dorothea" – it's Dorothea Blake!'

This snub is news to me, and I move to shove the sheet music under my chair in an attempt to hide the piece we were going to perform together. Dot strides out in glittering gold trousers and a battered tailcoat turned up at the sleeves, which must have once belonged to Felix. She has drawn on a monobrow and a curling moustache in black eyeliner and holds a little silver hammer in one hand. She drags a chair across the floor, scraping the metal legs across the marble. Standing on the chair, she throws open the lid of the baby grand.

Dot takes the little hammer and starts to drag it across the taut wires inside. The sound that comes out is not unpleasant, the notes are subdued but harmonious. She begins to strike the wires in random places, a clanging, disjointed melody fills the room. Her striking gets faster and harder and more chaotic. The noise surges into cacophony. David is standing, shouting at her.

'Dorothea, stop it right now!' And she does.

She hops off the chair and takes three sweeping strides towards him. Mr Blake sits down in his chair, silenced. His daughter, despite her size, looms over him, hammer raised, teeth gritted.

'Don't. Call. Me.' She breaks into a wan smile. 'Dorothea.'

She bows so low that the tails flip over her head. Fizz leaps to her feet, knocking over an empty bottle and filling the room with furious applause. The rest of the family joins in. I clap too. Eventually Dot rights herself and takes a seat on a cushion next to me. Her breathing is fast but her face gives nothing away. She leans her weight against the leg of my chair and shuffles the sheet music beneath it. Felix sits sideways in an armchair, limbs akimbo. His hair is tousled and his cheeks are flushed, from wine or laughter I cannot tell. I imagine running my fingertips over them. He rolls off the chair onto his front then springs up again. The evening is picking up pace now, a carousel spinning to the rich music of family, laughter and wine. I cling on tight.

'*Mesdames et messieurs*,' he says, adopting a slurring French drawl. 'All the way from the darkest saloon this side of the Seine, the filthiest whorehouse outside of Montmartre, a denizen of the Paris underworld who was kicked out of the Moulin Rouge for being too fucking sexy.' Annie lets out a derisive snort; Simon bristles.

'Gentlemen, avert your eyes. Ladies, take notes. It's the one, the only . . . Celeste . . .'

A high, quivering violin note slides out of the speaker.

Felix flicks a switch and the remaining lamps go out. He aims a torch at the velvet curtains. A glittering silver stiletto appears between them, followed by a tanned fishnet-wrapped leg. The leg is impossibly long and, unmoored from its owner, more uncanny than alluring. The leg is followed by a body, clad in silver sequins and white feathers. Celeste slinks across the makeshift stage. Felix tracks her with his handheld spotlight. There is shimmying and the slow removal of layers, out of time with the music. The room looks on, Lily oohs and aahs in the correct places. Celeste moves to sit on Bill's lap but he shifts uncomfortably and crosses his legs so she has to bounce back up. She slings her feather boa around Simon's neck and pulls him towards her. Eventually, mercifully, the song comes to a close and Celeste, now wearing a high-cut gold bikini, curtsies.

Felix leads the applause and the men in the room join in. Mr Blake claps but looks at the floor. Simon leans forward in his chair, enraptured.

'A little on the nose, don't you think?' says Annie, too loudly, to Fizz. For a moment, Celeste looks like she is going to cry. But her face cracks into a showgirl smile. She gathers up her discarded clothes and exits through the velvet curtains.

'Well, well, well. That really split the room.' Felix trips slightly as he gets to his feet again. 'Now for something guaranteed to kill the boner that Celeste has given Bill – my mother singing Ella Fitzgerald.'

There are a few more dissenting noises, mainly from

Mr Blake but they are drowned out by Fizz and Lily's laughter and some cheering from Bill. I get to my feet; the room feels bigger than it is and I take a deep breath to push away the hollow feeling in my chest. I sit on the piano stool and pick out the opening chord. The notes feel awkward under my fingers. Annie Carpenter takes my cue and begins to sing.

After one whole quart of brandy. She nods towards Felix who downs his glass in response. *Like a daisy, I'm awake.* I try to steer us through the opening bars but the sounds coming from the piano don't make sense. *With no Bromo-Seltzer handy I don't even shake. Men are not a new sensation. I've done pretty well, I think.* She moves towards the centre of the room. *But this half-pint imitation.* She winks at her son. *Put me on the blink.*

We trudge through the song together. Her voice, perfect and clear and horribly at odds with the irregular, clanging notes I coax from the piano. I look up and Dot is watching us with a satisfied smirk and, at a particularly jarring discordance, winks at her mother. Annie looks down at me, smiles and shrugs. Finally, the song ends.

'That's jazz, baby,' says Annie to rapturous applause. I take my seat and try not to look at anyone. I feel like I am on fire and each strike of the ovation slices through me.

'Nothing like a little family sabotage to make things interesting,' shouts Felix, springing up yet again. Dot looks at him like butter wouldn't melt and my face flushes hotter.

'But now . . . Hot on the heels of his exotic and no

doubt expensive new lover. Fresh from a lifetime spent licking Dad's arsehole, it's Mr Simon Chance!'

Lily gasps, then squeals with delight. Dot laughs so hard that she spits out half the beer she has managed to get her hands on, and Annie holds Fizz's hand so hard her knuckles go white as she tries to suppress her laughter. Mr Blake is on his feet telling Felix to apologise.

'Apologies are for chumps, Father,' says Felix. 'I think you told me that.'

'I said apologise,' says David, nose to nose with his son.

'Or what?' He bumps his father's shirt with his bare chest. Pushes him with both hands so Mr Blake is forced to take a step back. 'What the fuck are you gonna do?'

David Blake raises his hand and lets it fly, down and across, catching Felix full in the face. A clap – the loudest of the evening – echoes off the marble.

'Will you fucking pull yourself together, boy?' he shouts, flecks of spittle landing on his son's face. Mr Blake draws himself up to his full height, exhales sharply, and walks out of the room. Simon slides out of his seat and follows faithfully. The room is frozen. Except for Lily, who runs to her brother and swaddles him in arms and fur. Felix, softly, begins to cry.

The tears fall and do not stop falling for a long time. Felix cries and cries. Lily, Dot, him and I sit cross-legged on the cold marble. His two sisters flank him, propping him up as the sobs rip through him. They breathe with him. Steadying breaths which calm him for a moment before he is overcome again. Lily rolls and smokes eight cigarettes. I have no idea where Annie, Celeste, Fizz or Bill are. At some point Dot gets up and starts to pick out a tune on the piano. It isn't something I know but it seems to soothe Felix. After what seems like an age, Lily says we should go to bed. We help Felix to his feet and walk him to the stairs. The girls are on the floor below us so I walk Felix to his room, leaning my weight against the heavy door. I take him to his unmade bed. I move to leave but he turns suddenly and grabs my wrist. Hard.

'Stay,' he says. His golden eyes have sunk. 'Please.'

So I do.

Saturday

Heavy curtains block out all but a knife-edge of morning sun, but eventually it creeps in just enough to wake me. I am in Felix's bed. One of his arms is draped casually over my chest. Last night I announced my intention of sleeping on the floor. Felix, quietly, insisted it was ridiculous and rolled over to make room for me. We lay in silence, until Felix's hand found mine and squeezed it. I squeezed back, gently, and then Felix cried again. He buried his face in my shoulder and wept. With my free arm I cradled his head and held him there until his sobs slowed into gasps, eventually melting into soft snores. I worried that the drumbeat of my heart would wake him but it only seemed to soothe him more. At some point, I must have fallen asleep.

The shaft of light slides from my face to his. His breath is lulled and his eyes are still ringed with the pink echo of tears. I adjust the rhythm of my breath so that as his chest rises mine falls. We expand and contract to fill the spaces in each other. Up close, scattered freckles and an almost invisible scar near his lip betray the perfect symmetry of his face. The blanket I used is tangled and forgotten on the floor. I lie there and feel the rhythm of his breath in sync with mine. Whether it's the sun or the intensity of my staring, something pierces his sleep and his eyes begin to flutter behind closed lids. He lets out a low murmur and I close my eyes.

'Are you pretending to be asleep?' he says.

'Um, no?' I try to protest, opening one eye.

'You're a funny fish, did you know that?'

'I wouldn't necessarily put it in those exact terms, but yeah, I guess.'

He looks at me for a second. His pink lips part into a wide grin. For a moment I think something is about to happen, then he rolls over, wraps the white sheet around himself and sits up in bed. He is naked and again I am drawn to the sharp line between his golden tan and the pale skin below the dip of his hip. Felix grabs a towel and moves towards the bathroom. There is a direct sightline from the bed to the shower but Felix does not close the door. I am trying not to watch him as he showers and look away when he turns back to face towards the bed. He lathers his armpits and hums Ella Fitzgerald. He turns off the water and stands there, drip-drying, regarding himself in the floor-length mirror propped up against the wall.

'You should probably shower in your room, then we'll meet down at breakfast,' he says absently, without taking his eyes off his reflection.

'Why?' I say, studying his face in the mirror. 'Are you worried people are going to think we've slept together?'

I hear the boldness in the words, as if they are spoken by somebody else. Felix's eyes lock onto mine through the mirror.

'Well, I wouldn't necessarily put it in those exact terms, but yeah, I guess.' He doesn't look away and neither do I. 'And technically, darling, technically, we did sleep together. But we wouldn't want anyone to get the wrong impression, would we?'

Felix picks up the towel to finish drying himself and I get up to leave. He doesn't say anything or look up. I close the door gently behind me.

'Ah! Good morning, young man!' says Bill, his hand on the handle of his own bedroom door down the corridor. 'Just, um, popping back up to get a hat. The sun out there is strong today! Make sure you wear some sun cream! Although I don't suppose you really need to, do you?'

There is a slight pause, then I laugh. Bill laughs too, relieved by my conspiratorial reaction, then goes into his room and I quicken my pace down the corridor to my bedroom. He doesn't seem to have noticed I wasn't coming from there in the first place.

'Nice of you to join us, Rip Van Winkle,' Felix says, sitting casually at the head of the table, buttered toast in one hand, newspaper in the other.

'Good morning, darling. How did you sleep?' Lily stares at me, eyebrows raised until I am forced to look away.

'Very well, thanks,' I muster, casually taking a seat without meeting her eye. She looks at Felix then back at me but neither of us say anything, so she lets up. Dot's gaze is fixed on a single strawberry at the centre of her bowl.

I busy myself by pouring coffee and scouting around for an unburnt piece of toast. Warm arms around my neck and cool water at my back make me jump, spilling the drink as I spin around in my chair.

'Well done last night – thank you,' Annie Blake growls into my ear. Dark hair like blackened water cascades over my shoulder. I do not know which part of the night she is thanking me for. She kisses me on the cheek then straightens up. 'How are you feeling this morning, my sweet?' she says to Felix.

'Absolutely tip-top, Mother,' he says flatly without lowering the paper. 'Where's Dad?'

'Gone to the vineyard with Simon,' offers Lily. 'Terribly important business, you know?'

'Right.' There is a cool silence for a while. Lily fiddles with her camera, Dot pushes the strawberry around with her fingers. Mrs Blake studies her son.

'Right, girls!' she says abruptly. 'Lots to be done before everyone arrives, so let's get to it, shall we? Lily, you're on catering. Sandrine is sending over some extra hands from Le Bleuet and I think Etienne is arriving later in the van. Dot, chairs. The ladies at the church say we can use the ones from the village hall on the condition that none of them are damaged, so do be careful. Bill is around somewhere and can give you a hand getting them over. And you must retune the piano after your theatrics last night. Oh, and the glassware needs collecting from that place by the square. Boys, is it alright if I send you both to town?'

'What? That's so unfair – why do they get to go to town and I have to spend all day tuning the stupid piano?'

'Well, Dotty, darling, you did almost destroy Granny's baby grand, and I'm not hiring someone to fix it when we both know you're perfectly capable of doing it yourself,' says Annie.

'Plus you're not old enough to drive,' offers Lily.

'And you're the absolutely useless carefully shaved chimpanzee that Lily and I snuck home from London Zoo in 2005.'

Dot laughs and throws the strawberry at her brother. He bats it away and it hits Annie in the middle of the forehead, leaving a little smear of red juice.

'Dorothea, do not throw food or you will be banned from the party!' She dries her forehead with the back of her hand. 'Felix, leave her alone and make yourself useful. Why are you all always so intent on ruining my life? There's a list on the fridge. Don't forget the crème de violette.'

'Oh, if you're going to town could you please get me some fresh film? This roll is about to run out and a party isn't really a party unless people can see how much fun you had without them,' Lily adds.

Felix slides a cassette tape into the slot of the Jeep's stereo and presses play. James Taylor crackles out of the speaker. The sun, which drenched us at breakfast, slips behind a solitary cloud as Taylor sings of horses and cattle and canyons. The road unspools ahead of us and we pass hills and farm buildings I think I noted when I first came to the Chateau, little knots of recognition. Felix takes his time today. On a long stretch of road between endless lavender fields he slows and gradually stops by a break in the yellow-and-purple haze. He slides out of the Jeep and opens the top of a wooden beehive that marks the entrance to a dusty path leading deep into a field. He pulls out two jars of honey and slips a few coins from his pocket and puts them into a box on the side of the hive. Getting back into the driver's seat, he carefully puts one of the jars in the cup holder and screws the lid off the other. He plunges his finger into the jar then into his mouth.

'People in the village say you can taste the lavender but I think that's bullshit. Open.' He scoops his finger through the honey again then repeats the command. 'Open.'

I open my mouth and he puts his finger on my tongue. Beneath the burst of silken sweetness, I taste the rough salt of his skin. He's right – there are no notes of lavender. But when I take a breath, I am filled with the scent of the plants around us. I close my eyes and my lips around his finger as he slowly pulls back and puts it into his own mouth to catch the last of the honey.

'Delicious,' he says, and starts the engine.

Pulling off the verge and back onto the road, we send up a cloud of dust. Felix lets his right hand fall gently onto my leg. His finger is still wet and it sticks to the hairs on my thigh. There's a tingling, a bright buzz that connects the contact with the taste of the honey still lingering on my tongue. He does not look at me. The touch feels casual but deliberate and I do not know what to do with my body. I shift myself slightly towards him to relieve the ache of stillness. He answers the movement with an almost imperceptible tightening of his grip. We continue on. I feel like we are going much faster than we were before. It is only when we reach the little town that we realise we have forgotten the list.

'Cheese!' says Felix triumphantly. 'We always need cheese, so we'll start with that.' He is balancing on one foot atop a squat metal bollard cutting the main square off from traffic. One hand in the air, finger stretching into the sky, the other arm out to the side to steady him. He says it helps him think.

'And your mum said something about violets? So maybe we should go to the florist? Is there a florist?'

'Oh, not violets, darling, crème de violette. For cocktails? Mum is obsessed with this pilot guy who's coming tonight so she's hellbent on serving Aviations to see if he'll notice that she's in love with him. It's horribly sad really.'

'What about your dad?'

'What about him?' He hops gracefully off the bollard. 'He's a total prick, I wouldn't pay him any mind.'

'Felix, he hit you.'

'He's done worse.'

'Really?'

'Well, not really. But, um, he's not a good guy. I, er . . . I told my family something recently. Something about myself, you know? It took a lot. To . . . get there.' He pauses, breathes. 'I told them . . . a thing. And he told me to keep it a secret. Told me he was going to pretend I'd never said it and that we should all do the same, otherwise I wouldn't be welcome.'

'Felix, I'm sorry, that's—'

'Don't worry. Annie dearest talked some sense into him. Told him that if I was going, so was she. And Dot and Lil were on my side, obviously. Pair of angels, I'm convinced. And he came around. Sort of. We reached what they called a compromise. Lovely word that, "compromise". Covers all manner of sins. We agreed that my secret could be our secret and we'd see how I felt after a little stay at North London's dullest hotel. Have you ever been to the Priory? No, of course you haven't. Don't bother, the food's terrible. And besides, I'm a bisexual, not a drug addict.'

He says all of this with a half-smile but doesn't look me in the eye once. I'm struggling to adjust to what he's telling me. My mind races through possibilities.

'Anyway, crème de violette? And you're right, we should absolutely go to the florist, that's a great idea.' He takes out his mobile and finds a contact. Someone picks up on the first ring. Felix speaks in rapid French. I pick up a couple of numbers and, when he checks his watch, a time – about an hour from now. He hangs up. 'That's the flowers ordered,' he says with a wink.

We wander towards the fromagerie. I am half a step behind Felix and stare at this boy who has changed into someone else in front of my eyes. I smell the shop before I see it. It's a beautiful shop – everything in this quaint town seems to be – with a large bay window edged in red paint. As we enter, a man in a blue apron appears from behind a chainlink curtain. The counter hums with the effort of staving off the summer heat. More cheeses than I can count, some whole wheels, some tiny slivers, all labelled with little chalkboard markers, wait to be packaged up and taken home. I want to say that I didn't know there were so many different types of cheese, but as soon as the thought forms I feel embarrassed. Instead, I say nothing and smile as the man in the apron looks from my face, then to Felix's before recognition flickers into life behind his round glasses.

'Ah, Monsieur Blake!' he says, suddenly on the charm offensive. After a few words and some forced laughter, the man disappears through the metal curtain, scattering a shimmer from the fluorescent lightning inside. Felix looks at me and then around the little shop.

'So much cheese,' he says, 'and it's all basically the same.' The man returns with a large box full of individually wrapped parcels of various shapes and sizes.

'Except for this one,' says Felix, plucking a squat cylinder from the top. 'Most delicious cheese you'll ever eat, I promise.' He drops the cheese back into the box and picks the whole thing up with a fake grunt, staggering a few steps towards the door under its feigned weight.

He thanks the fromager over his shoulder and heads off down the street towards the car. He places the box into the backseat then wipes his brow.

'Gosh, nothing like hard labour to strike up a thirst. I think it's time for a drink, don't you?'

At the hotel on the main square, Felix orders us a black coffee and a beer each. Exactly what I was craving, I realise. We sit in silence for a while. I watch the deft movement of his fingers as he takes a pinch of tobacco from a leather pouch and sprinkles it into a brown rectangle of paper – liquorice flavour, he tells me – and gently rolls it between his thumbs, nails bitten to jagged nubs. His fingers move back and forth until the tobacco is smoothed, then he tucks the paper into itself and brings the cigarette up to his mouth. His pink tongue darts out and swipes along the dried glue, then he folds the wet edge towards himself. From a folded piece of white card printed with the hotel's screaming Medusa head insignia, he takes a blue-tipped match and strikes it once. It flares and he lights the roll-up, puffing the silver smoke out of one side of his mouth, then licks the sweetness of the liquorice paper from his lips.

'It's nice to get you on your own, you know,' he says after a moment. 'I wanted to apologise for last night. My family can be . . . quite a lot sometimes. And you really got thrown in at the deep end.'

I am about to respond when his phone buzzes. He looks at it then smiles and slides the phone across the white tablecloth so I can see the screen. It's a text from Lily that just says *FILM*.

'Lest our Magpie be unable to collect her beautiful moments,' he says. 'God forbid she has to put the camera down and make some actual friends.' He laughs. I laugh too then catch myself. He notices the shift and looks me full in the face. Mischief swirls in his eyes.

The flash of the camera burst around the tin-foil covered walls of the living room, filling the space with unforgiving light. Every corner of the room, every crevice of every intertwined and fumbling couple, was thrown into harsh relief for a millisecond, then bathed in a deeper darkness. There was a collective gasp of horror then a ripple of relieved laughter as dilated, red-lit pupils adjusted back to the silver gloaming.

We were at a house party thrown by some art students Lily had befriended from the year above. It was rare that first-years got invited to stuff like this and Lily said we had to be on our best behaviour. She seemed comfortable enough to be snapping shots of every person she saw and I felt constantly exposed by the brutal brightness of the bulb. The house was in Heaton, back then the cheaper, edgier cousin of Jesmond, the student area where Lily and I would end up when we moved out of halls later that summer.

It was summer and my exams had ended. Lily had another few weeks until her final hand-in for the year, and we would spend our mornings lying in her bed drinking bad coffee, our afternoons lying in the park playing Fleetwood Mac off a tinny Bluetooth speaker, and our evenings lying about what year we were in at parties we shouldn't have been invited to. It was June and the warm weather had settled in on the city and given students and locals alike a healthy glow and an unwavering desire to be sitting in a beer garden for most of the day. I'd let Jasmine leave alone that night because it hadn't seemed far and by 4 a.m. the sky was already beginning to brighten. It was June, and I was young enough back then to believe that dark things do not happen beneath brightening skies.

The house itself, and the party around which we were now wandering aimlessly, had been the focus of much discussion in recent weeks. The seven-bedroomed poorly insulated Victorian terrace seemed fairly innocuous both inside and out – crumbling plaster facade, ugly reddish-brown carpets and a peeling original fireplace in the cramped living room. One day in the spring term, however, one of the residents – a Somali boy who went by the letter J – had reached into the fireplace in a bid to find out what was causing the whistling sound coming from the chimney. The mystery of the whistle was immediately forgotten when his scrabbling fingers found a smooth rectangle of plastic taped to the rough brick. The object was revealed to be a USB stick, which someone had clearly deemed important enough to hide there. The other six housemates were summoned for a house meeting (usually a forum for moaning about who had finished and not replaced the milk, or for finding a new drug dealer because the last one had graduated). But that time, the focus of the discussion was whether or not to find out the contents of the potentially cursed USB stick. The risk of unleashing a vengeful digital spirit or computer virus that infected the whole internet and crashed the World Bank was weighed up but determined low. Instead, they opted in favour of artistic curiosity and the sacred duty to uphold the bohemian ideals of beauty, truth and doing something because it will definitely make a good story even if it goes horribly wrong. The drive was plugged into J's laptop (disconnected from the mains and the internet, just in case). The folder the screen revealed was named after the number and street of the house and had a single file on it entitled WATCHME.mov. And so they did. A grainy, low-budget porn film started playing. The housemates shrieked in mingled disgust and delight; the girls turned away. But J kept watching. *Wait a minute,* he said and after a while beckoned the others back over. *Look there, behind them, that mark on the wall. And they're lying on . . . that's . . . that's this sofa.* The housemates leapt up in a collective horrified eureka moment.

And from there, WATCHME.move, had been born. First suggested and immediately rejected as a collective art project for their second-year show, they had decided a house-party-cum-independent-art-show was a better use of their time. Each of the housemates had been given an 'exhibitionist space' around the house with the brief to create a piece exploring the themes of sex, voyeurism, capture and legacy. Lily had overheard them planning the party while smoking on the fire escape outside the art building and had offered to document the party for free. Which is how we'd found ourselves in the foil-clad living room with settee cushions and pillows covering the floor, ambient techno, almost absent lighting and three night-vision cameras that captured every movement. A soft moan from closer than I would have liked snapped me back into focus.

'I think I'm gonna get a drink?' I said, suddenly uncomfortable, shifting my weight from one foot to the other.

'Cool, cool. I'm going to stay here for a bit, I think.'

I left Lily and her camera and the writhing mass of bodies and picked a door at random from the three that led off the space we were in. It opened into a small corridor down a couple of steps then into a large, crowded kitchen, where the strip lighting had been wrapped in red vinyl, so everyone's skin glowed crimson and their eyes were beetle black. From the opposite side of the kitchen, leaning casually against the counter, Jasmine blew out a slow stream of smoke which dissipated into the hazy pink air and beckoned me over with her finger. I slipped through the crowd, all shouting to be heard above the loud music and the louder voices of the people around them.

'Who'd you bribe to get into a party like this, WhiteBoy?' she said, wrapping me in a hug, then drawing back to kiss both of my cheeks before finally putting her joint in my mouth. 'Deep breath, baby girl.'

I felt the smoke catch in my throat and coughed despite

myself. I took another toke and let the heat melt into my chest. A buzz spread out from my brain to my limbs as I exhaled. I passed the butt on and Jasmine introduced me to her friends – all Black – some of whom I'd met before. One of them was J, the boy who'd found the sex tape. Another boy reached out and took my hand. He was tall and beautiful and the straight lines and smooth grooves of his face glowed orange and purple under the lights. He welcomed me with a smile and introduced himself as Caleb.

I repeated the name back to him, enjoying the way it felt in my mouth. He asked if I'd seen all the exhibits and when I said I hadn't he led me by the hand back the way I'd come, through the tin-foil living room and into the entrance hall. He reached down and opened a door which led to a small cupboard under the stairs. He placed a warm hand on the small of my back and gestured for me to go inside.

'It's pretty trippy, brother – enjoy,' he said and closed the door behind me.

Inside, the ceiling was low and hung with strips of soft pink silk, which made it feel suffocating. I crouched then sat down on a large bean bag. A small boxy TV screen provided the only light in the space and showed a vibrant sunset over a calm sea, foam lapping at the bubbling sand. I picked up a set of headphones from the side of the bean bag and placed them over my ears. I leaned back into the softness of the cushions around me. At first, I thought the sound was that of the sea. But as I listened,

I realised it was the soft breath of some unseen person, their mouth extremely close to the microphone. The closeness sent a ripple of warmth down my spine. As the waves crashed on the shore and the water level rose and the colours of the sky deepened from blushing pink to pulsing indigo, the breathing also became deeper, more ragged, then shallow and harsh. A murmur built into a moan as the sound and the image were both about to reach their apex. The noise cut out into static and all that was left was my rapid heartbeat and the soft, pulsing glow of the room around me. I emerged from the cocoon-like safety of the cupboard, blinking at the now-glaring brightness of the corridor. As I went in search of Lily and her camera, I could still feel the warm, shell-pink waves crashing inside my mind.

Felix's phone buzzes and he drains the last of his beer. He stands and motions for me to follow.

'Gotta see a man about a dog,' he says. I follow him down a few back-streets until we reach a florist on a shaded corner. Felix knocks three times on the door next to the shop entrance. There is a long pause and then the door opens a crack. An eye appears from the darkness and looks us up and down and then a low voice murmurs something in French. Felix nods in agreement and the door closes, there is the sound of a latch being undone, and the door opens again, wide enough for Felix to slip through.

'I'll be back in a bit,' Felix says over his shoulder and then the door closes in my face. I wait for what seems like an age and nothing happens. I am slightly at a loss and suddenly feel very self-conscious just standing aimlessly in the street, so I go into the flower shop. The air is bright and fresh and a little bell announces my entrance. I walk around, stopping occasionally to admire a colourful bouquet, doing my best to look casual. A pretty young woman comes over to ask me if I need any help and I decline. After a little while, the bell rings again and Felix sidles up beside me. He is holding a bulky white envelope, which he pushes into his pocket when he sees me looking.

'Dog all sorted, and this goes without saying but maybe don't mention this particular errand to the 'rents – or Lil, for that matter – they'll only worry,' he says, smiling mischievously. Then, looking down at the flowers I am standing in front of, he laughs. 'Oh, you're funny! Which colour do you prefer?'

I look down and see two tubs of five-petalled flowers, one white and one purple.

'Purple, I think,' I say, and Felix grins.

'Me too, much more interesting.' He chooses a bunch and hands the girl behind the counter a note then motions for her to keep the change. She wraps them in brown paper. As we are walking back to the car, he hands me the bunch of violets. I put them up to my face and inhale a breath of the powdery-sweet perfume.

On the drive back to the Chateau, we sit in comfortable silence and I listen to the clink and rustle of bags and bottles in the backseat. When we slide through the green gate, we find the Chateau has become a hive of activity. The courtyard is full of cars so Felix steers us round the corner to park. All around us people come and go, delivering boxes of wine and crates piled high with fruit and packages emblazoned with the cornflower insignia of Le Bleuet. I look around for Etienne but don't see him.

From where we have parked, I can see into one of the outhouses off the courtyard. Luc is transferring more boxes of wine from a van while David Blake stands and watches. When Luc is done, he closes the heavy wooden door of the outhouse and locks it with a large padlock. The gleaming gold metal is conspicuous against the rusted latch and style of the chipped door. David Blake sees me looking and fixes me with a stare. His eyes are metallic, like his son's. But where Felix's glow with the soft bronze of sunlight, David Blake's eyes flash, keen and grey as iron. We stand still, watching each other, until a gentle tug on my arm pulls me back into the moment. Felix grins at me, appearing not to have seen his father. He signals to the heavy box full of cheese. I carry it into the kitchen.

'That absolutely stinks,' says Dot, materialising out of thin air. The cheese has been sitting in the car for probably too long and leaves a pungent trail through the house. Dot is wearing a white dress with little flowers embroidered across the neckline. The pink crystal rose she was given during Lily's birthday celebration is pinned carefully into her hair.

'Mum says you're in trouble because you forgot the

list and if you didn't get crème de violette she's going to string you up by the balls – her words, not mine.'

'Well, we did, Dotty. And enough lemons to sink a battleship, so I think our balls are safe for the time being.' Felix gives himself a self-satisfied tap on the front of his shorts. He and I finish putting away the shopping. It's a delicate dance and feels strangely domestic. He takes the violets and puts them into a terracotta vase by the windowsill.

'Right, let's join the party. I think the madding crowd has arrived.'

Out on the terrace, Lily swoops down on us. She drags Felix back to the house to get the film for her camera. Alone, I scan for familiar faces in the sea of new people that has flooded the house since we left. Bobbing somewhere near the back I spot Celeste talking to a tall man in matching white linen shirt and trousers. Simon pops up by her side and she deftly kisses the tall man goodbye and disappears into the throng, clearly pretending not to have noticed Simon appear. They continue this dance, bobbing and weaving through the crowd until Simon seems to tire and allows himself to be snagged into conversation by Fizz, who is guffawing at the jokes of a tanned white man who looks vaguely familiar.

'That's Richard Symmonds?' says Dot. 'From those terrible spy movies? Old school-friend of Dad's?' Each statement she makes poses a question, as if I should be the one who knows the answer. 'And that there', she says, pulling me round by the arm, 'is Virginia Marks? As in,

like, the hair products? Mum wants an invite to her pala-
zzo in Italy, that's why she's here?'

She guides me around the edge of the packed terrace,
pointing people out as we go. There are a few faces I
recognise but most of the people Dot deems important
enough to name I have never even heard of, until I spot a
face I definitely do know. Caroline Asiamah MP recently
went viral on a news clip talking about the importance
of improving safety and security at Notting Hill Carnival,
citing worries from her constituents. Jasmine sent me a
link to the video with the caption *Uncle Tom's creepy sister
at it again.* She is short and dark-skinned with shrewd eyes
that peer out from behind frameless square glasses. She's
wearing an off-white satin suit with a pussy-bow blouse
underneath and is fanning herself with a folded paper
plate. I type out a message to Jasmine.

Me

17:09

You're NEVER gonna guess who's here right now!

I snap a picture of her, then quickly shove my phone back
in my pocket as the MP's eyes lock with mine.

The first time I ever visited London I was maybe five
or six years old. Mum woke me from a cotton-wool
sleep. She had a look on her face which I already knew
meant something exciting was in the works. Later, that
look would start to scare me, but back then it gave me a

buzz of anticipation. We were awake in the middle of the night! Mum said we had something important to do. She dressed me in a hurry, putting my clothes on right over my pyjamas and stuffing my little arms into my coat. It must have been early spring or maybe autumn because Mum's purple Nissan Micra wasn't quite frozen but the windows fogged up when we got inside. I drew a little smiley face in the condensation. Mum turned the heat on full blast and set off as soon as a small patch of clear glass had appeared on the windscreen.

I remember I kept on falling asleep on the drive. I remember waking up on the motorway, the grey road stretching out into a big pink sky. I remember asking Mum lots of questions, but I don't remember her telling me where we were going or why. I remember vaguely thinking that Grandma might be worried. I remember Mum stopping somewhere and leaving me in the car and coming back with sausages and bacon and beans in a squeaky white box. There were even hash browns! I remember waking up as Mum unclipped my seatbelt and lifted me out of the car and into the cool morning air.

There were so many people and so much noise. I'd never seen that many people all in one place before. Not ever in my life. They were chanting, laughing and banging drums and pots and pans. They were also holding up signs. Mum put me on her shoulders and got me to hold a sign made of cardboard. Lots of people wanted to give me high-fives and I kept on dropping the sign and Mum got angry at me. A man from the news wanted to take a picture of me so I held the sign up extra high and put on my bravest face. The man from the news had a big blue coat and a big red face. That was when I realised that most of the faces around us were brown. Most of them were dark brown like Mum's, but some were lighter like mine and some of them were brown but different like my friend Asha from school. Some of the faces were white too, but mostly they were all different kinds of brown. One of the dark brown faces belonged to a man who kept smiling at me and putting his arm around Mum's shoulders.

At some point my hands got cold and my arms got tired and Mum had forgotten my gloves and I started crying, but I tried to be brave and put my hands inside my sleeves to keep them warm. We walked and walked and walked and I think Mum got tired of carrying me so I had to walk a bit but everyone was too close and too big and so the smiling man put me on his shoulders and Mum held on to the sign with one hand and on to my hand with the other and then my hand got warmer. When we stopped walking I could see Big Ben and then I knew we were in London. I couldn't wait to tell everyone at school that I had been to London. Asha had never been to London. Only Jamie Albright had been to London and he always bragged about it. I was excited to tell Jamie that I'd been to London because he'd never seen Big Ben and now I had!

When everyone stopped walking the crowd got even closer together and some people did speeches from a stage. They had faces like ours too but I couldn't hear what they were saying, but sometimes everyone cheered and I cheered too, and sometimes everyone booed so I booed as well. Lots of the signs had pictures of the same man on them. I didn't know who he was but he was dark brown like Mum, not light brown like me. The sun came out and then we walked some more and went to a big park and we sat on the grass and ate sandwiches and more people did more speeches and there was more cheering and more booing. And then we walked even more. There was so much walking.

When it started to get dark Mum said that we had to go because pigs were coming and they might put us in a kettle. I wanted to stay because I'd never met a pig before, I had only seen them in books, but I didn't like the idea of being in a kettle because they were dangerous and I wasn't allowed to touch the one at home because it was too hot. So we walked even more and I think I cried again because my legs were so tired from all the walking, so the smiling man carried me the rest of the way. When we got back to the car it had a big yellow circle on the wheel and a sticker on the windscreen and Mum said a word that I wasn't allowed to say. But I said it anyway and the smiling man laughed but I didn't know what was funny. The smiling man took us to his house and got blankets for us and Mum took off my clothes and my pyjamas were still underneath and I fell asleep on the settee but when I woke up Mum wasn't there. She was in the smiling man's room and the door was closed but I opened it and saw them sleeping in the bed together, and the room was messy and there were clothes all over the floor.

When we went back to the car in the morning a man in a uniform took the yellow circle off the car and Mum was in a bad mood. The drive was so long and I think I fell asleep because Mum carried me into the house, and Grandma was so angry and she shouted and shouted because Mum hadn't even called. Even after I was put in bed they were shouting and shouting at each other all night.

Dot pulls me by the arm down the path towards the ice shed, where a table has been set up with a white table-cloth and huge silver buckets filled with bottles of wine and light beer. Etienne is there and he smiles at me in a crisp white apron from behind the table, then raises an eyebrow and nods back towards the house. Mrs Blake is thundering down the slope towards us, draped in ivory silk with a gold brooch fastening at her left breast. She has a slightly crazed look on her face. Dot lets out a little 'Uh-oh' as she approaches.

'Just the man I was looking for,' she says brusquely. 'You haven't, by any chance, seen my idiot son, have you? And you didn't, by any chance, happen to notice if he remembered to pick up the glasses on your trip, did you?'

'I think he went to help Lily with her camera?' Dot offers.

'I don't think we got glasses, Mrs Blake, no,' I say.

'Felix,' she growls, low and dangerous. And then,

louder, almost shrieking her son's name. 'Felix!' She turns on a heel and stalks up the lawn almost knocking Bill off his feet, a spurned goddess hellbent on revenge.

'Sucks to be Felix right now,' says Etienne, eyebrows raised, a light smile playing across his lips. 'What can I get for you both? It will have to be something you can drink from the bottle, unless you want me to pour a cocktail directly into your mouth.'

'We'll have two beers, please Eti,' says Dot. Etienne looks at me and I'm about to protest but then he shrugs, deftly pops the caps on two bottles and hands one to each of us.

'Did you, uh, not get the memo?' he says, looking me up and down.

'What memo?'

'Oh, sugar sticks!' says Dot. 'Oh, how embarrassing, of course we just assumed you knew 'cause you're, like, part of the gang. Tonight's a White Party?' She sees the look on my face. 'You should be wearing white.'

I look around and realise she's not kidding. Everything – bunting, tablecloths and every single guest – is milky in the late-afternoon glow. I look down at my faded denim shirt and black shorts and suddenly feel weirdly naked.

'It's not, like, a hard and fast rule though. I'm sure no one will notice,' says Dot, trying to help.

'Yeah, I'm going to go and change,' I say.

'Yes, I think you'd better,' says Etienne with a laugh.

I grab my beer and pick my way up the lawn towards the house. I feel like everyone is looking at me as I force my way through the crowd. The garden and house are full of strangers and it takes me forever to finally get to the stairs. I eventually reach the safety of my floor and I'm about to head into my room and change when I hear laughter from down the corridor. I follow the sound to Felix's room and knock twice before walking in. The laughter abruptly stops and Felix and Celeste jump up from the bed, knocking a plate to the floor which smashes.

'Oh fuck, you scared the shit out of me,' says Felix.

'You should really knock before entering a room,' says Celeste coolly.

'Um, I did. Sorry, I heard voices and just came to see if—'

'Don't worry about it,' says Felix, smiling.

'Well, he should worry, actually, because—'

'Now, CeCe, let's not get worked up. Don't worry about it, mate, it's all good. Now what are you wearing? I think we need to get you into something more appropriate to the theme, don't you?'

'I was just coming to change, actually; I think I have a white T-shirt, and maybe some jeans that are kind of very light blue.'

'Jeans!?' Felix squawks, aghast. 'Absolutely fucking not. Here, try these.' He hands me some white chinos. 'And this.' He pulls the white linen shirt he is wearing over his head and throws it to me. 'Much better. Now, if you'll excuse us . . .' He nods towards the door then starts picking up the broken pieces of the plate.

I back out, a strange feeling sinking deep into my

stomach. When I get to my room and pull Felix's shirt on, it is still warm from his body and I can smell his aftershave on it. I button it up to my throat and settle the chain we found in town on the outside so the collar points are connected by a thin thread of gold. I put on the chinos and, because it's either them or flip flops, slip on my white Reebok Classics.

I go looking for Lily but I haven't seen her since she dragged Felix away earlier. I do a couple of laps of the terrace but can't find any of the Blakes, who must be tied up elsewhere with hosting duties as more guests pour in. Even Bill and Fizz seem to have disappeared. I am nursing my beer, which is now warm, and feeling uncomfortable in the thick chinos when a voice startles me.

'A bit on the nose, all this "White Party" stuff. Don't you think so?' The voice is perfectly clipped, BBC-ready. I shake the hand that has been offered to me and get a faint trace of cocoa butter.

'Caroline Asiamah,' she says, studying me.

'I know who you are. I mean, it's a pleasure to meet you, Mrs Asiamah.'

'Ms,' she says, unsmiling. 'But you can call me Caroline. It's a pleasure to see another . . . let's say "friendly face", shall we?' She appraises me, eyes narrowed. 'Now, tell me: how did you end up here?'

'I'm a, uh, a friend of Lily's from university.'

'Leeds?'

'Newcastle.'

'Ah, yes, of course. I read Law at Durham, you know? It seems we have quite a lot in common, you and I.' She looks around at the other guests while I wonder what she means aside from the obvious. 'The Blakes are so wonderfully generous, aren't they? Although David quite frankly hates parties – even mine.' She laughs at her own joke. 'I imagine he's locked himself in his study at this point.'

I don't really know what to say so I say nothing.

'Tell me, what are your plans when you graduate?'

'Oh, I'm not sure really. I'm still waiting to hear back from a few grad schemes and stuff. I might move back to Manchester for a bit, I think.'

'Manchester? Gosh, Toto, we really aren't in Kansas anymore, are we? If you end up in London, which any sensible man like you should by the way, you should give me a call. We could always use more faces like yours on our side.'

She hands me a business card, gives me another look, once up and down, smiles, then moves off into the party. I turn the card over a few times. It is thick and feels expensive, cream with shiny green lettering and the crowned portcullis symbol of the House of Commons.

CAROLINE ELIZABETH ASIAMAH
MP FOR KENSINGTON
THE CONSERVATIVE AND UNIONIST PARTY

'What are you doing talking to Creepy Caroline?' asks Lily, popping up at my shoulder.

'I'm not quite sure.' I shove the card in the pocket of Felix's chinos.

'Anyway, where on earth have you been? I've been looking everywhere for you. The uni gang is here and everyone is dying to say hello.'

I highly doubt this but let her lead me round the side of the house, down a few steps and through a large window into a room I haven't seen before. There are a few settees and two huge bean bags on the floor. The opposite wall has a huge TV screen mounted on it surrounded by a fitted bookcase lined with hundreds of DVDs. Six of Lily's friends, three girls and three boys are arranged in couples on the various surfaces, paper plates filled with sandwiches and salads on their laps.

'Everyone, look who I found!'

There is a chorus of half-hearted hellos. Lily and I, despite being close friends, have pretty different circles at uni. Most of the friends we have in common are from halls and we don't really see them that often anymore. This group, which Jasmine disdainfully calls Jack Wills Anonymous, are all Lily's friends from boarding school. They've been tight since they were thirteen and all decided to go to university together.

'Oi, Lil,' says one of the boys, lighting a cigarette, his voice clipped and clear like a ship's bell. 'I thought you were going to get us a drink. I'm absolutely parched.' The girl whose knee he has his hand on laughs.

This boy is Rupert. This boy is a boy I know.

*

When I emerged from the cupboard under the stairs, the disembodied moaning still swirling through my head, the WATCHME.move party was even busier and louder than before. I decided to try and find Lily so I headed away from the bass of the main room and up the stairs. I located her in one of the bedrooms where a few people were lounging on a huge mattress covering most of the floor. Projectors angled around the room covered the walls with slow-motion hyper-zoomed-in footage from the porn film. The music sounded like those recordings of deep space. Lily took my hand and guided me down.

'Let's lie here for a bit,' she slurred, snuggling into my shoulder.

'Do you want some K, bro?' said one of the boys on the mattress. He didn't really wait for a response before putting a key with a little heap of white powder on it in front of my nose. I inhaled. The powder burned in my nostril and made my eyes water. I fought the urge to cough, not wanting to show myself up for a second time that night. I waited awkwardly for a while, watching the close-ups of hands and mouths and dicks. After a while I started to feel like I was melting into the people around me, all of us seeping into the mattress, dripping through the floorboards. Together we watched the film blur. It seemed to slow even further into static frames that dissolved from one to the next seamlessly.

'Hey. I . . . We need to leave.' It was Jasmine, suddenly kneeling next to me, slurring her words. I tried to sit up but my body refused.

'Hey, Jazz. What's up?'

'I don't . . . I want to go.' I couldn't really make out her voice over the music. I felt like I was floating.

'Shh, just stay a while,' said Lily, waving a hand to quiet us.

'I really, think I . . .' Jasmine trailed off. Her voice didn't sound like her own through the haze of the music and the movie and the drugs.

'Hey, I'm heading back to halls. Wanna jump in my cab?' A new voice, clipped and clear, cutting through the fuzziness. I don't remember hearing a reply but then Jasmine was gone. I tried to get up again but Lily waved me back down.

'It's fine, he's a gentleman. Don't worry.'

The rest of the night is absent from my mind. I think we stayed for a few more hours. I woke up the next morning in Lily's room, both of us fully clothed, on top of her duvet. I went to find Jasmine once I'd showered and changed. She was sitting on her bed, knees pulled tight to her chest. She didn't say anything to me. She just stared until I left. She didn't say anything to me for two days. When she started talking to me again, I was so relieved I didn't want to ask what was wrong in case it triggered something again, so I said nothing.

The words that Lily said still reverberate in my mind: *It's fine, he's a gentleman. Don't worry.*

The flood of memory makes me feel sick. I step outside to get some air but it's too thick, it feels like glue hardening on my skin. A jazz band has started up on the terrace and the music drifts around the corner of the house. I turn to make my way towards it and almost collide with Simon, who seems to be on the warpath.

'You haven't seen my darling girl, have you?' he spits through gritted teeth. He is tired of their game of cat and mouse. He is sweating. Beads form in the sunburnt retreat of his hairline and there are patches of soft pink under his arms and above the protruding mound of his stomach where the sweat has made his white shirt translucent.

'I think she might be inside,' I say, and then realise I might be dropping her in it. 'But I'm not sure.'

Simon scowls. 'Probably whispering in a corner with her little friend.' He pushes past me – even though the space is more than wide enough for him not to – and staggers a little as he disappears to find Celeste.

The music changes and I follow the opening bars of 'La Vie en rose' onto the terrace. The low sun scatters gold across the faces of the guests and lights the various shades of their clothes into a pearly glimmer. They are all facing the little platform where Mrs Blake has joined the band and begun to sing. All except Dot, who is using the distraction to pick off unattended drinks. She furtively sips from a bottle of wine, catches my eye and puts a finger up to her smiling lips. Mrs Blake's eyes are closed and the song spills out of her lips. She takes her time with the melody and the band adjusts to keep pace with her. I close my eyes too and let myself float on the familiar tune.

When she is finished, the partygoers break into applause. She bows her head, a studiedly modest smile on her face, then holds up a hand to silence them.

'Dearest friends, old and new, you are truly welcome. It is always such a pleasure to have you all here. It doesn't feel like a year since we were last gathered here, but that's life, I suppose. Every year seems to go faster than the last. And I should know, I have had my fair share – though nobody knows exactly how many. A few thank-yous are in order. First, to all of you for coming. I know for many of you it is an awfully long way and your presence is very much appreciated. To Sandrine and the whole team at Le Bleuet, for the wonderful food and all of your help. To my darling children, with the exception of Felix, whose inability to follow even basic instructions is the reason that we are drinking out of mugs rather than crystal this evening. If you see him, please feel free to mock him.'

The crowd laughs and applauds in the correct places. Right on cue, Felix appears, having swapped the white linen I am now wearing for a sleeveless silk shirt, fastened with golden buttons up to a round collar tight against his throat. He carries a crate of mugs and teacups and makes a show of forcing his way through the crowd, muttering hellos and sorries and thank-yous and welcomes in a stage whisper. He theatrically pops a bottle of champagne and starts pouring drinks for everyone.

'And finally, to my loving husband, who hates this party but lets me do it every year anyway. Without him, none of this' – she spreads out her arms, gesturing towards the terrace, the grounds and the now imposing blank towers of the Chateau, which have just started to block out the setting sun – 'would be possible. I am eternally grateful, for everything you have built, everything you have done, and everything you continue to do for this family. Wherever you are David, thank you. *La fête commence maintenant!*'

She raises a teacup of champagne and the crowd applauds again, the band picks up, and people turn back to their conversations. Annie drifts off the stage and down towards the bar where Felix has deposited the rest of the mugs. He is brandishing a cocktail shaker; the oscillation of the metal is a blur against the solid tension in his tanned arms. He sees me looking and smiles.

'Aviation?' he says as I approach. 'It'll have to be out of a mug though; apparently someone forgot to pick up the glassware.'

'Careful, Felix,' Mrs Blake warns, laughing darkly. She gestures to the man she is talking to. 'This is Group Captain Henry Teller.'

'Call me Harry,' he says, taking my hand in both of his. He is broad and rugged and looks directly into my eyes as he talks. 'Annie was telling me you're from Manchester, is that right? I grew up in Manchester. Well, near enough.'

Felix snorts. 'Group Captain Henry's family owns Allenbury Hall. And Harry dearest will inherit it all soon enough, won't he, Mother? Everything the light touches will be his. Would that make you a marquis? Or an earl? I can never quite remember.'

'How are those cocktails coming along, darling?' Mrs Blake buries the insinuation, a warning flashing in her gaze. 'Our guests look parched.'

'We used to go up to Allenbury all the time as kids,' Felix presses on. 'We'd go for exeat and sometimes half-term. Annie would pick us up from school and drive north. The house is absolutely massive, with a vast estate. Dot, Lily and I would just roam endlessly and no one would have any idea where we were. We'd band together with Captain Henry's kids and cause all sorts of havoc. Once we herded an entire flock of sheep into the drawing room. It took absolutely ages but once they were in it was almost impossible to get them back out. If I remember correctly, one of them somehow made its way into the servants' corridor. It was found roaming the third floor two days later.'

I know the house he is talking about. We visited once on a school trip. Some outreach programme to get city kids out into the countryside. We were loaded onto a coach and each given a brown paper bag containing a soggy sandwich, a warm box of orange juice and a KitKat. I ate mine before we got on to the M60. The house was so big, with rows and rows of windows gleaming in the light as the coach rolled up the impossibly long drive. I thought it was too big for any one person to live there. We were herded to the visitors' centre where we were told about life on the farm and sent out to take rubbings with different coloured crayons in our little notebooks. Yellow, for History, of course. We were supposed to pet the animals, but we weren't allowed to because of a disease that was going round. We had to step in little trays of disinfectant when we went in and out of the fields. I was wearing my trainers and the pungent liquid made the dye bleed into my white socks. Grandma had to boil them in vinegar to get them white again.

'Well, you've always had a nose for mischief, Felix,' countered Group Captain Henry Teller.

'Speaking of mischief, Harry,' said Felix, pouring a double measure of pale purple liquid into two mugs with a flourish, 'how's your wife?'

'Felix!' Mrs Blake brings her palm down hard on the bar with a bang, but Teller just laughs.

'Effy is very well, thanks, Fe. I've actually just come from a week in St Barts with her and the kids. They were all asking after you. Wanted to know if you'd been in anything good lately, but I told them no one's really casting self-involved, talentless pricks at the moment.'

There is a pause, then both men laugh. Felix pulls Teller into a bear-hug across the bar, almost knocking over the drinks he's just poured. Teller ruffles the boy's hair.

'It's good to see you, Uncle Harry!'

'Don't you dare call me Uncle Harry, you little shit.' He takes a sip from one of the mugs, then winces. 'That, my friend, is fucking disgusting.'

They sink into reminiscence, about Allenbury and their fond memories there. Mrs Blake slides her arm through the crook of my elbow and steers me across the flag-stones. When we reach our target, she rattles through a round of introductions. All of the names slip out of my head and into the summer air. Except for one.

'And this,' she says with a flourish, 'is Cassandra Quant.'

The woman is short, with a waterfall of red hair and a white cotton suit that looks so soft it might actually be loungewear. She peers at me curiously.

'This friend of Lily's is an absolutely virtuosic pianist, Cass. You should be champing at the bit to hear him play. I'm surprised the Academy hasn't discovered him already. If you miss out on him, you'll owe the classical music community a huge debt.' Mrs Blake's eyes glitter with the insinuation.

Cassandra Quant blinks, raises an eyebrow to Mrs Blake, then stretches out her hand to shake mine.

'Unfortunately, admissions for this year are closed. And the audition slots for next year have already been allocated.'

Mr Quant, with Mrs Blake stood directly by his side, coughs. His wife smiles.

'But I always have time to hear a handsome rogue with raw talent.'

She slips me her card. I take it, red-faced, and make an excuse about going to find Lily. I walk down onto the lawn, trying to look interested in the view across the fields out to the low hills in the distance, which are stained an inky black as the sun flirts with the horizon. The drink is quite disgusting. The violet has a sickly, almost chemical taste to it, and there is so much lemon juice that it makes me screw up my face. I find a dry-looking rosemary bush in the shadow of the terrace to pour it into. Above me, through the mingled sound of people and soft music from the terrace, I hear voices talking animatedly but in hushed tones. Without knowing why, I press my back against the wall to avoid being seen. I recognise Rupert's voice and assume without looking that the rest of Jack Wills Anonymous are there too. I am not trying to eavesdrop, but I hear them anyway.

'Picked her up in a whorehouse, apparently,' Rupert is saying. 'Always a class act our Slimy Simey.'

'Don't be vulgar, Ru. I think it's romantic actually,' says one of the girls, maybe Phoebe, or Hebe – I can never remember which is which. One is blonde and the other desperately wants to be. 'It's like *Pretty Woman*!'

'Don't be so naive, Phoebs – that isn't love in her eyes, it's greed. And he's hardly Richard Gere.' This must be Hebe. Her voice is softer and sweeter, even as she spits poison.

'If he were, he wouldn't be paying her.'

'We don't know that he's definitely paying her,' Rupert chimes in.

'Oh, come on. We can all spot a gold-digger, even if he has wrapped her in Hermès!'

They all laugh and I take the opportunity to peel myself away from the wall and escape up the lawn, leaving them to gossip. In the back of my mind the thought of what they say about me when I'm not around begins to form. I push it away and take out my phone. Absently I flick through the apps and then see a notification. A message from Etienne. *Come to Felix's room.* He is 28 metres away. I check the timestamp. It was sent three minutes ago. My phone buzzes again. *Bring a plate.*

I swing via the kitchen to get the plate as requested, taking a couple of cold beers from the fridge as I go. I can hear laughter and Childish Gambino's nasal voice echo across the corridor. The door to Felix's room is ajar. When I push it open, Etienne and Felix are sitting cross-legged on the floor. They are giggling and their heads are pressed close together. I feel heat rise from my gut. It is jealousy mixed with something else I can't quite place. Embarrassment, maybe, at my possessiveness. It melts away when Felix turns to look at me and his smile grows even wider. Again, that light in his eyes, which feels like it turns up a notch when he looks at me, stirs a flutter inside my chest. It snatches my breath so that the hello I'd practised before opening the door escapes as a soft sigh.

'Look what the cat dragged in!' he says, getting to his feet then taking my hand and pulling me down with him so that we are sat in a triangle, our knees brushing against each other. Felix takes the plate and a beer, placing one in the middle of us and taking a long slug from the other. 'Okay, where were we? Ah yes, Eti – it's your turn. Truth or dare?'

He looks at me, mischief dancing across his eyes. 'Dare.'

'Alright,' says Felix, stretching backwards so he can reach into his pocket. He takes out a small packet and hands it to Etienne. The movement pushes his knee further against mine and he leaves it there as he leans forward. 'I dare you to rack us up some lines. And make them big. The first one's the only one that counts.'

I try to protest but Felix cuts me off.

'Oh, come on, it's only coke. And besides, you owe me one after wasting about fifty euros worth when you made me drop the last plate. Also maybe don't mention that to Annie – the plate was probably about fifty euros too, knowing her. She'll go absolutely mad. Best to blame it on the caterers.'

He winks at Etienne, who scowls, then taps out a mound of white powder and takes a credit card from Felix's outstretched hand. He crushes it finely then divides it into three rows. Felix hands him a little metal straw. 'Dealer's choice.'

Etienne appraises his handiwork then bends down to take the line nearest to him. He straightens up and pinches his nose with one hand while passing the straw to me with the other. I hesitate for a moment but feel the expectation from both of them so I swallow my reservation. The cocaine is acrid and makes the back of my throat go numb. I take a sip of beer and force it down. Felix takes the straw from me and does the same. By the time he is done, I can already feel a surge of boldness, a surety and a sense of self that was not there before. I hear Jasmine's voice in my head: *Cocaine is for white people, I already know I'm the shit.*

'Okay, your turn.' Etienne turns towards me. 'Truth or dare?'

'Um, truth, I guess.'

Felix jumps in before Etienne can speak. 'Do you want to kiss me?'

My mind goes blank and the flutter in my chest becomes a pounding. Panicked, I mumble something incoherent.

'I didn't quite catch that. I said, "Do you want to kiss me?"'

'Can I change to dare?'

'Okay . . . I dare you.'

'What?'

'To kiss me.'

Felix shifts his weight onto his knees so he is gazing down at me. He fixes me in place with his eyes and puts a hand on my cheek. Then he leans forward and brushes his lips against mine. I breathe him in and he fills my chest with sandalwood and tobacco. He brushes against my mouth again and I catch his bottom lip between my teeth. He pushes me back with both hands, hard in the centre of my chest and positions himself on top of me. He crushes his face against mine and I open my mouth and let myself be kissed. Though I am on my back I feel as if I am being pulled up towards him. When he moves to sit up, I am dragged with him by the hunger in my chest. I can feel him smiling against my lips. It fills me up with a warmth that seems to spill out of my mouth and into his. I am leaning back on my elbows, looking up at him, my breath coming in snatches. My mind is blank and it is impossible to do anything but look at his face smiling down at me. He laughs and then I do too.

From behind us Etienne clears his throat.

'I think, Felix, it is your turn, *non*? Truth or dare?'

Felix pauses. He does not take his eyes off me. He smiles. 'Let's have another line.'

'Ah, you are not playing the game,' Etienne protests.

Felix ignores him and shakes more cocaine out onto the plate. He makes three parallel lines, smaller this time and bends over to take his. Etienne and I follow suit.

'Okay, it is actually your turn though,' I say, trying out putting my hand gently on his thigh. He does not shake me off.

'Oh, fine. Truth.' says Felix, and before I can form a question, Etienne jumps in.

'Who is a better fuck: him or me?'

My heart flutters deep in my chest, heightened by the coke flowing through my system. It's like the solid floor is warping beneath me. Felix's head spins around and he glares at Etienne before turning to me. There is a look on his face that I don't recognise. A kind of searching panic like he has been knocked off his axis. I try to appear nonchalant and force a laugh but it comes out as a choke from the back of my throat.

'Hey, hey, you and me are ancient history now, Eti. It wouldn't be fair to make the comparison.' He says this coolly, freezing Etienne in place. When he turns back to me, though, there is a plea in his eyes.

'Ah, I wouldn't call thirty minutes ago so ancient, would you?'

I can feel the force of Etienne's words searing into

me and the flutter of my heart has become a pounding drumbeat that spreads anger through my body. I am acutely aware of every cell within me and all I want is to collapse in on myself. Etienne is laughing. And Felix is laughing too, and somewhere so are Lily and Celeste and Rupert and all of them. I try to re-centre myself but I can hear the echoing giggles rising to a deafening pitch in my head and I think I might cry but I know if I do that then I won't be able to stop. So I slowly get to my feet and somehow this time the words I try to muster come out whole and I say I'm going to get a drink and Felix points out that I already have one and says I should stay and Etienne says he is sorry and didn't mean to upset me and I hear myself saying that I am not upset but even as I say that my voice cracks again. I cover the fracture in my words with a cough and I am over by the door by now, with my back to them so they do not see my face crumple. I flee into the corridor which is awash with a muted red light as the sun finally sets. The blaze draws out the tears that I have been holding back. Tears I now can't quite understand, the scene I have just left already twisting itself into a haunting memory. That embarrassment at feeling something I have no right to feel returns and mingles with my ire, a burning knot lodging itself behind my breastbone.

I can hear Felix calling to me from the other end of the corridor but I can't face him. I move towards the stairs, intending to find somewhere in the garden to hide. But as I pass the landing of the floor below, I can hear a clamour from one of the rooms. I follow the raised voices. From a room towards the far end, Celeste is shouting frantically in high-pitched French. Although I do not understand what she is saying, I can make out the venom in her tone. The pitch rises and then becomes a scream, shot through with the sound of breaking glass.

'Don't you dare fucking embarrass me in front of these people! I can see what you're trying to do here and I will send you right back where you came from. Do you fucking understand me?'

Without realising it I have opened the door and find myself standing between Simon and Celeste. Beneath my trainers are shards of glass and beheaded tulips floating in a small puddle of slimy water. Celeste looks shaken but there is a determination on her face and no trace of fear.

'Listening at doors now, are we, boy? That's not very polite.' Simon Chance takes a step towards me and I feel myself square my shoulders. I'm not a fighter but I've taken punches from men much bigger than him. I'm weighing up the pros and cons of nutting him between the eyes and making a break for it when a voice cuts through the tension.

'Dear oh dear, Mum's going to be raging about that vase, Simon. Be a good boy and go and get a dustpan, would you?'

Felix moves to stand by my side and puts a hand on my shoulder. I shrug him off as Simon moves past us towards the door.

'I was just telling your little friend to keep his nose

out of the grown-ups' business. I recommend you do the same, Felix.' He spits this and stalks out of the room.

Felix starts to pick up the fragments of glass and looks up at Celeste, asking if she's okay.

'Never better, Fifi,' she says, forcing a smile.

Felix looks at me but I am not ready to talk to him. I surprise myself by taking Celeste's hand and leading her out of the room. I allow her to take over and she leads me down a smaller set of spiral stairs I've not noticed before, to a little door that opens into the drawing room. I close it behind us. Celeste taps her nose, crouches down and pulls a bottle of gin and two crystal glasses out of the cabinet.

'I think we both need a drink, don't you?'

The first time I got drunk I was eleven years old. It was early summer and after school the evenings stretched out with endless possibilities. It was the summer before I was due to start secondary school, the summer I would have my first kiss. And the summer that mum would get ill. The summer I broke my wrist racing my best friend, Marcus, down the hill at the end of the road, when I flew off my bike after hitting a pothole. I remember not feeling any pain at all even though my wrist stuck out strangely. I remember not feeling any pain at all even as the ambulance arrived to pick me up and take me to hospital, Grandma strapped into the seat in the back, handbag on lap, eyes closed, muttering prayers, her face lined with worry, the rolled-up tissue she always kept in her cardigan sleeve on hand to wipe away any stray tears.

I remember Grandma straightening her back when she heard the words 'safeguarding' and 'social worker' and someone asking where Mum was. I remember waking up in the hospital and my wrist being wrapped in an electric-blue cast and a pretty white nurse being told off by an older Caribbean one in a uniform two shades of blue darker for asking if she could be the first to sign it. I remember her sneaking back later to sign it anyway, bearing a box of warm orange juice and two digestives wrapped in plastic. I remember that her name was Jenny and that next to her name she drew a little heart. But that was the end of the summer. The first time I got drunk, really properly drunk, was before I flew through the air and landed in Jenny's kindness.

It was just before we broke up for the holidays, and one day after school I dawdled for a while, trying to numb the reality of what was happening at home. Mum and Grandma had been fighting a lot. Big screaming fights that blazed for hours and shook the walls of the house. Raised voices and slammed doors. I savoured the last quiet drops of the warm afternoon. I sat in the little play area of the park opposite the school and watched the other kids filter out, greeted by parents or finding their friends and stumbling down the road, leaning in to each other, giddy with excitement and secret jokes. I twisted up the chains of the rusty swing then raised my feet off the ground and allowed the helix to unravel. So much energy contained within the juddering release of the rectangular steel links. *Clink*, *clink*, *clink*. The rubber seat dropped a fraction of an inch each time the metal slipped over itself. I alternated between watching the dust spin beneath me and clamping my eyes shut against the dizziness. Above me, the cloudless sky faded from the flat, expansive blue of day into grey.

From the darkening edge of the park, someone called out to me. I spun in my swing to see a white boy a couple of years older than me. I recognised him because his sister was in the year below me and sometimes he would pick her up from school. He must have been fifteen or sixteen but even the kids at my school would hurl names at him. Poofter, bender, faggot. Words that, although they were meant for him, wrenched at something inside me. I wanted nothing to do with him. But he was walking across the park towards me and there was nothing I could do about it.

'Hey, kiddo, it's pretty late to be hanging around here on your own, you know. Don't you have anywhere to go?'

'You're on your own,' I said. I'd meant it to sound defiant, to push away his unearned familiarity, but it came out more inquisitive and childlike than I had intended.

'I'm actually meeting some mates. You can hang with us if you want?'

'I'm fine,' I mumbled, studying the ground.

'Look, mate, it's not safe round here after dark. What are you, like, ten?' His voice sat on the edge of manhood, occasionally cracking, giving away his youth. But to me he looked like a man, straggly hairs poked out of angry-looking bumps around his throat.

'Actually, I'm fourteen,' I lied. I looked up at him. His eyes were a bright, urgent blue.

'Whatever you say, big man,' he said, a kind smile showing off braces with alternating red and black elastic. 'But I'm not leaving you alone, in this park, after dark. The next stranger you meet might not be so kind. Come and meet the gang. Don't worry, they're all sound.'

For want of a better option, I followed this boy (whose name, I thought, might have been Danny) out of the play area. We were walking away from the streetlights that lined the road outside of school and I suddenly worried I'd made a bad decision. The tall trees stretched out their limbs against the cloudy sky. Through the rustle of the summer breeze in the leaves I heard snatches of reassuring laughter and the tinny sound of music. I followed Danny down a hill towards a group of kids all dressed in various shades of black with chequered trainers and chains hanging from their studded belts and second belts hanging seemingly from nothing. Gerard Way was singing about the broken, the beaten and the damned from a tinny mobile-phone speaker.

'Here comes trouble,' said a tall girl with a nose ring and jet-black hair that looked like she'd cut the fringe herself. 'I didn't know you were babysitting tonight, Dannyboy.'

'I'm not a baby,' I said, trying to deepen my voice. Everyone looked older than me.

'Leave it out, Kayla. Big man looked like he needed a mate. I think we all know the feeling, right? Anyway, don't you have goats to sacrifice or something?' The rest of the group laughed. The tension eased.

'Hey, big man, fancy some of this?' A ratty-looking boy held out a large bottle with a red label. 'This'll put hair between ya legs.'

'Don't be a fuckin' perv, Floody,' said Kayla, smacking him round the head with the flat of her hand. Biro-tattooed stars snaked in a burst of blurry blue around her slender wrist.

I took a small sip from the bottle, then a larger one before I'd felt the burn of the first. The taste made my eyes water and I must have coughed because everyone started to laugh. The heat spread out through my chest.

'Alright, slow down, Ernest Hemingway. Leave some for the rest of us,' said Floody, taking a swig from the bottle then passing it to the others.

We continued like this for a long time. The bottle making its way into different hands and lips. Jokes passed back and forth. Their friendship seemed easy, yet somehow adversarial. They sparred but the insults were loving and no one, except for maybe Floody, seemed to get offended. I relaxed, leaning in to feeling rather than thinking, laughing hard and often even though sometimes I didn't know what I was laughing about. At one point I fell backwards off the fallen tree we were sitting on. It knocked the wind out of me, but I didn't really feel the pain, and as soon as I caught my breath it came back out as laughter. I felt my face flush and a swimming feeling in my head as if I'd twisted the chains of the swing all the way to the top and was now spinning endlessly on its rubber seat. Except this time, when I closed my eyes, the feeling got worse not better. At one point Kayla asked if I wanted a smiley. I didn't know what she meant and gave her a puzzled look as she held her pink lighter aloft, the orange flame flickering in the dark. I flinched as she pressed the tip into my forearm but she was holding tightly on to my wrist so I could not pull my hand away. The vodka numbed the pain and I only felt a prick of heat, which later became a gentle throb. The two vertical lines and half circle left by the hot metal swelled, red and angry on my skin. A distorted smile that would blister, then burst, then fade to pink and eventually white, never fully disappearing.

The rest of the night is fragmented. Each time I think back, I record over it like a roll of broken film, changing the scattered memories. I think I remember the spinning most of all. No matter how hard I closed my eyes, I couldn't get it to stop. It twisted inside my head, like I was being tossed around in a storm, until eventually the vortex found its way out through my nose and mouth. Urgent and sour. I think I remember someone screaming and someone laughing. I remember looking down and thinking that I'd ruined my trainers. I remember Danny slapping me in the face, asking where I lived. I remember mumbling my address and being made to repeat it until it actually made sense. I remember someone feeding me water and most of it spilling onto my face. I remember being hoisted over someone's shoulder and watching the grass turn into a path then into pavement. I remember being dropped and landing awkwardly on my arm and my face. I remember Mum and Grandma shouting, whether at me or at them I couldn't tell. I remember being laid in the shower, fully clothed, and Mum sticking her fingers down my throat. Forcing up everything in my stomach until all that would come up was a lumpy grey nothingness. I don't remember getting put to bed. I remember the round of high-fives I got from Danny and Kayla and Floody and the rest of them when I snuck out a week later to see them in the park.

'Everybody here thinks I'm a whore and there's nothing I can do about it.'

Celeste drains her glass, lights a cigarette, and reaches for the gin bottle. Pouring it neat over ice and taking another large swig. We ran out of tonic about three drinks ago and neither of us cares enough to venture outside to get more. She winces. I open my mouth to protest but she cuts me off.

'We both know it is true: don't try to patronise me by saying otherwise. These people, they take one look at you and make up their minds about what kind of person you are. The truth doesn't matter to them. I have a fucking master's degree, for fuck's sake. But they look at him and then they look at me and they see just another whore he has paid to hang off his hairy little arm. It doesn't matter that I'm not fucking him. It doesn't matter that he's not given me a penny. There is nothing I can say or do that will ever change their minds about me.'

She must see the question in my eyes because she answers before I can ask it.

'I am here because Simon is funny and powerful and I had nothing else to do this summer. And I have done some modelling with Felix before and thought it would be fun to get to know him better. But none of that matters to these people,' she repeats. 'They think I am here to worm my way into their inbred little English hierarchy, squeeze out some cross-eyed child for Simon and divorce him, taking half of what he's worth. Which isn't even enough to go to all that trouble for, by the way. But what they fail to understand is that without people like me to keep them excited and youthful and glamorous, their little island with its ugly clothes and overcooked meat will decay, and collapse into the sea.'

She pulls a disgusted face and stubs out her cigarette on the marble floor. She gets up to leave, then pauses by the piano and turns to look at me.

'They fear me. They think I'm using him. Perhaps I am. But they are using me just as much. We all trick one another, to get what we want. Life is a game. And all games have winners, and they have losers. I suggest you think about the reasons you are playing, *mon chou*. And what they might say when you're not around the table.' She takes a long match from the tall glass jar on the fireplace and uses it to light another cigarette. My nervous fingers find the chain around my neck and tuck it inside the collar of Felix's shirt. She exhales a long, slow stream of smoke then glides across the room. Her poise is momentarily lost as she stumbles slightly near the door, the tiny crack in the bottom pane glinting in the light.

Her words swim with the alcohol in my head. I place both hands against the cool marble to steady myself but when I close my eyes the floor pitches and shifts beneath me. The memory of Felix and Etienne and the kiss flood back into my mind. It makes my head spin more. I take a few deep breaths to try and push the thoughts away. A sudden click and a flash bring me back to the moment.

'There you are, hiding away. Why are you sitting on the floor? You're literally surrounded by more comfortable places to sit.' Lily is standing above me. She has taken her shoes off and let her hair down. Her camera dangles from the thin leather strap looped around her slender wrist. The light from the chandelier shines through the waves of her hair. She extends a pale hand towards me and helps me to my feet. 'Come on, we're playing games in the Cave.'

She turns to go and I follow. I pick up the nearly-empty bottle of gin. Lily is quick and it's an effort to keep up with her. She disappears down a set of stairs that lead to the little cushion-strewn room I entered through the window earlier. It is busier than before and music blares from a large speaker. Someone has screwed a colour-changing bulb into one of the lamps; little grooves along its surface scatter rainbows around the room as it slowly rotates. Bodies tangle and twist in the swirling kaleidoscope.

The night seems to come and go in stop-motion flickers. Someone, Hebe, or maybe Phoebe, pushes a small cup into my hand. Everyone raises their glasses, Felix says something, and we all drink. The tequila burns but I blink it away.

I dance into the crowd, avoiding Felix and Etienne. I take Lily's hand and spin her under my arm. The room is a flurry of limbs and hair and music and light and faces. Someone puts a key with a little heap of white powder on it under my nose. I inhale it, not knowing what it is.

I find myself outside. The night air is warm, close around my throat. I feel like I might be sick. Etienne puts a cigarette between my lips and lights it. I let it fall to the ground. He grabs my hand as I turn to go inside and pulls me back towards him, pushes his lips against mine. I think I kiss him back, something stirs inside my chest. He tells me that we're even now.

I am now on the terrace. The band has finished playing and are packing away their instruments. My shirt has come mostly unbuttoned. The grown-ups that remain are dancing to Toploader. Bill pours champagne into used mugs. I take one.

Would you get me some water please, my dear. I think I ate a bad prawn. Fizz retches into a large pot full of lavender and rosemary and vomit. She rests her cheek on the terracotta rim and turns her gaze upward as heavy droplets begin to fall out of the sky. They hit the plant pot, slowly staining it a bloody red.

In the large foyer I drip onto the flagstones and help Mrs Blake pass around towels. Celeste curls her hair into a rope and wrings out the rainwater. Bill says that the best way to prevent a cold is to have a hot toddy as soon as you get wet. There is a chorus of agreeable noises.

There is plenty of room around the kitchen island but Felix stands next to me, spooning honey into the mugs as I squeeze lemons. He moves so he is behind me, his hands on the counter, closing me in. I do not move away. He kisses my neck and I turn to face him. I let him kiss me until the kettle screams that it is done.

The speaker and the lights are brought up from the Cave and the two parties become one once more. The bass rattles the crystal vases on the sideboard and someone smashes a glass. Celeste grabs me by both of my hands and spins us in a circle. The crowd around us scatters. I do not know where Felix is and I think to myself that I shouldn't care.

But I am looking for Felix. I lumber down yet another unidentifiable corridor, my heart pounding from the coke or maybe adrenaline or both. Hushed voices float through a gap in the wall. I am about to open the door but through the small opening I see Mrs Blake. The room looks like a study. Her body is pressed up against a wall of leather-bound books, her face turned away from me. Even from behind I can recognise Group Captain Teller burying his head in the angle of her neck. They stop. *Did you hear that?* I retreat back down the corridor.

Lily has sent me to get more ice. I am distracted by the sound of shouting and crashing from the kitchen. No one else can hear it above the music in the hall. Simon storms out of the kitchen but stops in his tracks when he sees me. *Careful, mate, our little Polka Dot is drunk and has gotten herself all worked up.* His cheek is scratched and his eyes are glazed.

Dot sits on the flagstones in the kitchen, her knees pulled up tight to her chest. She is surrounded by cutlery and broken glass. Glittering shards and silver knives, forks and spoons spread out around her like a strange art installation. She is clutching a sharp knife which has cut into her palm. Bright red blood clings to her pale forearm and soaks into her white dress. She stares straight ahead. She doesn't say anything when I walk in. *Dot, are you okay? You're bleeding.* She doesn't say anything. *Dot, can I see your hand. I think you're hurt.* She stares straight ahead. I take the knife from her hand and place it on the counter. *I'm going to get someone, okay? Stay here.*

In the hall, the party continues like nothing has happened. No one here knows that anything has happened. I don't know what has happened. I can't see any of the Blakes in the crowd, just a blur of unfamiliar faces. I go out onto the terrace, hoping someone might be out there having a cigarette. It is deserted. Puddles of rainwater shrink into the warm night air. It is quiet out here after the clamour of the party. The surface of the silence is broken by a sudden splash.

The body in the swimming pool doesn't move. Dark hair and white silk fan out around it, arms and legs hanging down like a marionette. A bloom of crimson drifts from the deep slash on Dot's right hand. I stare down into the pool as images flash through my mind.

Simon. The three pink scratches on his cheek. Dot in the kitchen. The kitchen knife. I cry out for help before diving into the water. When I reach Dot and flip her onto her back, she takes a long breath and turns to face me.

'I knew you'd save me,' she says. She stares at me, wide-eyed, her face almost distorted with pain and wonder. Then she winks, pitches forwards, and dives into the blackness. She swims to the edge and pulls herself out.

I follow her out of the water, grabbing towels from the nearest sun lounger. I suddenly remember that I was supposed to be getting ice for Lily. I break off a few cubes from the huge freezer in the outhouse and wrap them in a napkin. I drape a towel around Dot and ask to see her hand. The cut is straight and clean and deep across her palm. The bleeding has slowed to a trickle. I place the iced fabric against it and she winces.

Dot doesn't say anything for a very long time. Eventually I suggest that we go inside but she doesn't respond. I don't want to leave her where she is, so we just sit in silence. The crickets strike up their noise again. The music from inside is a distant, relentless pounding. A figure approaches from the house. Felix's face turns from surprise to curiosity to concern as he sees us huddled by the side of the water. A rosette of blood has bloomed in the centre of Dot's dress where her hand rests against the white fabric.

Sunday

I am torn from a dream in which I'm falling. Somewhere between sleep and wakefulness, my body hits the cold ground. The impact causes bile to rise in my throat. Laughter seeps through the heavy curtains that I pulled across the large windows last night, which mercifully block out the blistering sunlight of the new day. I scramble, sluggish yet panicked, to the mirror, expecting a torn, shredded mess but find only my own face, whole and undisturbed by my nightmare. I feel utterly changed, altered in some irrevocable way, but the only difference between myself and the boy that arrived here at the start of the week is a slight deepening of my tan and a delicate chain hanging from my neck. I splash cold water on my face and sip greedily from my cupped hands. The cool liquid soothes my dry throat and I try to relax into the reality of being awake.

Another burst of laughter, loud and insistent, pushes into the room. I reach for my phone to check the time and see a flurry of messages from Jasmine.

Me

17:09

You're NEVER gonna guess who's here right now!

Jazz

21:03

OMG who??

21:47

Oh. Just seen Lily's story.

21:49

What are you even doing hanging out with him??

23:26

So I guess you're in with Jack Wills Anonymous now? Can't believe you're mates with that creep.

23:27

Missed call

23:28

Missed call

23:28

Missed call

23:29

Missed call

23:32

Fuck you.

Confused, I scroll back up. Next to the picture I took of Caroline Asiamah, a digital exclamation mark glares up at me. Another peal of laughter tears through the room and this time I recognise it. The penny lands heavily in the pit of my stomach. Rupert. I try to call Jasmine back but it rings out. Twice. On the third attempt it goes straight to voicemail. A fourth yields a hollow voice, which informs me that this person's phone is switched off. I text her a scrambled apology and try to explain what happened. A single grey tick mocks me from the screen, the message sent but undelivered.

I lie back, trying to stitch together scraps of memory from last night. The image of Dot sitting on the floor surrounded by sharp edges is fresh in my mind. I don't realise I've fallen asleep again until I wake up and anxiety has tied its knot in the centre of my chest.

I shower and dress then drift through the house. It is eerily quiet and tidy inside; there isn't a single trace of the chaos of last night. In the hall, everything is back in its designated place or rearranged to disguise the space left by what is missing. The incessant, glaring order of it all makes me want to scream. In the kitchen I almost expect to see Dot sitting there, the blacklight of memory illuminating a bloodstained floor. But it has all been scrubbed clean, swept up, the knife carefully placed back in a drawer. In the garden, a long line of trestle tables have been spread with white linen. The Blake family and a number of guests who stayed at the castle (or close enough to come back) are arranged around the table, which is littered with the detritus of a half-eaten brunch. One by one, it seems, they turn to look at me. Benign faces belie the judgement I am convinced simmers beneath.

'I'm so sorry, I must have slept through the clean-up,' I say to no one in particular.

'Not at all, sweetie,' answers Fizz, giving me a bemused look. 'Annie had some girls from the village come and clear everything away before any of us were up. Isn't that marvellous?'

'Yes, it's remarkable what you can make disappear when you have the right people to clean it up.' This comes from Felix who is looking at David, who sits at the far end of the table. Next to Felix, protectively wrapped in his embrace, sits Dot. Absent-mindedly she rubs a bandage in the centre of her right palm. She avoids catching my eye, reaching out with her unbandaged hand for another piece of toast, which she busies herself with until she thinks I am no longer looking at her. She looks different, aloof. Her back is straighter and the smile that rumples the smooth curves of her face is gone, replaced by a grim, straight set of her jaw.

The conversation descends back into easy chatter. I get the feeling that the guests are avoiding talking about last night and instead focus on people who aren't present and their plans for the remaining weeks of summer. The rain last night has broken the heat a little and the air is stirred by a gentle breeze. Jack Wills Anonymous are heaped together around one corner of the table. Shockwaves of frantic laughter emanate from them. They are, I realise,

infected with the collective, joyful delirium you sometimes experience with the right hangover and are finding
everything hysterical. This could not be more at odds
with the brittle, persistent fear that taps away behind my
breastbone. Whether I am simply outside the joke or the
butt of it I cannot tell.

When I've forced down a slice of cold toast with a
thin smear of apricot jam, I escape the oppressive silence
of the table and head for the pool. As I pass the lower
edge of the terrace, I inhale deeply, trying to stretch into
this strange new day. Instead of lavender and rosemary,
I take in the acrid stench of stomach acid, champagne
and undigested vol-au-vents. There is dry vomit on the
side of the planter but the soil inside is moist, which must
have reawakened the smell. I retch and feel sorry for Luc,
who is working his way around the large garden, watering
plants and occasionally pouring the remnants of half-
empty mugs into a large bucket he is toting around. I walk
to the edge of the swimming pool and let my right hand
skim the surface, sending shimmering ripples across the
water and allowing its coolness to ground me. This is the
same water I was in last night. And I am the same body
that was in it. But I feel severed from yesterday: there is
no way to return there. Through the prism of my hand-
made waves, a rosy light flickers from the dark slate at
the bottom of the pool. My heartbeat quickens. I lower
myself into the water and am startled by its chill. I dive
towards the drain at the centre, chlorine stinging my eyes.
My ears pop painfully but finally my hand reaches the

lattice of the drain. My fingers scrabble around and come into contact with something hard and smooth. It's slightly stuck but I am able loosen it. I kick off from the bottom of the pool, my lungs burning with effort. I burst through the surface and take a desperate heave of air, slamming my closed fist on the stone edge of the pool. I feel a tap in my hand, like a single tick of a clock, and a sharp sting of pain. I pull back my hand, steadying myself with my other arm, my legs kicking at the water. Dot's pink crystal rose glitters in the light. My hand is bleeding and I have broken the flower in my carelessness. The head and the stem lie apart, severed like a real flower that has fallen victim to the cruel stick of a passing child.

I didn't understand what was going on back then but I knew that it was bad. It started, as it often did, after one of the fun times. The fun times were when Mum would call up the school and tell them I couldn't come because I was ill. I wasn't ill but that's what Mum would tell them. The fun times were when we would have cake for breakfast and KFC for lunch and dance in our pyjamas. 'Girls Just Wanna Have Fun' and that's what we would do. The fun times were when there were so many new toys and games and clothes and so much laughter. Eventually, though, the energy would shift and it wouldn't be fun anymore. I would have to go to Catch-Up Club to do the homework I'd missed, and the toys would disappear, receipts having been carefully hidden away by Grandma.

This particular fun time was at Christmas. I remember because the shift came when we were pulling crackers. Grandma was the first to notice the smell, the smoke coming from under the door. Burnt turkey, so black it crumbled into dust when Mum tried to cut it. Usually, she'd find this funny. She'd throw her head back and laugh her special laugh. It was like a music box, that laugh. She'd open her mouth and magic would tumble out. But this time, there was no laughter. The turkey crumbled and so did Mum. She started to cry and could not stop. I remember Grandma gently but firmly taking the knife out of Mum's hand and guiding her out of the kitchen, leaving me alone surrounded by presents I knew deep down we couldn't afford.

We stayed at Grandma's that night, as we frequently did. In the morning, Mum drove us back to our little flat and left all the presents behind. When we got home, she went into her room and didn't come out again for a long time. I knew she was poorly, so I didn't want to disturb her. I remember the phone rang a lot that day, but I didn't dare to answer it. I didn't know what I would say. I turned on the telly and put on a video and I think I slept. When I woke up, I was hungry so I had some chocolate from my secret hiding place. It felt like a midnight feast. I wanted to take Mum some secret chocolate too, but she didn't answer when I knocked on her door and I was still hungry, so I ate hers too.

The next morning, Mum didn't wake me up or make breakfast so I knew she was really poorly. When I'm poorly I like to eat beans on toast. I wasn't tall enough to reach the beans at first, but then I remembered the little step that Grandma had got me so I could help her make ginger cake. I would watch her soft brown hands squeeze soft brown sugar together with soft yellow butter in a bowl. The step meant I could just about reach the shelf with the beans on it. I accidentally knocked some more cans onto the floor but that was actually a good accident because then I didn't have to use the step as much. I wasn't supposed to use it when Mum or Grandma weren't there because I could fall, but I thought because Mum was poorly they wouldn't mind. Opening the can was the scariest part because the edge was sharp but I did it and put the beans in a bowl like Mum had shown me. I couldn't get the toast the right colour and it was too light but I was scared of burning it like the turkey and making Mum sad again. When the beans were hot and steaming from the microwave I put the toast in it. The triangles weren't very neat like when Mum did it but I thought it was a good try. When I took the beans on toast to her she was still in bed. I think I upset her because she cried more but she told me that I was a very good boy. I don't think she liked the beans on toast though, because when I went back later everything was still in the bowl. I know because I had counted the toasts.

The next day Mum didn't wake me up again and that's when I started to get really scared. I knocked on Mum's bedroom door and she didn't answer but I went in anyway. She looked really scary, like a witch or something.

Her hair was a mess, fuzzy black strands half stuck to her face, and her eyes looked like mud. I looked at her dry, cracked lips and she told me that I was a good boy and that she loved me very much and that she was sorry. I told her she didn't need to be sorry and that she should eat the beans because they always made me feel better but they were cold and she didn't. When I went back later Mum was sleeping. I couldn't get her to wake up and there was a foamy yellowish liquid on her mouth like when you pour salt on a slug in the garden. I leaned in close to see what it was and to whisper that she should wake up, and she opened her eyes, bloodshot and bleary. It was like the sleep didn't want to let her go. She told me that I needed to bring her the phone. She seemed scared too, so I ran and got the phone even though I wasn't supposed to touch it usually, and Mum pressed some buttons and then I was talking to a nice lady who asked me lots of questions and made me read out the words on the packets scattered across the floor around the pink vanity. I only knew some of the answers but I must have got enough of them right because a little bit later someone was knocking on the door and then a big tall man in a shiny yellow-and-green coat was telling me that everything was going to be okay even though they were taking Mum away in the ambulance. They took me to Grandma's and that was the last time I ever saw our little home.

After three weeks, Mum came back to Grandma's house. Everyone pretended that nothing had happened and I started to forget that anything had. Mum looked better and her lips were full and smooth. She took her tablets every day until one day she stopped. I thought that meant she was better.

There are five huge plastic tubs filled with empty bottles piled around us in the Jeep. The clinking as we drive down the track towards the road is so loud that Felix and I have to shout to hear each other. He has already done one trip to the bottle bank this morning but insisted that I join him for this one, saying he had something he wanted to show me. The noise of the bottles dies down a little as we pull out onto the smooth tarmac of the road, and Felix takes both hands off the wheel to light the cigarette hanging from between his pursed lips. This is the first time we have been alone together since the party. I feel like we have passed through some sort of boundary, but I am not yet sure where we have found ourselves. Twice I try to start the conversation and twice the words fail, catching somewhere in my chest.

'Simon really is an arse, isn't he?' Felix says suddenly. 'I don't know why he thinks he can treat her like that and get away with it.'

I murmur in assent, unable to form a coherent response. Is he talking about Dot or Celeste? What happened or almost happened last night that I don't know about?

'I honestly don't know why she came with him to be honest with you. She must have had much more glamorous places to be this summer.'

'I think she thought it would be fun,' I say, trying to figure out which parts of my conversation with Celeste I can repeat. 'And she said she knew you and wanted to see you again.'

'Is that so?' Felix's face is inscrutable. 'Gosh, summer in Paris must be as boring as they say it is.'

We trundle along, taking a right turn before reaching the town, which takes us in a direction I haven't yet been. Occasionally a bump in the road causes a cascade of glass-on-glass as the bottles rearrange themselves. Felix takes another turn and we are in a large complex with signs written in French pointing down tracks that lead in different directions. There is a sour edge and the air feels closer than it did out on the road.

'Look,' says Felix, killing the engine at the edge of a massive pit full of half-broken glass, 'about last night—'

'Don't. You don't need to . . . It's whatever.'

'I feel like I need to explain myself. Me and Etienne, that was—'

'I really don't want to hear this.'

'I want you to know that it's nothing, it's over. It barely even began really, and last night was stupid and I'm sorry.'

'Apology accepted.' I don't know what I want to feel but even if I did, I wouldn't be able to ignore the excitement bubbling up inside me. I want to turn to him and kiss him again. I want to feel his weight on top of me and his lips against mine.

'I want to make it up to you.'

'What do you mean?'

162

'Can I see you? After we leave here . . .'

'What? I—'

'I want you to come to London.'

'What? When?'

'This summer. Soon. Whenever. I don't want this to be it.'

'Okay, yes. Fine. Good. I mean, I'd really like that.'

We have both been staring ahead through all of this but now we are looking at each other. I can feel the creases of my sheepish grin and know it probably matches the one he is wearing. I feel giddy. He puts his hand out to touch my thigh and then the blast of a horn makes us both jump.

'Jesus fucking Christ!' shouts Felix. 'Okay, okay, we're moving.' We hop out of the car, leaving a trace of the moment pressed into the warm leather seats. The tubs are heavy and it takes two of us to carry each one to the edge of the skip. We smile at each other as the bottles crash down into chaos below, pealing and clattering like broken bells.

We drive out past the town and up a small incline which becomes a steeper one, and then a winding road leading up and up and up. Felix won't tell me where we're going, only that I'm going to love it. I want to tell him that I would love anything he showed me, but the words don't feel right in my mouth. I am not the type of boy who says things like that. Not to Felix. The town becomes a collection of smaller and smaller buildings reflected in the Jeep's dusty mirror until we turn a final bend and it disappears completely. Ahead of us, rocky hills roll out a carpet towards the horizon. The lazy sun has stirred up little pools of delusive water that evaporate into nothing as we speed along the hot road. We turn onto an unassuming dusty track, which leads through a dry thicket. Felix parks the Jeep into the space between two gnarled trees and we hop out. He takes something from the glove compartment and hides it behind his back. He moves towards me until we are almost nose to nose. I am rooted to the spot by his beauty. Thick, dark eyebrows framing eyes that seem to expand and swallow me whole. We lean towards each other and I can almost feel the softness of his pink lips. He stops.

'Do you trust me?'

I answer honestly. 'I don't know.'

'Can I show you?'

'Show me what?'

'How to trust me.'

I nod, once. He tells me to close my eyes. I do. I feel the slip of silk across my face and breathe in a scent that has already become familiar, necessary. It is the scent of Felix, of his aftershave and sweat. He ties the scarf at the back of my head and makes me look around to prove that I can't see. Then he takes my hands in his and leads me through the trees. I fear I may trip and fall at any moment, but Felix knows this place and he guides me through it. I feel a change in the air and I know we have left the treeline.

'Okay. Are you ready?'

'Yes.'

Felix stands close behind me, pressing his body into mine. He reaches up to undo the knot and then suddenly, wonderfully, the blackness opens up into a brilliant expanse of glass-like water. The mountains and sky are double, and perfectly still. Between us and the water's edge a red-and-white blanket is laid out, the corners held down by large stones. There is a basket, half open, filled with bottles and paper-wrapped parcels.

'Do you like it?' he asks, searching my face for approval.

'Felix, what is all this?'

His face falls slightly. 'It's for you. For us. I wanted to properly make it up to you. To show you that I'm serious. About you. About us. Look, since you got here, to the Chateau, I've been meaning to . . . I've felt . . . I really like you. I wanted to show you.'

'Felix, this is . . . This is amazing, it's beautiful. I love it.'

'Good,' he says. 'Now strip. I actually mean it this time.'

He grins and kicks off his shoes then straightens up and peels off his T-shirt and shorts and sets off towards the lake. He takes down his boxers and stands for a moment looking out across the vastness with contemplative quiet. Downy hair shows stark against the untanned parts of his skin. A gentle breeze scatters ripples across the lake's perfect surface. He looks over his shoulder at me, the sunlight and the water and his eyes all willing me to follow. He walks until he is knee deep, then dives forward with only the slightest splash.

I am much less graceful, both in undressing and wading

into the water. It is surprisingly warm, though, and I am waist deep when Felix surfaces. He sinks back down so his eyes are just in line with where the water laps gently at the curve of my hip bones. Rising back up to his full height he strides towards me and runs wet fingers through my curls. With his hands pressing against the back of my neck, he urges me forward. My mouth finds his and we are all tongues and lips and teeth. We part so all that still touches is our foreheads and his hands on my shoulders and we breathe like that and for a moment there is nothing. Not sky, not mountains, not water. There is nothing.

Then we swim, around and through each other, for a while. The sun overhead keeps time but we do not. When we flop, panting, onto the towels Felix has brought, we lie there and let the sun dry our skin. Usually, I would reach for something to cover myself, shield myself from view, but I do not. We lie there and I look at new freckles appear on his skin where before there were none and I let myself grow ever darker. He has brought wine and baguettes and cheese and the jar of honey from our first trip to town. We sip from plastic cups and brush crumbs from the dark hairs in the creases of each other's thighs. He takes a crust of bread, smears it with soft cheese, and scoops it around the edges of the almost-empty jar. He kisses me softly on the lips.

'Open,' he says.

And I do. The gold in his eyes catches fire as he feeds me the last of the honey.

'I want you,' he says to me.

So, I give him what he wants. His tongue is on mine and it tastes like red wine and I breathe the feeling of him into me. My fingers trace soft skin and hard muscle and the colossal endlessness of a body that with my eyes closed feels like it goes on forever. He touches me so gently that it feels like I am being shaped out of soft clay and holds me so tightly that I worry I may shatter. With one hand around my neck, he lets a thick trail of spit form and hang above me. I open my mouth to take it when it falls but he catches it in his free palm and uses the wet to push himself inside me. I gasp and so does he and his weight pins me down. My hands are on him and his hands are on me and he is holding me close in his spit-slicked palm. He shudders above me and his breath is soft but ragged and it catches fire in my ear.

'I want you to cum for me,' he says.

So, I give him what he wants. He lets out a cry and presses his mouth against mine and swallows the sound of my moans. He collapses above me and I let the weight of his body push me into the sand and everything touches and his forehead is on mine and we breathe like that for a moment. Then he rolls to one side and he laughs and I laugh and we lie there panting, a tangle of sandy legs. Eventually, we have enough breath to speak.

'Please come to London, for me,' he says.

So, I give him what he wants again.

PART TWO

Flies

July

Eleven Months Later

On a midsummer's evening, the branching streets of Soho hang heavy with revellers, ripe from after-work Aperol spritzes and ready to drop at the slightest breeze. A welcome windfall for idling taxi drivers, who wait, ready to scoop them up in ones and twos and threes and take them home with their chips or deliver them to someone else's home to continue an evening which, just moments ago, was still kissed by the late rays of July. It's on days like these that I am sometimes struck full in the face by the forceful beauty of the city I now call home. London is an easy place to love someone. I want to take a moment. To stand unmoving and let its energy flow around me, but tonight I don't have time, so I dive into a stream of people going in roughly the right direction and let myself get carried along.

My mind returns to my conversation with Felix this morning. I'd barely slept, staring up at the light fitting while he snored gently beside me, undisturbed. I'd drifted off at some point and been woken by my alarm. While I got ready, Felix slipped in and out of sleep, confident in the knowledge that he didn't need to be up for hours. I brought my breakfast and a cup of tea for him back to bed, desperate to eke out a few more moments with him next to me before I had to face the day.

'Aren't you going to tell me to break a leg?' His voice was still thick with sleep but his pout was unmistakable from beneath his bed-tousled fringe.

I murmured a question through a mouthful of oats, nonplussed.

'It's press night. For the show?'

'Tonight? I thought that was next week?'

'The show opens next week. But press night is tonight. I told you this. You said you'd come.'

'Felix, you didn't. I would have remembered. I'm sure you said it was next week.'

'Why would I get that wrong? It's the most important night of my career and you couldn't care less.'

'Of course I care, Fe. Tell me what time and I'll be there.'

'Well, you didn't say anything so I didn't reserve any tickets. There probably aren't any now. It's fine, don't worry, I'll brave it alone.'

'I'm so sorry, Felix, I thought . . .'

'It's okay. I'll talk to Annelise, see if she can do anything.'

'I'm really, really sorry, Felix.'

'It's fine. It's whatever.'

He put down his tea and rolled over, ending the conversation. On my way to work I scanned through my phone's calendar. An entry, in all caps, a week from now: press night – FELIX'S PLAY – 19:30.

*

Felix hasn't responded to any of the messages I sent since I left the flat, so I take out my phone and call Annelise, his agent. She picks up on the first ring.

'Hello?'

'Annelise, hi, I was trying to get hold of Felix. Have you—'

'Oh, it's you.'

'Always lovely to chat, Annelise, but I'm outside the theatre. Felix said he'd talk to you about a ticket for tonight but I'm guessing he's been busy with everything today because I haven't heard back.'

She sighs down the phone then moves it away from her mouth to say something to someone nearby. 'It's packed. Sorry.'

I see her cut the call as I round the corner. She is standing out the front of the theatre, looking like she is waiting for someone. When she catches sight of me, she rolls her eyes.

'You're really, really late. Did you know that?'

'Has it started?'

'About five minutes ago, but one of the ushers is holding some space at the back so if you go now, you can sneak in.'

I try to thank her, but she shushes me. Her many-ringed fingers clack together as she waves me away. She opens her arms excitedly and warmly greets a blonde woman in an oversized linen suit with a brilliant green crocodile skin handbag swinging from her arm. The woman looks at me so I open my mouth to introduce myself, but Annelise waves a hand to silence me again.

'A colleague of Felix's father.'

She shoos us both through the entrance to the theatre, past the bar where we are each given a glass of wine, and into the auditorium, where thankfully the play hasn't yet started. We are escorted to two seats near the back and the lights go down as soon as we move to sit. A hush falls across the audience and my stomach does a little flip.

About six months after we met, Felix took me to Rome. We fled the freezing damp of winter in London and were greeted by a surprisingly bright Italian spring. His god-mother let us stay in her apartment overlooking Piazza Navona and every morning Felix brought me coffee on the little balcony and we watched the square come alive. For four days, he led me through the city's serpentine streets. Rome and the language were as familiar to him as they were alien to me. He told me he preferred it in the low season. In summer, he said, it's too hot and too crowded and American tourists step on your feet in St Peter's Square and ask you where the Vatican is. But that February, the whole city was ours.

We drank silken red wine and ate in the tiniest restaurants on the narrowest lanes. We watched an Audrey Hepburn film and then he took me everywhere that Gregory Peck takes her. He held my hand and placed it inside a huge marble mask of Oceanus and told me that here, I couldn't lie. I told him I had nothing to lie to him about and he laughed and told me that must be nice. My hand buzzed inside the cold grey mouth of the angry god. The sky stayed cloudless above us and he told me the history of the Roman Empire and I forgot everything he said. I couldn't concentrate on words, I was distracted by the overwhelming beauty around us – a beauty through which he seemed to soar ever higher. We walked along the Tiber and watched a huge piece of ice float through the city. He took me to a tiny gay bar in the shadow of the Colosseum and we drank negronis and danced together on the empty dancefloor.

On our last morning we went for breakfast – inky-black espresso and thick, cloudlike pastries filled with pistachio cream – then sat on the edge of the Fontana del Moro. Beneath the sound of the rushing water, our cheeks flushed by the whisper of cold in the morning air, I told him, softly, that I loved him. The words tumbled out, the shock of them making the next breath catch in my throat. He didn't say anything back. He didn't say anything for a long time. He just looked straight ahead, gazing into infinity, and then said that we should make a move if we were going to make it to the airport in time. While he locked up the apartment, closing the shutters against the likely spring rain, I lay on the bed and stared at the mural on the ceiling. Focussing on Actaeon's hounds tearing him apart, I willed myself not to cry. Back in London, two days later, our holiday already sinking into me as a memory, he turned to me and said, 'I love you too, I think.'

*

'You must be a very valued colleague,' the woman with the emerald bag says to me as the cast exits the stage. Most of the audience is on their feet. Felix, topless and breathing hard from the climax of the final scene, jogs back onto the stage, bows low and his hair flops almost to the ground. He has a knowing, almost relieved look on his face as if the audience has finally been let in on a joke he was telling.

'I'm sorry?'

'You mouthed almost every word of the script.'

'Oh, I didn't even realise. I'm so sorry if I distracted you.'

'Do you know him well? Felix.'

'Felix and I, um, we . . . I helped him run lines sometimes.'

'I see . . .'

Thankfully, we are interrupted by Annelise, who whisks the woman out of the auditorium and towards the door. The drinks and the company are much better up the road at Soho House, she insists. The woman looks expectantly at me, the question she wants to ask dancing behind her steady gaze. I tell her I'm going to wait for Felix. Satisfied, she turns and follows Annelise up the street.

I knock twice on the stage door where a couple of people have gathered despite the best efforts of the theatre staff to usher them towards the drinks' reception up the road. Felix opens the door a crack and allows me to slip through. In this dim corridor he seems to burn brighter than ever, outshining the pallid strip lighting that lines the cobweb-strung ceiling. Felix is so beautiful that sometimes looking at him can be blinding. Cheeks still flushed with exhilaration, a lock of sweat-darkened hair hangs over his eyes, he fills the space around him. Between frantic, snatched kisses he tells me he didn't think I would actually come. His breath, hot on my neck, feels like an apology even though he doesn't say the words. As often happens, the fight – which had been brewing in me since this morning – fades with a sigh as he bites the stubbled angle of my jaw. I try to tell him how incredible he was tonight, how I couldn't take my eyes off him, how his final monologue almost drew me to my feet. But the words die in my throat as he pushes his right hand down the waistband of my jeans and slams his left arm against my neck, pinning me against the wall. When he is finished with me, he crushes the hot burst of his lips hard against mine and stalks back to his dressing room, leaving me panting in the corridor which has suddenly become darker. Somehow, he takes the light with him.

At Soho House, surly staff muster fake smiles when we arrive. Immediately – wrapped in a crisp white shirt, hair carefully styled into casual disarray – Felix is absorbed by the crowd. He smiles and shakes hands and I watch the movement of his mouth as he accepts congratulations and compliments. I watch the faces of the people around him light up as he bestows his gaze upon them. Felix Blake's beauty is matched only by his charm. He steps so lightly through the busy floor of the bar that he seems to float. Annelise deftly guides him towards the most important people in the room. A tap on my shoulder makes me jump.

'Picante?'

The woman from the show is holding out a cocktail garnished with a bright red chilli. Her nails shine the same brilliant green as her handbag, which is slung over the crook of her elbow. I take the drink and she introduces herself as *Sarah Osbourne, Daily Mail*. We shake free hands, hers slightly wet from the condensation on the glass, and my guard goes up. I see Annelise eye us warily from across the room. I muster a warm smile. One of the many things I have learned from the Blake family this past year is a defensive mistrust of journalists. *They will either try to befriend you or ruin you. And we have plenty of friends.* Annie's words swim into my head. I am halfway through my rehearsed line, habitually minimising my relationship with Felix, positioning myself as a family friend of the Blakes, wrapping a big truth in a little lie, when my phone buzzes in my pocket. It's a message from Jazz.

Jazz

22:09

Babe, have you seen this? Absolutely awful.

Below her message is a link. It's to an article. black man killed by police in georgia. A familiar sinking feeling swoops through my heart. The article is short, just a single paragraph, bare bones, initial facts as presented. *Police say . . . routine stop . . . shots fired . . . died at scene.* It promises more as the story develops. Somewhere inside me one word lodges, gets stuck. Story. The story will develop. Like a photograph. But unlike a photograph – the film kept hidden from corrupting light, the moment protected so it is free to bloom unchanged onto polyethylene – this story will develop through lenses and prisms and perspectives, across histories and narratives and oceans. And by those lenses and histories and narratives and oceans this moment will be changed, will become a story. It will become more, as the story develops.

A second message from Jazz.

Jazz
22:10
Don't go on Twitter.

Obviously, I ignore her. I mumble an excuse to Sarah, who barely hears me, already checking her own phone. I feel a prickle of cold at the base of my skull despite the warmth of the room. Opening the app, I see the story is already trending. A million voices chattering at once across the Atlantic, an incessant drone, the hum and click of a swarm of angry insects. There are people who are calling it murder. There are people looking for a reason why he deserved to die. There is a video. I try to resist the urge to click the thumbnail. To avoid seeing a body like mine brutalised and left lifeless. But there is life in me right now, bloody, surging life that cannot look away. The chill that started at the back of my head spreads its cold tendrils throughout my body. I press play with numb fingers. I watch the grainy footage, shot on a mobile phone. I watch a story unfold that I thought I could not possibly imagine. And yet I watch it happen. I hold it in my palm. I watch a story of a man, of a whole life, get reduced to a final moment, a name, across an ocean. From four thousand miles away, just moments after the event took place, I watch a man die.

The only problem with Tooting is that you're pretty much an hour from anywhere worth being. By the time I rumble into the station at Broadway, my heart has stopped pounding and the panicked, frantic exhilaration I was feeling has been replaced by a chilly emptiness. I take a detour through the market, desperately seeking comfort in the familiar sounds and smells. I slip through the vendors' entrance, draped in strips of heavy plastic, and take a shortcut that leads me directly to the Caribbean food stall. The man behind the counter smiles warmly when he sees me. It is almost closing time, but I see him flick the heater back on as I approach. He gestures towards the metal showcase, its gleam dulled with grease and dust, where three patties sit sweating in paper bags, their bottoms transparent with melted fat.

'Me haf two goat an' a vegetable or yuh cyan wait a minute fi di last chicken,' says Uncle Joe, wiping his large hands on his huge apron-wrapped belly.

Uncle Joe, sometimes called Jupiter by those who dare, is a hulking planet of a man. But it's the flavours he creates that draw people from Mitcham, Streatham and sometimes as far as Brixton into his orbit. Grandma always says that the more faded the sign, the better the gravy and this rings true for Uncle Joe's place. Bleached almost white by years of light and smoke and hungry eyes, you can just about make out a palm tree and a few remaining letters.

'Is that an actual minute or a Jamaican one?'

'Don't be fas wi mi, son. Dis the problem with yutes today, always dey pon haste.'

'I'll take the two goat, please. It's been a long day, Joe.'

Shaking his head, a sad smile crinkling the walnut skin around his little eyes, he takes his time wrapping the patties in napkins then in another bag, unbothered by my impatience. I stop shifting my weight from one foot to the other: it won't make him go any faster. He looks up at me then nods. Every interaction here is a lesson. He slips a can of Old Jamaica into the bag and hands it to me with a wink.

'Thanks, Joe,' I mumble over my shoulder, pushing my way through the rabble. The faces have long since changed from the black and brown hues of the old crowd going about their daily business to the wry alabaster smirks of the new night-time locals – first-time buyers who were priced out of Balham and tourists here to try that new pop-up Bao place after work. They are drunk now and oblivious to the flow of rich local lifeblood that their presence here stems from. My mind flicks to the videos I've been watching on repeat on the

Tube. Shouts, gunshots, blood spiralling out into black asphalt. I push the image away. I trudge through the street towards home, through the dwindling evening crowd. A woman with two purple-faced babies in a double-stroller and mobile phone between her shoulder and ear forces me into a clumsy pirouette and a taxi blares its horn at us.

I round the corner onto our quiet street. In the marmalade buzz of the solitary functioning streetlamp, a skinny fox momentarily stops sniffing at a discarded polystyrene carton and watches me curiously. She is relaxed. I pose no threat. She sniffs the air, considering whether to take me on for my patties, then decides against it and returns to her puddle, lapping up the turbid water. I find Jazz at the kitchen table, her face lit only by the cold blue glow of her phone, flicking between Twitter and various encrypted messaging apps. Grief and anger pour out of the screen and into the room, filling up the silence between us. When I flick on the light she turns to me, and I see the empty sadness on her face and know it must be reflected in mine. There are some people you never have to explain yourself to. She locks her phone, stands up and puts her arms around me. Jazz is short and compact and her soft arms fit close around my waist. With my chin on her head, I let her tears soak into my T-shirt, while mine roll down into her hair. At some point, we stop crying and I put the food in the microwave while Jazz makes us tea. She takes a bite of a patty. Soft flakes of yellow pastry drift to the floor.

*

I once told Felix that I hated being in his family's house alone. The House, they call it, as if it's the only one that matters. The sheer size of it, the grandeur, made me feel so small that it was dizzying. Almost a year on, I am more used to it. Though I do still feel as if I need to shrink into myself so that I don't dirty the walls. When filled with the Blakes and their many and ever-changing houseguests, the House feels like the kind of charmingly crumbling home you get in films where people wear hand-knitted jumpers over striped pyjamas and say profound things about the state of love while eating a piece of burnt toast. But empty, the creaking floors and high ceilings and bowed lintels seem to press in from all angles, trying to force you out. Dot is convinced there's a ghost, but Annie says it's just the boiler.

I stayed here when I first came to see Felix after our time at the Chateau last summer. I crossed London after a nervous, lurching train journey through city then suburb then countryside then commuter town then suburb then suburb then city and city and city. Even now I am constantly surprised by London's scale and strangeness. The city is unknowable. That first time, I came straight here, to Notting Hill. I felt removed from the city, like a spectator or an unwelcome guest.

Walking through the pristine streets of the Blake's neighbourhood, I'd wondered at how, in a city so full of dirt and people and noise, this place could be so neat and quiet. How the sky could be so blue, and the lines made by the straight roofs of the tall, deliberate houses could be so crisp. How the hand-painted numbers on faultless columns could be so pristine. After checking I had the correct address for the third time, I took hold of the burnished brass ring in a blazing lion's mouth and brought it down three times. Before the third knock had even begun to sound, the heavy black door swung open to reveal Lily, bare-legged in a huge white shirt, holding an enormous grey cat, which was trying to twist itself out of her grip. Spreading her arms into a theatrical welcome, she dropped the cat, who regarded me with large orange eyes and let out a long low yowl of warning.

'Oh, don't mind Dunstable. He's mostly harmless — unless your name is Simon, in which case he's trained to kill on sight.'

She pulled me into a tight hug and whispered her welcome into my ear. I lingered for a moment in the familiarity of her embrace. Her hair across my face brought with it a whisper of jasmine. She told me once that when she was at school the older girls told them to spray perfume in their hair when they were meeting boys, and when they laughed to shake their heads, so that the scent would pour out and drive the boys crazy. The thought of this tugs at a feeling that is now almost forgotten. This was before things started to unravel between us. That first day at the House, Lily and I were still knit close: our loose threads had not been pulled, the stitching had not yet been unpicked.

She was excited to see me. She told me Felix was in the park with some friends, and that we were going to join them. Looking back, I feel a tug of guilt. When he'd invited me to come to London, Felix had thought it best to let Lily think it was her idea. It's not that I ever lied to Lily, but she didn't know then about Felix and me and the party and the lake. Sometimes it is the lies we don't tell that actually do the most damage. I took Felix's lead and let Lily believe what she chose to. We all choose what we believe, I think.

She took my bag and threw it under a table in the hall, upsetting the casual symmetry. She held me by the shoulders and looked me up and down, shaking her head. She told me my outfit absolutely wouldn't do and asked if I had brought a shirt. When I said I hadn't, she rolled her eyes, said I hadn't learned anything from my time at the Chateau and turned to drag me upstairs with one hand. She gestured towards various doors, pointing out bathrooms and studies and bedrooms. She took me to one near the top of the house where an unmade bed was surrounded by half-empty teacups, one of which was being used as an overstuffed ashtray. Rails and rails of clothes filled the rest of the space with framed *Vogue* covers and posters of foreign films I did not recognise plastered on the walls from floor to high ceiling. This was Felix's lair, she told me. Here be monsters.

'Try this,' she said, handing me a blue-and-white cotton shirt, roughly cobbled together from different fabrics. 'It was a gift from Vivienne.' Seeing the blank expression on my face, she raised an eyebrow and then said, 'Westwood?'

She made me change into the shirt then fastened a heavy brooch onto the front. She gently stroked my curls, placing some expensive-looking sunglasses on top of my head. She said I looked perfect. She gave me another hug and a warm smile, then linked her arm through mine and marched me down the many flights of stairs, out of the front door and all the way to Hyde Park.

When he saw us approaching across the grass, Felix got to his feet, haloed by the setting autumn sun, laughing back over his shoulder at a joke we could not hear.

'Hello, stranger,' he said, stopping a few feet away. 'Thanks for waiting for him, Magpie – you are a doll.'

Recognising her subtle dismissal, Lily looked puzzled, then slightly annoyed, then skipped over to Felix's friends who were lounging in a rough circle on the ground and plopped herself down among them. Felix leaned in and took my hand, then led me across the park away from the group. Confused, I turned back to Lily who was pointedly studying a ring of daisies in the grass.

'Not worth the blankets they're sitting on, that lot, honestly. And besides, I want you all to myself today. Pizza? I'm absolutely ravenous.'

'Sure,' I said. My pensiveness must have reflected on my face because he stopped us, taking both of my shoulders in his hands.

'Do you trust me?' he said.

'Of course I do.'

'Do you want to be with me?'

'You know I do.'

'Then that is all that matters. You belong here as much as anyone.' I understood he meant all of it – the House, his life. 'Because I want you here.'

He kissed me and I felt my worry drift away like fallen leaves.

It is still strange to come to the House without Felix, but the muggy heat of this past week has finally broken into thunderstorms and now offers welcome shelter. The rain threatens to wash the city away. Caught unaware, people are scrambling to rescue sheets from washing lines before they are sodden, and I have had to run from the station, with the optimistic denim jacket I put on when I left Tooting my only flimsy protection from the downpour. Somewhere over the city, thunder booms.

I ring the bell, but I am early, and no one is home. I fetch the spare key from under the loose tile on the top step. Second from the right, two squares back. Dunstable, it seems, was as poorly prepared for the weather as I was. When I open the door, he shoots from his hiding place under the hedge in the front garden and into the house. I close the door behind me, shutting out the rain, and the cat moans at me, belligerent, from his vantage point at the top of the stairs. I slip off my dripping trainers and carry them with me through the house, not wanting to leave them by the door but also at a loss for somewhere to put them. I go downstairs to the kitchen. As I click on the kettle and wait for it to boil, little pools of water seep out of my wet socks and onto the slate tiles of the kitchen floor. I slip them off too and hang them to dry on the rail of the cream Aga, grateful that, despite the recent heatwave, Annie has not turned it off for the summer. Behind the vent of the Aga's flue, a fly struggles against a cobweb. I finish making my tea and head upstairs to the drawing room and sit myself behind the Blake's gleaming black grand piano. Eventually, Dunstable forgives my lack of control over the weather and comes upstairs to join me, hopping onto the stool next to me. I start to tap at a few keys, then relax and lose myself in the music.

'I am glad you've made yourself at home, darling, but must you put your dirty socks where I make my supper?'

Annie's sudden appearance startles me. The cat flees and my mug almost goes flying. I mumble an apology, but Annie isn't listening. She is discarding sopping layers of clothing and throwing them into a pile by the door.

'This is entirely David's fault, you know? He's been complaining all week about the heat and now look what he's gone and done. Thunderstorms in July. Two hundred and fifty fucking quid on a cut and blow dry and just look at it!' I tell her that her hair looks as perfect as ever and offer to make her a tea.

'That's very sweet of you, darling, but you make a much better pianist than you do a liar. I must get on to Cass about the Academy. And yes to the tea. Green. Now, tell me, how is my dear eldest child?'

I haven't seen or heard from Felix since the show on Thursday night. It is now Sunday and my initial annoyance has turned into mild worry. I didn't tell Felix I was leaving the press night party and now he is punishing me. My messages lie delivered and read. I know from Celeste's Instagram Story that they were out last night, some party with people I did not know. Felix was smiling in the pixels, surrounded by strangers. A wild glint in his dark eyes told me he hasn't slept since I saw him. The once-crisp white shirt now in fashionable disarray. I wondered if it was the same one he was wearing on press night.

Back down in the kitchen, I busy myself with the kettle and tell Annie about the play, about his performance, about how he shone in the spotlight, about how everyone was so excited to talk to him afterwards. She seems satisfied with my answer.

'Have you seen Dorothea? She – sorry, *they* – hasn't – haven't – been returning my calls. I'm worried about her. This little episode has gone on for longer than previous ones. I think she's rather confused.'

I say I haven't seen them, which isn't a lie entirely. Dot hasn't been at the House for almost three weeks. They are staying, I know through Felix, with friends somewhere, though their exact location is unknown, lest someone let it slip to Annie or David. They say that if their parents insist on being difficult then they will be difficult too. I make a mental note to call Dot when I leave. When Felix talks about them, he always seems worried, though I think in part it's because he'd rather avoid being the middleman. When I last spoke to them, Dot seemed to be thriving away from Annie's watchful eye.

'It really is ridiculous. If you see her, do tell her to come home.'

I tell Annie I will. Early on, Felix told me not to cross her and I haven't yet. Annie Blake is a woman who always gets her way. When she summoned me here today for a 'catch-up' I hadn't realised she was expecting me to turn informant.

'And how are you, my dear?'

I tell her I'm fine, a bit wet. She tilts her head to the side and smiles gently at me, as someone might smile at a child who has misunderstood the question.

'I meant with all this horrid news coming out of America at the moment. It really is awfully sad. It must be hard to see. And there's just so much *news*. I usually try to switch off but this time it really is everywhere. I can't imagine what it must be like for you.'

Her pity opens up a space between us. The cold feeling I've been pushing away for the past few days creeps back in. She is looking at me, expecting an answer that will not come. She wants me to lean in to the space she has created. Or, more likely, brush it away, fill it with a platitude to let her off the hook. Annie Blake is warm and smiling on the surface but the more time I spend with her the more I see another, cooler side of her. She seems, sometimes, completely indifferent to other people. Felix told me that when he was sent to boarding school when he was eight, he missed her terribly. He wrote her letters and went to his housemaster's office crying, asking to call her. He says she ignored his calls and that when she finally came to pick him up at the end of the first term, he felt like he'd forgotten what her voice sounded like.

She can't imagine what it must be like for me. She doesn't try. We stand in silence until the front door opens and the sound of the storm rushes down to meet us.

'Ah, Lily, what a lovely surprise,' says Annie before her daughter turns the corner of the stairs. 'I must put some dry clothes on.'

She smiles, her trap snapping shut around me, and passes Lily on the stairs. Lily kisses her on the cheek. She is carrying a sodden paper bag which she places on the marble island. She is trying to seem nonchalant but her left hand reaches up involuntarily to twist a damp lock of hair.

Over the last year, somewhere, the fabric of our friendship has worn thin. At one time, we thought our thoughts together. What she felt, I had no choice but to feel too. We would tell people at parties that we were twins and watch their faces try to rationalise the lie without crossing a line. For a whole month, driven out of her own student house by a petty argument with a housemate, she shared my bed. The day she asked me to come to France, I felt like we were becoming family. And I suppose we are now, in a way. Though maybe not in the way Lily would have chosen.

It wasn't that Lily reacted badly when Felix told the rest of the Blakes about us. But she didn't react well either. Felix had decided that he was bored of sneaking me into his room when nobody was around and that logistically it would be easier if everyone knew. I didn't realise at the time that his definition of everyone extended only to immediate family and a scattering of the inner circle. My heart was pounding as we sat in the drawing room at the House one Sunday in late November. Felix cleared his throat as Lily came back into the room with a tray of coffees and teas.

'I thought it was maybe time that I welcomed you lot into the fold.' He paused, carefully considering his words. Then he took my hand in his, which did nothing to combat my agitation. 'We, erm . . . Well. For a while now, actually, the two of us have been—'

'Bonking since the summer? Yeah, we know.'

Annie dropped a teaspoon onto the tray with a clatter. David coughed into his hand and Dot looked satisfied that their words had had the desired effect.

'I wouldn't have put it exactly like that, Dotty, but yes, I suppose.'

'Well, we think it's lovely, don't we, darling?' said Annie, placing a firm hand on David's knee.

'Delightful,' murmured David.

'I think you make a lovely pair,' Dot purred. 'But I don't know why you felt like you had to make a big announcement. You're both terrible at sneaking around.'

There was laughter, the lovely sound easing my apprehension, and the conversation melted back into Sunday-afternoon banality. Only Lily didn't join in. She excused herself and took the tray of empty cups down to the kitchen. I followed, wanting to explain, to apologise for not telling her sooner. When I got down to the kitchen, though, she looked up from the sink, turned off the tap, and let herself out into the garden, closing the door firmly behind her.

'Give her some time,' said a voice from behind me. 'She can be funny about Felix. She'll come around. She's happy for you – we all are. And very glad that we can all give up this silly charade.'

Annie pulled me into a quick hug then picked up the washing-up where Lily had left off.

But Lily didn't come around. For weeks she ignored any texts or calls from both me and Felix. Our friendship cooled. Wisps of closeness where there had once been roaring flames. We settled into a new rhythm. I was eager, she was polite. We drifted further apart. Felix told me not to worry. I knew I'd broken something I could not repair.

'I'm sorry about the ambush,' she says. 'But I didn't think you'd come if you knew I'd be here. I was gonna text you, but you haven't replied to my last one.'

'That's not fair Lily, I—'

'Look, I don't want to fight or argue or anything. I just wanted to tell you that I miss you. It's been ages.'

'I miss you too, Lil.'

'Well . . . good.' Relief brings a flush of colour back to her cheeks. 'Now eat your sandwich. It's slightly damp but I think it'll still be good.'

I accept the peace offering and bite into a soggy baguette. We eat and catch up and try to mend what has come undone. We promise to see each other more. We both mean it.

August

There is a slight curve to the facade of the building across the river. At this time, on a clear summer day, the office I share with the rest of the property licensing team becomes the focal point of that curve. It sends a ray of focussed sunlight directly at us. Floor-to-ceiling glass combined with safety windows that only open a crack mean that the heat in here can be absolutely unbearable. Sometimes I stare out of these windows and wish that I could fling them wide open. On days like this one, my computer gets so hot that the fan goes into overdrive, its loud humming drowning out my thoughts. It gets so hot that if anyone pops their head in to deliver a message or ask for a favour they invariably stop and say, 'Gosh, it's hot in here.'

'Gosh, it's hot in here,' says Arthur. He should know: this is his office too, and he only stepped out about fifteen minutes ago. 'You're up,' he nods towards me.

Three of us share this office and today has been tense. Rumours started yesterday afternoon of a 'structural reorganisation', which is corporate slang for 'a tonne of people are going to get fired'. We've already seen four people leave and it is barely two o'clock. Arthur, though, seems relieved. I'm the most junior person on the team and so have been waiting for this moment with a mixture of resignation and dread. I take a deep breath and get up from my desk.

'Good luck, mate,' says Tim, who completes our trio. He doesn't mean it.

I make my way across the office, looking out over the river and the postcard skyline of Central London, wondering whether I'll miss the view or if I'll be happier job-hunting in my poorly insulated Tooting flat. People watch me from their desks, concerned but relieved it is not them who has been summoned. I knock gently on the door and a voice beckons me in. If it weren't for the situation, I'd be almost grateful to be invited into the air-conditioned room.

'Do you like working here?' Simon Chance greets me.

I am slightly surprised to see him standing next to David, leaning against the large wooden desk, a hand casually in his suit pocket. I try not to let it show.

I feel resentment rise in my throat, but I swallow it down and mumble something about my gratitude for the opportunity they've given me. Simon eyes me suspiciously. I can feel the disdain radiating off him. David, as ever, is uninterested. After a moment he looks up from the papers he is pretending to read.

'Don't be cruel, Si. Put the poor boy out of his misery.'

'Fine. As you know, we're making a few . . . adjustments to the company. We're downsizing your team. Clearing out the rubbish. Emptying the trash bin, as it were.'

'Okay . . . just tell me,' I mutter.

'We've always valued your loyalty and your fucking work ethic or whatever. Besides, firing you would have terrible optics, since you're the only . . . Well, you know. Plus, you're fucking the boss's son, so—'

'Simon,' David interjects. My ears feel like they might catch on fire.

'Congratulations on your promotion, kid. Property licensing officer. You're in the big leagues now. Could you send in Tim? It's, ah, not great news for him, I'm afraid.'

Mingled anger and relief flood through me, making my skin prickle. I want to say something to wipe the satisfied smirk off Simon's smug face, but, considering the fact that until about ten seconds ago I thought I was about to lose my job and still very much could, I opt for thanks and a curt nod instead. I rearrange my face into what feels like inscrutable neutrality and make my way back to my stuffy cubicle, the eyes of the office burning a hundred little holes into my back. My heart pounds out the minutes while Tim takes his turn. I move my cursor around the screen, avoiding looking up at Arthur, who I can tell is watching me. The door slams open only a few minutes later, Tim's rage blowing in hotter than the air inside.

'This is fucking bullshit!' He makes his way over to his desk and starts tearing papers out of drawers. 'This is bullshit and you both know it. What the actual fuck?! "Subpar performance", my fucking arse! Those bastards. I'm gonna tear this whole fucking place down. Don't you dare look at m, you little fuck. This is your fucking fault.'

This last part is directed at me. 'This is a joke. Honestly, fuck this. I was out anyway. This ship is sinking and I hope you rats drown. Precious little diversity hire gets a cosy promotion. This is all your fucking fault. Did you suck Simon off for that one too?'

'Timothy. That's enough now.' David has appeared at the door, flanked by two thickset white security guards with cropped hair.

'It's fine, I'm bloody going,' says Tim, picking up his laptop and making for the door.

'I'm afraid I can't let you leave with company property.' David says this calmly but his eyes flash, sharp as a knife-edge.

Childishly, Tim puts the laptop behind his back, as if to hide it. He starts towards the door but one of the shaven-headed men blocks his way while the other goes to take the computer from him. There is a short tussle and one of Tim's shirt buttons pops off before the laptop is wrested from his hands.

'Fine, fine, take it, whatever. I know what I know, David, and you're gonna fucking regret this.' David nods to security and they take hold of Tim and start towards the lift. He drags his feet, swearing and thrashing, trying to shake them off. Eventually he manages to escape their grip and makes towards David. We are out in the corridor now and everyone in the office is staring, their work forgotten. The security guards go to take hold of Tim but David raises a hand and they pause.

For a moment, the two men face each other, Tim

red-faced and breathing hard, David cool and still. Tim leans in so that their noses are almost touching. David remains unmoved. 'I know what I know.'

He takes a step back, then spits on the floor at David's feet. He stalks towards the lift then pauses by the reception desk and sweeps his arms across it. Letters and pens and a bowl of individually wrapped mints scatter through the air. He steps into the open lift, mashes his hand against the buttons, then holds up a middle finger to his now-former colleagues as the lift doors slowly close.

'Well,' says Simon after a long and awkward pause. 'That was quite the show, wasn't it. I think that's quite enough excitement for one day. I doubt any of you will be getting any more work done so you might as well all fuck off. Run an errand. Go to the post office or whatever it is you people do in your free time. Oh, and Rachel, would please clean up that mess before you leave? Thanks.'

Still reeling from Tim's rage a few hours later, I connect to the wifi on the platform while I wait for the Tube and I type out a message to Jazz.

Me

15:04

Still got a job. Coming home early. Mad day. Pint?

Jazz

15:05

You want it? Cos ur asking for it.

Me

15:05

Dying for it. Antelope in half an hour?

Jazz

15:06

I'll get us a table.

As we pull out of the station, I watch the eyes of the man across from me watching the adverts on the station wall. They drift along, following a poster for erectile dysfunction pills then flick back to one about second-hand MacBooks. Drift and then flick. Faster and faster. Drift and flick, drift and flick, drift flick drift flick drift flick. Then the walls go dark as we scream into the tunnel.

'These people are total sociopaths – you do know that, right?' says Jazz an hour and one pint later. 'You know you could be doing literally anything else. Something actually worthwhile. Not working with *landlords*.' She spits out the last word. 'I know you think you're making a difference from the inside but if you lie down with dogs . . .'

She's doing that thing where she listens but already knows what she's going to say. We have had this same conversation again and again for nearly a year. I can't deal with her lecture today, so I don't respond. She picks up on my lack of fight and changes tack.

'It's nice to see you back in ends, WhiteBoy. We were beginning to think we'd lost you to Camden.'

'Tooting isn't ends, Jazz. For me or you.'

'Speak for yourself; you can practically see the hospital where I was born from here. And anyway, you know what I mean. You've barely been to the flat in weeks. I'm guessing this means you two have patched things up. Again.'

I ignore the implication. 'Felix and I are fine. We're good, actually. Great.'

'Tell that to your face, babes.'

I get up to get us another drink.

'What are you doing tonight?' Jazz asks as I place a pint of cider in front of her. 'Thought we could get noodles and watch something stupid.'

'I can't tonight, I've got a thing. I think.'

'Ooh, mysterious! Date night with lover boy?'

'Leave it out, Jazz. I'm not in the mood.' There is a pause. I see her weigh up whether to pick at this particular scab and decide against it.

'You'll never guess who I met up with today.'

'I dunno. Lady Di?'

'Good one. No, do you remember those art kids from the year above? The ones who threw that party we went to.' There's a beat. We haven't really spoken about that night or Rupert or any of it for years.

'Uh, yeah, I remember.'

'Well, they're bringing it back. The party I mean. WATCHME.move. J – do you remember J? The tall Somali one – well, I was out a few weeks ago and bumped into his little sister. Turns out she's queer and peng as hell, and also has a girlfriend – well, partner – who might now hate me. But that's a whole other thing. I'm pretty sure you know them . . .' She trails off, as if she is worried she has said too much.

'But anyway, we were texting a bit and she's all, like, "J is planning something cool and wants to know if you wanna be involved," and I'm, like, "Yeah." 'Cause one, he's also peng as hell, and two, he was always making the coolest shit at uni. So anyway, I went to his studio in Manor House today and it's in this massive warehouse, and basically, a bunch of the gang from uni have been throwing a few parties but now they wanna grow and expand beyond their mates. Make it more official. And they've asked me to get involved 'cause ya girl's connected. Bottom line is: queer POC rave, sick music. First one is in a couple of weeks and you're on the guest list. You can thank me later.'

'That's awesome, Jazz,' I say, only half listening, watching my phone for a reply to the message I've sent Felix asking about drinks. The reply has yet to come. 'Who do I know?'

'What?'

'You said I know someone. The J guy's sister's girlfriend's whoever or something.'

'Oh, um, no, I think I got that wrong. And also, kind of random, but Caleb told me to say hi to you. So . . . hi.' The half-forgotten name draws up fragments from the depths of my memory. Dark skin, a hand leading me through a crowd, crashing waves.

I drain the rest of my pint to hide the colour I feel

blossoming in my cheeks. Felix still hasn't messaged me back so I let Jazz drag me back to the flat and we scroll through food delivery options on her phone.

'Come on, Jazz, the house is massive and it's literally right by everything and you only have to come for a bit. Please. It'll be fun, I promise.' Jasmine raises her eyebrows until they almost disappear into her hair. 'Okay, maybe I can't promise it'll be fun, but just come. For a bit. For me?'

Jasmine is sitting on the peeling Formica counter of our little kitchen. It's been a long summer and the air is thick with heat and the weird smell that has started coming from the sink, which we are both ignoring. Outside, our neighbours' three children shriek with delight at their new paddling pool, which has been crammed into the tiny rectangle of AstroTurf that stands in for their garden.

'What I don't get, WhiteBoy,' she says, studying a menu on her phone, 'is why on earth you expect me to spend Notting Hill Carnival with your white boyfriend and his creepy family.'

'Right, now you're just being rude, Jasmine. And also, they're not creepy.'

'Ooh, "Jasmine" now, is it? Am I in trouble? And they are creepy. They control half of London. They're basically Illuminati.'

'You're being ridiculous.'

'Ridiculous? Babe, what's ridiculous is that you're on one of the highest-paid grad schemes in the country at a property firm that happens to be run by your boyfriend's dad.'

'Yeah, but I applied like everyone else!'

'Two months after the deadline. And they're downsizing but somehow you've miraculously kept your job. Not even – they've actually promoted you. Whatever happened to last in first out?'

'I've got an Economics degree!'

'You've got a 2:2 in combined English Literature and Economics because you dropped out of Eco after a year and your tutor liked you enough to let you carry some modules over.'

'Yeah, but it's from a red-brick uni!'

'Are you actually joking, WhiteBoy?'

'Wildcard.'

'What? No!'

'Wildcard.'

Back at uni, Jazz and I each had a wildcard to play. One each per year. They replenished when the new uni year started in September. The rules were simple: if you had an event – a night out or a course-mate's party or a gig – and the other person wasn't keen, you could play your wildcard and they had to come. I don't think I ever used mine (Jasmine was always at everything I wanted to go to anyway); she, however, deployed hers every year. It was most recently used in our final year to get me to attend a slam poetry competition that the girl she was seeing at the time was hosting at the students' union. We were the only people in the audience.

'Wildcard,' I repeat again. We both know she's beaten. She kisses her teeth.

'Fine. Fuck you, man.'

'Thank you, thank you! You only have to stay for brunch, I promise.'

'Brunch? Are you actually joking?'

My phone buzzes in my pocket. It's him.

Felix

18:43

Heard you got a promotion. Dinner on me to celebrate. Love you. F.

I tell Jazz we'll have to do noodles another time and call Felix. He picks up on the first ring and I grab my keys from the counter before oozing out into the sluggish heat. He asks me where I want to eat.

'Somewhere fresh,' I tell him. 'Somewhere expensive? Somewhere outside.'

The door of the House is ajar and wrapped in a Jamaican flag. To either side the doors and windows of 37 and 41, as well as most of the others on the street, are boarded up, the occupants having fled south to country seats or warmer climes to avoid the noise and dirt and joy of the celebration we are headed to. From inside, Bob Marley blares from a speaker. Jazz gives me an incredulous look, her eyebrows arched, and I shrug. It's too late for her to back out now. The blunt we smoked on the walk from the Tube station seems to have softened her edges. She smiles at me and shakes her head. We walk in and make our way down the stairs. The kitchen is full of boys in Hawaiian shirts with signet rings and girls in varying colours of seemingly the exact same polka-dot dress.

'Nice yard, man,' Jazz says to Lily who comes over to greet us. 'But you wanna be careful leaving your whole door open during Carnival. You don't know what kind of reprobate might walk in off the street.'

I can tell that Lily doesn't know whether Jazz is joking but as we move further into the room, I see Lily slip up the stairs to close the front door. Looking around the room, I see a few familiar faces. Celeste is talking to a clique of other tall, impossibly pretty women who have congealed around a side-table where Lily's sticker-covered MacBook is hooked up to an ancient-looking set of speakers. Through the French windows I can see Felix handing out glasses to a few people I don't know. I can hear Hebe's laugh echo somewhere in the house.

'Right, I'm gonna tackle West London's Bratz dolls and put on some actual music. Catch you outside?' Jazz marches off, tiny and determined, and plants herself firmly in the middle of the group of models, who regard her with suspicion until she says something I can't hear, and they all laugh. Jazz has this way of making a space completely hers. She effortlessly controls a crowd and can diffuse pretty much any tension with a skilfully timed quip. But the opposite is also true: if she is having a bad time, everyone else is going to as well. For now, though, she seems to be in a good mood. She leans over the laptop, searching for something, then presses enter. Satisfied, she straightens up as a repeated rapid-fire D-minor seventh heralds the starts of Dawn Penn's syrupy vocals. Leaning back, her arms spread wide, Jazz mouths along and winks at me. *No, no, no. You don't love me and I know now.*

I head outside and slide a hand around Felix's waist. He turns to me and smiles. Things have been good these last few weeks. The play's run has just finished and everyone loved it. He's been in pretty much every audition room in London and a few in California since. He greets me with a gentle kiss on the cheek and somehow manages not to break the flow of his monologue. He is explaining how usually the Blakes would shut up shop here for the whole of August, boarding up the place like the rest of their neighbours and heading to the Chateau. This year, however, the Blake children weren't invited. Annie and David have gone there with Group Captain Teller and his wife, Effy, for a holiday; which, given the complicated state of their intermarital liaisons, sounds more like an emergency peace negotiation.

'. . . It's all very modern.'

It took me three months to work up the courage to tell Felix what I'd seen happen between Annie and Teller at the Chateau. We had just left through the service entrance at Soho House after some of Felix's friends had walked in. It was exciting, then, to be his secret. It made what we had seem more real, in a way. I could justify the gaps in his attention by how hyper-focussed he was when he was with me. I thought, then, that our shared secrets would bring us closer. I thought that secrets bind, unaware that they can also sever.

'Felix, I have to tell you something,' I said.

'Can't it wait?'

He stepped forward to kiss me and I stepped back, knocking into a table where an ashtray – full of the discarded butts of a week's staff breaks – eagerly leapt to the ground and smashed into bright shards that glinted on the grimy back-street concrete.

'I think your mum is having an affair.' The words flew out, tumbling through the air to where I could not catch them. 'I saw her and Teller in your dad's study in France and I was gonna tell you but then everything else happened and then I didn't want to spoil this, but I don't want to keep it a secret anymore.'

Felix was looking down, pushing a fragment of ashtray around with his shoe but then he locked eyes with me. If he felt any surprise at all it was well hidden in the casual set of his jaw. He looked at me for a long time.

'The thing you need to understand,' he said slowly, after a while, 'is it that secrets, once you've breathed life into them, don't stay secret very long.'

'Wagwan, bredren?' Rupert's voice is hot in my ear and he hangs uncomfortably off my neck with one arm.

'Wagwan, Rupert.' I untangle myself from him as he takes out a pouch of tobacco to roll a cigarette. As he rifles through various pockets looking for papers and filters, he pulls out a bag of what is, presumably, given his over-familiarity and general twitchiness, cocaine. He takes a tiny spoon from a key that hangs on a chain around his neck and scoops out a little heap of the powder, which duly disappears up his nostril. He sniffs twice, then rubs the back of his hand across his nose. As he puts the bag away, he mistakes the look on my face and shrugs apologetically.

'Sorry, mate, only got enough for yours truly. Gotta last me all day. I'm sure you understand.'

'Hello, darling.' Lily, all smiles, swoops in and saves me. She wraps me in a tight hug. We have been better with each other since her and Annie's little plot. It feels like the air has cleared a little. It's nice to see her here and I'm glad of the interruption.

'I see you brought Jasmine,' she says, with a look I can't quite decipher, and nods over my shoulder as Jazz barrels towards us. She pushes her way through the people on the Blakes' back terrace and out through the gate into the lush communal garden.

'WhiteBoy, you gotta save me, man. Someone is trying to feed me rum punch they made using a Nigella recipe.' Jazz looks around at the flowing lawn and verdant trees. 'Huh. I'd always wondered what was behind these massive houses. Your own green slice of Middle England, right here in Kensington. Aren't you lucky?'

She falters slightly when she sees who I'm talking to. 'Oh, great. Today is getting better and better. I would say it's nice to see you, Rupey, but my mamma didn't raise a liar.'

'Hello, Jasmine. The pleasure's all mine.'

I feel her prickle beside me and take hold of her hand to try and quell the maelstrom. She takes a breath to steady herself, but makes it sound like a sigh.

'Now, I'm not usually one to dish out unsolicited advice. But if I were you, Rupert, I'd make myself scarce before someone here tells your new girlfriend the "rumours" about what you liked to do at uni to girls who'd mysteriously had too much to drink.'

'Fuck you, Jazz. I don't even know what you're talking about.'

'Five, four, three—'

Rupert pales. He looks angry but turns and storms off before Jazz gets to zero.

'So nice to see you, Lily,' says Jazz, unclenching her jaw. She rolls the tension out of her shoulders. 'But we're gonna have to split. Meeting some friends and don't wanna get snarled up in the crowd. Careful out there. Day one is usually fine for your lot but tomorrow you wanna watch yourself, yeah?'

She turns and walks off, through the doors, into the kitchen, pushes past a group of people huddled around the island doing shots, and disappears up the stairs. I apologise to Lily, promising I'll let her know where we end up, then mumble a few other goodbyes. Felix follows me up the stairs. He curls his finger through my belt loop and pulls me backwards towards him. He kisses me softly on the neck then grazes the soft skin beneath my earlobe with his teeth. I lean into the embrace, he kisses me again, then pushes me gently towards the door. I emerge out onto the front steps where Jazz is sitting, playing with a tile that has come loose. Second from the right, two squares back.

'Jazz, I am so, so sorry. I had no idea he'd be here. I wouldn't have put you through that if I had.'

'It's absolutely mad,' she says, not looking up. 'That these people board up their whole houses but leave a key under the mat. These houses deserve to get broken into.'

'Are you alright? I'm so sorry.'

'I'm fine, WhiteBoy. Stop saying you're sorry. It wasn't you that did it.'

'Were you actually gonna tell his girlfriend?'

'I dunno. Maybe? But do you wanna know something grim?' She bites her lip and nods her head as if testing out the thought and reaching the same conclusion. 'I reckon she already knows.'

The crowd has thickened. The rolling mass of skin and colour and faces seems impenetrable, but Jazz is determined to find her friends. I squat down and she clambers onto my shoulders, one leg then the other. Steadying myself against a passing stranger, I push up and hoist her into the air. She tugs my hair left and right to get me to turn, scanning the crowd for faces she knows. Excitedly she bounces up and down, which causes me to stagger slightly, which in turn causes her to clamp her thighs tighter around my head.

'I think I see J!' she says excitedly, steering me via my

curls through the sweaty mass of bodies. I step over legs and cups and discarded bags. Jazz taps on the top of my head to get me to stop.

'Woah, boy! Steady!' I stop, thinking she's found the group.

'You're a baddie, you know?' she says to a girl next to us, who looks up at Jasmine then down at me, then back up to her. Jazz hands the girl her phone, the Instagram search bar is already open, and the girl types her handle. Her acrylics make a satisfying click against the screen.

'Hi-ho, Silver!' says Jazz triumphantly and excitedly kicks me in the side with her Air Max. I threaten to buck her off if she doesn't calm down and she apologises, ruffling my hair, which annoys me even more. My carefully styled curls are reduced to a frizzy mass.

'I've got eyes on Caleb! Go, go, go!'

Finally, we make it to the group. Jazz taps my head. I lower myself down and she hops off my shoulders with a clumsy grace, hopping on one pristine trainer to regain her balance. I snatch the cap she is wearing and clamp it down over my fluffy hair. She shoots me a look but doesn't complain: she is wearing her hair in two long plaits that hang over each of her shoulders and her precisely combed and gelled middle part is still immaculate.

'WhiteBoy, you remember J, right? From uni? And this is his girlfriend, Neisha. We used to run around together back in the day.'

I say my hellos, navigating the unsure waters of heterosexual greetings. J bumps his fist against mine, Neisha kisses me on both cheeks, another boy opts for a high-five then pulls me into a hug I am not expecting.

I do not realise that I have been looking for someone until he returns, clutching four cans of Red Stripe with two more shoved into the deep side pockets of his black cargo shorts. Caleb passes out the beers and hands the last one to me. The cold can is welcome in the dense heat of the midday crowd. I thank him and take a sip. He is looking at me with a curious expression and I don't look away. He mirrors my sip then winks.

'Enjoy it, mate. They've just run out of ice. This will be your last cold drink of the day.'

We melt into the jubilant crowd. It presses close around us then we are absorbed. Bass from the stack nearby rumbles the tarmac and the feet of feather-clad dancers pound, riotous, through the street. One of the performers tilts forward with a little too much enthusiasm and takes a few frantic steps to regain her balance, but her gleaming smile never falters. As the day presses on, the parade gives way to the street party, and we dance and sip and laugh into the shimmering air. Warm rum punch in hand, Jazz and Neisha climb on top of a massive recycling bin. Neisha drops low, the beat of the music travelling up through the ground and the metal and into her body, while Jazz hypes up the crowd She is ecstatic, a different Jazz from the one I saw earlier at the House. I am different too. It is strange to see these streets so packed with brown bodies. Usually I would stroll through them, Felix's arm in mine. Being here without him feels disloyal in some way. Throughout the day, Caleb is either by my side or watching me across the group. He gets excited when a particular song starts playing and I feel his hand on my waist and we dance together to a tune I have never heard before. I ignore the persistent buzzing of my phone in my pocket until it stops. I ignore the persistent niggle in my conscience and dance with Caleb to songs I wish I knew so I could throw my head back and sing along like he does. Jazz flicks her plaits forward, hands on her knees, a fluid spiral spreading through her, smoothing her hips back and chest forward. She grins at me and Caleb and raises one eyebrow. All I can do is shrug.

Some people have brought signs, placards. A banner is unrolled. I feel a flood of cold as I recognise the face and name of the man we all watched die on our phone screens not long ago. Here, too, a story is unfolding. This celebration was once a riot. In a Tube station not far from here, milk bottles and iron bars and slurs were thrown at a white woman who'd dared to marry a Jamaican. A mob formed, baying for blood. Petrol bombs and knives and pistols. Five nights they raged.

Here, now, in the joyous crowd, someone takes out a megaphone and calls for silence. We hold it in our raised fists and lowered eyes. Someone reads out the names of the dead. We punctuate the litany. *Say their names.* Echoes of a memory. *Lord in your mercy.* Grandma's fan. *Say their names.* Eyes closed and heads bowed. *Lord in your mercy.* A half-forgotten liturgy. *Lord in your mercy. Hear our prayer.* The music strikes up again. A major-key requiem on steel drums. We dance, defiant. The swirling multitude continues to flow.

There is always danger in a crowd. In being one anonymous moving part of a larger whole. There is safety in anonymity. In being seen but not being known. Out of sight of people who know us, we can become someone else. I realise suddenly that we are alone, Caleb and I. That his hands are on my waist and his forehead is against mine. How close is too close? Somebody else decides for us. A shoulder in my back causes a jolt of pain and the accompanying shout of 'faggots' shatters the pain into shame and we break apart. Caleb straightens up, ready for a fight but the crowd has already swallowed our attacker. Our shadows have lengthened then melted into one. The sun has dipped behind the tall houses and the street feels suddenly muted. I say that we should probably find the others. I take out my phone and see a tonne of missed calls from Lily, Felix and Jazz. I do not read Felix's messages but type something about the signal being weird all day and drop my live location. Something seems to shift. A collective unconscious recalibration. A chill travels through the crowd from person to person and suddenly there are more of us, and we are being carried along on the tide that pours in from neighbouring streets. Somewhere, the music cuts off. A burst of static from somewhere else. A tinny voice, impossible to discern, barks instructions that get lost between the mouth and the megaphone.

I am now alone. The space around me condenses as

the gaps fill with people pushed forward from behind. We are being herded. I search for Caleb to no avail. I look up to try to get my bearings but cannot. I find a lamp-post and haul myself above the bodies. Behind the revellers, batons in hand, a line of policemen urges everyone forward. I think I catch a glimpse of Neisha near the back, trying to reason, complaints falling on unhearing ears. An officer steps forward and shoves her back. I watch J step between them. I do not know who raises their hand first but the single blow that matters is the one that sends up a spray of red into the fading rays of the day. A single blow that sends J's head spinning. It cracks like thunder. Or bone. Neisha's scream slices through me and suddenly everyone is running. I cannot see J or Neisha or Caleb or anyone and then I lose my footing and I am falling through the panicked air. The impact of my head on the pavement tastes like iron. White stars burst before my eyes. Someone pulls me to my feet. I try to push back towards J but I cannot fight the flood of people. I stagger with it. There is a dull pain at the back of my head that shoots forward with every thud of my frenzied heart.

I don't know how long it is before I get my bearings. I see a street I know and try to turn down it. It is blocked by three police officers and their bright tape, caging me away. One of them tells me there has been an incident. She says she is sorry but I can't go down there unless I live there. I tell her I do. She does not believe me. I have no proof. I start to cry and they tell me to move along.

My hand touches the back of my head and comes back bloody. I plead with them again. I say his name and, like a miracle, he appears. Felix, his hand interlacing with mine. When he talks to the officers, they call him 'sir'. The tape falls and so I do. He cradles my head until I am calm. The officers look embarrassed. We step over the police tape and walk back to the House.

I'm so glad you asked that. I am here with you today to address the unfortunate incident that occurred within my constituency yesterday. It is my duty as an elected representative to prioritise the safety and security of all citizens – be they Black, white, rich or poor – and it deeply concerns me that a number of my constituents resorted to violence on the streets during yesterday's celebrations. I must emphasise that the blame for this regrettable incident lies squarely with the people who, through their violent and criminal behaviour, have invited such repercussions. I can confirm that a man was taken into custody following his arrest and later transferred to hospital to be treated for injuries he sustained during an altercation with police. I am told he is in a stable condition and remains in hospital. My sympathies are with his family at this difficult time.

The individual in question, I am told, was associated with gang activity during the Notting Hill Carnival, an event known, unfortunately, for its recurring incidents of unrest and lawlessness. It is disheartening to witness the consequences of such associations manifesting in the form of a physical altercation with the police. While I understand the complexities surrounding community events and the passions they may evoke – especially given the current climate across the Atlantic – it is essential that we acknowledge the role that personal choices and behaviours play in contributing to such unfortunate outcomes.

In light of this incident, I believe it is crucial to reinforce this government's manifesto commitment to public safety by bolstering our police force and taking tougher action against those who engage in criminal activities. We must send a clear message that our community will not tolerate criminal behaviour. The Metropolitan Police work tirelessly to maintain law and order within our communities, often facing dangerous situations with limited resources. They deserve our unwavering support and gratitude as they put themselves in harm's way to protect us.

Furthermore, it is essential that we resist attempts to politicise incidents such as this. It is not a matter of racism or discrimination, but rather a matter of ensuring the safety and well-being of all citizens. Attempts by those on the left to link this unfortunate event to the horrific tragedy that occurred in Atlanta last month are transparent and disingenuous agenda pushing from a woke opposition who have run out of ideas. The comparison is, frankly, an insulting one. By focussing on the facts at hand and the need for a robust response, we can work together to create a more secure environment for everyone, irrespective of their background.

The thing that the people of this country need to understand is that this was a response to an act of violence by a small minority of thugs in an otherwise peaceful and welcome demonstration of Afro-Caribbean pride and culture. There is, sadly, a problem with gangs in this city. And that problem – and it is not racist for me to say this – that problem is predominantly within the Black community. And if we do not face up to that fact, then we are saying it is okay for it to continue. The actions of a selfish, violent, *irresponsible few cannot be left unchecked. We cannot have crime without punishment. Rights without responsibilities. Communities without control.*

In closing, let us not allow ourselves to be swayed by misguided notions of political correctness. Instead, let us stand together in support of our dedicated police force and their unwavering commitment to public safety.

Caroline Asiamah is replaced by a blank screen and we all let out the breath we have been holding. Someone asks if I am okay, but I don't respond. Someone hands me a cup of tea that I don't drink. All night the scene has played over and over, projected onto the peeling plaster of Felix's ceiling. The spray of blood, the crack of bone, the rush of bodies. Over and over. Spray of blood, crack of bone, rush of bodies. Again and again and again. Blood, bone, bodies. Felix had to hold me down, shake me awake, whisper to me that I was safe here. I let him hold me, I let him tell me this even though I knew it was a lie. Outside, shouts and smashed glass and sirens wailed until the early hours.

Now there is sunlight streaming into the kitchen at the House and birdsong flits in with the morning air. Felix had to leave early to go to an audition. The sun and the song turn cold with my tea. Someone asks again if I'm okay. I must be upset, they say. But I am not upset. I am rage. Every hair on my body is rage. Every inch of my Black skin. All my fear, all my sadness. All my hope and injustice and desperation are rage. All I have is rage and nowhere to put it. I want to smash the teacup into pieces. To crush it like the bone in J's cheek. He is still unconscious, Jazz tells me. A depressed skull fracture, a fracture of the left zygomatic arch, a comminuted, displaced fracture of the right ulna, a single undisplaced fracture of the right distal radius, isolated fractures of left ribs seven, eight and ten, no evidence of injury to pulmonary or abdominal viscera, no evidence of massive blood loss, no evidence of cerebral bleeding or oedema. The words wash over me, sterile and meaningless. He is lucky, we are told. I wonder what unlucky looks like if this is our lot. The police say most of the injuries were sustained when he fell. The hospital does not want to comment but one of the doctors has suggested that that is impossible. Two videos posted last night on Twitter show J disappearing under a flurry of batons and boots. They are everywhere, the videos, stories unfolding across screens and streets and oceans. A body, so close to mine for so much of the day. Reduced to minute particles and fragments. That's what 'comminuted' means. I had to look it up. Neisha, Jazz says, hasn't spoken since last night. I can still hear her screaming.

The second day of Carnival has been cancelled – that's what they say. Everyone is still coming, Jazz tells me. I step out onto the front step. The road is strewn with crumpled cans and broken glass. Minute particles and fragments. The houses are strewn with eggs and paper and graffiti. On the plywood over the door to number 37 someone has hastily scrawled black lives matter. The door to 41 reads all my neighbours r niggers.

Click.

'Hey. I'm here for you.' It's Lily. Her camera is slung around her neck and her fragile hand finds mine. 'It's gonna be okay,' she says. How can she possibly know?

All of the streets near the House are closed off. There are policemen everywhere. Lily's provisional driving licence acts as a talisman, though I am eyed with some suspicion. Eventually we make our way onto Ladbroke Grove, where a huge crowd has already amassed. We are hit by a tidal wave of noise. There are signs and balaclavas and people in hi-vis tabards and news crews and rows and rows of riot police. She points the camera, finding her field. *Click.*

Jazz

12:09

NH is locked down. We're in Hyde Park.

She has dropped a pin. We head towards it, using Lily's ID to cut through cordoned-off streets, two helpless bystanders caught in the chaos. From behind a row of geared-up officers, the mass of faces, mostly Black and brown, smears into an anguished streak. What is the tipping point between pain and fury? There are silver clouds overhead, edged with black. *Click.*

Hyde Park is a seething ocean of flesh and cloth and cardboard. I think of Mum as I hoist Lily onto my shoulders to try to find Jazz. I think of cold hands and loud voices and a yellow wheel clamp. Lily gently leans her weight to turn me slowly, searching the overflowing park. There is always danger in a crowd. *Click.*

We find Jazz. She gives Lily a surly look. *Click.* I shrug. It's most of the group from yesterday. J and Neisha are not here, obviously. There are more faces though, some familiar and some strange. They did not let Jazz into the hospital to see J. She waited outside all night. J's sister brought updates and bad coffee to the pavement outside A&E where Jasmine sat and smoked a chain of roll-ups. I can picture her there, under the sickly glow of the red sign, daubing the grey curb with ashy runes. I can hear her muttered spells and prayers and curses curling into the August night. She stayed there until it got light and then came here. She looks rough, but her middle part is still immaculate. Tear-streaked and grim, her face shines despite the flatness of the light. *Click.*

The signs around us vary in their wording and skill and size but they all declare the same thing. I feel some of my rage seeping out into the hard ground. The crowd seems to spiral out from our epicentre, shockwaves. Like we have chosen to sit on a ley line. Caleb sits down next to me and tries to hold my hand. I let him for a moment but remember Lily and pull away. Nearby someone has set up a makeshift stage. People make speeches, start chants. Some of the people are famous. Some of them are not. *Click.*

'Smile for the cameras.' Jazz spits on the ground and Lily colours. But then Jazz gestures upwards raising both middle fingers to the sky. We all look up. Above us, two helicopters skin the bellies of low clouds. Police or media, they are too far above us to distinguish. 'Fascist mosquitos.' *Click.*

The person on the stage says something and a huge cheer goes up. There are police all around us. Some, wearing baby-blue tabards, wander through the park, smiling and trying to talk to people. Ahead of them, a vanguard of volunteers hands out protest rights cards and Sharpies so people can write emergency contacts and solicitors' numbers on their skin. Black ink on brown arms. *Click.*

After a while, a group of women in yellow T-shirts takes to the stage. They make speeches and repeat what has already been said. Both here and in other places, at other times, thousands of miles away for hundreds of years. I can barely hear their words over the cheering from the people around me. The police claim the protest is illegal. We are going to do it anyway. There will be no more Black blood shed today they say. How can they possibly know?

They tell us to use our voices and I think of Neisha. Her voice has been used up. One single scream was all she had left and now she is silent. I wonder how many screams I have left. I wonder if one day I will find out; if I will open my mouth to cry out but all there will be is silence. What pain will tear the final howl from my chest? For now, I use what's left of my voice to join the too-familiar call and response. *Say their names. Say their names. Say their names. Lord in your mercy.*

The park boils over into the streets and the decision

is made to move on. The tired clouds lose their hold and fat raindrops cover the procession that snakes through the streets. The buildings here are made of sugar cane. The streets are slick with blood. They are named after squares and sovereigns and slavers. But those names mean nothing today. Blood is what links the hands that built these streets to the feet that pound them now. *Click*.

The people are headed to the Number 10. Or to Caroline's constituency office. It is unclear. Suddenly we are soaked with hot rain. Jazz says we should get a drink, that we can leave the others to march on without us. In the shelter of a building that looks like it used to be a bank we huddle together to hide from the heavy clouds, framed by placards and umbrellas and two stone lions. *Click*. And then we are immortal.

We are lying on the roof of a garage somewhere in Ladbroke Grove. From inside, the bass threatens to burst through the window we have closed to muffle the party that is showing no signs of waning. We moved from protest to pub to wherever we are now. Somewhere, Lily and her camera peeled off. The sombre mood has been loosened by a few drinks and the rain has given way to a muggy heat than has not abated. We pass a joint gently between tentative fingers. We only brought one sofa cushion out here with us, so our shoulders are pressed tightly together as we look up at the stars that try to shine in spite of the yellow buzz of the city.

'Have you ever noticed', says Caleb, tilting his head

towards mine so that I feel the stubble of his shaved head brush against my ear, 'that if you stare at one star for long enough, the rest seem to disappear?'

I try it and am surprised to find that he is right. I train my focus on a twinkling star directly above us. One by one, the ones around it dim, then fade, then die, replaced by an unsure blankness that only holds itself together for as long as I keep looking at it.

'I think I might be looking at Venus,' I say. 'Do planets still count?'

'Yeah,' says Caleb, his fingers grazing mine. 'I think they do.'

A flat palm slamming against a window pane shatters the fragile moment. Jasmine beckons excitedly from inside. Her face is urgent and her eyes are filled with tears. Caleb stands and pulls me to my feet. For a second we are chest to chest, my chin tilted up so I can see the light from inside dance across his face. Jasmine slams on the window again. She is pointing to her phone. A story is developing. In a hospital five miles away, J has woken up.

The thing I remember most about the unit is the smell. People often say that hospitals smell like disinfectant or decay, but I always thought they smelt like people. Units like the one Mum was on were never empty, there were always patients there with their breath and skin and life-force. It was a secure unit so you had to be let through one door into a small in-between space while the door behind you closed before the one in front opened. The first time we visited, I remember thinking that it was like an airlock on a spaceship, that if we didn't make sure the doors were locked and unlocked in the correct sequence then we would all be sucked out into the vacuum of space. I imagined the unit like that. Slowly revolving in space to keep our feet on the ground. And when I was missing Mum, I would look out the window at home and imagine her out there floating through nothing.

It was even structured like a space station. Modular pods around a central control room. Fixed furniture and no sharp edges so you couldn't tear your spacesuit. Porthole windows that didn't open and looked on to nowhere. They would dim the strip lighting to let everyone know it was getting late, time to leave or return to your room. It felt so far away. There were toys there, which I found strange, because all of the people who lived there – or were just visiting, like Mum – were grownups. But I would play with them anyway, even though I was right on the edge of being too old for toys, while Grandma would chat and Mum would stare at nothing and sometimes stroke my back or my hair or my arm. I hated going there. It felt like visiting some other version of Mum. Like somebody had drawn her but forgotten to colour her in. Sometimes I would cry when we had to leave but I knew it upset Mum so I would try to keep it in. Boys my age didn't cry.

Once, I was taken into one of the little rooms that had a desk and some plastic chairs. Grandma was waiting just outside, they told me, and I could call for her whenever

I wanted. A white woman with a kind smile and a big bundle of notes asked me lots of questions about all sorts of things. About school and Mum and home and Grandma and about what I ate and who looked after me when Grandma was working. The lady with the kind smile visited us at home too, and once she even came to see me at school. Eventually Grandma signed some papers that meant that I could keep living with her. I didn't know someone had been planning to take me away.

Once when we visited, Mum's arms were wrapped in bandages. Everyone told me it was nothing to worry about but I could see the dark brown flecks around Mum's nails. Once, under an orange streetlight, on the way home from a gig we'd been way too young for, my friend Kayla had shown me her scars, thick raised crescents from left to right. Pink and purple and white. Tallies of the times she couldn't say what she wanted to scream. Kayla had told me that when people really meant it, they went top to bottom, not left to right.

That time it was Mum who had cried. Grandma clucked and cooed and sang old songs which soothed her. Mum moved onto the floor and sat between Grandma's knees and let her smooth and gather the tangled mess of her hair into neat little knots. Dignity was important, Grandma said, even in the hardest of times. After that visit I think I told Grandma that I didn't want to go there anymore. She hugged me really tight and told me I didn't have to go if I didn't want to. Grandma would still visit but I would stay at home by myself or go to Marcus's or

Uncle Henry's or hang out with Danny and Kayla and that lot. I would still look out at the stars though, and imagine Mum up there, spinning to keep her feet on the ground.

The step-down trauma ward is half empty. Only three of the beds are occupied. The others wait in neat-cornered apprehension for someone to have the worst day of their life. In the bed nearest the door, a man in his early forties dozes in a shirt and tie. Jazz says he is between meetings, which he is doing via video to his law firm. From the waist down he is naked except for a thickly padded pelvic binder out of which snake various tubes. The bus that hit him cracked his pelvis in five places. He was wearing a helmet, which saved his life. He is lucky.

Opposite the lawyer, moaning gently in disturbed sleep, lies an old woman. Her paper-white skin is blotted with bruises. She was found on the floor of her flat between three-foot-high stacks of magazines by a neighbour who raised the alarm after the smell of rot made its way through the extractor fan into her bathroom. Nobody has any idea how long she was on the floor. A huge wound on her thigh was packed with maggots, who had fatted themselves on the parts of her that were beyond saving. A solitary shiny green fly repeatedly taps its hard carapace against the window, impatient for release. If the neighbour had not smelled the decay, the old lady would be dead. She is lucky.

J is in a good mood today, according to Jasmine. If this

is his good mood, then I am glad to have missed the bad ones. His right eye is swollen shut, the skin shines purple and ripe. At first, I thought his bruising wasn't too bad, that the dark hue of his skin was maybe hiding the worst of it. Up close, however, I can see that his skin is a patchwork of ruin. My eyes scan the wreckage, struggling and failing to find a witch's mark, a scrap of him untouched by the beating or bruising or blood tests. He stares back at me with his one working eye. I ask him how he's doing and hate myself for it.

'At least I've still got my looks.' His weak smile splits into a grimace of pain. 'They say I might be allowed to eat some solid food tomorrow, so that's good. I don't know how many more milkshakes I can handle.'

The effort of speaking slows him down, he can only talk out of the left side of his mouth. He takes long pauses after each phrase to allow the pain to subside.

'You saw it.' It isn't a question. What has Jazz said? She knows I don't want to talk about this, but I did agree to come today. Looking down at him, I cannot bear to withhold. I say I did. I expect him to ask a follow-up question, to ask me to make a statement like Jazz has been doing, but he doesn't.

'The video is pretty gnarly. Racking up the views, though. I always thought I'd get famous for my art, you know? Apparently, I make a better poster boy than I do a painter.' He takes a long shaky breath. 'I don't want to be a poster boy though.' J's voice begins to crack. 'I just want to be me. This is all so fucked. I just want it to stop.'

The tears come and then are cut short by a gasp of pain when they are unable to find an escape from the wreckage of his right eye. He frantically scrabbles for something in the bed sheets. His desperate fingers find a small pen-like device and he jabs at the red button on its end. One of the machines by his head bleeps and administers a dose of morphine through his drip. He relaxes slightly but his thumb still taps the button and his breaths come in ragged snatches. Eventually the machine allows another dose and J sighs his relief.

As soon as he drifts into a troubled sleep, Jazz launches into her speech. We have had this conversation multiple times already. It usually ends in a fight. She whispers her argument to avoid disturbing the sleeping patients. I let her finish.

'Jazz, I know you think that me making a statement will help, but honestly, I barely even know what I saw.'

'You were pretty sure the day after. Jesus fucking Christ, WhiteBoy. There's videos for goodness' sake!'

'Then what difference would I make? Why would anybody listen to what I have to say about this?'

'A video can't stand up in court. A video can't express how it felt—'

'This isn't about my feelings, Jazz. It isn't about me at all. I don't want to be a part of any of this.'

'It's about all of us – how do you not understand that? It's about something bigger than us. Like it or not, you're already a part of it. You may think you're protected from all of this because of *them* but you're not. They are not your people. They will turn their backs on you as soon as you become inconvenient to them. How do you not see that? You might think that you're safe, but when they don't need you anymore, you won't matter to them. They won't care that you've kept your mouth shut. They won't care that you've been a good little boy. They won't care about your white dad or your light skin or the fact that you threw all of us under the bus. None of that matters to them, and if you can't see that, then I don't even see the point in talking to you about this anymore.'

She picks up her bag, kisses J gently on the forehead, shoots me a poisoned look, and walks out of the room. It takes a moment of her words ringing in my ears before any reaction kicks in. I know somewhere, some part of me feels angry, but right now all I feel is completely alone. A sob I can't hold back leaps out of my throat and is followed by tears that I don't know how to stop. I want to call Felix; he would know what to say. I could bury my pain in the crook of his neck, fold myself into the safety of his arms. But I did not tell him I was coming here. A worried-looking nurse tells me J is going to be alright. She offers me a cup of tea. I don't say anything, so she brings me one anyway. It is hot and sweet, and she gives me four biscuits even though she's only supposed to give me two.

September

The best way to wake up is slowly and in the arms of someone you love. Though I'm not sure you could technically call the last few drunken fumbling hours we've just spent in bed sleep. As our fifth alarm of the morning sounds, I try to heave Felix out of bed, but he flops back down in lethargic obstinance. Even puffy and bloodshot he is shockingly beautiful. I offer no resistance as he pulls me back on top of him. He cradles my head into the warm hair on his chest and I breathe in the feeling. I've begun to think of Felix's flat as ours, though most of my things are still in Tooting. It is here, in Felix's arms, in his bed, in his blue-walled room, that feels like home. It isn't an alarm that next wakes me but the realisation that one hasn't gone off. I check the time. We are already ten minutes late. I leap out of bed and this time force Felix up too. He follows me into the shower, muffling my complaints with whispered kisses. He turns up the heat on of the water and pushes me to my knees as we try to wake each other up.

Last night was the wrap party of *Uplands*, the TV show Felix has been filming. He plays the son of a retired detective who is brought back to the force to solve a case from her past. As ever, Felix mingled and dazzled while I tried to fade. The woman playing the detective, who I think might have been in *Downton Abbey*, cornered me at one point.

'You're Felix's . . . friend, yes?' She had kind eyes and an affable Lancashire accent that she hadn't had moments ago on screen. 'He talks about you lot, you know, and very fondly.'

This caught me off-guard, and I had no response. She lowered her voice, drawing me closer.

'I had a friend like you once. She were right beautiful, like you. I was too scared to say what I should have said and eventually she walked away and never came back. People think British society runs on manners and propriety but the real currency in this country is gossip. Especially in this industry. People talk. You need to decide if you're ready to hear the tripe they've got to say.'

She took a small step back and looked at me; her smile turned into a frown that wrinkled the skin around the corners of her mouth. 'Oh flower, you look terrified. I hope I've not put my foot in it. All I meant was you need to look after yourself. Take care, okay?'

She was whisked away. Felix scooped up another pair of cocktails from the bar and swept over to me. He whispered that he couldn't stand another second with these people and, highball glasses in hand, we fled out into the street together to find a better party, somewhere we could both be nameless. He hailed a black cab and gave the driver an address in Mayfair. He slipped a thickset

233

man in a black puffer a fifty-pound note and we slipped into the club through a side-door. Felix led me through a crowded dancefloor, pulsing with bodies, to a small private booth with a black glass table and plush velvet seating.

'Do you ever just want it all to stop?' said Felix, shaking the contents of a small plastic bag directly onto the table. 'Sometimes it just feels like everything is so loud. I feel everything so much, I see everyone staring. I feel like everyone is waiting for me to fuck up. The world is so bright and loud and I can't get away from it. Coke is good. Whatever, it's fine.' He laughed, rolled his eyes, did not look me in mine. 'But if I do more, if I do enough, it's like I get to this other level. This quiet space. Where no one else exists. It's like my mind goes blank. I don't have to feel fucking anything and it's . . .' Felix closed his eyes and let out a long, gentle breath, then leaned forward and snorted the heap of powder.

I don't want to be out of bed and I'm not even sure Felix should be driving. I lay my arm casually over his leg and hold the hand he is using to change gear, but he doesn't tell me to stop. As we crawl through the torpor of Sunday traffic, the narrow streets filled with tote-bag farmers' market acolytes and hung-over brunchers melt into wider sweeping streets on hills that seem too steep to fit into my narrow topography of London. Somewhere between us stumbling home and crashing back out again it must have rained heavily. Now, though, an indulgent sun lights the jagged edge of a thick raincloud silver and stirs up a hopeful warmth in the air.

I know we're in the right place when the houses get further apart, and the cars parked outside them get shinier. A group of four or five white children in jelly shoes and swimming costumes splash in a huge puddle at the bottom of a hill, watched over by a tired-looking dad reading the *Telegraph* from a deck chair. Felix puts his foot down and steers towards the puddle, sending a curve of water sailing towards the kids who scream with delight. The wave reaches the dad and whips the newspaper from his hand. He stands up to shout as us and knocks over the deckchair, which only makes the kids laugh harder. Felix is giggling so much that he misses the turn and has to slam on the brakes and reverse up the wide avenue. He pulls up outside a detached house. He takes my right hand in both of his.

'Don't look so miserable,' he says. 'It's only lunch. I love you.'

Lily must have been waiting for us to arrive because before we are halfway up the long front-garden path she swings open the purple door. She is beaming wide and starts to laugh when she sees our faces.

'You two look absolutely horrendous. Quick heads-up: your day is about to get much more chaotic. Fizz is already pissed and forgot the Aga was still off from the summer so we're at least two hours off any food. Bill didn't realise Mummy and Daddy aren't talking and invited them both and didn't tell the other. He also let slip that dad's been staying at the Dorchester rather than the Bermondsey flat so naturally she's accused him of having another affair which is incredibly rich. Dad is spitting feathers, so watch out. And there's something else but I can't for the life of me remember what it is. You both look like you could use a drink. Luckily there's plenty.'

We exchange hugs and greetings and soon Lily, Felix and I are arranged on a sofa, balancing glasses of red wine and listening to Fizz lament the unfortunate timing of her eldest daughter's wedding and its cutting short of their planned trip around Italy.

'Oh, I wouldn't worry too much Auntie Fizz. Venice will always be there.'

Lily sniggers at this and spills a drop of wine onto my leg. 'Well, exactly, and I'm sure the west coast of Scotland is lovely at that time of year. God, are they going to have a ceilidh?'

'They'd bloody better,' shouts Bill from the kitchen. 'I do an absolutely world-class Dashing White Sergeant!'

Fizz groans theatrically. 'As if things couldn't get any worse. Now, do tell me, where are you living these days? Not still in *Manchester*, I hope?'

'Tooting,' I respond, looking to Felix.

'Well! Everyone has to live somewhere, I suppose.' We both laugh, but hers is real.

I allow myself to sink deeper into the comfortable softness of the afternoon, carried off on the tangle of limbs and chatter. Felix chimes in with a story about his time as president of the Caledonian Society at university and I feel the words rumble through his chest. There are still times, and this is one of them, where the gulf between me and the Blakes seems impassable. There are so many things about them that I will never understand. But these stories – of white-tie dinners that serve breakfast at four in the morning and business deals done in back-rooms of members' clubs with unmarked doors – are my stories now. The intoxicating sense of belonging, of moving through a space I didn't even know existed, guided by the hand of Felix or Lily or Annie – this is something I cannot give up.

A crunch of gravel and three short, sharp raps at the door announce the arrival of the something else Lily couldn't quite remember when we arrived. Her voice is unmistakable; clipped vowels speak of careful elocution while the occasional swallowed G at the end of a verb belies a diasporic upbringing that can never quite be practised out. She makes her apologies for being late and Bill falls over himself trying to explain about the kitchen troubles and offering her a list of drinks, all of which she refuses. I detach myself from the puddle of Blake siblings and slip outside with the excuse of needing some air. I find Annie sitting at a small table under an apple tree towards the back of the garden, smoking a long, thin cigarette. She offers me one and I take it gratefully. You can become addicted to anything if you try hard enough.

'Avoiding Creepy Caroline, are we? Sensible move. Can't stand the woman. David insists on keeping her sweet so that he and Simon can have their wicked way with the zoning regulations in Kensington. I've never met a woman more allergic to fun. Or putting together an outfit. Oh Jesus, she's coming. I'm so sorry to do this, darling, but it's every man for himself.' And with that, she stubs out her Vogue and escapes back up the garden, giving Caroline an insincere kiss on each cheek as she passes her.

'There you are,' purrs Caroline, closing in. I think, for a brief moment, about hopping over the back wall, but it looks too high and she'd definitely see me do it. 'I was hoping to get you on your own today. You're a difficult man to get hold of.'

I say nothing but muster a weak smile to avoid being rude.

Caroline presses on, undeterred. 'I've been meaning to speak to you about that awful business at the Carnival last month. I understand you might have a connection with that boy and his family. It seems they are determined to make life very difficult for me in pressing on with this case. As far as I'm concerned, we should all just put this unfortunate misunderstanding behind us. It would be wonderful if you could put a word in on our behalf. Get them around the table, as it were. I'm sure we can come to an arrangement that is beneficial for everyone.'

I mutter that I don't really know J and don't have much sway but will see what I can do. I look at my feet and nearby lies a half-decayed apple. A team of ants scatter frantically from inside the fruit, devouring its flesh.

'Good man. It's great to have you onside. And I don't

know how many times I have to offer, but if you're ever interested in getting out from under David's watchful eye, there's a job waiting for you at the constituency office. I'm sure he's been very generous, but a boy like you is wasted in property. It's time you stood on your own two feet, and the Party is always looking for diverse voices to bring in some fresh perspective. I won't give you my card again as I'm sure you have it. But do give me a call. We'll look after you.'

She stresses this last part and looks over her shoulder towards the house where Lily is beckoning us in. I barely have time to register what Caroline has told me when Lily announces that lunch is ready. Simon, who has arrived with yet another smug but benign-looking young woman on his arm, makes a show of ignoring me when I re-enter the room.

'Caroline! It's smashing to see you!'

'Is it, now? What do you want this time?'

'Just the pleasure of your company, sweetheart.'

Caroline bristles.

'Si, I'm surprised you're even here today,' says Felix. 'Isn't there a village somewhere missing an idiot?'

I cannot look Lily in the eye as Bill serves up plates of practically raw vegetables and lethally pink-looking chicken. When Simon greedily tucks in to his plate, Felix has to jab me in the side to stop me losing myself into a fit of giggles at the look of genuine horror on Lily's face. I push a firm potato through watery gravy and fill up Fizz's wine glass, so she doesn't notice Felix slipping chunks of meat from our plates into the waiting mouth of their practically blind Border terrier. Titus seems to be used to Fizz's cooking and trots around the dining table happily accepting offerings from most of the guests.

'And how is dear Polka Dot?' asks Simon, slicing through the jovial atmosphere that has settled on the room and turning it cold. 'Still banging on about all that gender rubbish?'

The girl to his right chimes in. 'Oh, is this the poor girl you were telling me about who cut off all her hair?' Maybe not so benign after all.

'We're dealing with it, Simon. Thank you very much for asking.'

'I'm not sure, Mum, that this is something that needs to be "dealt with", if I'm entirely honest with you,' Lily says in a carefully measured voice. 'Dot has told us how they feel and how they want to be addressed and your refusal to do that is the issue here.'

'Well, my issue', offers Fizz, 'is that it's just bad grammar. I can't keep up with all this new-fangled language. I don't care if Dot calls herself the King of Siam as long as she doesn't get offended if I don't follow suit.'

Felix sighs and puts down his wine glass. 'It's about respect, Fizz—'

'Oh, so now you're concerned about respect, are you?' David, who has been silently stewing for most of the afternoon, sits forward in his chair. He has a way of talking that commands attention, even without him raising his voice. 'I agree, Felix, the problem is a lack of respect. Whether it's Dot's latest act of rebellion, or baboons throwing punches at police.' Felix finds my hand under the table and gives it a little squeeze though his face remains impassive. 'Or little lefty activists crying foul at proper working people who are trying to make this country prosper, people here have forgotten how this place works. I have worked my whole fucking life to get where I am, and this new generation thinks that they can just stroll in and demand whatever they want. What you lot fail to understand' – David gestures towards the end of the table where Felix, Lily and I sit – 'Is that I built everything you enjoy with my bare hands, and you think you have the right to tell me how to speak, how to think. You think you have a God-given right to the life of luxury that you live. But God did not pay for your school, God didn't buy your house, God doesn't pay your wages, God doesn't pay for you to sit around on your arse pretending to be a bloody photographer, God didn't pluck you out of a doomed fucking singing career and give you every fucking thing you asked for. I did all of that, and what do I get in return? Disrespect and fucking pronouns.'

His words hang in the silence for a moment. Felix has let go of my hand and he and Lily are looking down at their plates. Annie is staring David full in the face, her nostrils flared, but she says nothing, clearly deciding that this fight is better won in private. Caroline is studying the pattern on her napkin and Fizz is indiscriminately filling glasses. Simon looks disinterested while the girl he brought looks absolutely delighted.

Bill, oblivious and clad in an apron and matching oven gloves, pops his head around the dining-room door. 'Anyone for Baked Alaska?'

We don't stay for very long after that. Lily hops in the car with us, refusing Bill's kind offer that we take some food with us. As Felix backs the car off the kerb, I scroll through takeaway options to order so that the delivery will arrive at the flat the same time we do. I settle on Chinese, adding extra prawn crackers to cheer us up. Lily's phone is connected to the car's radio, and she interrupts her noughties singalong playlist to call Dot. We listen together as the phone rings out to voicemail.

October

When Felix promised a 'casual affair' for his birthday, I knew better than to take him at his word. Nothing is ever casual when it comes to the Blakes. It starts simply enough, with dinner at one of our favourite places: a little Italian on the corner of the street that does three choices of proper pasta with brilliant wine that shouldn't be as cheap as it is. Ten of us – Celeste, Lily and I plus a few of Felix's boarding-school and university friends – sing and cheer as the owner, Francesco, brings out a Bible-sized slab of tiramisu with a sparkler sticking out of the top of it. Towards the end of the meal, various friends and hangers-on arrive and help themselves to the stash of pre-paid negronis on the bar that Francesco and his daughter cannot make quick enough to meet demand.

It's hard to know who Felix's actual friends are. People are drawn to him and he, in turn, shines brighter because of their nearness. It seems like it has always been this way, but since I met him, his name has grown and so has his flame and the circle that flutters around it. With the exception of the people invited to eat with us tonight, nobody seems to have been around for very long. Writers, models, actors and people who seem to do nothing at all swirl about him always, but none get close enough to

243

risk burning up. They are rarely seen more than once. At maybe midnight, with guests spilling into the street and fresh out of Campari, Francesco, with a smile, shuts up shop and ushers us out into the night.

We deliberate for a minute, under the cold and starless sky. Felix looks to me, not for permission but for something else; acquiescence perhaps. I smile back, because it is all I can do when he looks at me like that. Satisfied eyes lit to a sparkling orange by the buzzing streetlamp, he leads the rabble back to our flat. Back to his flat. The decision was never mine, but he asked, with his eyes at least. The flat is pristine (Dora, the cleaning lady, has been busy since we left), and all the glassware sits sparkling and apprehensive, laid out on white linen waiting to be filled. I realise with a sting that this was his plan all along. I wonder for a second whether he didn't mentioned it because he thought I'd protest or because he hadn't felt that he needed to. He takes a bottle from the sink – which Dora has filled with crushed ice – pops the cork, and begins to pour buttery froth first into Lily's open mouth and then into the impatient glasses held aloft by old friends and new disciples. The bottles are from a score of boxes shipped over from the Chateau by David. A paltry peace offering that until tonight has waited, unacknowledged, at the bottom of the stairs, stacked in two looming columns taller than me. Someone, an old friend I think, from the way he is casually pushing the furniture around, sets up decks in the bay window, dims the lights, and hits play on an old song that makes Felix laugh and start to dance. Suddenly, this is a party.

The bath, too, is filled with ice. Bottles stick out of it at careful angles. I force my hands into it to shock myself into the present. I hold them there for ten, nine, eight, seven – someone knocks on the door – *I'll just be a minute!* – six, five, four – the pain turns to an echo as the blood retreats completely – three, two, one. I pull my hands back and they are white like the feeling in my chest. They flush red again when I finally breathe. In, two, three, four. Hold, two, three, four. Out, two, three, four.

I put down the lid of the toilet and check my phone. It has been silent in my pocket all day. I have a few messages from Jazz about a warehouse party in Manor House tonight. Caleb will be there, she tells me with a pregnant ellipsis. I realise, with a stab of hot guilt, that I have two missed called from Grandma. It's 2 a.m. now and far too late to call her back. I make a mental note to do it in the morning but forget about it when I tune in to the conversation on the other side of the bathroom door.

'Blake says she fucks like a pornstar.' The voice, snagged somewhere between drawl and slur, must belong to one of Felix's schoolmates: only they call him by his last name.

'Yeah, mate, French birds are absolutely feral. I was in Montpellier last year and the girls were absolutely frothing.'

'I would love a go on Celine, to be fair.'

'Mate, are you joking? Her name isn't Celine.'

'Yes, it is, mate. Like the singer.'

'What the fuck are you on about?'

'Like, *Titanic*, mate? Are you actually thick? "My Heart Will Go On"?'

'Whatever her name is.'

'But what about that Black kid?'

'Who?'

'Lily's mate. Hangs around Blake all the time. I reckon there's something going on there, you know. You remember those rumours.'

'Yeah, but those were just rumours, mate. Blake says he can't get rid of him. Feels sorry for him. It's a bit tragic, if you ask me.'

'What the fuck is taking so long? Hello? Are you doing a shit in there?'

'Mate, let's just use Blake's room. Do it off a book or something.'

My ear is still pressed against the door and I listen to them creak away to Felix's room. I look at my toothbrush in the cup by the sink and feel the searing prick of tears. I splash cold water on my face and swallow down a shaky breath. I try to minimise their words. I don't even know their names. They can't know Felix like that. Not this Felix, my Felix. But their words, his words, reverberate in my head. *Blake says, Blake says, Blake says.* The white-hot brand of shame, always waiting deep in the burning coal of my subconscious, sears my breast. I feel ridiculous for letting the words of these total strangers burn me like this. But they do.

I trip down the stairs two at a time – maybe the negronis have kicked in: my feet don't want to do what I tell them.

In the kitchen, Felix holds court. On a plate on the counter behind him, a credit card and a rolled-up note call out to me that tonight is one of those nights for him. Their frequency has increased lately and I feel powerless in the face of Felix's impulses. He sees me notice and a challenge flares in his eyes. To his right, a pretty girl is laughing at one of his stories. I walk to him and go to put my hand around his waist, but he turns towards his companion and my hand finds the polished wood countertop. He introduces her as Cecily Scott, a playwright, then lists her accolades. She looks expectantly at me, and I pause, waiting for Felix.

'This is my dear friend.'

Shame burns my flesh and I feel my cheeks flush. My heart pounds as I contort my face into a smile. My jaw is set hard. I take the note, scrape up the dregs of cocaine and snort it. Felix looks at me with bemused approval, but his face falls as I offer him a fist bump and a curt goodbye.

'I've got another party to get to. Happy birthday, mate.'

I push through the strangers dancing in the living room and out into the corridor. I feel Felix following behind me, waylaid by well-wishers, and not wanting to make a scene. I grab my keys from the bowl and step out into the chilly air without a coat, leaving the door open behind me. Felix stops at the threshold, apparently above chasing me into the street. I can hear him calling after me, half shout, half whisper. I don't turn back.

*

I regret not bringing a jacket. No one can hear my hammering on the warehouse door, a fire exit that I cannot open from the outside. Jazz's phone is ringing out and I don't have anyone else's number. I scroll through Instagram and find Caleb's profile. It's sparse, a few photos – the most recent is from over a year ago – and there is nothing on his Stories. I take a chance and tap out a message anyway.

Me

02:48

Hey! Are you at this party with Jazz? I'm stuck outside and kind of need saving.

I shiver. My thin linen shirt does nothing to keep the chill night air off my skin. Felix's shirt. I am about to give up. I check Citymapper. It's going to take me almost two hours to get all the way back to Tooting and my phone is almost out of battery. The bass from inside gets momentarily louder then fades again as a door inside is opened and closed. Excited voices approach and the door swings open with a clunk. A group spills out, colourfully dressed and moving as one fluid animal. One of them, a tall girl in zebra-print jeans, knocks into me, and her friend, wrapped in a canary-yellow fur coat, starts to apologise then cuts themself short.

'Holy shit – hello, stranger.' I almost don't recognise them. Their head is shaved to a tight crop and they have bleached their eyebrows white, but their face and voice are unchanged.

'Dot? What the hell are you doing here?'

'It's nice to see you too, sweetie.'

The questions pour out of me. Cords of concern and relief and anger that have wound themselves tightly around me over the last few weeks unravel. I take out my phone to call Lily, but Dot stops me with a look. The phone is dead anyway. They tell their friends to go ahead, that they're going to stay for a bit, that I'm basically family. I feel warmth wash up from my chest. The friends look me up and down, decide I don't pose any particular threat, and step off into the night. Dot swiftly catches the fire door to keep it from closing. They follow me inside. We pass a couple stretched out together, embracing on the concrete floor, lost in their own world. A door at the end of the corridor is guarded by a skinny boy with a hot-pink buzzcut and a clipboard. He looks at me quizzically for a moment before Dot shows him a black plastic wristband and he stamps my hand and waves us through. The door opens onto a massive dancefloor. The music and the heat pulse through me like a wave. Dot takes my hand and leads me around the edge of the vibrating mass of bodies. We head for another door and up a concrete staircase that takes us round and round until we walk out onto the roof. There's a metal brazier with a fire burning inside it, around which people sit in little groups, chatting and smoking cigarettes, or silently staring into the flames, cradling friends' heads in their laps. The city stretches out. Dot lights up a joint and offers me a sleeve of their fur coat. I slip into it, and we sit with our arms around each other while they fill me in on the last few months.

'I should have called, I know. I'm sorry. But I just didn't know what to say. I've been fine though – honestly, better than fine. I'm thriving, man. The House is a prison, honestly. Like, everyone thinks their family is fucked up, right? But, like, mine – ours – is next level. I've been crashing with a friend in Finsbury Park. Cressie, Cressida – the one who almost flattened you outside – has a spare room in her dad's house. It's not like I've been living in a squat. And I've joined a band. They were just getting some cool gigs when Jazz introduced me to this guy from the band, Ebenezer, and they needed another singer, so I—'

'Jazz?'

'Uh, yeah. So, she introduced me to the guys and they are super chill and their sound is awesome. We're called the Scrooges and we've—'

'Hang on a second. Jazz has known where you were this whole time? I've been so worried about you, and she never once thought to maybe tell me you were okay?' Things have been awkward between Jazz and me since our fight at the hospital, but this information still stings.

'Woah, chill. I made her promise not to tell you. I'm sorry, I just couldn't hack the Blake family psychodrama. And, like, we all know Annie and David have got your balls in a vise and I didn't want her turning up on my doorstep.'

My stomach twists and I feel a rush of embarrassment. Do they all know about my meals with Annie? And what do they know about my promotion at work? These thoughts flicker through my mind and I think of how to explain myself, but instead find myself saying that their parents might just need some time to adjust.

'Adjust to what?' Dot looks quizzically at me and then twigs. 'Oh, shit. Oh my God, you all think this about my gender. Is that what my parents told you? Fuck, those two are properly mental. I honestly couldn't give a fuck about what pronouns they use for me. They can't misgender me. Nobody can. That stuff is for me. It's personal. Like, you can choose to respect me, or you can choose to be a dickhead, but that's on you. I tried to let them in, and they want to be pricks about it, but that's their problem. No, as always, the truth is way worse, darling.'

Dot explains the conversation they had with Annie and David the night they left the House. Simon had been over for dinner and Dot had refused to say hello or eat with them, staying in their room until he left. They were summoned downstairs after he'd gone and were dressed down for being so rude, and decided they'd had enough. They said they were putting their foot down. That they refused to be in the same room as Simon. Because of what he'd done. Or had tried, that night at the Chateau, when I'd found them in the pool. It had been swept away into a corner, at first a looming presence, and then, gradually, fading until it was nothing more than an ugly stain the Blakes tried to forget. As Dot tells me the truth, confirming what I hadn't wanted to believe, I feel the dormant guilt unfurling like a poisonous weed in my belly.

That night wasn't the first time Simon had tried something, Dot tells me. For as long as they could remember, Dot had been wary of Simon. He was always too close to them, his compliments lingered like saliva on a cheek from an unwanted kiss. Dot describes how he would bounce them on his knee when they were younger, holding too tightly on to their hips. How he would somehow always manage to find them alone together. Always subtle, never explicit, never anything Dot could tell someone, never anything anyone would believe. But it made Dot feel guilty, dirty somehow, as if they had done something wrong.

That night in France, though, he crossed a line. He found Dot alone in the kitchen, as he had done a thousand times before, but this time, Dot says, it felt different. He was drunk, his eyes glazed with booze and anger. He told Dot he knew how they felt about him, how there was nothing wrong with it, how they were old enough now. He stepped towards Dot, who backed away but found themself pressed against the cold marble worktop, knocking their glass to the floor. He kissed them hard, trying to force his foul tongue into their mouth. Dot scratched at his face but he did not pull away. He tried to slither his hand up their dress, which tore up the seam exposing their thigh. He bent down to bite at the naked flesh and Dot used the moment to elbow Simon in the back of the head. He stumbled back and Dot fumbled behind themself, finding a drawer; their fingers scrabbled and found a bread knife. Simon laughed, Dot tells me, and asked them what they were going to do. When Dot sliced the serrated edge deep into their palm, Simon stopped laughing. Dot told Simon that if he took one more step towards them, they'd cut off his balls. He'd spat that no one would believe them and stormed out into the party.

This is how I'd found them that night. Trembling and bleeding on the flagstones. When I went to find help, find someone who could handle things better than me, they'd got up and walked to the edge of the pool. Dot says they didn't want to drown. They just wanted to wash off the blood and the feeling of Simon's filthy hands. But when they were in the water, it filled their dress, the little embroidered flowers bleeding into the silk. They were dragged down, and the water filled their ears and nose and mouth and for a moment they forgot everything except the sharp pain in their hand and the frantic beating of their heart. When I pulled them out, they thought that everything was going to be okay.

'Did you know I had the biggest crush on you that holiday? You were so shiny and new and normal. So far away from all the posturing and the games and the bullshit and the fuckery. I think that's why everyone loves you so much. Because you're nothing like us,' they say.

'Dot, I'm so, so sorry that happened to you. I should have—'

'Don't be. It wasn't you that did it. Anyway, I told all of this to David and Annie. She believed me, I could see it in her eyes, but he didn't, and so I left. It's as simple as that.'

'Dot, this is serious. We need to do something.'

'Don't. Please. Don't tell anyone. It won't do anything.
It's ancient history. And I can't have everyone treating
me like I'm some damaged, delicate little doll. Fuck sympathy, I'm fucking fine. I guess I wanted to you know
because . . . I dunno, I guess I trust you. So don't fuck
that up by telling the others. Our little secret, okay?'

I agree not to say a word. Dot makes me promise, we
wrap our little fingers around each other's, then huddle
closer together under the fur coat.

We watch the sun slowly rise over the city. There is
something special about dawn, I think. Sunset is for
everyone. For lovers and painters and commuters and
mothers calling children in for tea. But dawn, I think, is
preserved for a chosen few. Only those with the determination to see the night to its blissful end or those
incapable of waiting to start the new day are afforded a
glimpse of the subtle, wonderous, eternal change from
one into the other. Eventually the fire dies and though
the music still shakes the building downstairs, we decide
it is time to leave. Dot fumbles in their pockets but they
cannot find their keys. They reluctantly agree to come
with me back to Tooting and we step out into the secret
dawn. On the bus, they rest their head on my shoulder
and immediately fall asleep. It's almost 10 a.m. when we
finally reach my flat. Jazz still isn't home. Dot makes a
pot of tea, while I find a charger for my phone. I turn it
on, expecting texts or a missed call from Felix, but find
nothing. I open Instagram and he hasn't messaged me
there either. I have a single notification.

Caleb
03:05
Hey cutie! Coming to find you!

03.08
Guessing you made it in? Find me on the dancefloor.

04.36
I'm heading home but we should hang soon x

I don't know what to respond, so I flick back to the home page and something catches my attention. Celeste's profile icon sits at the top of my screen, ringed in green. I tap the icon and see a picture she has posted to just a handful of her 'close friends', of which I am suddenly one. The picture shows her and Felix in our bed – Felix's bed. They are both clearly naked, though the sheets are pulled up to hide most of her body, Felix's head is slightly turned away from the camera but he's clearly identifiable. *Hung-over birthday cuddles* reads the caption. I pull up Caleb's message again and type out my reply, pressing send before I lose my nerve.

Me
10.03
Sorry, phone died then a friend found me. Headed home too but would love to hang. Lmk when x

November

'It wouldn't be proper,' Felix says, biting my neck harder. 'Two young men, sharing a room like that.' He pushes his middle finger into my mouth to wet it then finds the gap in my waistband and moves his hand to press between my cheeks. 'What would people think?'

His touch forces out a breath, which clouds up the mirror in front of my face. My hands are on the dresser, and I'm bent forward, close enough that I can almost kiss my reflection. Felix doesn't break eye contact. It feels like he is staring through me, pulling me into the glass with his eyes as he pushes his fingers further inside me. His other arm is around my neck, the point of his elbow forcing my chin up, so I am looking up at him. I see my expression twisted with want. I am desperate for him.

'What would they all think if they knew?' he says, twisting his hand at the same time that he bites my ear. I let out a low, involuntary moan and feel Felix's cock get harder. He takes it in his hand and pushes himself into me. It's slow and he uses his grip around my throat to force my eyes back to his. He starts to fuck me, rocking his hips back and forth. The speed builds and he pulls my hands behind my back, holding both of my wrists in one hand while the other reaches inside my mouth, forcing it open.

I hear a change in his breathing and his body starts to tighten. He releases my hands to hold on to my hips so he can push himself deeper. I reach for my dick and feel pleasure swell within me. Felix's breath turns to a grunt, and he jerks forwards. As we both cum there is a crack of pain in my forehead and I see stars bursting over his face, distorted in the mirror. His breathing slows but mine is still ragged, craving more. He slips out of me and steps back, pulling up his trousers. He points at the mirror, which has a crack, like a lightning bolt, right through its centre. A bright pearl of red beads at my hairline then slides down towards my eye. Felix catches the blood with his thumb and puts it to his mouth.

'Silly boy,' he says. 'Look what you've done.'

We arrived at Allenbury earlier in the day, driving up the motorway under a hard, blank sky. It felt as if it never got light; we passed from night to twilight and back again without glimpsing the day. In the car, Lily and Dot sat in the back, chattering and swapping stories about the house and their trips there. Dot reluctantly agreed to come on this trip after Annie found out where they'd been staying through her network of informants. It took some serious convincing that I wasn't been the source of the leak before Dot believed me. But they came anyway, on the condition that neither Simon nor David were mentioned in their presence.

During the drive, Felix said little. Our truce is still uneasy, and we skirt around the edge of his birthday like cautious children exploring a frozen lake. I know that if either of us ventures too far into what happened that night, we will fracture this fragile peace and be pulled under. I stayed at my place in Tooting for two days afterwards and when I got back to his, Felix slapped me once, hard, across the face, then kissed me. We wept, kissing away each other's tears then held each other close, wrapped in the burning sweetness of our fury. There's a strain within me when we're apart, like a steel cable pulled taut. I feel the tension still, even though he is here. He feels so far away. We have been fucking almost constantly but I don't think he's said more than ten words to me. The sex is rough. I like it. I hate that I like it so much.

At some point we pulled off the grey motorway, which immediately gave way to winding country roads and villages with vaguely familiar names, like people you've heard mentioned in stories but never actually met. The sky here clings to low, rolling hills. I know that somewhere nearby there are moors – haughty and purple and wide – that separate these country dales from the mills and memories and mess of the city I used to call home. We turned on to ever-narrower, twisting lanes and eventually followed a high sandstone wall to an ornate gate flanked by two winged lions, carved out of the same stone, which glowed in the claggy half-light. The expansive lawns of Allenbury Hall were a muffled grey, lapped by swirling silver mist. On either side of the long, straight drive towering trees bowed their solemn heads as we passed. Felix rolled down the windows and the cold air and the rustle of leaves flooded the car, silencing his siblings' chatter and turning our breath to frosted clouds.

'If you close your eyes, the wind in the poplars sounds like the ocean,' he said. I did and found that he was right. When I opened my eyes again, he was smiling at me for the first time in weeks.

Felix shrouds the mirror in a thick embroidered throw and winks at me. Some say that a covered mirror prevents a soul from getting trapped between the worlds of the living and the dead. I wonder what lost, dead things here are in need of release. He pulls me into an embrace. I find myself murmuring an apology. I don't know if I'm talking about the mirror or something else. He squeezes me and tells me it's going to be okay. I do not believe him. I go to my room – linked to his by an adjoining door – to splash water on my face. The porcelain basin is scattered with a fine web of cracks and the ornate brass tap groans before yielding its icy water. The blood from my forehead turns the drops of water coppery brown, and I press some tissue into the cut to stem the flow. By the time it has stopped and I walk back through Felix's room he has already gone, so I find my way through the creaking house alone.

If possible, the Hall is even more oppressively grand from inside. Long, straight corridors stretch the length of the house, the floors covered with a patchwork of plush Persian rugs. Wood-panelled walls hide doors to servant corridors and staircases, which connect the family's rooms to the working bowels of the house. Ancient radiators pump out heat, which condenses on huge windows hung with tasselled velvet curtains. Gilt-framed portraits of elegant ancestors and pot-bellied horses huddle on every inch of wall. I listen for a voice I can follow, but the mist and the vastness of the house wraps me in silence. Instead, I wander without direction, hoping to come across someone who might point me in the right one. I descend a flight of stairs to find a small room with a flagstone floor and a heavy wooden door. Muddy boot prints, red-brown leaves, and a surprising chill in the air suggest the door has been recently used.

'Are you lost?'

The voice makes me jolt. I begin to mumble an apology to the tall, pretty young woman who is peeling off a dripping tweed jacket. She balances on one socked foot as she pulls off her second black boot and stretches out her hand towards me. I can't tell if she wants a handshake or assistance balancing so end up giving her both.

'Millie Teller,' she tells me. 'You must be that friend of Felix's.' She gives me a curious look, as if suddenly a puzzle she's been stuck on has started to make sense. She winks. 'You're the one who brought the prodigal child back from the brink, I hear. Lots of Brownie points for you.'

'I was just trying to find the, er, the drawing room? Felix said something about drinks before dinner, but I lost him after we— After I went to freshen up.'

She raises an eyebrow and I blush, hoping she doesn't notice. 'Have you seen Magpie? Or Dad or Annie?'

'Lily said she was going to find your brother, I think. And Annie and Henry said they were going to look around the rose garden before tea.'

'The rose garden! There's one I've not heard before. So, everybody in the house is shagging apart from me. It's all getting a little bit Shakespearean, don't you think?'

She turns and heads off down a passageway, her dark, damp curls bouncing just above her waist and leaving a wet triangle on the seat of her tight sand-coloured jodhpurs.

Millie passes around crystal glasses with a drop of ruby-red damson gin in the bottom while her brother, Hugo, tops them up with champagne. Annie and Captain Henry sit together on a deep blue high-backed velvet sofa. Dot is sitting cross-legged on the floor, their back against one of the sofa's arms, stretching out their legs in front of the fire, which writhes in the hearth. Lily sits and flirts with Hugo while Felix eyes them both silently. He, like me, has probably had her cry on his shoulder over this man. These two families have a twisting, convoluted history. Shared childhood, shared adolescence, shared secrets. The walls of Allenbury Hall hum with collective memory. The room is hazy with the warmth of the fire and the things everyone refuses to acknowledge.

Millie is telling the story of the time they thought they'd lost Dot. On one of the many long holidays spent here, cousins and family friends had descended for some birthday or anniversary. Most of the adults had gone out for an afternoon ride, setting out on favourite horses across the dusky moors. Millie's mother, Effy, had drawn the short straw and had agreed to stay home and watch the children. Twelve of them, varying in age from Hugo, who was eleven, all the way down to Dot who was barely three years old. They'd decided, as children often do, to play hide and seek. Across a house like this one, a single round can last a whole afternoon. They had scattered, through the corridors and passageways, into corners and niches and nooks that only children could know. Felix, who was always great at seeking and knew the house as well as the Tellers, had found most of them pretty quickly, but Dot was nowhere to be seen. The rest of the children searched for what felt like hours, first as one big group, then as smaller teams. Eventually, they decided that they should commit the cardinal sin of childhood games and tell an adult. They found Effy and owned up that they could not find the toddler. It was only when they saw the fear in Effy's eyes that the children themselves became frantic. Were the doors left open? Had Dot wandered out? Had anyone checked the pond? By the time they found Dot, who had fallen asleep in a pile of empty hatboxes under one of the beds, Effy's face was tear-streaked and Hugo was in a lot of trouble.

'Wasn't that when you and Felix had your first kiss?' teases Hugo.

'Don't be disgusting,' laughs Millie. 'I was six! No, our first kiss was in the walk-in fridge off the staff kitchen when *you* cut the wires to the fuse box while the grownups were having supper and almost electrocuted yourself.'

'Oh, sorry, my mistake. There have been a lot of firsts in this house, haven't there?' Hugo looks to Lily who giggles as her cheeks go rosy.

'Was that when you two had your first kiss as well?' says Dot, gesturing towards Annie and Teller. 'How poetic.'

There's a rigid silence. I watch Annie decide to let this go, anger flashing in her brown eyes. Nobody says anything. Mercifully, a metallic clang breaks the moment. The gong has been rung for dinner.

They don't usually have a full service, Hugo tells me as we walk through to an enormous dining room, but they get one in for shoot weekends. The room is strung with stag heads, some of them furry and whole with glassy eyes, some stripped to white skulls with blank sockets and many-pointed antlers. There are only eight of us at a table that could seat twenty, and we are spaced comically far apart. Over dinner, expensive red wine flows into the stories they swap across the table. The laughter seems to fill the empty spaces between us. There is another roaring fire in the grate here and I absent-mindedly wonder who lit it, whether it's been burning all day in a room that will only be used for an hour or two. The conversation turns to tomorrow and who is coming, their previous faux pas, and who not to be stood next to if you want to claim your own successful shots.

'Have you ever fired a gun?' Hugo asks me. 'Shotgun, I mean.'

He says this with a laugh and everyone else at the table laughs too. I force a smile and tell him I haven't.

'Don't worry. I hear Felix is very good at guiding people through their first time.'

His father coughs and Lily spits out some of her wine. Millie changes the subject.

'Well, Dot won't be firing a gun at all. Last time they did, poor Jimmy ended up with an arse full of lead.'

'In my defence, it was a very foggy day.'

'Did you not hear them say that ground game was off-limits? I think that includes the gamekeeper,' jokes Teller.

'I thought he was a fox,' says Dot with a completely straight face.

'Where did you come from, anyway?' Hugo asks when the laughter dies down.

'Excuse me?' I say, looking him in the eye. His history with Lily and his attitude today has encouraged a hostility that surprises even me. Still, I do not look away.

'What I mean,' he says, reaching for more wine, happy to have riled me, 'is where on earth were the Blakes lucky enough to find such a charming young man?'

'We met at Newcastle,' says Lily.

'Ah, the Magpie strikes again. You always did have an eye for shiny trinkets, didn't you, Lil? This one's stuck around for a while, hasn't it? Must have got its teeth into you all.'

Felix, who has quietly shifted his chair to be closer to mine, makes me jump by sliding his arm around my shoulders. 'I expect he'll be around for a lot longer. And personally, if I had the infamous Teller receding jawline,

I'd watch what I said about other people's teeth. Now, would you stop be an insufferable prick and pass the wine?'

When we have finished and our custard-smeared bowls have been cleared away, Annie and Teller excuse themselves while their children raise their eyebrows at one another. We move through into the billiards room, which, true to its name, is mostly occupied by a huge baize-covered snooker table. Hugo sets up for a game while the others cluster by yet another fire and roll cigarettes. There is masculine push and pull between Hugo and Felix, as if they are both jostling for the position of leader. Felix turns down the offer of a game.

'Why don't we do something actually fun?' he says, pulling out a small packet of small brownish crystals and flicking it with his middle finger.

Felix's drug-taking had seemed glamorous and fun until it suddenly wasn't. Those first few months after we met were a blur of parties and nightclubs and vivid kisses. Once we flew to Berlin and stayed a full weekend inside a club that felt like a cathedral of black glass. As the bass pulsed it ripped through everything, tearing the air into shimmering crystalline shards. Under a strobe light Felix moved to me, God-like, and kissed my neck. Chemical bliss surged in my veins. At another party, Felix once pulled me through a skylight and out onto a sloping roof where, starry-eyed, we watched as the gentle sun lit the sparkling towers of the city and turned the Thames from black marble into shimmering rose quartz. I wanted to dance out into the middle of it, and in that moment believed I could. At a dinner party in Chelsea, a borrowed wing-collar scratching my neck, we exchanged blue-mouthed kisses and metal straws as a silver platter of perfect white powder passed from left to right around a table. In Felix's flat, we'd waste whole weekends, clouded in weed smoke, ordering takeaways. He kept his drugs in a large turquoise-blue Tiffany's giftbox, and he'd sit with it on his knees, pushing through bags of various pills and powder to roll us a fresh joint, while I sank further into the sofa and we swapped our favourite songs. Nina, Billie, Solange, Erykah, Sade, Tyler, Frank, Bey, Rih. Love on the brain and all around us. One of Felix's hands casually tapping ash into a blue teacup, the other finding its way up the leg of my shorts.

The first time we fought was when I told him, in front of some friends, that maybe he'd had enough, that maybe we should call it a night and get some sleep. His eyes didn't leave mine as he crushed two green pills, rolled up a ten-pound note, snorted it all, then told me bedtimes were for cunts. When he came down at some point the next afternoon, he told me that if I ever spoke to him like that in front of his friends again, it would be over. When he wanted me to go to some party or stay out past five, they were our friends. When I needed putting back in my place, they were his.

*

'Can you feel it kicking in?'

The teacup we are using as an ashtray is fuller now and the abandoned balls of Felix's and Hugo's game flicker in the firelight. Hugo has built it up high with dry logs and we are sitting on the floor, staring into the flames.

'I definitely feel something,' says Millie. 'But maybe it's just the fire. Did you know that anthropologists think that staring into fire might be what made us human? Early human species discovered fire and that allowed us to cook food and keep predators away and whatever. But there's this theory that human consciousness, the very essence of what it is to know you exist, was a side-effect of staring into the flames. That we developed the ability to contemplate by watching the flickering of this terrible and beautiful thing. This beast that we domesticated so we could cook our meat and sleep without fear of wolves. And that by that fire, the first thoughts, the first ideas, the first dreams were forged in those early human minds.'

'You're definitely high,' says Dot. 'Oh my God, I've got a great idea.'

Having learned from past mistakes, the Blake–Teller children now only play hide and seek if there are some ground rules. We agree that we all have to stay on the ground floor, no one is allowed outside, and that once you're caught, you have to join the seeker. Dot starts to count to 100 and we scatter from the billiards room. Lily slips into the dining room while Felix sprints down the long corridor. I find myself back in the entranceway where I first bumped into Millie. There's a dark wooden door on one wall. I open it and am confronted with a sea of tweed coats. I slip myself between them and am enveloped in a comforting, earthy scent that wraps itself around me. I can feel the drug coursing through me, it hits the center of my chest like a heartbreak. I want to weep, to laugh, to cry out with the rediscovered joy of this juvenile game. I feel like I might burst as I huddle and wait to be discovered in this small dark space. I hear footsteps on the stone floor. Someone is approaching my hiding place. A hand on the door. It swings open and Millie throws herself inside where she collides with me.

'Oh God, sorry, didn't realise you were in here.' Her voice is slightly slurred and I imagine her jaw churning in the darkness.

'God, you're really beautiful, aren't you? Look at your skin. Can I kiss you?' She presses her body closer to mine. 'Oh my God, of course not, that's definitely the mandy talking. I'm so sorry. No, don't go. If you go out there we'll both be caught.' She pauses and our breath fills the space. 'Felix has already caught you though, hasn't he? I'd know that look anywhere, I've seen it in the mirror. You're mad for him. And I'm assuming it's reciprocated, otherwise why the hell would you be here?

'I'd always suspected he might be . . . you know, but I thought it was just me being self-centred? Making up excuses for why he didn't like me back. Now it's confirmed I'm not sure I feel any better. Good for you though. It's so lovely to be in love.'

I smile despite myself but also wish she would stop talking in case Dot approaches.

'Can I offer you some advice? Be careful. That family, they . . . destroy things. They see something they want, and they take it. Look, I'm not going to pretend that my parents were happy. I mean, whose are, really? And my mum is pretending to be fine. She's off in Greece living her best life, but I know that this destroyed her. I can see it in her eyes every time she talks about it, every time she thinks about him. Did you know they denied it? For years. Told her she was jealous, told her she was imagining things, that she was going crazy, and when it all came out she didn't say, "How could you?" She didn't say, "I fucking knew it, you cheating bastard." No. When he sat down and told her that he'd been cheating on her for years she just sighed and said, "I know," and walked out. I think after all this time, after all those tiny heartbreaks, she wasn't even able to feel the full weight of the betrayal,' she sighs, her eyes burning into mine. 'That's what I mean when I say they destroy people. They grind them down until there's nothing left there that's actually a person. So, be careful, yeah?'

I don't have anything to say to that.

Millie and I are the last to be found. That makes us joint winners, but I don't feel like I've won. We all go back to the billiards room and talk and dance and laugh and smoke and eventually, one by one, Lily, Millie, then Dot peel off to bed. Us boys stay and talk about nothing until the crackle of gravel outside announces the arrival of morning and the first beaters. Hugo, suddenly sober and swearing, staggers off promising strong coffee and bacon sandwiches. Felix says he has something to show me. He takes me by the hand and leads me through the house. We go through a door behind a panel in the wall and take a service staircase all the way up. When we reach the top, we have to stoop through a low corridor which is more like a tunnel. At the far end is a small door. Felix forces it open, covering himself in dust. We emerge into the darkness of the early-winter morning. It is freezing cold, and a shiver sets into my bones. Felix lights a cigarette and leans against the crenelated wall. He looks out at the dark shapes of the landscape. The wine and the drugs have softened him. He is moony. Misty-eyed. I pull him into an embrace. He says he's sorry. I squeeze him and tell him it's going be okay. I don't believe it.

While we take turns showering and trying to snatch five minutes of sleep, the rest of the shooting party arrives in Range Rovers and BMWs and the beaters come in muddy Land Rovers. Beaters, Felix informs me, are the people paid to drive the birds out from the safety of their nests with sticks and dogs ready for the paying guests who wait with their guns. I tell him it doesn't seem fair that the pheasants' only choices are to be torn apart by dogs or shot while trying to escape. Felix just laughs and tells me that most of them choose to fly away. I tell him that a choice between death or freedom is not really a choice at all.

The cold that seeped in this morning has not left and I take Felix's lead and wear pyjamas under my clothes. I pull on the stiff three-quarter-length trousers and bright purple socks. There are woollen garters to keep the socks up and I struggle to tie them without a huge lump showing. Felix ties my tie for me, which is printed with tiny birds, partridges caught in flight. This seems, to me, a bit obvious. We wrap ourselves in layer after layer of brown and green and grey. The birds can't see very well, I am told: we will be well camouflaged.

Outside, on the wide terrace overlooking the sweeping lawn, we eat bacon rolls and drink strong black coffee, passed around by Hugo and Millie, who look remarkably fresh. The gamekeeper, Jimmy, is ruddy and jovial. He claps his rough hands around mine and asks if I'll be taking a shot today. Felix tells him that I will.

The shooters shake hands with the beaters but drift back to their side of the terrace and talk about their drives and deals and indiscretions. I have no interest in the gossip of men, and I am so tired I can barely follow the conversation anyway. An elderly man says he's never seen me before and asks how long I've been working at the estate. Teller appears by my side to correct him, and the man apologises profusely then shakes my hand with an overly tight grip. A hulking tweed jacket lumbers toward me. It stretches out a sleeve and a big red hand appears.

'You're the piano chap, right?' booms a voice from within the layers of scarves and flat cap that hide the man's face. 'Mark Quant. We met at the Chateau. I've been on to Cass about getting you in front of that admissions panel, you know. She's very keen to hear what you've got to say. Or play, I suppose!' He guffaws at his own joke.

I start to thank him, to try to nail down a date or get an email address, but Teller clears his throat and welcomes everyone. He goes through the rules of the day, which I don't listen to. The shooters line up and take little metal rods from a leather wrap. They are numbered corresponding to the pegs from which each person will start the day then moving up two at a time as we progress.

We set off on foot up a muddy path onto the moor. In the pocket of my coat I have a flask of damson gin and a plastic handwarmer, boiled in a pot of water on the Aga this morning. I click a little metal button inside it and a chemical reaction crystalises the gel inside, releasing the trapped heat within. Felix and I have been lent Dipper, a sleek black Labrador belonging to the Tellers, who dutifully trots beside us as we traipse towards our first peg: a wooden post knocked into the ground with a yellow number 8 stapled to it. Mist curls its tendrils around our boots and the grass on the bank in front of us is silvery with frost. Once everyone has taken their place, a distant whistle sounds. A minute or two passes, then the frightened birds begin to fly. Agitated black dots cascade over the ridge.

Felix is an excellent shot. Birds crumple mid-flight and fall around us. Downy feathers dance through the chilly air and bodies hit the hard earth with a nauseating thud. The sound of delicate flight cut short is surprisingly loud.

The birds have been fattened by autumnal plenty and now is the time for harvest. Dipper obediently waits for a nod from Felix, then slinks away to collect the dead. Another whistle marks the end of the frenzy. Felix has killed eight birds, four brace, he says. He piles the bodies by the post and we set off to another peg. We continue on like this all morning, while the pale light breaks over the purple heather. At one point we stop for sausage rolls and prosecco and soup. The men compare kills and admire each other's weapons.

After the break, Felix tells me it is my turn. Reluctantly, I take the shotgun from him. It is heavy and cold to the touch. My hands are shaking when he hands it over. Felix dryly asks if I am chilly. He adjusts my posture for me, turning my hips to the side with his hands, putting both arms around me to rearrange my own, pressing my cheek into the cold wooden stock.

The whistle goes and the birds make their break for escape once more. I slide off the safety catch and point the barrels of the gun aimlessly into the whiteness of the sky. As I pull the trigger, I involuntarily close my eyes. There is a deafening crack and a searing, tearing pain in my right shoulder. My arm is thrown back, and the gun slips from my grasp. It hits the frozen ground and the second shot fires. I fall backwards.

When I look to Felix, he is bent double. Horror floods through me. I scramble to my feet and run to him. He is on his hands and knees now. His whole body is shaking. I vomit grey lumps of sausage and pastry onto the grass.

Felix makes a sound like a wounded animal, then turns and falls onto his back. He is convulsing and his face is twisted with pain. I put my hands on him, looking for a wound. There is no blood. Then I realise he is laughing. I pound my fists against his chest and he laughs harder. It's a panicked laughter.

'I thought I'd killed you.'

'So did I for a second. Jesus Christ.' His laughter subsides and I collapse onto the ground next to him. 'I think you got one.'

Dipper streaks off into the heather and comes back with the limp, lifeless thing between her jaws. It is tiny. Light, speckled brown with a long, straight beak which is rimmed with blood.

'It's a fucking woodcock,' he tells me. 'Nice shot.'

I am still trembling when the final whistle blows, and we make our way back to the rest of the group. Felix is holding the little bird by the neck. As we approach the party, he holds it triumphantly aloft. Hugo points out that this is my first kill and a cheer goes up from the men. Tradition dictates that I must be 'blooded'. I decline before I even know what it means, but am overruled.

'Not much blood in a woodcock,' says Jimmy.

He takes out a pocketknife and makes a nick in the bird's neck. A thin stream of red trickles onto his fingers. Felix takes the bird from him and gives it a squeeze, which turns my stomach. He takes a step towards me and smears his blood-soaked fingers across my cheeks and forehead. It's slick and cold and a trickle of it runs onto my lips. I gag at the coppery taste. His thumbnail catches the scab from the broken mirror and a flash of pain makes me gasp as my own blood mixes with the bird's. There is a quadbike pulling a trailer on which pairs of pheasants and partridges have been tied together with twine and strung up. He tosses the little bird onto the trailer. Despite the cold, a few flies buzz around the dead animals. I have a flash of memory: Felix's arms drenched in red, a lifeless deer pulled mercifully to the side of the road. There is no mercy in the killing today. We walk back to the house. The blood dries on my face. We thank the beaters and the shooters tip Jimmy with twenty-pound notes disguised as handshakes. At dinner, I cannot eat. The dried blood flakes off my face and falls into my food.

Uncle Henry got his hair cut every other Saturday in the front room of a terraced house in Blackford Bridge. He used to take me with him. A man's relationship with his barber, he told me once, is as important as his relationship with God. Back then I believed in God, and I believed the words of men like Uncle Henry. I would sit silently on the low brick wall outside the house or on the floor in the carpeted living room, depending on the weather. The makeshift barbershop was much livelier than the sparse church hall Grandma would take me to on Sundays, but somehow felt just as sacred. Uncle Henry would sip on cans of beer or ginger ale and wait his turn. He'd swap stories with the other men, huge and faceless and brash. All of them knew me and would ruffle my hair with rough palms that smelled of pipe smoke. They would ask after Grandma and sometimes Mum. I remember feeling anger bubble up inside me when they expressed their pity. They would nod and murmur and say it was such a shame and I would hate them in silence.

When Uncle Henry's turn came, he would sit in the wooden chair in the centre of the room, draped in the plasticky black robe, hands clasped in his lap and stare out the window into nothing. His trims were so frequent that to me his hair always looked exactly the same. The barber would run his clippers across the bumps and rolls and bones of Uncle Henry's head, and microscopic fragments of hair would tumble down into the brown carpet. In late summer, or early winter maybe, the light would fall exactly right so that from where I was sitting, the hairs would dance through golden shafts of air. The barber would take a sharp blade from a paper packet and slide it into the razor. He'd dust the edges of Uncle Henry's hairline with baby powder and scrape away invisible stubble, sharpening the lines. When he got to the nape of his neck, Uncle Henry would bow his head as if in prayer.

Sometimes there were other children there. Almost always boys but occasionally a girl. Always brown-skinned and always darker than me. One time, when I was seven, a boy a little older than me whom I had seen there a few times before asked me if I wanted to check out something cool. He told me that the barber was his cousin and that he could go anywhere in the house that he wanted. This caught my attention because I'd never seen any of the house apart from the living room, the little hall that led on to it, and the tiny toilet under the stairs that smelled, always, of pot pourri. It must have been summer because the net curtains were drawn wide and the front windows were flung open as far as they would go. Old Spice, like incense, wafted through the reverent hush. A battered Bakelite radio crackled with that week's sermon: Brian Lara giving his judgement on so-and-so's top spin, on whether twelve overs was long enough to turn this around. I had been running a toy car across the wall in the garden – making the racing noises in my head to avoid a clip round the ear from Uncle Henry – when the boy approached me.

He told me that his name was Solomon but that everybody apart from his mum called him Sol. His smile made me think that whatever he had to show me must have been very cool indeed. He fizzed with excitement. I said I did want to see something cool and followed him around the side of the house into the little back garden. He told me that the barber wasn't just a barber but also a fisherman. And not just a fisherman but a magic fisherman who caught magic fish. I didn't know whether to believe this older boy. My faith in magic had already begun to wane. But there was this boy, with his wide smile and knowing eyes, telling me it was real. And I believed him.

Sol told me that in order to catch magic fish, you have to use magic bait. Which makes sense if you think about it. Sol told me that the magic bait was special worms that glowed in the dark. But it had to be really, properly dark. And they would not glow if more than one person was looking. They would just look like ordinary worms. He led me towards the small shed at the bottom of the garden and unlocked the padlock on the door. He stood on an overturned bucket to reach a shelf and took down a little metal box with a faded picture on it that I could not make out. He showed me how to open the box then retreated from the shed and closed the door with a click. Sol shouted to me from outside to open the box. I was worried the magic wouldn't work because cracks of light were seeping in through the gaps around the door. Sol told me it would be fine. He impatiently urged me to open the box. I held it in both hands, feeling it buzz with magic power.

The lid was stiff and it took a few attempts to jimmy it off. But when I did I was met, not by magic glowing worms, but a frantic, hissing black mass. Huge, angry bluebottles, the size of my thumbnail, spiralled out of the tin box. I gasped and the flies filled my nose and ears. I tried to scream and they crawled down my throat. I tried to run but Solomon had locked the door from the outside. I thrashed and spat and howled as the flies destroyed me. I knocked fishing rods and rakes and jerry cans of oil to the floor in my desperation. I remember not knowing what was my own howling and what was the sound of the furious swarm.

When someone finally came to deliver me, I could not be soothed. I wailed and Sol was nowhere to be found. I was told to calm down, but the tears wouldn't stop. I could still feel the bluebottles crawling all over my skin. Uncle Henry, still draped in black, dragged me to the car by my ear, shoved me inside and locked the doors. He went back to the living room to finish his trim. When he finally came to drive me home, the heat of his anger was worse than the air trapped with me inside the car. I remember realising that I wasn't in trouble for being where I shouldn't have been. I wasn't in trouble for opening the box or for breaking a fishing rod in my panic to escape. I was in trouble for being inconsolable. I was in trouble for infecting this placid, masculine afternoon with the contagion of my tears. This was not how men behaved, Uncle Henry told me. That was my trespass. And it would not be forgiven.

The house looks empty from the outside. No flowers in the window of the little porch like usual. Curtains drawn. The lights upstairs are all switched off. I wonder for a moment whether Grandma might have gone out and forgotten to tell me. But when I unlock the door, I hear her call out from the lounge. The house feels flattened, devoid of the usual symphony of sights and smells. This place should be a riot of colour and sound, but it's muted. I call out again and Grandma calls back, her voice thin as a reed. Grandma says I'm too big for this house but as I move through the hall it's the house itself that seems small. It closes in around me from all sides, the air hot and tight.

I didn't want Felix to come. I forbade it, actually. After

our trip to Allenbury, I told him that I just wanted some time to myself with Grandma, that I didn't think now was the right time for them to meet. The real reasons rattled around my head, but I didn't dare say them aloud. In my head we were still fighting and allowing him this close felt like losing, like giving in. And maybe I was right, maybe now wasn't the right time to introduce them. Who was I introducing? Who was this boy to me? What did their meeting mean for the boy who'd outgrown this house? This life? Who would I become to Grandma if I told her who I was? She once told me I was the man of this house. What kind of man was I now? I didn't want Felix to come, but right now all I want is his hand in mine.

Grandma is sitting on the plastic-covered sofa in the blue darkness of the morning. The heating's cranked up high but the sight of her makes me feel cold. When did she get so frail? I wrack my brain trying to think of the last time I actually came home and tears prick my eyes as I realise I can't remember. She smiles at me, wide and warm like a shallow wave across hot white sand.

'Sweetness, yuh too skinny. Watta they been feeding yuh inna London?'

This makes me laugh. 'Grandma, I'm fine. I'm sorry I've been away so long. Are you okay? Are things okay?' My accent, I notice has slipped northward, it is rounder, warmer. I wasn't aware it had changed.

She closes her eyes, as if thinking about her response for a moment. Then she sighs. 'Mi irie, son, mi irie.'

I ask if she's eaten. She tells me she has but I know she

is lying. Seeing her here, in context, I am worried about her. It's easier to hide over the phone. When she tells me she's fine, all I have to go on are her words and the spaces between them. But here I can see the evidence of aging. It's in the chair that has clearly been slept in. It's in yesterday's teacups, which normally would have been washed and put away. It's in the dust on the mantle above the glowing electric fire. It's in the sense that this corner of this room is where she spends most of her day.

The kitchen is the same. At first glance, it is as neat and calm as usual. But the sink is dull with grime, and I can smell something below the spice and lemon-scented Flash. A whisper of neglect. Next to the phone on the little table in the corner, someone has written out important numbers in thick black marker and taped them to the wood. When I open the fridge, the whisper becomes a hum. The bottom drawers are filled with plastic packs of unidentifiable brown vegetables and a thin, rancid liquid that has managed to escape them. There's a carton of milk but I don't think I should trust it. I turn to the cupboard instead and find something tinned and safe and comforting. There's bread in the bread bin and I'm relieved to find that it's sealed and still within its use-by date.

I place the steaming plates of beans on toast on the table and we sit and eat. I give Grandma the vague details of my life and feel the space between us opening up. I know I am pushing her away by keeping the details from her, but where do I even begin? I tell her I've been up from London seeing friends. She asks if I've seen Marcus or 'dem oddah boys'. I assume she means Danny and the goth kids and am reassured that her mind is still sharp enough to recall her dislike of my old friends. I think at one point, in some story or other, Felix's name slips out. She doesn't ask any follow-up questions, but she does pause for a second before scooping more baked beans into her mouth with a triangular slice of toast.

I clear away the plates and make Grandma a cup of ginger tea, then set about clearing the rotting food from the fridge. I give the kitchen a good clean and water a dry-looking Scotch Bonnet plant on the windowsill. I collect the sheets from the beds, planning on stuffing them all in the washing machine. Before I go into the spare room, the third room, the one we never use anymore, I take a shaky breath. My heart flips when I realise the bed has been recently slept in. The things that have been bothering me suddenly click into place. The two used teacups, the numbers by the phone in handwriting that is not quite Grandma's.

I strip the bed with shaking hands and take everything down to the kitchen. I put the wash on and roll a cigarette. I smoke it on the concrete step leading out into the garden, which is overgrown with brambles. It does nothing to calm me down. A Lego man I once Super-Glued to the tap of the hose smiles blankly up at me. I planned on staying the night, sorting more stuff out around the house, but I am overcome by the need to run. Inside it feels like I am sucking air through a straw. I splash my face with water, shove my hands into the top drawer of the freezer, count to ten and then back and then ten again, but I cannot force away the feeling that I might die if I don't get out of here. I make an excuse to Grandma about misreading the Sunday train times and set a reminder on the smartphone I bought her to take out the washing when it's done. She looks confused and wounded and it breaks my heart to leave her, but I can't stay here.

'It did nice to see yuh, sweetness,' she tells me. 'Nuh stay away too long. We need yuh.' But I'm already backing away down the path. I can't wait for the bus, so I walk to the end of the road and order an Uber. As I escape towards Piccadilly station, her words ring in my ears. *Nuh stay away too long. We need yuh.*

One word in particular that suggests a truth that tears open something I have spent years trying to keep shut. *We.*

December

Everyone thinks their own Christmas is completely normal. The shape of the day is so set in stone, so deep in the bones of tradition, that it feels impossible that anyone could do it differently. Maybe it's because it's such an early touchstone. I think Christmas is the first thing I remember. The mythology and the ritual and the expectation blend together into something. I thought everyone had a Christmas breakfast of spiced beef with rice and pea until I was laughed at in assembly when I was eight. I thought everyone opened their presents first thing in the morning after crawling into bed with Mum and Grandma, until Mum's bed was somewhere else, and we had to get permission to go and see her and the bed was too small for the three of us to fit.

At the House, there is smoked salmon and champagne for breakfast, and we won't open our presents until after lunch, and we have to sing 'Truly Scrumptious' from *Chitty Chitty Bang Bang* to Dunstable, who has been forced into a cat-sized Christmas jumper and tiny Santa hat and looks thoroughly appalled.

When I was little, if we had people over on Christmas, I was put to work. I would pour Bombay mix into bowls and cut thick slices of hard dough bread ready to be dipped into Grandma's sweet, spicy beef stew. It was always when we felt most like a family, I think. When Mum was still around, she, Grandma and I would bump up against each other in the little house, all doing our bit to get things ready for our guests.

The tree at the Blakes' is enormous. It fills one corner of the huge space they call the drawing room, which they never use apart from when they have guests over (and even then, only the important ones). Old friends and trusted companions are welcomed into the much-friendlier basement kitchen with its chipped slogan mugs and well-used prep-school self-portrait tea towels. The angel at the top of the tree is a brushed copper figure. Its face is a glossy cut-out of a smiling seven-year-old Felix showing off a gap where his front left tooth should be. It brushes the ceiling and some of the tree's branches are bent against the duck-egg walls of the room. The tree sits in a big shiny black pot. It is fully sustainable and can be planted outside, apparently.

We went to pick it up a few weeks ago. The Blake siblings and I piled into David's Range Rover and drove through West London. The garden centre was pristine, with uniformed staff standing in rows beside their fir and spruce counterparts, ready to spring into action. The siblings raced off down an avenue of branches. They are so childlike when they're all together, as if they fall back into themselves. Dot has been cautious since they came back but they love Christmas, and they haven't been able to help themself since the weather turned cold and the decorations went up.

I found myself alone with David, a situation I then realised I pretty much always try to avoid. He cleared his throat and asked me how Grandma was doing. A firm but plausibly deniable reminder of his generosity: when I'd come back from Bury and had told Felix how worried I was about her, he had insisted that the Blakes would help. I'd protested, obviously, but within days Grandma had had a visit from a very friendly, very expensive care worker who'd immediately made her laugh, had made her get up and take a little walk, and had made her a cup of strong sweet tea. There'd been no going back. I told him she was doing fine and thanked him, assuming validation was what he wanted.

'It's, um, the least I could do,' he said, clearing his throat hesitantly. 'You've been a real help these last few . . . Well, Felix is happier and actually working, and Lily loves you. And Dot, well she . . . um . . . Thank you, for bringing my daughter back.'

I didn't correct him and immediately felt a lash of guilt. Lily came bounding over saying they'd found the perfect tree and dragged us over to it. The smiling attendant had already wrapped it in plastic netting and put it on a little trolley. He helped us strap it to the roof of the Range Rover and David tipped him five crisp twenty-pound notes.

Felix is impatient. Incapable of waiting for the rest of the family, he has made himself toast with a thick spread of butter and Marmite. He offers the last bite of a slice to me, and I take it, licking the salt and crumbs from his fingers. Lily and Dot trot down the stairs laughing in their pyjamas. Upstairs, someone slams a door, David shouts that Annie is being immature, and Annie launches into yet another tirade. Last night we went to sleep to the sound of them berating each other and it appears they haven't yet let up yet.

'Can you believe they loved each other once?' says Lily sadly, sneaking a slice from Felix's plate.

Dot snorts. 'Did they though? Or did Annie just see a way to avoid having to re-release her greatest hits album every five years until she died?'

'I think they still do,' mutters Felix. The three of us look at him, varying levels of credulity on our faces. 'Why else would she still be here, if not to try and preserve some of that? And why else would he hate her so much for trying to be happy? For trying to leave him behind?'

'If what they have is love, then I'm not sure I want it,' I say, before I can stop myself.

The shape of Christmas Day is set in stone, so the annual Blake family walk around Hyde Park cannot be skipped, regardless of how fiercely anyone is fighting. We shove jeans and jumpers and coats over our pyjamas – an extra layer of protection against the vicious cold that has soaked into the bones of the city. As we step out onto the steps, Felix pulls me back inside. He loops his orange silk scarf around my neck and uses it to pull me towards him. He kisses me softly and whispers 'Merry Christmas' into my ear. I feel my heart swell with love for him.

There is no snow outside, but a frost descended towards the end of November and turned the earth and the faces of hurried passers-by to iron. But now those faces have fled this part of London – for ski chalets and country manors with roaring fires – and the wide streets and Royal Parks are deserted. The Blakes like it this way: they like the whole park to feel like their own back garden. As we wander the glittering paths and disturb the frozen air with clouds of vigorous breath, we come across just one other person. An elderly woman in a big brown coat sits on a bench and throws bread to the edge of the frozen lake. She is surrounded by hundreds of pigeons. A burst of unnaturally green parakeets pours out of a nearby tree to eat their fill. I don't see any ducks. My phone buzzes in my pocket. I slip off my glove and slide to answer Jazz's call.

'Merry Christmas, WhiteBoy. What weird shit have they got you doing today? Ritually sacrificed an albino stag or something?'

'Merry Christmas, Jazz.' I hang back, motioning to Lily, who has stopped to wait for me, that she can go ahead. 'Very funny. No nothing like that, although we did have to sing to the cat, and now we're walking around Hyde Park pretty much in silence.'

'Just your totally normal, not insane at all Christmas morning then?'

I laugh and ask her about her day. They are at her sister's place in Morden. I can hear the chaos of twenty-plus Nigerian relatives through the phone. She covers the mic for a second to tell them to be quiet and I hear a chorus of complaints and some shuffling as she moves into another room. She has an army of cousins and nieces and nephews, the youngest of whom are about five and are so excited that she has been up since 5 a.m. trying to placate them with songs and crackers snuck from the table until they were allowed to open some presents. She asks me about Grandma, and I feel the guilt swell inside my chest again. She has gotten worse, I tell her. The carer has the day off today, so Grandma is in respite care at a nursing home until the day after Boxing Day. I spoke to her via FaceTime first thing this morning and she seemed okay. Someone had put a paper hat from a cracker on her greying, hot-combed hair. Jazz asks if I'm going to go and see her, and I don't respond. She lets the silence simmer for a second.

'They've set a date.' She pauses, expecting me to know what she's talking about. 'For J's trial. They're not seeing him until March – it's totally fucked. The fourteenth. Keep it free. We're planning something big.'

I don't say anything.

'Look I'm not gonna flog a dead horse, especially today. But I miss you, yeah? We miss you. You haven't been at the flat for weeks, man. Look, Caleb's having a New Year's Eve party at his yard. I'm sure he'd love to see you there. I'd love to see you there. Come through. I'll send you the deets.'

In the background, someone calls her name. Her full, actual Yoruba name, which flows like water and means

'Peace of God'. 'Sorry, angel, gotta bounce. Someone has to show these kids how to steal extra pigs in blankets. See you at New Year's, yeah?'

She hangs up and the joyous disarray behind her clicks into silence. It feels like a slammed door. I realise that I am crying, hot tears burning on my frozen cheeks. I wipe them away with my naked hand and look towards the Blakes who are some way off now. Annie walks a little ahead, while David trails behind. Felix, Lily and Dot walk arm-in-arm, stepping together under the empty silver sky.

We arrive back at the House at the same time as a beetle-green van pulls up outside. A smiling white girl with a ponytail and storybook freckles hops out of the passenger seat and floats towards us. Her companion, the driver, is a surly-looking Black teenager with acne scars across his sloping forehead. He starts unloading dark green plastic trays from the shelves in the back of the little van. He catches my eye and gives me the Nod. I smile and nod back, trying to communicate silently that I don't really know how I've got myself into this either.

'Oh, bugger,' says Annie when she goes to sign the form on the clipboard the white girl has just handed her. 'Bugger, bugger, bugger.'

Originally, this Christmas was supposed to be the usual massive Blake family affair, with cousins, friends and strays from all over descending on the house. But at the last minute Annie decided she wanted to keep it small. Family only, she declared, which made me blush until she explained that included me. She has, however, seemingly forgotten to update the caterers. We watch as the pair unload enough Christmas dinner for nineteen people. When they bring out the second whole turkey, Dot starts to laugh, which sets off Lily, then Felix, then me. After potato tray number four, Annie joins in too. David, unmoved, goes inside to turn on the second oven.

The meal is, obviously, delicious. When we have all had seconds and eventually, forced by Annie, thirds, there seems to be more food than we started out with. Someone muses that we should package it up and take it to a community centre or a homeless shelter, but we don't. The next tradition that isn't a tradition is what the Blakes call the Stocktake. Lily uses her silver fountain pen to write all of our names onto scraps of paper, which she neatly folds and places into a large bowl. Felix plucks a name at random.

'Okay, Lily, you go first,' he says, handing her a small square package wrapped in brightly coloured paper from under the tree. We are sitting around the drawing room on sofas and the floor. Dot has handed round mugs of Baileys.

'Right. So. One thing I'm glad to leave behind this year is . . . God, I dunno. I'm glad you're back Dotty. Dot. It's good to have you here.'

'Hear, hear!' Felix cries and we raise our mugs.

Lily rips the paper off the present, revealing a sleek black box from which she pulls a compact shiny black-and-silver camera lens. She looks at the box again, then holds the lens up to the light, regarding it. A smile breaks across her.

'It's perfect,' she says. 'Thank you. And I guess it ties nicely in to what I'm looking forward to next year.' She pauses. 'I've got a bit of exciting news . . . I sent some photos over to the gallery over on Westbourne Park Road, the ones I took at Carnival. They really liked them. They've offered me a solo exhibition there in the New Year.'

There is a surge of excitement in the room. Annie insists on opening a new bottle of champagne. She pours it into our used mugs. The golden liquid curdles the dregs of creamy liqueur in the bottom of mine. We toast to Lily. She looks at me and I think I see a glimmer of something like doubt glide across her face. But then she smiles.

'Lily, that's amazing. Really,' I say softly, giving her hand a squeeze.

'Alright, alright, that's quite enough of that,' shouts Felix over everyone. He reaches his hand into the bowl and pulls out another folded piece of paper. 'Next up we have . . . Well, would you look at that. Me!'

Annie and I laugh as Dot rolls their eyes and Lily accuses her brother of being a cheat. Felix clears his throat and waits for his family to fall silent.

'One thing I'm grateful to leave behind', he says slowly, 'is the endless squabbling. So, if you two don't pack it in' – he gestures to his parents – 'I'm just going to start phasing you out.'

There's a stiff silence while he quickly unwraps his gift,

a bottle of expensive-looking aftershave from a French perfume house I've never even heard of. He tosses the bottle casually onto the sofa without acknowledging it.

'I've got some pretty exciting news too, actually.'

I feel a tingle at the back of my neck.

'I got a call from Annelise yesterday. Turns out Hollywood loves me. I'm going to be a fucking movie star!'

Annie screams, David says nothing, Lily drops her mug, and Dot abridges all of our reactions with a succinct 'What the fuck?'

I feel like I'm falling through the floor. My head is spinning, and I think I might pass out. I push my hand against a nail sticking out of the hard wooden floor to bring myself back into the room.

'Well, Pinewood, technically. I'm not moving to LA just yet. I can't really say any more right now, but it's big.'

The room comes back into focus, and I catch Lily's eye. She's smiling but it's a weak disguise, her eyes as glossy as I suspect mine are.

'I think David should go next,' Annie blurts abruptly.

'But the bowl!' cries Dot.

'Fuck the bowl. It's time, David.'

She hands him a little black velvet box. It's unwrapped. David looks at it for a second. Then back at his wife, to her hands which are folded in her lap, then at the box again. His shoulders slump a little.

'I suppose . . .' he starts. 'I suppose I'm glad for the year we've had. Business has been good and, um, the vineyard has been booming, and . . . Annie, do we have to do this now?'

'It's already done, darling.'

David Blake takes a shaky breath and as he tries to speak, his voice breaks. A single sob escapes his stubbled throat. He gathers himself, swallowing down the emotion.

'I am glad to have had the time we've had as a family,' he says. 'I am prouder of you all than I can ever say. Than I ever do say, and for that I am sorry. I am sorry. Your mother and I, we . . .'

But words fail him. He opens the box and reveals a simple gold band. It glints in the twinkling electric lights of the Christmas tree. It takes a second for the meaning to sink in. Then Annie shifts her hands slightly and I see the pale halo of skin on her left hand where the ring should be. The cruelty of the display rolls over me like a wave.

'You're getting divorced?' The words come out as a whisper and Lily looks surprised by the weakness of her own voice. Annie nods and begins to explain but is cut off as Dot suddenly erupts into a fit of laughter.

'Are you actually kidding?' they manage between cackles. 'This is how you announce your divorce? That is so fucking dramatic! What the actual fuck? Can't someone in this family just be normal for once?'

'Dorothea, this isn't funny,' hisses David, his jaw set.

'Don't call me Dorothea, you fucking loser,' they spit, sinking back into the sofa.

'Dorothea, how dare you speak to me like—'

'Oh, fuck off, David.'

Mr Blake blinks, opens his mouth to say something, then closes it again.

'Merry fucking Christmas,' he says. He puts the ring down on the coffee table, puts on his jacket, and walks out. The heavy front door swings shut behind him with a sigh.

'Well,' says Felix, clapping his hands. 'Looks like we've got two things to celebrate!'

'Three,' says Lily quietly.

'What?'

'Three things. We have three bloody things to celebrate, Felix.'

'Sorry, Magpie, of cour—'

'You always fucking do this. It isn't fair.'

The tears come before the end of her sentence and her porcelain face shatters into embarrassed rage. She stands up abruptly, which sends Dunstable – who's been purring in her lap – thudding to the floor. She turns and half runs from the room, apparently unsure if it's worse for her to flee or to have us watch her fleeing. When she reaches the stairs, we hear her footsteps quicken as she races to her bedroom. I flinch as the door slams even though the sound is muffled by two floors. Both Felix and I move to go after her, but I catch his eye and he motions for me to go ahead.

I knock, once, gently on the frame of the door, which has crept ajar since it was slammed. She says nothing so

I push it open. Lily is lying face-down on the bed. She's silent but her body jerks with little sobs until she takes a trembling breath. I sit on the edge of the bed, and she turns to look at me. Her face is blotchy, but she looks relieved to see it is me and not her brother.

'I'm so embarrassed,' she sniffs.

'Don't be.'

'Felix always does this. He ruins everything. Did you know he used to take my presents? When we were kids. That's why we have the fucking stupid Magpie prizes in the first place. He was so incapable of letting me have things, even as a toddler. He would scream and cry until Mummy gave him one of my gifts. Eventually they just started buying a present for Felix and Dot on my birthday too. They do it as a joke now, but it was never funny to me. When I was six, he blew out all the candles before I could. He couldn't even let me have today, couldn't let me have one piece of good news that was just mine. As soon as the spotlight is off him, he can't bear it. One day. That's all I wanted. One day. He takes everything I want. Every time. Even you. He didn't even look twice at you until he knew how much I wanted you. And don't look at me like that because I'm not saying I want you, because I don't anymore and I'm happy for you, I really am, but it hurts so much to watch him take you away from me.'

I shift on the bed, try to give her a hug, try to make this better.

'Don't,' she says. 'Don't say you're sorry, don't patronise

me. I don't need you to feel sorry. The only thing worse than having you not love me back is having you pity me.'

I can't really hear what the red-faced man on my phone screen is saying but I don't want to turn the volume up because Felix is in the next room and I can't have him hear this. I rewind the tutorial and try again. The first couple of steps are easy enough but then suddenly it's so complicated and I end up with another tangled mess. The bathroom is still steamy from Felix's shower and I am sweating into the stiff waffle collar of my shirt. Without knocking, Felix walks into the room. I scrabble for my phone but knock it off the little shelf below the mirror and into the sink. Felix laughs and takes a step towards me, still in his towel.

'Just got off the phone with Annie. She sends her love and told me to tell you that Auntie Cassandra has got a date in for your Royal Academy audition. Fourteenth of March. Ten o'clock, I think. I should probably have written that down.' He notices the bow tie in my hands, and cottons on to the video which is still taunting me from my phone, amplified by the basin of the sink. 'Do you want me to do that for you?'

'I don't need . . . Yes. Please.'

He takes the loose ends of the bow tie and tugs until they are the correct length. He loops one over the other, then over and round and through. I try to follow his nimble fingers, but he has done this a hundred times and they are too quick for me to keep up. He smooths the perfect bow and kisses me once, softly on the cheek.

'An audition? Really? Felix, I don't know what to say. This is a dream come true.'

'Don't say anything. Just nail the audition and look pretty. The second part should be easy, but you must brush up on your arpeggios. Thank you for agreeing to come tonight. I know there are a thousand other things you'd rather be doing.'

I avoid the trap, but a question burns in me, genuine and persistent. The good news about Cassandra has done nothing to quiet it. When it comes out, it sounds like a challenge.

'Who am I to you tonight?'

'Who are you? Are you trying to start a fight?'

'No.'

'No?'

'I just want to know where we stand.'

'Where we stand?'

'Yes.'

'Well, right now, I'm standing the bathroom and you're standing in my way.'

'I'm being serious, Felix.'

'Are you?'

'I want to know who I am to you, in that room.'

'You know who you are to me, everywhere. But it's complicated. It doesn't matter what the people in that room think or don't think.'

'It matters to me. And it clearly matters to you otherwise you'd just tell everyone that we're together.'

'It isn't that simple.'

'Yes, it is! It is that simple!'

Felix closes his eyes for a second, shutting me out. 'I need to get dressed. We're going to be late.'

'Do you love me?'

'Stop this.'

'No. Do you love me?'

'What are you trying to prove?'

'I love you. I love you so, so much. Please, just say it.'

'You're being ridiculous.'

Our cab pulls up silently outside the House just as Lily emerges onto the steps. Her silvery dress shines in the thin porch light. I am so relieved to see her that I think I might start to cry again, but then she turns to look over her shoulder and laughs at the other person who is stepping out of the house. Celeste glitters in an emerald dress and brown fur coat, a diamond choker fastened tight at her throat. Her painted lips part to dazzle us and she and Lily clutch one another as they totter down the steps in death-trap heels. Felix steps out to offer the girls a hand and Lily plants herself between us. Celeste takes the seat opposite Felix, facing away from the driver. I wonder why someone would choose to have completely bare legs on an evening this cold.

I have often found it impossible to predict how Lily will act in a certain situation. She can be as easy as breathing or as stubborn as a fly-bitten mule. I never know which version she will decide to be. Tonight, she has opted for peace. Her anger at Felix appears forgotten and she chatters away, seemingly not noticing that she is the only person talking. She wonders who else will be there, who we might meet. Felix tells her she has to play it cool. She straightens up and promises she will, then she and Celeste fall about laughing, a tangle of silk and limbs. We arrive at the pier, where a long purple carpet has been rolled out and pairs of satin-wrapped partygoers wait behind crimson ropes for their turn to be photographed.

We wait our turn. Lily's excitement is infectious. I let it warm my cool demeanour until the four of us are laughing so much that we don't realise we are being called to have our picture taken. The first is of the four of us. Felix and I are in the middle, his arm over my shoulders, with the girls either side. They frame us, flirting with the cameraman. Once he has the shot, he asks to get shots of the couples, motioning for Lily and I to step to the side. Felix doesn't correct him. He slides his arm around Celeste's waist, and she twists around him like a vine, throwing back her head to laugh for the camera. She pulls herself close into him and as she whirls her head round to stare directly at the lens, she flashes me a defiant look. They are moved along, ushered inside by a woman in a headset. Lily and I take our places; she plays with my bow tie, smooths my lapels, then turns to face the bright flash of the bulb. When we too are ushered towards the boat, I excuse myself by holding a cigarette between my fingers. I ignore the woman telling me I can smoke on the top deck. Lily looks at me strangely but goes inside anyway.

I smoke a cigarette. Then another. Then a third. The

woman with the headset comes over to tell me the boat is about to leave. I nod and light another cigarette. As the boat pulls away from the pier, Felix steps out onto the deck, searching. He sees me and I raise my hand to wave at him. His whole body is a question. I shrug because I don't have an answer. His shouts drown into the churning water and the groan of the ship's engine. I turn and walk down the Embankment towards the towering buildings of the city. It is dark and cold and the streets are teeming with people heading towards the South Bank for the firework display. I push through them, heading in the opposite direction. I fool myself that I am just following my feet, but I know exactly where I am going.

While I wait for the next Tube, a rat scurries back and forth across the empty tracks. Despite the danger, despite the light, it exposes itself here, in search of food, desperate to keep going. To stay alive. I remember reading once about a group of scientists who wanted to find out if you could condition rats to act in a specific way. They trained them to press a button that would release food. The first experiment was consistent: press the button, get the reward. Positive reinforcement. The opposite worked too. When the button led to an electric shock, the rats learned not to press it. But if the button was unpredictable, if it randomly dispensed food when the button was pressed, the rats would continue to push it, waiting for their reward, even when one didn't come. Eventually, the button stopped dispensing food entirely. The rats continued their obsession, though, pressing the button constantly, neglecting their own hygiene and the other rats entirely. The button drove the rats insane.

My Tube rat stops scurrying, twitches its whiskers, then disappears into the soot and shadow of the tracks. Moments later I hear the distant rumble of the approaching train. It screams into the station. For the briefest of seconds, I think about jumping. The thought pops into my mind half-formed and completely unbidden. Absently I muse that I am at the wrong end of the tracks and the train wouldn't even kill me. My feet stay planted until the train comes to a reluctant halt. I wipe away the bite of tears and press the button on the doors, even though I know they will open anyway.

'Jesus Christ, did Caleb tell you it was a costume party? Why are you dressed like a Tory?'

'Long story. It's nice to see you too, Neisha. You good?'

'Thriving, babes,' she says coolly, and disappears back inside, leaving the door ajar.

The house is packed. Coloured bulbs provide a weak glow that fails to illuminate the faces of the strangers I push past. I've never been here before but I follow a hunch and find Jazz exactly where she always is at parties like this: holding court in the kitchen. When she sees me, she lets out a happy screech, hopping down from the counter and folding me into a hug. She pulls back and looks me up and down, taking in the patent-leather shoes and expensive dinner jacket. She snorts.

'You look like such a twat. Come say hi to everyone!'

She leads me back over to the group she was talking to. One girl hovers near the edge of the group and it takes me a moment to place her. She's the girl with the acrylics from Carnival. Jazz has been trying to get her to hang out for months and it seems she has finally given in. Jazz sees me clock her and gives me a rapid wink. I shake a load of hands and explain I've come from another party. Someone else asks if it was fancy dress and this time I can't tell if they're joking. A tall boy steps forward with his hand outstretched. At first, I don't recognise him in the half-light. They had to rebreak and wire J's jaw, and his left eye socket is now mostly titanium. He looks like someone has tried to draw the old version of him from memory. He tells me it's good to see me with a slight stutter he didn't have before. The conversation they were having before I arrived starts up again.

'I'm just saying that you have to make yourself heard if you want to provoke change,' says Jazz.

'And I'm saying that violence isn't necessarily the best way to get yourself heard,' says a short Black guy in round glasses. 'I mean, look at what happened in Georgia. They burned a city to the ground. Did it bring him back? Did it provoke any significant change?'

'We're talking about it now – that's significant,' offers J.

'Talk is cheap though. Did it change a single law? Did it make life materially better for any Black Americans? Or did it confirm – from the viewpoint of the racist majority – that Black people are violent thugs who are willing to burn down cities.'

'You can't just put "from the viewpoint of the racist majority" in air quotes and pretend that isn't your own opinion,' Jazz smirks.

'What do you suggest then, Miss Gandhi? A hug-in at Parliament?'

'I just think there are other ways of making yourself heard. Direct action doesn't have to be destructive, you know?'

'Woah, woah, I thought we were meant to be keeping it light?' Caleb appears behind the short guy in the glasses. 'Less politics. This is supposed to a party.'

'The party is the political,' counters Jazz.

'Who said that? Was that the Beastie Boys?'

The group laughs, and a few people use the break in tension as an excuse to escape to another corner of the party. Jazz takes Acrylic Girl's hand and leads her into another room. Caleb makes his way to me.

'I didn't think you'd actually turn up.'

'Wouldn't miss this for the world.'

'Is that so?' He smiles down at me. 'You know, we don't enforce a very strict dress code here. You can take your jacket off if you want.'

'I'll look like a waiter.'

'What's wrong with being a waiter?'

'Nothing, I—'

'Yo, I'm kidding. Chill out.'

Caleb slips his thumbs under the lapels of my jacket and tugs them over my shoulders, so the sleeves are halfway down my arms, trapping them against my sides.

He pulls me slightly towards him, lets the jacket drop to the floor. He brings his hands up and starts to loosen the silk bow at my throat. He is so close now that our noses, foreheads, lips almost touch. The bow tie breathes a trembling sigh as it slides from my collar. One button, then two, he pops them open with a flick of his thumb. I want to beg him to stop but he stops before I can. I want to beg him to keep going.

'Much better,' he says, and pulls away. He checks his watch. 'Only an hour to midnight.'

The short guy's name, it transpires, is Ben. He seems to know an unnerving amount about me. About the Blakes. He has this way of talking that is at the same time convincing and confusing. He deflects or jokes in a way that means that after almost an hour chatting with him and Caleb and a few others, I barely know anything about him. I know he's smart though; everyone shuts up and listens whenever he talks. It's nice to see Jazz on the back foot for once.

It is too warm inside. The heating is on, and the bodies and the booze have made the air stuffy. I find a side-door and allow the cold of the night to cool me down. I can hear Jasmine inside, corralling people for the countdown. I suddenly don't feel like being around anyone. I want to hide out here and let the New Year start without me. I think of Felix. Is he out on the boat's deck looking up at this same sky, thinking of me? Or is he inside with Lily and Celeste while they laugh at his jokes, his hand on her knee? A voice says my name, quiet and low, a distant rumble. Caleb steps out to join me.

'I'm sorry, I don't think I can handle a crowd right now.'

He holds out his hand and, despite myself, I take it. I let myself be led. Back inside and up the stairs, avoiding the flock of partygoers who have collected on the back lawn, which slopes down Brixton Hill, the night opening above it, providing a clear sightline down to the firework display by the river. I can't bear to look at it. Caleb opens a door into a bedroom and leads me across to a tiny balcony. It's actually more like a single step with a little railing around it. It is tiny. We stand close together, my back pressed into his chest so we both fit. We are hidden from the rest of the group by the corner of the house, but the view is still good. The countdown drifts around to us.

Ten. 'I'm really glad you came tonight.'

Nine. 'Thank you for having me.'

Eight. 'I've been wanting to get you on your own all night.'

Seven. 'Don't—'

Six. 'All year, if I'm honest . . .'

Five. 'Caleb—'

Four. 'I know. I'm sorry.'

Three. I turn to face him.

Two. 'Don't be.'

One. He puts a hand to my cheek. We are so close I can hear his heartbeat.

'You look so beautiful tonight,' he says.

And here, for the first time, the bursting clouds of colour reflected in his dark eyes, I actually believe those words.

Happy New Year! He dips his face towards mine. There is nothing I can do.

January

I wake up with strong arms wrapped around me, the soft cotton of Felix's bed caressing my naked body. For at least a few glorious minutes, that is where I think I am. Until the unfamiliar bedroom comes into focus around me and I suddenly remember. I want to believe that my memory is hazy, that I can claim some deniability, but as I am wrenched into wakefulness, my mind is completely clear. Caleb's large hand on my chest, moments ago a welcome comfort, is now a leaden bar pinning me down. I am being crushed under the weight of the blankets and I push the fabric away from me, swinging my legs out of the bed, embarrassed by my nakedness. Caleb stirs, asks me if I'm alright.

'I need . . . Have you seen my phone?'

He gestures lazily to the bedside table where it lies plugged in next to his. It's almost nine in the morning. I scroll through my notifications without unlocking it. A few missed calls from Felix make my heart spasm with guilt. There are messages too, but I don't read them. A few texts from other friends saying *Happy New Year*. A missed call from Grandma at 1.43 a.m. Three missed calls from an unknown number. The most recent just a few minutes ago. And a call from a number that, even though it isn't saved, makes my head spin. I know that number by heart. I scramble for my underwear. Caleb asks if everything is okay and I don't respond because of course it isn't. He puts a hand on my shoulder and his fingers catch the delicate gold chain around my neck. I jerk away from him and it pulls for a second against my throat, then snaps. He swears, holds the broken necklace in his hands, apologises, offers to pay for a new one. I just pull on my socks and shove my feet into my ridiculous shiny shoes and escape down the stairs without much of a goodbye. The house is quiet, the detritus of the party has been mostly cleared away, but over-full bin bags straddle the hall and there is a general sense of slight disarray.

Ben is standing in the kitchen eating a bowl of cereal. He raises his eyebrows behind his circular lenses, which catch the soft light that trickles past the clouds and in through the grubby window. 'Good night?'

'Have you seen my jacket? I need to go.'

Out in the street I listen to my voicemails with blossoming dread. Felix what-the-fucks at me. I skip the message, letting it dissolve into nothing. The next message is less coherent. He is drunk and Lily warns him to calm down in the background. I delete that too.

The next is an unfamiliar voice. 'We've been trying to get hold of next of kin. Could you please give us a call back.' The pavement lurches and patent leather struggles to find its footing. 'Just give us a call back. As soon as you can.'

I dial the number they left with numb fingers and feet that carry me to the bus stop. I get through to the switchboard and give them Grandma's name. They take a few minutes to find out where she is and put me through. A kind voice tells me she's still in surgery. I feel the questions catch in my throat. None seem big enough. Visions of purple bruises and rotten wounds and stacks of years-old magazines bubble up unbidden. *Is she going to be okay?* But no one can answer that. I feel a sudden, implacable need to be with Felix. Despite everything, I know that he is the only person who could calm me down. He has this quality about him, a softness that I love and crave. He can look right into me and find the bruising part and know exactly what to say. I want to crawl into bed next to him and let my tears wash out the fear I feel. But I can't do that right now. I don't have the words to explain last night and I don't know how to apologise for something I'm not yet sure I regret doing. I stare at the picture I have saved with his contact in my phone. It is one that Lily took in the village near the Chateau last summer. Felix straddling light and shadow, caught between moments, his unwavering smile staring at me.

I was eighteen when Uncle Henry died. I was on a Geography field trip somewhere in Wales. We were eating dinner in the youth hostel they'd put us up in. Discussing whatever it is that eighteen-year-olds discuss after a day of standing in rivers and making notes about rocks. Mr Bryan – tall, softly spoken, with kind eyes – tapped me on the shoulder and told me he needed to talk to me. My mind raced to some forgotten crime that might warrant this intervention but found none. I left my tray of pallid sausages and lumpy mash and the safe chatter of youth. When he told me what had happened, I didn't really know how to react. I think I told him that Henry wasn't really my uncle, that that was just what we called him. Trying to distance myself from the reality of the news.

'Even so, son, even so,' he said and placed a large, warm hand on my shoulder.

It was too late for me to get on a train that night. I remember sitting alone. I remember going to bed alone. Curling up on the bottom bunk, facing the wall as the other boys talked about girls and *Call of Duty*. In the morning Mr Bryan drove me to the station. It was tiny – one squat building without even a ticket machine. He hadn't checked the schedule, so I sat there alone for two hours, wondering when to eat the cheese sandwich the youth hostel staff had made for me. A man with dirt under his nails and a haystack of a dog on a leather lead got on the single-carriage train with me when it arrived. He stumbled as we boarded and pulled an unlabelled plastic bottle out of the pocket of his coat. He took a swig from the bottle then offered me some. I declined, then he vomited. On the floor, the table and all over the only toilet. I sat on the hot train for four hours, ignoring the soggy sandwiches in my bag and the urge to pee. The dog licked at the vomit, which slid around the carriage whenever the train swept round a bend. When we finally got to Cardiff and I was able to change trains, the man waved me off with a laugh.

Grandma has always been pragmatic about death. She wrapped me in her arms, smelling, as she always did, of spice and Mr Muscle. She told me not to cry but I did anyway. I don't know, still, whether I was crying for the man who was likely the closest thing I had to a father or from relief at being in her arms. I don't remember how many days it was before the funeral. One, maybe two. I watched TV and ate the procession of food Grandma placed before me. When the day came, I put on my only suit – the one I'd bought in case I got an interview at Oxford, which I hadn't – and got into the back of one of the black cars that made up Uncle Henry's funeral procession.

A heart attack. I think that's what it was, but my memory is murky. I suppose it doesn't matter how someone died, just that they did. I felt empty more than anything else. Washed out. We were his family in a way and people kept apologising for our loss. I thought it was strange: I hadn't seen him in months and despite our regular physical proximity, Uncle Henry and I were never close. He'd sensed something in me, I think; something that required either stamping out or keeping at a distance. They apologised for my loss anyway.

Jamaicans deal with death well. Faced with the fragility and finality of life, instead of bowing our heads and sinking into pity, we lean, joyous and defiant, into life. There is food and music and dancing. There were so many flowers that day, piled high in every corner of the West Indian Centre in Moss Side. Flowers of every size, colour and shape you could think of. Flowers in hats and lapels and in big vases on tables. Men only get flowers when they die.

There was an abundance of food too. Curried goat and rice and pea and patties and callaloo and pork chops and chicken and huge slabs of bread to mop up all the juices. Sweaty from grief and Red Stripe and dancing, the congregation descended into chaos when it was time for cake. The woman who served me my slice – huge and overflowing with icing – wore a T-shirt that said, in glittering gold letters, black is a happy colour. That day, despite everything, it felt like it was.

The last few hours seem to have passed in one terrifying smear. I saw Jazz at home, told her where I was going, brushed off her sympathy and her offer to come with me. Acrylic Girl stood awkwardly near the kitchen door and I didn't wanted her to see me cry. I don't remember the journey here. It feels like I have been here for hours, waiting for Grandma to wake up. They tell me she was groggy and a little confused after the operation, but that she'll be more with it after a little sleep.

She fell in the night, they tell me, but they're not sure when; she was found by the carer at eight this morning. I tell them it must have been around 1.43 a.m. My voice cracks when I say this because I know that is when she'd called me, scared and hurting on the floor. Her grandson instead of an ambulance. They tell me she broke her hip. Clean through the neck of the bone, near the socket, which they tell me is better than further down. Or worse. They say everything so fast that I can't keep up. They tell me they've already replaced it. As if it were a lightbulb, or a fuse, or a bin bag. They tell me she's lucky. That she'll be up and about in no time at all. I tell them she's a fighter, but I don't really know what I mean.

Eventually she wakes up and I am so glad I am there because she is terrified for a second, but then she sees my face and feels my hand in hers and goes still. I explain what happened, where we are, that she's had a fall and an operation, and she apologises to me. She apologises for all the fuss, for dragging me up from London, for taking me away from my boy. My boy. That's what she calls him, and I wonder how she knows this or if she's just confused. I am about to ask what she means but I stop. I think for a second that I am hearing things, that her mention of him has made me mistake a stranger's voice for Felix's. But then he pulls back the curtain. He looks worried and, for the first time since I met him, I think I see something like hesitance on his face. He hovers, as if waiting for permission to come in. Lily, however, dives right in.

'Mrs Roberts, I'm Lily. Lily Blake? We met at graduation. And this is my brother, Felix. It's so nice to see you again. I hope you're feeling okay. The nurse said you took quite a tumble. Can I get you a cup of tea?'

'Felix,' says Grandma, putting on her glasses so she

can see the boy at the end of the bed properly. 'It nice to meet you. An' good to see you, Lily. A cup of tea would be just lovely.'

She is using the voice she uses on the phone or when someone in the supermarket doesn't understand her. It's deferential and it makes me angry. I want to tell them both to leave but I don't have the strength. I step out with both of them, telling Grandma I'll help with the tea. I turn on Lily; Felix stays silent.

'What the hell are you doing here? How did you—'

'Well, someone disappeared from a boat party on New Year's Eve and wasn't answering their phone. So we decided to drive up to Manchester and check out all the hospitals in case they'd gone mad and checked themselves in.'

'Very funny.'

'Jazz told us what happened.' Felix's tone is cautious, plaintive. 'We were worried about you. We are worried about you. You can't just vanish like that.'

I swallow down my response, not wanting to blow up in the middle of the hospital ward. We find the tea station and make ourselves a mug each and one for Grandma. I pop in an extra sugar. When we get back to Grandma's bay, the ward sister who showed me in bars the way.

'I'm sorry, I'm afraid you can only have three visitors per patient at a time.'

'There are only three of us,' says Lily.

'There were, until she arrived.'

I'm about to ask who 'she' might be, but I already

know the answer. I've known this was coming for a while. I've known since I last visited Grandma at home, since I saw her number on my phone screen this morning. I expected to feel panicked but now that the moment is here, I just feel beaten. I use my free hand to pull back the curtain. She is sitting there next to Grandma, holding her hand, but her eyes, edged with mascara, are directed straight at me. I say something I haven't said in almost a decade.

'Hello, Mum.'

Most of what I know about Mum's illness is just a patchwork of memory – both mine and other people's – of things I saw, snippets of overheard conversation, things that grown-ups told me when they shouldn't have, and a bundle of case notes stolen from my social worker's bag when I was fourteen. It is a thin quilt and offers little comfort. My version of what a mother should be is probably very different from most other people's. But the soft, gentle Mum, the one who loved music and singing and hugging me so tightly I felt like nothing could ever hurt me, the one who sang with her head thrown back, whose eyes sparkled with the promise of adventure, who laughed at my child jokes like they were the funniest thing in the world, who knew the different flavours of my tears and how to stem them – that is the Mum I try to remember.

She was always beautiful, Grandma had told me, with a long, slender neck and high, arching cheekbones. Her skin was dark and perfect, and her eyes were large and light and mischievous. She was prone to laughter as a child, and was fearlessly defiant of all authority. She was clever and shrewd and suspicious of the status quo, incessantly questioning why things were the way they were. She argued with her teachers and squabbled with her friends and got suspended for punching a boy twice her size. She was wild and unruly, and when she was a teenager, Grandma worried that she'd go down a bad path. She had a few bad boyfriends, from the wrong side of Moss Side. She drank heavily. She smoked weed in the house. But then she met my father, an awkward but gentle man, who lulled her spirit. He was softly spoken and unopinionated and he let her temper rage and never once raised his voice at her. He adored her, and she, in her own way, loved him too. She loved the peace she felt when he placed his hand on hers. She loved the idea that he would love her, and only her, forever. When she fell pregnant, everyone was delighted. My parents got married in a hurry. I have a photo from their wedding day. They are sitting together at a table spread with a white tablecloth and half-empty wine glasses and flowers and cigarette ends. Dad is already balding and his face is red from alcohol and excitement. He is gazing at my mother like he has never seen anything so beautiful in his entire life. Mum glares joyously into the camera. Her hair is scraped back into a puffy bun and her skin shines in the fluorescent lighting. Between her and the table, she holds a bouquet of yellow roses over her pregnant bump, which shows beneath her white dress.

They did not have the time or the money for a honeymoon. I came quick and early but the labour was long. Three days between the waters that broke a month too soon and the moment I was forced, screaming and wrinkled, into life. I have a photo of this too: Mum sweaty, her hair and eyes feral, and me, tiny and red, bundled in blankets to keep in the warmth my little body could not yet produce for itself. She got ill very soon after. It started, Grandma told me, subtly enough. Mum was tired, so tired she couldn't do much more than sleep. Grandma or Dad or the health visitor would wake her to feed me and then she would fall back into a troubled sleep. She only called me 'the baby'. Then, after a while, she called me 'that thing', then simply 'it'. *It isn't mine. It shouldn't be here. They say I need to kill it.*

I read in her case notes that she left me on the doorstep one night, convinced I'd been eaten alive by insects and that they were devouring her too. My father found me when he came home from work and screamed at her for the first time in their relationship. Her behaviour was erratic and she started to hide her worst thoughts from Dad and Grandma and anyone who asked. Grandma, I think, was in denial. She told me that she had to hide all the knives in the house because she was worried what Mum might do to me or to Dad or to herself. But she never thought to get help, never mentioned anything to the health visitor or the doctor or the police. They tried to downplay how bad things were. The shame made them hide, wary of what might happen if they asked for help. Dad took more time off work, more to keep Mum from doing anything than to look after me himself. They screamed at each other, the neighbours called the police, they took Dad away, and me and Mum to Grandma's once. It makes sense, I suppose, taking mum and baby to a place of safety.

That night was the first time Mum tried to kill herself. I do not know the exact details, but I have searched the words 'ligature marks' enough times to have a strong guess at how she tried. That first psychiatric report diagnosed her with puerperal psychosis. I looked into those words a lot too. There is only so much sense that Google can make of the worst thing that has ever happened to you. They took us to a special mother and baby unit, so we could be together. Apparently, that helps some mothers get better faster. It worked with Mum. We went home after a few weeks and she was started on a load of different medications and we had weekly visits from the community mental health team. She got better and eventually we were discharged from the service. The damage to by parents' marriage was not so easily undone and my parents fought and fought and fought. Gone was the calm Mum had found in my father. Gone was his reverence for her beauty; he only saw the ugliness he thought her capable of. I understand why he left. But I still hate him for it.

She was well for years. Well enough. We were fine. We were solid. Just the two of us. A little team. We saw a lot of Grandma, obviously; we ate tea at hers most nights and she would almost always pick me up from school if Mum was working. But it was me and Mum against the world. And the fun times were so much fun, and the other times, when Mum would withdraw, were scary but short-lived. Until the withdrawals got longer and her lows got lower too and suddenly I was six years old and on the phone to a paramedic and then we didn't live in our little flat anymore, we lived at Grandma's. As is often the way with these things, I remember the worst bits better than the best. I don't remember the long stretches when she was well, not really. I have memories, yes; some of them more solid than others. I remember the good times in that I know they happened. But the worst moments are etched into my mind. They are vivid and Technicolor and if I allow myself to revisit them, I can feel everything I felt then. I can feel the sting of a slapped cheek that still burns fifteen years later. I can smell the sweet, choking smell of our bodies, unwashed for days, curled up in her bed because she would not leave it.

Eventually, I stopped visiting Mum and Mum stopped coming to the flat when she was allowed out of the unit. I don't know who decided, but it was thought best – for me or her? I wonder – that we did not see each other. There was a brief court case and a child protection order, and suddenly, legally Mum wasn't my mother anymore. The pain of this is hard to explain. It is terrible and cruel, to be stolen away and told you have been saved. But we pushed on, a new team. Me and Grandma. We didn't talk about Mum much. If people asked about her, Grandma would say she had gone away or wasn't with us and people would stop asking. I started doing the same. It was easier to think of her as simply not here, rather than somewhere else.

'You told me she was dead!'

'No, I didn't.'

Felix and I are standing in a corridor between two wings of the hospital. It is more like a bridge, a tunnel of glass suspended just above the ground, connecting the shiny orthopaedics ward to the rest of the crumbling hospital. The winter sun beating in makes me sweat despite the frost on the ground outside.

'Yes, you fucking did.'

'No, really, I didn't.' My voice is calmer than I expected it to be. I knew this day would come. 'You heard what you wanted to hear.'

'What the hell does that even mean? We've had so many conversations about this. About what it was like to lose your mum. And the whole time she's been – what? Just up the road?'

'I did lose her. I haven't seen her in almost ten years.'

'You let me think she was dead. There's an important distinction.'

'Not to me.'

'You're being insane.'

'Don't call me insane. Don't you fucking dare, Felix.'

There's a pause as he takes a few breaths, trying to calm himself down. I can see him working through it all in his head. I feel something inside me dissolve. I thought I would hate the moment this all came crashing down, but it's a relief.

'Look, when I met you and you assumed what you assumed and invited me in, I saw a chance at a new start. I saw a chance at a life without all this bleak, shitty tragedy hanging over me, and I took it. Can you blame me?'

People are moving through the corridor, from one building to another. Porters pushing patients, nurses hurrying off for a mid-shift cigarette, families looking for their relatives.

Felix looks around and I wonder if he's worried people will recognise him. He lowers his voice. 'You lied.'

'I didn't lie.'

'You did. You lied from the start. What else have you lied to me about?'

'Nothing.' A flash of guilt, white hot and unwelcome.

'Did you ever think for a second what impact that would have on us? On our life?'

'This isn't our life, Felix, this is your life.'

'What the fuck is that supposed to mean?'

'None of this was ever mine! The parties, the dinners, the flights, the houses. This isn't my life, this isn't *our* life. It's *yours*. You've barely let me in to it! You claim we have a life together, but you won't even show yourself with me in public. What am I to you? What life do we have together?'

'That isn't fair. I love you.'

'Don't you dare,' I repeat, and I am crying now, burning

fat tears that rush up from my chest. 'How can you say you love me? This is my life and if you'd known what happened, where I come from, you wouldn't have wanted anything to do with me. Can you blame me? For wanting to keep something for myself? For wanting a chance to leave this behind?'

Felix moves towards me. He is crying now too. He kisses me and I taste his tears, or mine, I don't know. His hands find my hair and he cups my head. I snake my arms around his neck. He kisses me harder and I kiss him back with equal urgency. It doesn't matter what I've done. What he's done. It doesn't matter what we've said. How we've hurt each other. It doesn't matter that someone, some faceless, prying stranger, has stopped at the end of the corridor to snap this moment into blurry permanence. All that matters is his lips on mine and his hands around me. *I'm sorry, I love you.* Our words blend into a muffled chant. *I'm sorry, I love you. I'm sorry I love you. I'm sorry I love you.*

Grandma's house is disturbingly still now that Felix and Lily have gone. Mum insisted they stayed the night, that it was too far and too late for them to drive back to London. On the way to Grandma's, she and Lily chatted and asked each other questions like they were old friends catching up. I realise now why I was so drawn to Lily in the first place. Her effortless joy in the everyday, her childlike eagerness for life to be a constant game. She reminded me of Mum when she was well. Felix stared resolutely ahead, following the map on his phone from the hospital back to our house. I ignored them all, letting Mum's and Lily's chatter melt into background noise and tracking the raindrops on the window as they slid across and through each other leaving a delicate web of smaller droplets in their wake. When we pulled into the drive, I felt the need to apologise, to make some sort of excuse.

'It's lovely,' said Lily politely as the four of us pushed through into the hallway. I had no bag, no change of clothes. I went into the kitchen and flicked on the kettle, searching for a charger for my dead phone. When I went to find the others, I registered Lily's hurried warning a second too late. The floor of the lounge was a mess. The console table was over-turned and a smashed mug lay in the centre of a now-dried coffee stain. Grandma's pyjama bottoms had been cut from her and discarded at the end of the sofa. Some plastic wrappers for medical needles and painkillers marked out the space on the floor from where she must have been scooped up. A small streak of dried blood from a wound I must not have noticed at the hospital. The idea of her scared and alone in here, bleeding and calling out for me, flooded my mind again and I had to sit down. Lily and Mum tidied the room while Felix made tea. I could feel the anger coming off him like steam. I could tell that he didn't dislike her, but the mere fact of her existence rekindled his anger at me. We ate a silent curry on our knees and I made up Grandma's bed for Felix and Lily to share. In the middle of the night my bedroom door creaked open and I felt the mattress shift as someone got in next to me. I smelled a waft of Lily's perfume and allowed her to snake her thin arms around me. I let myself cry.

Now that Felix and Lily have left and we are alone, I cannot avoid talking to Mum. I make us tea and find some not-too-stale biscuits in the cupboard. We sit in silence for a while, letting the steam from our mugs rise into the space between us.

'So, you're back,' I say.

'Is that a question?'

'No.'

'Do you want me to be back?' Mum doesn't look at me directly. She stares down into the tea I have made for her. Strong and dark with two sugars.

'We've been doing fine without you.' A part of me wants these words to hurt and another just believes this to be true. 'How are you? Are you well?'

'I'm alright, yeah. Been coming here recently. Helping around the house and stuff. I'm just round the corner. Council sorted me a flat on the Merson Estate a few years back.'

This slaps me in the face. The estate is a ten-minute walk from here. Less than that if you take the cut-through between the Chinese takeaway and the newsagent.

'And you didn't think to pop over?'

'I didn't think you'd want to see me.' She's right.

'Don't do that. Don't put this all on me, that isn't fair.'

'I'm not, love, I . . .' She trails off. We look anywhere

but at each other. There is a row of three dead flies on the windowsill above the sink.

Eventually she speaks. 'Lily seems nice. And Felix is . . . he's very handsome. Who would've thought that Annie Carpenter's son would end up being your . . . Well, life can be like that, I suppose. Do you remember when we used to listen to her in the car?'

'You don't get to do this, Mum. You don't get to just walk back in here after all this time and call me "love" and pretend that *I* pushed *you* away. It isn't fair. I was a child, Mum, I needed you. I needed you then. I don't anymore.' I see my words hit her in the face. We are both silent for a long time.

When she next speaks, her voice has shrunk to almost a whisper. 'I was sick.'

'I know, Mum. I know.'

'I thought that maybe we could . . .'

She doesn't say what it is that we could maybe do and I don't ask. I drain my tea, leaving the dregs and some soaked crumbs of biscuit in the mug, grab my coat and walk out. I find myself in the park near my old school, twisting the frozen chain of the swing above me. I spin until I am dizzy. I watch the sky fade from pale blue to pink to purple then walk home in the familiar dark. When I get back to the house, Mum isn't there.

February

It's strange, even though my name is on the rental agreement, I think I've probably spent less than half my nights in London in this flat. When Jazz found it – clean, convenient, within budget – it felt like it was the start of a new life for us. It was exciting. We imagined a continuation of what it was like at uni but with a whole glittering city as our playground. We imagined cosy nights in together, outrageous nights out, a favourite restaurant around the corner, dinners with our friends, crammed into our little kitchen. But then we got here and she already had friends in London and I didn't feel like I fit in with them, and besides, I was busy. I was in love. I am in love.

I've now been here for almost two weeks. It's the longest stretch of time I've gone without staying a night at Felix's or the House. I can tell that Jazz is finding it weird too. She must be used to having the whole place to herself. It isn't that we've drifted apart. We haven't. I hope we haven't. The kettle hisses and I pour the boiling water into two chipped mugs, letting the tea steep.

'Could you do another one, please, babe? Caleb will be here in a second.' She looks up from her phone. I feel like she is looking for a reaction, so I keep my face neutral. I pour another cup.

'Oh, cool, I didn't realise he was coming over,' I lie. Jazz looks at me, eyebrows raised, but moves on.

'Yeah, apparently he's got some new intel about the exhibition. Since you won't help us out . . .'

I sigh and turn back to the tea, squeezing the bags against the side of each mug then flicking them into the bin, the lid of which has been broken open for at least four months. Jazz has been like a dog with a bone since I let slip about Lily's exhibition. Initially she flipped out. Went into one of her rants about the Blakes and privilege and nepotism. I felt bad, like I'd opened Lily up to criticism that wasn't necessarily fair. I told Jazz that those were her photos, which she took with permission. Granted I haven't seen them yet but I know Lily has talent. *It's just not her story to tell.* That was Caleb's reaction when I discussed it with him. There's a rapid series of knocks on the door, then Jazz opens it to Caleb, as if my thinking of him has conjured him up.

'Well, if it isn't the dark mystery stranger,' he says, winking.

The photos from the hospital were published by an online gossip site the day after they'd been taken. Within a few days, screenshots had made it to social media, and from there the tabloids picked up the story and ran with it. The whole thing was completely horrifying. Blurry, distorted images of Felix and me. Almost unrecognisable really, but they cross-referenced Felix's outfit with a photo of him getting out of his car earlier in the day. In one of the many shots, you can tell there's some sort of argument happening and in another, well, it's clearer what is going on. Jazz says you have to admire the imagination of the poor Journalism grad they got to write the copy. I think she's being unnecessarily generous.

What's Eating Felix Blake?

Rising star of upcoming BBC crime drama *Uplands* pictured in fraught embrace with unnamed male friend in Manchester Hospital. Blake, 26, was recently announced to have joined the cast of the upcoming remake of *Black Jets*, the 1983 spy movie starring Blake's godfather Richard Symmonds. The young actor was rumoured to be dating Paris model and socialite Celeste Marchand, 36. The two were pictured together at the Turner Foundation New Year's Eve River Gala. But these pictures raise questions: who is this dark mystery stranger and what exactly is the young star getting up to behind not-so-closed doors?

Felix freaked out. He sank into one of his moods and disappeared for a week. Then he popped up in some paparazzi photos in a strip club in Ibiza. Initially, Annelise tried to get the stories buried, but rumours like this take on a life of their own. So far, the Blakes and their network of friends and hangers-on had kept quiet, but as far as Felix was concerned it was only a matter of time before someone agreed to comment. I told him that maybe this was a good thing, that we should just lean in to it. The story was already out there anyway. He said I was being naive. I stayed in Bury until Grandma was discharged home. David sent a message saying I could extend my Christmas break for a week and the tenderness of the gesture surprised me. I got a hotel so Mum could have the house.

Felix and I haven't spoken since. A few days after Grandma's accident, I got an email from Anna Osbourne, the journalist I met at one of Felix's shows, telling me she'd been thinking of me and wondered if I wanted to meet for a coffee. I immediately declined. Eventually, with no new leads the story died down and people moved on to other non-stories about people I'd never heard of.

I still haven't seen Felix. It's now been several weeks. He's been filming since I got back, long days and early starts, and he's been staying at the House rather than at his place. He says it's easier to get out to Pinewood from that side of the city. London is a hard place to love someone. I've barely spoken to Lily either. She's been holed up in her studio prepping for the exhibition, and while I don't begrudge her this, I could really do with some of the lightness she'd bring to the situation. Nothing is ever doom and gloom for Lily. There are bright sides and silver linings and everything will work out in the end. Except this doesn't feel like it has an end. Even Annie has stopped checking in. She was concerned for Grandma, offered to have her moved to a private hospital, made it clear that whatever happened with her and David, Grandma's support at home would continue. She didn't bring up the pictures or the rumours. Didn't even mention Felix. But I haven't heard from any of the Blakes in days.

Caleb fills the tiny kitchen with his frame. He brings with him a gust of cold air that thickens the condensation on the windows. He gratefully takes the warm mug from me. My fingers brush against his, shocked with cold. I picture them tracing the soft contours of my ribs in warmer moments, on different nights.

I'm not sure when I made the decision to start sleeping with Caleb. After the first time, in the rush of Grandma's injury and the tabloids and all the mess with Mum, I pushed it almost completely out of my mind. I promised myself I'd never do it again. But it also seemed, in some strange way, to have been the only thing that had happened to me recently that felt at all right. So, when he got in touch to ask how I was holding up and offered to come round one evening when Jazz was out, just to talk, I didn't said no. He asked me if I regretted what we did. I realised in that moment that I truly didn't. I also didn't say no when he asked me if he could kiss me. And now we are here, in this in-between space, and I do not regret it. There is something about this that feels out of my control. Since I first saw him in that student house years ago, this feels like the direction we were always headed towards. I find comfort in the inevitability. Where being with Felix feels like free-falling, Caleb's solidity is like being caught.

Jazz has been seeing a lot of Caleb too. And J and Neisha and Ben and the others. J's trial is coming up, and by the sounds of it, they're planning some sort of protest. I've tried to distance myself from it and Jazz hasn't tried to get me involved. I am grateful to have an excuse, even if thinking about my looming piano audition brings me out in a cold sweat. Jazz has softened towards me a lot since Grandma's fall.

I leave the two of them to their planning and take my tea into the lounge and turn up the TV. My phone buzzes and I look down to see a message from Felix.

Felix
19:46
Can we talk? Dinner at Francesco's? Tomorrow. 8pm.

I read the message again, put my phone down, then pick it back up again, type my response, delete it, then type it again and press send before I change my mind. When Jazz and Caleb come through and join me, I don't say anything about Felix and I don't ask about what they were talking about. I just curl into the arm Caleb has placed around my shoulder. Jazz sits on the floor in front of the sofa and lets me play with her hair. I realise with a warm pull that this is the life I pictured for us.

I am exactly fifteen minutes late. Felix stands up when I walk in and hands me a bunch of flowers. I smell them casually in an attempt to appear less nervous than I am. Violets. He has ordered us both a negroni and his is already half finished. I pour myself a glass of water and take a sip.

I feel the anger I've been suppressing start to bubble up, but then Felix says the last thing I was expecting him to. 'I was wrong.'

I pause before responding. 'About what?'

'Everything.'

'Right.'

This feels unfair. A plea for total absolution without acknowledgement of any particular sins. But then he surprises me again. 'I was wrong for reacting the way I did. I'm sorry I pushed you away, I know you were right. About everything. I really want to do the right thing, even though I wasn't there for you. I can't imagine how hard the past few weeks must have been. I'm so sorry,' he pauses. I take a generous sip of negroni. 'I love you.'

He says all this with tears in his eyes and I believe him. He asks me how things are at home. He asks me about Mum. I want to tell him that things are messy; that we've been speaking on the phone and it feels sur-real, that she's looking after Grandma and that Grandma is walking again and is not in as much pain and is doing okay, that Mum has been well for a while, stable, on her meds. I want to tell him that this hurts, that I feel like she's taken something from me, that if she's been well, she should have reached out, that it would be easier to know that she'd been ill all these years because then it was no one's fault that we've been so far apart. I want to tell him that I don't know how to move past this; that I have been trying to find the words to tell her that I want her in my life but keep coming up short. That Jazz says that I'm partly to blame as well, that I could have contacted Mum myself, that I know this is true but it hurts and make me hate Jazz for being able to see directly into my soul. I want to say all of this and tell him how much I've missed him.

'Things are fine. Mum is fine. Thanks for asking.'

He looks at me and the intensity of it burns. 'If we're going to make this work, you're going to have to open up to me.'

'This?'

'Us. You and me. I want to make this work.'

'But—'

'I'm serious. Please. Just . . .' Felix trails off, but then his eyes light up with a familiar mischievous excitement that draws me forward in my seat. He takes my hand. 'What are you doing tomorrow night? There's a viewing party for *Uplands* and I want you there. I need you there. Come with me.'

He rubs his thumb over mine and I know I don't have a choice in this. My excuse dies before it reaches my lips. We drink our cocktails and I let Felix order wine. I let him refill my glass until we have drunk two bottles and he pays the bill. He leads me out of Francesco's and down the road towards his flat. He kisses me on the doorstep of his house.

There is something about Felix that makes me trust him completely. A gentleness in his voice that reminds me of the way Grandma used to sprinkle lavender oil on my pillow and chest like holy water when I couldn't sleep. I do it to myself too sometimes. There is a bottle of lavender oil here, on Felix's nightstand. I am all over this flat. My good toothbrush is in the cup by the sink. There's a drawer of my clothes, a pot of Palmer's on the dresser. Maybe we do have a life together. There is nothing of his in the Tooting flat. I don't think he has ever been there.

Felix pushes me onto the bed. I stare at the window in a drunken haze, where our reflections play in the glass. I feel hot and detached as I watch our bodies. One is slight and dark, so dark that I can barely make out the features on his face, my face. Felix's nose is buried in my black curls. His pale arm reaches round the angle of my hips, his hand resting between my thighs. The dark blue duvet lies discarded on the wooden floor. Beneath the bed, as if hastily pushed out of sight, I spot the turquoise Tiffany's gift box. My eyes flick back up and meet Felix's in the window-mirror. There is a moment when I feel like I could stop this, but Felix flashes a smile. I know that I am dancing on shifting sands, but at least I am dancing.

'We really shouldn't. But shall we?'

He kisses me on the neck and my chest heaves with the warm drag of desire. I feel the last shred of my resistance melt away. Naked, I wander to the kitchen and grab a bottle of champagne and two glasses. When I return, Felix has shaken some coke out onto a little silver tray. He passes me a metal straw and our reflections blur inside the window.

*

Annelise lets her unfinished cigarette fall from her fingers, swears, then grinds it into the pavement with her patent-leather heel. She looks us up and down, taking in the expensive suit Felix has dressed me in, his messy hair, and the lopsided smile on his face that he adopts when he knows he's done something he shouldn't have but which he'll get away with it.

She rolls her eyes, kisses us both on each cheek, then looks pointedly at Felix. 'You're late.'

'Fashionably?'

'Don't try me, Felix. This is a big night for you. No . . .' She takes a step closer to him, lowering her voice. '. . . distractions.'

'No distractions,' says Felix, raising both hands in mock defensiveness.

We've barely slept. One bag turned into two, two bottles into three, and by the time we finally passed out the winter sun was already glaring into the flat. Felix woke up in a panic and scrabbled around in the Tiffany's box. When I said I would prefer coffee he looked at me like I'd slapped him. I could feel him pulling away, so I let him make us each a line while I pulled the duvet over the bed. My head is pounding now, my chest is tight, and there is an itch behind my right eye that makes me want to drag my fingernails across the inside of my skull.

Felix's hand in mine brings me back to the present. He leads me past someone with a clipboard and through a set of doors into the plush lobby of the cinema. Heads turn when we walk in. It is clear from the looks on most people's faces that firstly, they've heard the rumours, and secondly, I was not supposed to be here tonight. Lily sweeps over to us. She is wearing a fringed canary-yellow silk dress and is the only person who doesn't look surprised to see me on Felix's arm. She kisses me then hands me a glass of champagne. Felix takes the other glass, which is filled with sparkling water. His eyes follow mine to the glass and he shrugs. I ask Lily about the exhibition. Tonight is not about her, she tells me.

Felix, for once, remains by my side. Whenever someone comes to talk to him, he places a hand on my back or lets his fingers brush against mine. A squeeze of the hand to let me know he's there. Lily stays with us too, shepherding us around the room from person to person, cutting them off after their allotted time. She seems protective, treating us as if we might shatter or explode if knocked too hard.

Dot bounds over. They are wearing an oversized pin-stripe suit, their structured white shirt protruding at the collar and cuffs. 'So, you two are back together then, are you?'

There's a challenge in the question. I am caught by the implication within it: back together implies that at some point we've come apart.

'We're figuring it out, Dot,' Felix says, linking his fingers through mine.

'I just think that—'

'Oh, leave it out, will you?' Lily tries to cut her sibling off, but Dot will not be silenced.

'I just think that everybody deserves to be on the same page about what's happening here.'

Dot's eyes are fixed on me and burn with a combativeness I've never seen in them before. I don't like it. I look around for an escape and see Annie and Teller talking to Cassandra Quant. Annie whispers something to Teller, who guides Cassandra to where Hugo and Millie are holding court by the bar. Annie glides purposefully across the room. She comes over and wraps Felix in a firm, urgent embrace. She draws back, clutching his chin with her thumb and forefinger, studying the angles of his face.

'You look tired. Did you even sleep last night?'

'Annie,' Felix shrugs off her glittering silver nails.

'We were very well behaved.' The lie passes my lips, easy as a breath. 'Got a solid ten hours.'

Annie's eyes narrow and I see her store the moment away. She turns back to her son. 'You really ought to call your mother more. I haven't seen you in weeks.'

'I thought you said you'd been staying at the House.' I feel a small tear appear in the fabric of the story Felix has been telling me. The Blakes share a look I can't quite decipher, then snap back as if nothing has happened.

'We were beginning to think you weren't going to show up tonight, darling. And we weren't aware you were bringing . . . company. Hello, dear. How is your grandmother?' Annie's attention, like her son's, feels like it can light me up from the inside. Being left outside of it is like being shut out in the cold. I answer her question, thanking her for her generosity and she listens distractedly.

'I'm very glad to hear it. Would you be an absolute angel and get me a vodka-tonic? I need to talk to my son.'

I spot a cascade of red hair by the bar and make a bee-line for Cassandra. When she sees me coming, the colour drains from her face. I try to ask about my audition. She looks around awkwardly. Is she looking for an escape route? I watch the Blake family across the room, heads together, deep in discussion. Felix laughs at something and is admonished by his mother. He glances at me and the rest of the family look too. Felix takes the opportunity to signal to me with his eyes, nodding towards the bathroom at the other end of the lobby.

I try again with Cassandra. 'I'm very much looking forward to playing for you, Mrs Quant. Again, thank you so much for the opportunity.'

Again, she refuses to answer. I follow Cassandra's eyes back to the Blakes. Annie gives us a quick smile and makes the slightest movement with her head and shoulders. A nod, or a shrug. I can't tell. I feel the walls of my throat close in on me.

'Well, I must go and find a seat,' Cassandra says coolly. 'Do excuse me.'

I dredge up a polite 'Of course' and escape to the bathroom. Felix is coming out as I get to the door and he gracefully slides something into my pocket as we pass one another. I lean on the marble sink. The yellow lightbulbs hanging above my reflection look like they're pulsating. I think about leaving, about slipping out of a side-door and getting on a bus back to Tooting. But Felix said he needed me tonight and I can't run away now, not when we've just started to rekindle what we had. But everybody else is acting like I shouldn't be here, like I've broken some unwritten code of conduct by showing my face. I resolve to stay. I go into a cubicle and pull out the small leather pouch Felix slipped into my jacket. Inside, my fingers find a small plastic bag and a tiny silver spoon. I take a heap of coke and put it to my nose, flushing the toilet to disguise the sound of my sniffing. I hear the door of the room open and close. There is a soft click and I realise someone must have locked the door. I rub the back of my hand across my nose and push everything into my pocket. I leave the cubicle and see Caroline Asiamah peering at me through the mirror. I start to say hello, my eyes shifting to the locked door, but she places a finger to her lips. She pushes open all three of the stalls, checking we are alone. I give her a puzzled look.

'Sorry for all the cloak-and-dagger stuff,' she says, her voice low. 'I don't like being overheard.'

She stands up straight. She is taller than she seems, used to shrinking herself so people won't notice the tricks she is playing. I think she is expecting me to say something. Or is very carefully planning what she has to say. She looks at me through her square glasses for a long time.

'It's a shame.' She shakes her head. 'You would have gone really far, you know.'

I don't have an answer to this, so I wait. She glances towards the door again then takes a step closer to me.

'Look, this is honestly nothing to do with me, and I

shouldn't really be telling you. I don't want to take sides here, but I believe things like this should be a fair fight. And people like us should help each other out. I'm not sure how young Mr Blake managed to sweet-talk you into coming here, but you should know that the family are sharpening their knives, as it were.

'All this commotion in the press about the two of you reflects rather poorly on Felix and the family. These old families place so much importance on reputation. In a changing world, it's all they have, really. They'd rather not have to deal with anyone taking too close a look. Privacy has always been so important to the Blakes, you know. And with everything going on with your poor mother, they're understandably jumpy about how this all looks. Image is everything – you know that.

'There are people whose job it is to make things look a certain way. Spin a certain narrative. Control the story. It will come as no surprise to you that I've had my reasons to employ those people in the past. So, I thought, in the name of fairness, that you ought to know that our friend Annie has been paying a considerable amount of money to a contact of mine over the last few weeks. It's hard to say what she's planning – it's actually impossible to ever know what that woman is thinking. From what I've gathered, the plan was for Felix to get you back onside so you wouldn't make too much of a fuss about things. I didn't expect him to march you in here and parade you around like this. So maybe PR management is out the window now. I thought, however, that you ought to know what's been going on behind the scenes. Information is, after all, our greatest weapon.'

It takes some time for what she is saying to sink in. The chequered tiles beneath my feet have gone soft, they warp and I feel as if I'm about to stumble. Caroline turns to leave, unlocking the door and pulling it towards her. I hear myself say her name. She stops.

'What are you saying? What can I even do with that? Without Felix, I've got nothing.'

'Don't be so naive. Secrets, my dear: you have secrets.' She turns and leaves. 'Oh, and I'd double-check your nose if I were you.'

I wipe the back of my hand across my face and check myself in the mirror, then follow her out into the foyer which is now mostly empty. Everyone is filtering into the cinema room. I don't see Felix, but Lily is hanging back. Relief floods her face when she sees me, but her eyes narrow when she spots Caroline. She swoops over to me, the fringe of her dress dancing in the air. She links her slender arm through mine, a familiar gesture that now feels unwieldy.

'Come on, the screening's about to start. Thought you'd done a runner for a second there. Sorry if Mummy's being a bit intense. Big night, you know? Let's go, Felix has saved us seats.'

I barely register a moment of the episode. My mind is frantic. Caroline's words flicker through my head, and I can't focus on the screen in front of me. In the dark of the room, I feel the weight of what she said pressing in around me. Towards the end, Felix abruptly stands up and leaves the theatre. The eyes of the room follow him out, but he doesn't look back. Annelise gets up to follow him and I do the same. I feel everyone staring at me and I want to not care. I want to turn around and stare them down, to look each one of them in the eye and confirm what they all suspect. But I am not that person. The pressure of their watching bores into the back of my skull. Every step falls unevenly in the dark as I shuffle after Felix, trying to make myself as small as possible. In the foyer, Felix is standing next to the bar. He's towering over Annelise who is trying to calm him down.

'Five fucking minutes,' he spits. 'They gave me five fucking minutes.'

'Felix, calm down.'

'No, Annelise. I won't calm down. This is so humiliating. You can't let them do this to me.'

'It's already done, Felix. This happens. Take a breath, have a drink, smile graciously, and say how much you enjoyed it. Do you understand me? Don't mess this up. If you'll excuse me, I'm going to go and apologise for you being a whiny little cry-baby.' She strides back towards the screening room, stopping to clutch my arm as we pass each other. 'Will you make yourself useful for once and get him to pull himself together?'

I walk over. Felix is now clutching a glass full of amber liquid.

'Can you believe they cut me out?'

'Felix, I need to talk to you about something.'

'Those fuckers. Have you got the coke?'

'What? Felix, I need you to answer me properly.'

'This is so humiliating.'

'Felix, did your mum hire a PR firm to make the story about us go away?'

'Everyone from the new film is here and now I look like a total prick.'

'Felix! Are you listening to me?'

'What? Yes. Yeah, I'm listening.'

'Well, did she?'

'Yes. But it's not like that. We just needed to be ahead of the narrative.'

'What narrative?'

'You know what.'

'Of you coming out? Or of your dirty little secret and his mad mum?'

'That's not fair.'

'Where have you been staying the last few weeks?'

'What? Give me the bag.'

'No. Where have you been staying?'

'At the House.'

'No, you haven't. Your mum said—'

'At my flat – whatever. It doesn't matter. What are you trying to do here?'

'It does matter if you've been lying to me.'

'Oh, that's fucking rich. You dare to lecture me about honesty. Look, Annie does what she wants. She was trying to . . . to help. This . . . all this . . . attention is bad for my image. I don't need this right now.'

I feel my anger spilling over. People have started filtering into the foyer. Our voices are raised, their eyes are lowered. We are making a scene and neither of us seems to care.

'What do you want me to do? Book us a photoshoot with *Hello!* to announce our pregnancy? Post some videos of us fucking on Instagram? Would that get you off?'

'What the fuck are you talking about, Felix? I just want you to not be ashamed of me. For once, I want people to know that I'm yours.'

'That's just it though, don't you get it? You *are* mine. I own you. You think you have any power here? You get all upset and you have your little outbursts and then I click my fingers and you come running right back. I sometimes think that maybe you're a bit unhinged. I feel sad for you. That stuff runs in families, you know. Maybe you got it from your mum.'

Something within me irrevocably breaks. I realise the champagne flute I was holding has fallen to the floor. I stumble backwards, away from Felix. I try to find words but there are none. My mouth is dry and my jaw is clamped tight by an invisible muzzle. I pull the drugs out of my pocket and fling them towards him. They land on the floor and he lunges for them, but it's too late. A small crowd has formed, and they murmur as the white baggy slides out of the leather pouch and across the tiles. A black patent Oxford snaps down over the drugs, hiding them from view. David Blake holds out a hand to his son and helps him stand. I've never noticed before, but the squaring of their shoulders, the set of their jaws, are identical. In anger Felix Blake is his father. I turn away and keep walking. I can hear Felix shouting after me. He tells me to stop. He tells me to come the fuck back. He tells me I'm being ridiculous. He tells me he loves me. This makes me pause but I don't turn around. Then he screams. Guttural and unintelligible. His whiskey glass lands a few feet away from me and shatters. I keep walking, eyes fixed ahead, and I know I will never get back what I'm leaving behind.

March

Winter has suddenly cracked into spring and the daffodils are brittle in the cold air. I haven't seen Felix in days and part of me feels used to his absence. It is also used to the feeling that he will turn up at some point, eyes dark, and sleep for two days before carrying on like nothing has happened. It's actually in the brief bursts of normality and domesticity that I feel most loved by him. This is just how we work. We fight, one of us walks out. We come back. With him, I thought that was a sustainable way to love. Sometimes, after bigger fights, Felix is cold and cruel, but he always thaws. Sometimes he goes home, back to the House, and barricades himself in his room. I once went after him, and Annie let me stay in a spare room for two days until he came out and back to me. *You're good to him,* she told me several times. It always felt like a warning.

After I left the screening, I fled back to Tooting. Back to Jazz and Caleb and some sense of safety. I hid in my room but started to worry. Lily called me to ask if I'd heard from Felix. They'd tried to calm him down at the screening, to reason with him. But then Dot said something, Lily won't say what, and things got out of control. They hadn't seen him since. Messages weren't delivering and calls went straight to voicemail, his smiling voice on the other end of the line exclaiming that he was 'having far too much fun to answer the wretched phone'. It has now been four days and there's still no news on Felix. I realise, despite the anger I feel towards him, that I need to see him. Check on him. Make sure he's okay. I grab my keys and head to his flat, hoping, perhaps in vain, to find him holed up there, quietly seething but safe.

Instead, I find cold, empty rooms and mild disarray. He's definitely been back at some point, and has made quite a mess in the process. The bed is unmade, a few half-empty lube packets are strewn around the room, the drawer where he keeps his cock rings and poppers is half open. I know I should feel angrier – this grim still life was deliberately left to taunt me – but there is still a growing fear that something awful has taken place here. I find myself on my knees beside the bed. I pull out the blue giftbox. I'm not sure what I plan to do with it. Flush the drugs away? Confiscate them like some self-righteous governess? With wavering hands, I slide the lid off the box. It takes me a second to realise what I'm seeing. A collection of misshapen white stones nestled in a sea of soft orange fabric. I take them out, one by one. On one of the stones, I can make out an eye; on another, half a mouth. Understanding closes in around me and the cold broken face of Annie's Venus stares up at me from the folds of Felix's silk scarf. I position its pieces carefully on the bed and lay down next to them, staring at the ceiling.

The key scratching in the lock wakes me from a sleep

I didn't know I'd fallen into. I am curled on top of Felix's duvet, his silk scarf resting between my fingers. I scramble to put the fragments of the Venus back into the box. Felix stumbles in wearing the same clothes I last saw him in, a thin silk shirt and dark suit trousers, but he is missing his jacket. He must be absolutely freezing but doesn't seem to feel it. I don't know what the look in his eyes means but it's different. My body recoils from it. There is a bruise on his cheek, which drags the usually perfect symmetry of his face off to the side. He rushes over to me and kisses me and his mouth tastes sour, its dryness sucking the moisture out of mine. His tongue pushes violently into mine until I turn my head. There is pain in his bloodshot eyes, but they are glazed and dart around the room, a jerking dance that is mirrored by the twitching of his rakish body. It takes me longer than it should to realise that, despite the fact that it's the morning, he is still high. I see my realisation dawn on him. He wraps me in a tight hug and buries his face in my neck. I feel tears soak into the collar of my shirt. His body shudders with a big heavy sob and he pulls away from me, his gaze wild.

'Fe, what the fuck? I couldn't get through to your phone. Where have you been? You're absolutely freezing.'

'Let's go for a drive.' He grabs both of our sets of keys from the bowl in the hall and whirls around, leaving the front door open behind him. I run after him, calling his name. A neighbour watches from across the road as Felix falls into the driver's seat and turns on the car with shaking hands, pulling away before I've even closed the door.

'Fe, slow down.' I try to sound firm but my voice cracks with fear. He doesn't say anything for a while. The roads are surprisingly clear, and he is picking up speed as we whip past cold brick and bare trees. A couple step onto a zebra crossing and Felix flings the car around them, holding down the horn and throwing back his head to laugh. I wonder why I let him get behind the wheel. But this is how it always is, isn't it? When faced with Felix's impulses, I am completely powerless. This time, however, I am truly afraid of them.

'Slow the fuck down, Felix – this isn't funny.'

'Funny? Do you know want to know what's fucking funny, *darling*?' He spits this last word and saliva lands on the steering wheel. 'What's funny is that you thought I wouldn't find out about your little nigger boyfriend.'

My lungs feel like they are being crushed. In this wretched moment, I see things clearly. I realise that this is what it means to be in love. You give someone else the power to destroy you. Felix turns triumphantly to watch my reaction and then there's a horrible tearing sound. My neck jerks violently. For a moment there is silence, like a held breath, then everything goes black.

I taste metal and try to spit. The blood runs upwards into my eyes and I realise I am upside down. I feel a pounding in my head and panic rises with each beat. Felix is hanging beside me, his face turned into a gruesome, vacant grin. My fingers fumble at the seatbelt buckle and I forget to brace an arm against the ceiling, so I slam down onto my neck, sending a hot crack of pain through my spine. Felix watches it happen and laughs. It's a ripple at first but it spills over into hysteria, then deep ragged sobs. For a few seconds I fight the urge to go to him, then I unclip his seatbelt and lower him down onto the ceiling of the car. I pull myself through the ragged hole that was once the window, shards of glass spilling over the floor. I can smell rubber and the thick slick of diesel. Felix climbs out after me and a sharp edge slices his silk shirt cleanly into two pieces.

'Fuck, fuck, fuck, fuck, fuck, fuck, fuck.' I can't form enough of a thought to say anything else.

Felix is laughing again, bent double like a cartoon.

The noise has drawn people out to the road. A kind woman in a hijab and a Prada trench coat asks me if I'm okay. She looks horrified and I follow her gaze down and see a black line unfurling on my T-shirt. I didn't feel the pain before but now it's as if a blade is being sliced repeatedly across my breastbone. I must have caught myself on the glass, but I don't want to look. A man in transition-lens glasses with a little white dog pulling at its lead is speaking into a phone, looking up at a road sign to give the name. The kind woman suggests I sit down and I let her guide me to the kerb. It's cold beneath me and I start to shiver. Felix is standing by the car, shirt hanging down around him like bat wings. The woman gently moves him to the kerb too but on the opposite side of the road. The shirt falls off his back and she wraps him in her expensive coat. The transition-lens man comes over and offers me a blanket that smells like dog. He tells me to stay calm because an ambulance is coming. I try to, knowing that the first sirens I hear will be the police.

The first time I was in handcuffs I was thirteen years old. I was with some other Black boys from school in the park. Some of the older boys were drinking and their girlfriends – all white – leaned against souped-up cars with mismatched spoilers. I remember the surging pride I felt at being allowed proximity to these boys I saw, at the time, as men. When a police car rolled around the corner, I was the last to see it, not yet alert to the constant threat of existing for boys of my hue. I only realised something was happening when everyone started to run. Marcus, who'd invited me along, told me to peg it, so I did. Clumsily, I tried to jump over the little fence out of the children's playground we'd been sitting in. The older boys were in their cars and speeding away across the car park before the police car got anywhere near. It didn't pursue them, clearly not in the mood for a car chase against neon Ford Fiestas. The easier target was slipping across a muddy playground on foot.

When they caught up with us, they recited to Marcus and me what would become an all-too-familiar refrain, but which felt so just in its first declamation. Persons fitting our description, etc. Would we mind explaining what we'd been doing prior, etc. We did not have to say anything, but it may harm our defence, etc, etc. Our answers were clearly unsatisfactory. Seen, caught and judged as men, our cries that we were thirteen and our terrified tears proved nothing.

While we waited for the fat young PC to phone back to the station to corroborate our story, they sat us on the cold grass. Marcus would not stop sobbing but when the officer standing over us shouted at him to stop, he did. A dark oval spread out from the crotch of his G-Star RAWs.

Eventually they dropped us both home. Grandma was incensed, shouting and screaming at the officers who'd brought me back. They looked stricken but defiant in response. I couldn't understand the emotions swirling around me. After they left Grandma sat at the kitchen table for a long, long time and didn't say anything. I never told anyone about Marcus and his wet jeans, but we were no longer friends after that. He ran with the older boys, his young arrest a badge of pride. I retreated back to Danny and the goths. I saw Marcus a few years later, just before my first summer with the Blakes. He was on Princess Street, handing out leaflets for an organisation called the Manchester Black Caucus. He did not recognise me but called me 'brother'.

It is absolutely out of the question that Felix will take the fall for this. We both understand it without saying it out loud. So, when the police arrive and ask who was driving, he stays silent while I raise a hand. *What happened? We were arguing. I lost control of the car. Have you been drinking? He has. I haven't. Would you both mind blowing into this? Not at all.* My breath is clear but Felix is six times over the legal limit, so they put us both in handcuffs. *You do not have to say anything. . . but it may harm your defence if you do*

353

not mention when questioned something which you later rely on in court. Anything you do say may be given in evidence. The arresting officer calls us both 'sir' but there is no respect in it. We are taken by ambulance to the hospital where we sit and wait for hours. They let me call someone, so I use Felix's phone to call Simon, who delights in everything but sends a company solicitor anyway. We stick to our story and my T-shirt sticks to the drying blood on my chest. A smiling nurse makes them take off my handcuffs and gets the police to leave the room so he can clean the wound. I flinch when he touches me, but it doesn't hurt. I release a breath I didn't know I'd been holding. By the time I've been butterfly-stitched back together, the company lawyer – whose name, I think, is James – has legalised us into freedom. James tells me Felix has left already and has taken my keys with him. I don't have my phone, so I get him to tap me onto a bus with his card and I ride it all the way back to Tooting.

It's still light when I get to my flat, but the late-winter sun provides no warmth. I wonder absently where the dog blanket ended up. Then I remember the Prada coat and think about Felix, and then I push all my thoughts away and watch a squirrel wriggle up and down the fence next door. Eventually Jazz comes home. She is looking in her bag for her keys as she comes up the path and almost steps on me before she notices I'm there. If she's surprised, it doesn't show on her face.

'You look like shit, WhiteBoy,' she says.

*

Heartbreak is a kind of drowning. My whole body aches for release and my chest screams with the need for oxygen but there is no air. I let myself decay in bed for days. It isn't that I don't want to get up. It's that the very idea of moving from here is totally alien to me. There is my bed, this tangle of reeking sheets, and there is everything else, which seems so far away. It's as if I am submerged, seeing the world through a shimmering patch of light on the sea surface. I have the overwhelming need to tell Felix about this. I am convinced that only he would know what to do. The thought swirls round and round in my head, sucking me down. I crave the steady pull of his presence. Each time I open my eyes, after snatches of fitful sleep, I remember what has happened and feel myself pulled under again. The pain is physical. It throbs through the slash in my chest. Jazz brings food and cups of tea and glasses of water that lie untouched. I cannot read or listen to music or even think too much without spinning down into the darkness. I use one of his fleeces, soft and terrible with the scent of him, to dry my tears. In a moment of utter powerlessness, I open my laptop and watch *Uplands*. It is brilliant. He is brilliant. Tiny and glowing on my screen, he charges back into my conscious mind and my heart breaks, minute after minute. Watching is like tearing out my soul and I cannot look away.

After a day or a week, Jazz knocks on my door. I haven't been to work since before the screening and I'm fairly sure I no longer even have a job. Again, Jazz leaves a tray of food I know I will not touch. This time there is a brown package with the food. I reach for it and bile rises in my throat when I see his tiny scrawled handwriting. I cling to it like a life raft. Then I tear it open and shake out the contents. A toothbrush, a bottle of lavender oil, a tub of Palmer's, an envelope addressed to me, and my phone. I feel a tug of agony as my heart quickens. I plug the phone in and wait for it to turn on. When it does, the background is blank. I check my messages and find I have none. Not no new ones, none at all. I look at my photos and they are gone too. The whole thing is wiped clean. At first, I am confused. I turn it off and back on again, but find it is the same. The dreadful realisation unfurls slowly. Here is this record, this relic of our time together, all our happy memories, all my access to what we were, what we had, my only evidence that things between us were ever good, ever beautiful. And it's totally empty. I open the envelope with sweaty palms, but instead of Felix's messy, beautiful handwriting, the page holds a few lines of typed print.

Dear Applicant Number 23879,

We regret to inform you that due to unforeseen circumstances we are no longer able to offer you an audition at the Royal Academy of Music's Piano Department. We understand you may be disappointed by this decision.

Regards,
Professor Cassandra Quant

The thing about heartbreak is that it can quickly turn into fury. Despair has no power. It is a void and into it falls any concrete feeling, any sense I had that I knew myself or him or the world. But fury – fury is a forge. It burns, and as it burns it creates. I get out of bed, seeing stars as I stand upright for the first time in I don't know how long. I am suddenly appalled by the mess around me. I scoop up my discarded clothes and throw them into the basket at the foot of my bed. I balance old plates and cups onto the tray Jazz brought up and march downstairs with it. My anger has spurred me into action and I need somewhere to channel it. I find Jazz in the living room. She looks up from her phone, surprised to see me. I tell her that whatever she's up to with J's trial and Lily's exhibition, whatever she's been planning, I'm in. She hops up and hugs me.

'I love your enthusiasm, babe, but you've got to shower first. You absolutely stink.'

I refuse to let myself be erased, sent back to where I came from with no right of reply. I want to ruin him. I want to ruin them all. Caroline's words from our encounter in the bathroom echo in my mind.

I am unsurprised to find that Anna Osbourne's number has also been deleted from my phone, but it only takes me a few seconds to find her contact information online. We agree to meet in an unassuming cafe in Brixton, and when I arrive, after a much-needed shower, she is sitting waiting for me. I buy myself a coffee and sit down opposite her.

'How are you? It's nice to see you,' she says.

'I'm well,' I lie.

'Thank you for agreeing to meet me. I must say, I was surprised when I got your message. I heard what happened at the *Uplands* premiere.'

My cheeks flush. 'I understand. I just feel ready to talk now, I guess—'

'Talk about what, exactly?' she interrupts me.

So, I tell her everything. Anna Osbourne listens, nods her head, takes a few notes, and records everything I say.

The public gallery is full, so most people have congregated on the front steps of the court building. Jazz and I arrived early with J, hugging him tightly before he headed inside. Caleb, Neisha and a few others are inside too, sending updates via text. Jazz, Ben and I wait by the entrance with a few others. The atmosphere is strained. The day itself is bright and clear and cold. There are police here, almost as many officers as there are protestors. Some of our group have signs with slogans on them. One is pasted with a blown-up photograph of J after the attack, his ruined face distorted by the brutality, then stretched across cardboard and held aloft. It is grotesque. It is almost laughable that he is the one on trial today. The proceedings get under way. Both sides are presenting their closing arguments and the verdict is expected shortly. The story is unfolding here. Part of a history that stretches centuries. Whatever the outcome, we will use the momentum as a cover for what else we have planned.

The day trudges on. We take turns nipping to the shop

round the corner for snacks and coffees to stave off the creeping chill that threatens to numb our hands and feet. There is a sense of anticipation in the air. It crackles through the crowd every time we get an update. I check my phone and see a message from Mum wishing us luck today. We spoke, once, on the phone last week and I told her about today. She told me she was proud of me. Then, like now, I couldn't think of a response.

Caleb has messaged to say the jury have risen to deliberate. It's almost 3 p.m. and we are starting to worry this might drag over to tomorrow. Jazz is nervous. She chews at the skin around her fingernail, pacing back and forth. The wait is short-lived. The agreement is unanimous.

Caleb
15:57
Not guilty.

15:57
Not fucking guilty!

Relief is a flood. An unwinding of fear and anger and hope that somehow, maybe, the right thing could happen for once. There is an explosion of tears and shouts when the news passes through the waiting crowd. Someone has a bottle of Tesco prosecco and shakes it over us. Jazz ducks under her placard to protect her braid from the spay. A story that started months ago on these same streets feels like it is ending. Eventually J appears on the steps of the court building. He is crying, Neisha is crying, his family, dressed in their smartest, most serious clothes, wrap around him like a banner. We push through the crowd towards him. Caleb pulls me towards him and kisses me hard on the mouth. Jazz gathers us into a huddle, cutting the celebration short.

'Show time.'

We begin leading the ragtag group, but once people are clear where we are going, our group falls into the middle of the pack. Safely disguised by the crowd we wander through Notting Hill to our destination. Tangled nerves dance in my belly. Fireworks bursting and dying in my gut. When we reach the art gallery, the protest is met, initially, with confusion. There is a woman with a clipboard who calls upstairs and is joined by two burly private security guards. Jazz, Caleb, Ben, J, Neisha, and me peel off from the gaggle and down a narrow sidestreet past two huge bins overflowing with rubbish. Jazz grabs a duffel bag from underneath one of the bins. The fire exit of the gallery is slightly ajar and as we approach it swings open. Dot smiles as they see us. They bump fists with Ben. The two of them catch me looking at them. I must look as confused as I feel because their faces congeal into awkwardness.

'What's going on?' I ask.

'I wanted to apologise,' Dot says.

'For what?'

Dot doesn't say anything. Instead, they turn their head towards Caleb, and that's when it clicks into place. Dot's awkwardness at the *Uplands* screening. Felix's knowledge of Caleb.

'I'm sorry. I really am,' they say. 'I didn't know Felix was going to react like that, I never meant for anyone to get hurt. But Ebenezer told me you'd been staying at theirs a lot, hanging out with Caleb, and then when it looked like you and Felix were back together . . . I thought it was unfair that you and Caleb were—'

'Who the hell is Ebenezer?'

Dot looks to Ben, who avoids my eye. Of course. Ebenezer from their band, the Scrooges. Ben just shrugs, his eyes emotionless behind their circular frames.

'I thought Felix needed to know,' whispers Dot. 'But I just made everything worse. I'm sorry. I feel so guilty.'

I don't want to look at them.

'He's my brother. What was I supposed to do? And it's not like you're innocent in all this.'

'That's not fair.'

'I'm sorry. I wish none of this had ever happened. You're a good person, I still believe that. But Felix is my brother and he's not well and I love him. And I'm sorry for whatever Annie and David have said to you. I really am. But I almost envy you. At least you can finally escape all this. Look, I'm helping you now, aren't I?'

I am about to respond but Jazz cuts me off.

'Hate to break up this little reunion, but we've got a job to do.'

We agreed that I'd be the distraction. It made sense: eyes would be on me while the others got things in place.

A plan is different when acted out, though. My heart is hammering as I step out into the hubbub of the gallery space, but there is no big dramatic moment. The room is adequately full and people mill around. No one seems to notice me at all. I hover near the edge of the room, taking in some of the photographs. They are mostly black and white. They bring back the flashes of that day, the heavy, dark sky, the collective rage, the sense of community. The door of the House, clean and untouched, next to the roughly sprayed graffiti. black lives matter. Rows and rows of faces huddled under the gathering clouds. Jazz staring into the lens from under her thick eyebrows, mascara running down her face. Caleb and I sitting side-by-side, caught in a moment of comfort. Did Lily know then, what was about to happen? Did I? A girl with braids down her back on a makeshift stage, her fist raised to the sky. In the centre of the display, one of the photographs is bigger than the others. I remember the moment it was taken. Me, Caleb and Jazz shielding ourselves from rain that had just begun to fall. Our placards and umbrellas form a protective barrier around us, lions bare their teeth above. Seeing this moment again, hung here on this wall, surrounded by people who could not care less about its significance, makes me want to scream. Jazz clears her throat and nods towards the other side of the room.

'Incoming.'

I turn and see Annie, Teller and Caroline, who have clocked me. Annie excuses herself and starts to cross the room. Lily intercepts her, stays her with a hand and approaches me herself.

'What the hell?' Lily's voice is not at all angry or accusatory. It's a genuine question.

I falter. My tongue is dry, pressed hard against the roof of my mouth. I look to the photo on the wall and remember why I'm here. I opt for the truth, which feels easier.

'I wanted to see your photos.' I let this hang and Lily takes it in whatever way she wants to. When tears fill her eyes and she flings her arms around my neck, I start to feel sick. There's a sucking dread. It's like I'm being pulled down into thick black mud.

'Oh gosh, this is a lot. Have you seen Felix yet? He's going to lose it. Look, I don't know what is going on with you guys, or even if there's anything left, but he's not in a good way. I know this isn't your problem, but—'

'He looks fine to me,' I say, pointing across the gallery.

Felix looks just as beautiful as he always does. He is walking out of the ladies' bathroom at the other end of the gallery, laughing. Celeste hangs off his arm and giggles at something he says as they lean against each other for support. His golden hair is gelled back, slick against his head. A single strand has fallen forward over his face and he pushes it back into place with his free hand. There is an echo of Celeste's crimson lipstick on Felix's mouth. The two of them see me and stop still like they've hit a glass wall. Felix gives me a look like a struck match. He drops Celeste's hand and starts to march across the room. My vision narrows to his face, an expression I can't quite decode. Then all the lights go out. The screeching sound of feedback tears through the darkness, then Jazz's voice, amplified by a megaphone, fills the room.

'The photographs in this exhibition were taken without our consent. In a moment of protest, of collective action, of vulnerable solidarity. As we gathered to fight back against the policing of our bodies, our cultures and our essence, our images were stolen. Outside the doors of this gallery, the very people who marched that day are being refused entry as we speak. The man who we marched for, who was brutalised by a racist police force that people in this room continue to praise, found justice today. But in here, none of that seems to matter to you. You use our faces and our pain and our stories but you don't even hear our words. We say that we have had enough. We do not consent. We refuse. We are taking back our story.'

The lights flick back on. The six of us are standing between the crowd and the photographs. J's face, bloody and battered in his hospital bed is projected over us and onto the walls of the gallery. Over the speaker, Caroline Asiamah's voice, juddering and spliced, crackles into life.

I'm so glad you asked that. It is my duty as an elected represent-
ative to prioritise the safety and security of all . . . white, rich . . .
citizens. And it deeply concerns me that a number of my constitu-
ents . . . are . . . Black . . . and . . . poor.

There is sadly and problem with . . . this government. This gov-
ernment . . . is . . . a . . . racist . . . gang. This government is . . .
a selfish, violent and irresponsible . . . gang. This government . . .
is . . . out of ideas. This government . . . cannot be left unchecked.

The Metropolitan Police work tirelessly to maintain . . . their . . . racist . . . gang activity. The blame for this regrettable incident lies squarely with . . . our . . . violent and criminal . . . police force.

Let us not allow ourselves to be swayed by misguided notions of political correctness. We must send a clear message that our community will not tolerate . . . Afro-Caribbean pride and culture. Our community will not tolerate . . . Black . . . people. And if we do not face up to that, we are saying it is okay to continue.

Let us stand together in support of our . . . violent . . . racist . . . police force. They deserve our unwavering support as they put . . . the Black . . . community . . . in harm's way.'

The real Caroline, in flesh and blood and an ill-fitting skirt suit, has a grim smile plastered across her face. Most people have now turned to face her. She looks like she is about to say something, but instead she puts her handbag over her shoulder, signals to her assistant, and strides across the room. The tap of her kitten heels echoes across the polished concrete floor. The gallery security must have contacted the police because I hear sirens outside. Our group makes a coordinated break for the back exit. I try not to look at any of the Blakes, at Felix, as I hurry across the room, but my eyes are drawn to Lily's. The force of her expression stops me in my tracks. She is looking at me with childlike confusion, as if she's trying to make sense of what has just happened. It feels like the moment before a dropped vase hits the floor. I turn away from the wrecking of it all.

April

I'm at Caleb's when I get Lily's message. She's been silent since the day of the exhibition. I haven't been able to get through to Dot either. I'd been worried about what sort of punishment Annie might have dreamt up for their part in the whole thing. I've been wondering whether anyone even knew they were involved. Dot has a way of tiptoeing out of trouble. Felix used to always complain that whenever it was time for the siblings to do something – clear the table or put away their toys – Dot would mysteriously disappear, slinking off to the bathroom or manufacturing some other excuse. I've been hoping they've found out a way to slink away from all this, too. Lily's message tells me there's a bag of my clothes at the House, no one is going to be in this afternoon, the key is where it always is. This last part makes me burn with shame. Even after everything I've done, all the lies I've told her, Lily manages to be kind.

It's Saturday and the journey across London takes longer than anticipated. Couples and families and tourists and gaggles of teenagers invade the city streets. It's one of those warm days in early spring that trick people into thinking summer is coming. There are bare legs and burnt arms and melting ice creams. I get off the Central line a few stops early because the heat is unbearable, and I realise I'm not actually in a rush: there is no one waiting for me at the end of this road. I wander through Hyde Park. A part of me wonders when I'll next come here. This place feels like it belongs to the Blakes. I can see Felix sprawled with his friends on the grass, getting up to greet me with a smile. I can see Lily, camera swinging from her neck. I can see Annie, far ahead on Christmas Day, walking away from her marriage through the cold. I stop down by the Serpentine. There are boats on the water. A handsome boy peels off his T-shirt, sweating from the exertion of rowing. His date looks around, feigning embarrassment as he flexes dramatically. They both laugh. There is an elderly woman in a big brown coat throwing bread. She is surrounded by ducks and swans and pigeons and parakeets. I realise with a twist of discomfort that I've never paid her enough attention know for sure if this is the same woman I've seen here before. I study her now. Her face is weathered, drooping around the mouth and eyes, the skin crinkly like paper. She has gold earrings with green stones in them and dirt under her fingernails. The shopper next to her seems to be completely full of bread. I watch her for a while and at one point she catches my eye and smiles. When I get up to go, she waves me goodbye. I wave back then start off towards the House.

The tiles on the top step are pristine as usual. I wobble the loose one. Second from the right, two squares back. The key isn't there. Just plaster and dust. I stand as the front door opens and the jaws of the trap snap shut around me.

'I think you'd better come in,' says Annie Blake.

I follow her through into the hall then down to the kitchen. My palms are sweaty with surprise at the ambush. She motions for me to sit down. I pass close to her and get a familiar waft of perfume. Oranges, I once thought. I now know it is orange blossom, musk and bergamot. That it comes from a monastic apothecary in Switzerland. That it costs over £300 a bottle. She offers me a cup of tea, which I decline. She makes me one anyway. While she busies herself with this, neither of us says anything. I look around the kitchen and feel a lurch of premature nostalgia. It is strange how a place can feel so entirely familiar and so alien at the same time. Dunstable glares at me from the armchair by the door.

'I've always been very protective of my family,' Annie says, placing the tea in front of me. 'I think that's what happens when you're estranged from people. You put down roots, you find your tribe, and you do anything to stop those roots from being torn up, to protect those people from being hurt. I know what it's like to feel out of place, like the odds are stacked against you. It makes you clever. It makes you ruthless. They take it all for granted, people who are born into a world like this.' She gestures around the room.

'But you and me, we're smarter than that. We know what it feels like to have nothing. We know what it feels like to be hungry. We find a way inside and we dig our heels in. That was what I did. I saw a way in, and I took it. When David found me in that godawful jazz club the first night we met, I already knew four generations of his family tree and the combined market value of his budding property empire. There is no such thing as chance, my dear, only opportunity, as you well know. And you've got to make the most of it. Did I love him? He was handsome and charming and funny. But it doesn't matter whether I did or not. What matters is that before we met, I was singing in jazz clubs in Soho to scrape together enough money for a shared room in a nine-person house in Vauxhall. And now . . . well, now I'm here.

'People called me a gold-digger. I didn't care and told them as much. And what's funny is that this really never was about the money for me. Of course, this is all a nice bonus, and I do look fantastic in Hermès. But it was never about the money, no. The only thing that matters is power. Nothing else. Not money, not beauty, not charm, not talent. None of that means anything unless it makes you powerful. When you have power, you have control. Over the people around you, over the truth, over the whole fucking country. But most importantly, you control yourself. When you are powerful, you are actually, truly, free.

'I admire you, you know. I really do. You played your role so convincingly. You smiled at all the right people, looked pretty, showed just enough grit to be taken seriously. I certainly fell for it. I even admire the way you've tried to wriggle out of all the mess you've made. Your little stunt at Lily's show was actually quite entertaining. It's created a huge amount of buzz for her work and a massive headache for Caroline. So I really must thank you and your little friends for that one. Running off to Anna was a cowardly move, it's true, but you used what tools you had at your disposal. Your truth, I suppose. But the truth is that there is no truth. There's your version of events and there's someone else's and they very rarely match. The things you told her, those horrible things you said about us, they could have been really damaging. Poor Felix doesn't deserve any of that. I know my son. I know he can be . . . passionate. Reckless even. But the things you said . . . And you claim to have loved him?'

My hands start to shake under the table.

'Luckily for you, Anna is a sensible girl. She knows which side her toast is buttered. She has a respect for power, for the proper way of doing things. She let us have a look at all the nasty little things you said before it went to print. The right to reply and all that. She agreed to update a few details since she couldn't find a shred of evidence or a single person to corroborate what you'd said. Would you like to know what she's written?'

I don't respond. The blood is hammering in my ears, pressure builds in my chest, and my face is burning with heat. Annie takes out her reading glasses and opens her laptop.

'"Blake Burns Bright . . . BBC's new rising star is on the up and up." Blah, blah, blah. "Bright things in his future." Blah, blah, blah. A little over the top, actually.

It's almost hagiographic. My son is beautiful and talented, but he is certainly no saint. I know that as well as anyone. And you did too, I feel. I tried to warn you, actually – do you remember? Never get in my son's way. I knew from the moment you walked onto the terrace, beautiful and strange and new, that you'd cause all sorts of problems. It goes on. The article. Singing his praises, painting him in such a flattering light. But the interesting part, the really interesting part, is what it makes of you. Would you like to know what it says?'

I lean forward, my eyes scanning the screen, searching for my name. When I look up, victory flashes like lightning in Annie Blake's eyes.

'Oh, my darling,' she says. 'You're not mentioned at all.'